PRAISE FOR *T*

"Engrossing and provocative."
—Cynthia Swanson, *New York Times* bestselling author of
The Glass Forest and *The Bookseller*

"A knockout novel: beautiful, unique, suspenseful, and full of wonder."
—Julie Cantrell, *New York Times* and *USA Today*
bestselling author of *Perennials*

"A stunning novel with luminous prose and a story that speaks straight
to the heart."
—Camille Pagán, bestselling author of *Life and
Other Near-Death Experiences*

"A smart, tension-filled family drama—Yoerg at her best."
—Julie Lawson Timmer, author of *Five Days Left, Untethered,* and
Mrs. Saint and the Defectives

"Gripping, emotional, and deeply authentic, *True Places* will have you
flipping pages long into the night."
—Kristy Woodson Harvey, national bestselling author of
The Secret to Southern Charm

"Tender and triumphant . . . readers will be swept along in the gorgeous
narrative and fall in love with the artfully drawn characters plucked
from real life."
—Nicole Baart, author of *Little Broken Things* and
You Were Always Mine

"Readers will enjoy every moment of getting lost in the pages of *True Places*, with its richly drawn, realistic characters and loving attention to the details of the natural world. A beautiful book, all around."

—Susan Gloss, *USA Today* bestselling author of *Vintage* and *The Curiosities*

PRAISE FOR *ALL THE BEST PEOPLE*

"Not just the best people, but real people: authentic, quirky, and troubled. I cared for them all."

—Chris Bohjalian, *New York Times* bestselling author of *The Flight Attendant*

"Deftly and with the delicate brush of a master, Yoerg draws us into this brilliant, multigenerational saga of love, madness, mysticism, and the markings they leave on a family."

—Christopher Scotton, author of *The Secret Wisdom of the Earth*

"A stirring tale of mothers and daughters, their secrets and their strength . . . a mesmerizing read."

—Lynda Cohen Loigman, author of *The Wartime Sisters*

"A powerful and haunting novel about betrayal and shame, acceptance and unconditional love. Book clubs will devour it."

—Barbara Claypole White, bestselling author of *The Perfect Son*

PRAISE FOR *THE MIDDLE OF SOMEWHERE*

"Yoerg knows how to keep the pages turning in this fast-paced, action-packed, heart-tugging novel."

—Heather Gudenkauf, *New York Times* bestselling author of *Before She Was Found*

"The perfect blend of self-discovery and suspense."

—Kate Moretti, *New York Times* bestselling author of *In Her Bones*

"Yoerg skillfully explores how the weight of remorse makes the search for personal redemption a test of not just the will, but the heart . . . stunningly descriptive prose."

—Susan Meissner, *USA Today* bestselling author of *The Last Year of the War*

PRAISE FOR *HOUSE BROKEN*

"A stunning debut that will have readers wanting more! Yoerg is on par with Jennifer Weiner and Sarah Pekkanen."

—*Library Journal* starred review

"With beautiful prose and an unflinching eye, Sonja Yoerg has created a riveting tale exploring the power of family secrets. *House Broken* is a novel that will burn itself into your memory. The book is, by turns, brilliant, heartbreaking, shocking, and hopeful."

—Ellen Marie Wiseman, author of *The Life She Was Given*

stories
we
never
told

ALSO BY SONJA YOERG

stories

we *A NOVEL*

never

told

SONJA YOERG

Text copyright © 2020 by Sonja Yoerg
All rights reserved.

Published by Lake Union Publishing, Seattle

www.apub.com

Amazon, the Amazon logo, and Lake Union Publishing are trademarks of Amazon.com, Inc., or its affiliates.

ISBN-13: 9781542019729 (hardcover)
ISBN-10: 1542019729 (hardcover)
ISBN-13: 9781542004664 (paperback)
ISBN-10: 1542004667 (paperback)

Cover design by Rex Bonomelli

Printed in the United States of America

First edition

stories

we

never

told

CHAPTER 1

Just dinner.

The innocence of the phrase is deceptive, as deceptive as the dinner itself would turn out to be, as Jackie would discover ninety-eight days later. Dinner with friends, a table for four. Dinner with people she thought she knew and loved. As it turns out, no one is who she believed they were, least of all herself. So much secrecy, and in its service so many lies. And shame, at least for some.

They say—the infamous, authoritative "they"—that the worst lies are those you tell yourself. Even before the dinner, before everything began to unravel, Jackie had been skeptical of the veracity of that old chestnut. Being true to yourself is noble, but other people's lies can cripple you whether you are self-actualized or not. All it takes is a little misplaced trust, a scrap of faith made of white cloth.

That night at dinner a match would be struck, and the white cloth lit, although it would burn slowly. Slow, too, would be the dawning of Jackie's understanding. She knew (in her mind, not her heart) that appearances could be deceptive, and that love, desire, and ambition make it harder to see others for who they are.

Smart, rational people—even those who study people for a living, like Jackie—can get it wrong.

Dead wrong.

———

For a second time, Jackie checks her hair and makeup in the visor mirror, stalling. She hates being late, and there's no reason to dawdle now. It is, after all, just dinner with two people she knows intimately: Miles, her husband of eighteen months, and Harlan, her colleague in the Psychology Department and, more saliently, her former boyfriend. Oh, and a surprise guest.

Jackie frowns at herself and fusses with her eyebrow. She also hates surprises.

She hasn't seen Miles in ten days. It's his busy season, scouting young athletes, football players mostly, hoping to sign them. He's meeting her at the restaurant—she checks her watch—ten minutes ago. Harlan's been on sabbatical the past year, and during that interval they met only once, briefly, at a conference. Has she missed him? Of course. You don't date a man for five years, then pretend he has nothing going for him, especially when that man is Harlan. Jackie's not a revisionist.

The three have had dinner before, many times, and weathered the initial awkwardness. It was Harlan's idea to socialize when Jackie and Miles began dating four years ago. He invited them to a Redskins game, and the men became fast friends, with no apparent jealousy on either side. The Psychology Department isn't big enough to harbor enmity, so Jackie welcomed the chance to normalize her relationship with Harlan.

Phone in hand, Jackie grabs her bag, opens the door. She's parked too close to the next car and maneuvers through the narrow gap, scuttling sideways, sucking in her stomach to avoid getting dirt on her dress. She texts Miles, In 5! 🐾, and hurries out of the parking garage. She glances at her screen, reading Harlan's message from earlier today for the fifth time.

Bringing a friend tonight so changed the table to four. Eager to catch up with you and Miles. It's been too long.

A friend? Never did a word convey less. If Harlan meant to arouse her curiosity, he'd succeeded.

She pockets the phone and makes her way out to Potomac Street. Partway along the second block she spots Miles; his white-blond hair is a beacon. He's resting against a lamppost, extinguishing a cigarette on the sole of his shoe, a move at once masculine and regrettable. Three cigarettes a day aren't going to kill him, but why not just quit? It almost seems weaker to smoke three than the pack a day he'd smoked when she met him. Miles pulls a roll of mints from his trouser pocket and slides one into his mouth with one hand, extracting his phone from the breast pocket of his blazer with the other. Jackie smiles. For a former rugby star built like a dumpster, he has grace.

He looks up from his phone, zeroes in on her, and sends her a lopsided grin. She lifts her face to his for a minty, smoky kiss. "Hello, husband mine."

"Hello, beautiful." His usual greeting, springing from his European gentility and inherent goodness, but delivered in a way that never allows her to question his sincerity.

They set off and turn left onto Horatio. Within seconds Miles is out in front, as usual. Jackie takes several quick steps to catch up and tugs the sleeve of his jacket.

"Slow down. Notice my footwear?"

Miles peers at her feet, clad in emerald-green stilettos. "Oh. Those."

"You can't say 'those' with that tone. You must pay homage to their fabulousness."

"You're teetering."

"Hardly."

He resumes walking, albeit more slowly, and tucks her arm under his. "It's just that we're late."

She checks her watch. "Harlan's never on time. And I only wore these in case his friend is one of those six-footers that are so common nowadays. I don't want to look like the doomed runt about to be pushed out of the nest."

He squeezes her arm. "You look fine."

"Fine? If I get another downgrade before we get to the restaurant, I'm not going in."

Miles guides them around a group of college students—Adams University, judging by a sweatshirt and a baseball cap—lined up outside a pizza place. "What are you worried about anyway? It's dinner. Relax."

"You know I don't like to relax. And all the intrigue around this late-breaking plus-one." Jackie had texted Miles about Harlan's friend. "Who do you suppose? Someone from the sandbox? A college roomie? No, wait. A paramour?" She figured it had to be the latter. Why else be cagey? But not even that made sense. Jackie had obviously moved on to, well, marriage, so Harlan had no reason to be delicate with her feelings. Not that he had ever been.

Miles laughs. "We're about to find out."

———

Miles holds open the glass door of the Estrela for her and approaches the host, a Christian Bale look-alike in a slim-fit charcoal suit and a white shirt open at the collar.

"Reservation for Crispin, please. For four." Miles doesn't have to ask her who booked the table. Harlan has this top DC restaurant on speed dial.

The bar stretches behind the host stand, slightly elevated and delineated by a brass railing that curves into the room. Opposite the bar, a row of small tables lines a wall, where geometric artwork hangs inside an alcove illuminated from below by golden lights. More tables, squares for four, fill the center. White linens, beechwood chairs, hushed waitstaff. It's Saturday night, and the place hums, redolent of warm sourdough and roasted meat. Jackie turns away, not wanting to scan for Harlan and appear overeager. She slips off her coat, and Miles hangs it among others off to the side. She catches her reflection in the glass entry, runs her fingers through her shoulder-length hair, arranging the waves, a move so practiced as to be invisible.

The host leads them into the room. Jackie pulls her shoulders back and pictures Miles behind her, his casual ease, his "it's dinner" straight-forwardness. Her husband. A role Harlan refused.

"Enjoy your evening." The host steps aside, and Harlan stands in front of her, smiling, looking as he always does, his graying hair, long and thick as a pirate's, swept back from his forehead, his dark-brown eyes clear, glinting.

"Jackie," he says.

Something inside her pulls open, his voice like the swipe of a finger moving along a feather in the wrong direction, unzipping the interlocking barbs, splaying them apart.

"Welcome back." She gives him her cheek, leaning awkwardly because she doesn't trust herself to take a step just now, not in these shoes. And not when the citrus pinch of his aftershave, Guerlain Vetiver, rings in her head like a fucking bell and she is Pavlov's bitch. Couldn't he switch brands? There ought to be a law. Olfactory memories are made of hardened steel—she knows that—but her reaction surprises her nonetheless. Her reptilian brain has apparently misplaced the memo that she is over him.

Miles reaches around to shake Harlan's hand. "Hey, great to see you." Miles's smile is warm, genuine, like everything about him. Jackie stabilizes herself against her husband's shoulder.

Harlan gestures toward the table, toward the woman seated to his left.

Jackie smiles reflexively in greeting, then realizes who it is. "Nasira?" Jackie glances at Harlan, but he's taking a seat, arranging his napkin.

"Hi, Jackie." Nasira's voice is soft and breathy.

Harlan says, "Miles, I don't think you've met Nasira Amari, have you?"

Miles answers, but the words don't register. Jackie stares across the table at Nasira, her new postdoctoral research associate. *What is she doing here?* For a moment Jackie thinks that perhaps she invited Nasira and forgot, but no, that is impossible. She wouldn't include Nasira in an intimate dinner with friends, not before getting to know her.

"What a surprise," Jackie manages, and turns to Harlan with raised eyebrows. *Getting to know her.* Surely he will offer an explanation, a reason for inviting her postdoc at the last minute, or perhaps an account of how they have come to know each other. Jackie spots a flicker of mischief in his eyes, which dissolves as quickly as Jackie's certainty that it ever existed. Classic Harlan.

Jackie feels everyone's eyes on her and sits. Miles holds her chair—ever the gentleman—and takes his seat. Jackie, having been sideswiped by Nasira's presence, is eager to prove she can still steer. "Sorry we're a little late. Harlan, what's this new zest for punctuality?"

Harlan laughs. "You know how keen I am on self-improvement." This is a solid brick of irony, but it flies right past Nasira, as it would, since she couldn't possibly know Harlan at all well. She's only been in the department, what, not even three weeks?

Nasira says, "The Portrait Gallery closes at seven, but they start hustling you out earlier. The timing was perfect."

"The Portrait Gallery," Jackie repeats. She wants to ask Harlan what the hell they put in the water in Madison to render him amenable to a museum outing—*portraiture* no less—but stops herself. She stacks that question behind the others; her curiosity is her sharpest, largest sword. But she can't interrogate her ex-boyfriend in front of her new postdoc or her husband. Even as her mind races to illicit and alarming conclusions, she's wary of jumping the gun and making an ass of herself.

Miles asks about the exhibits (more good manners—he cares less about stuffy art than Harlan does, or did), and small talk swirls around the table. Jackie studies Nasira. Of course, Jackie is familiar with Nasira's appearance from work, but either the lighting in the lab is worse than Jackie thought or she hadn't been paying attention to her postdoc. Whatever the cause, tonight Nasira is gorgeous in every detail: heart-shaped face, dusky olive complexion, catlike eyes so dark the irises are nearly black, perfectly arched eyebrows, full lips. Until now, Jackie hasn't been able to pinpoint whom Nasira reminds her of: Jasmine, the Disney princess. And like the princess, Nasira is tiny, as if it would be an offense to the balance of the universe for her to be so beautiful and take up any more space. Jackie feels like a mastodon by comparison and regrets the shoes. What is Nasira wearing exactly? Some garment consisting of lengths of soft dove-colored cloth, twisted and draped loosely across her body. Its construction confounds Jackie. Nasira wouldn't undress so much as unravel.

Jackie hurries away from that thought.

The waiter arrives, a godsend of distraction, and asks for drink orders.

"I think so," Harlan says. "Jackie?"

Sure, age before beauty. But there is nothing other than affection and solicitousness in his expression. "I'd love a martini. Dirty."

Harlan's grin slides sideways, and he winks at her.

"I'm fine with water, thanks," Nasira says.

Jackie thinks, *Of course. How embarrassing if she should get carded,* and chides herself for being bitchy. But, really, Nasira can't be more than twenty-six, twenty-seven. Harlan is twice her age. Not that it matters, because they couldn't possibly be dating. That wouldn't be plausible, ethical, nor fair.

Jackie reaches under the table for Miles's hand.

He squeezes hers lightly and looks up at the waiter. "Gin and tonic for me, please. Sapphire."

"The same," Harlan says.

7

Harlan asks Miles about his recruiting trip, and Jackie follows the conversation so she doesn't have to talk to Nasira. The drinks arrive.

Harlan straightens and raises his glass, his face bright. "To friends— new and old."

Jackie touches her brimming glass to the others with care and smiles at Nasira. The impending delivery of gin to her system has made her generous.

"To new friends," Nasira says.

New friends? We'll see.

CHAPTER 2

On the sidewalk outside the restaurant, Jackie and Miles say goodbye to Harlan and Nasira in a blur of air-kisses, handshakes, and shoulder clasps. Jackie notes that Harlan and Nasira do not discuss where they are going or how they are getting there, together or separately, apparently having worked it out ahead of time.

Jackie takes Miles's arm as they leave. A moment later, she pulls up short and digs in her bag for her phone.

Miles stops. "What's wrong?"

She wakes the phone. "Something in my eye." She clicks open the camera and toggles to selfie mode. In the camera, she sees Harlan and Nasira walking away, and dabs at the corner of her eye for Miles's sake. Harlan dips his head toward Nasira in conversation and places his hand on the center of her back.

"Shit." Jackie drops the phone into her bag.

Miles leans closer. "Does it hurt?"

She blinks hard, completing the performance. "Nope. Got it, I think." She is dying to turn around, but is not prepared for what she might see. What is going on with those two? Her mind is racing, like it was during dinner as she scrutinized Harlan and Nasira on the sly. She doesn't know what to think. She needs to talk it out, run through the possibilities, and she doesn't want to wait until she and Miles are at home where there will be distractions. Miles will want to go through his mail, unpack.

Jackie touches his arm. "Are you up for a drink?"

"Out or at home?"

"Out. I haven't seen anything other than moms, babies, and freshmen all week." Between advising, teaching, and the start of a new study, her schedule has been packed. She made a point of introducing parents (usually mothers) and their babies to the study herself. Even behavioral laboratories can be intimidating, and she understands the importance of putting the moms at ease. A tough week combined with *that* dinner has left her desperate for time and conversation with her husband—and another drink.

Miles shrugs. "Sure. We can Uber home, pick up your car tomorrow. How about the Rye Bar?"

They make their way to M Street and turn right on Thirty-First toward the river. The bar is as plush and dark as a speakeasy, and they settle into armchairs in a corner. Jackie orders another martini. One is usually her limit, especially with wine thrown in, but it was hardly a usual evening. Miles asks for Lagavulin, and the waiter engages him in a discussion of single malts. Jackie squirms in her chair. The waiter leaves.

Miles checks his phone and tucks it away. He leans back, crosses his legs, and smiles at Jackie. "You definitely have something on your mind."

"I hardly know where to start. I keep bouncing between disconcerted and horrified."

"About what?"

How could he possibly ask? He knows Nasira is her postdoc. "Nasira!"

"Nasira?"

"Yes! And Harlan. I mean, why did he invite her and not tell me, knowing she works in my lab?"

"Sounds like they spent the afternoon together."

"Okay. So now we have two questions. Why did they spend the afternoon together? And why, having done that, was Nasira at our dinner? Harlan could've begged off."

Miles nods. "He could have, sure. But why not invite her? You know her. You work with her."

"I hardly know her at all. She just got here. Am I wrong to think I should've been the one to decide whether I wanted to socialize with her?"

"That's a fair point. But is it really a huge deal? Harlan's broken the ice now."

"Yes, but why?"

"Why what?"

"Why her?"

Miles spreads his hands. "Why not her? Look, Jackie. If Nasira was, I don't know, dreary or full of herself, I could see your point. But I thought she was easy company."

"'Easy' is an interesting choice of words."

"Jackie . . ."

The drinks arrive. Miles raises his glass. "Cheers."

"Cheers." Jackie inhales the resinous scent of the gin. Miles's attention is wandering around the bar as he tastes his scotch. She watches him, icy gin sliding down her throat, and wonders if he will comment on Nasira's looks. He's not the sort of man who routinely comments on appearances, thank God, but Nasira would send up a blip on any man's radar.

Jackie takes another sip and sets down her glass. "You're right, Miles. She's pleasant, if a bit reticent, and smart, of course."

Miles smiles. "You hired her, after all."

"I did."

"Her French is excellent. Did you know her mother was French?"

Miles is Dutch by birth but was schooled first in France, then in England, before returning to Utrecht for university. When Nasira ordered *pot de crème* and he heard the native sounds, he initiated a brief but rapid-fire exchange that left Jackie's I-can-get-by proficiency behind in the first sentence. It's ridiculous, but having a French mother seems to give Nasira intangible advantages, like having royal blood.

"Her mother never came up," Jackie replies.

"Well, I don't understand why you're objecting to someone who is so unobjectionable."

"I'm not objecting to her, Miles. I did enjoy talking with her at dinner. She was sprung on me, on us. Harlan could've warned us."

"We've covered that." He sighs and recrosses his legs. "Harlan seemed great. The sabbatical agreed with him, despite his aversion to travel, don't you think?"

Jackie nods. Harlan did seem more buoyant, refreshed. That's what sabbaticals are designed to achieve, but change was anathema to Harlan, or it had been, along with punctuality and visiting museums. Until tonight, Jackie has only seen Harlan in passing since his return; his research space, with its large, expensive equipment, is tucked into the labyrinthine basement of Wolf Hall, the Psychology Department building. Harlan studies the neural control of lying and truth telling, poking around in the electrochemical tangle of the brain in search of the mechanisms of moral judgment. Intriguing work, but esoteric compared to her own, especially her interest in uncovering behavioral markers for autism. For parents of autistic kids, knowledge is the foundation for coping—and hope.

Jackie pictures Harlan's hand on Nasira's back. She drains her glass and feels more focused and less tactful. "Miles. What do you think? Are they sleeping together?"

Miles laughs. "How would I know?"

"Harlan might have said."

Miles shakes his head, more in disbelief than denial. "Why are you so keen to know?"

"*L'enfant* is half his age."

He shrugs. "It happens."

Jackie studies him, trying to remember if he's said something recently about chatting with Harlan. She's been so frantic at work, and there wouldn't have been any reason for her to file the information away. She has the ghost of a memory of Miles saying he spoke with Harlan perhaps a week ago. Did they talk about Nasira? Jackie can't ask. A friendship between your ex and your husband means you've put the past behind you. But the past is never completely behind you; it is alive in your memories, in your reptilian brain, where a whiff of cologne can make you an idiot and where phrases like "we've moved on" mean next to nothing.

She leans forward. She knows damn well she should let it go but can't stop herself. One martini was not enough, and two, it seems, was too many. "Do you know something?"

"About?"

"Harlan and *L'enfant*."

He stares at her, his features squaring slightly, the playful curve of his mouth hardening. "Can we talk about something else?"

"Why? I'm just fascinated with what happened tonight."

"You're not just fascinated." He takes a slow sip of his scotch. "You're jealous."

"That's absurd."

"Is it?" He holds her gaze.

She resists the urge to squirm. When in doubt, double down. "Yes." She sits back in her chair and spreads her hands. "How can I be jealous? I don't even know if they're seeing each other."

"Then leave it alone."

His tone is firm, and Jackie pauses. Miles rarely challenges her, and never without cause. He's right that she doesn't know anything about Harlan and Nasira. If Jackie hadn't dated Harlan for five years, Nasira's presence at dinner would only have been a social blunder, easily overlooked. Miles is also right that she is jealous; she hasn't had cause for jealousy before tonight because she's never met any of Harlan's girl-friends. Maybe if she'd encountered a succession of Nasiras over the past five years she'd be inured.

As for Nasira, she probably walked into the evening blind, having no idea of Harlan's history with Jackie. It was, after all, just dinner.

Jackie reaches for Miles's hand. "I'm sorry to be such a nutjob. Want to go sailing in the morning?" It was how they met. At the time, Jackie rowed at dawn every morning. She'd begun the practice after college to quell her grief over her father's death. Losing him a second time, and losing him absolutely, had crippled her, and only the exhaustion from pulling the shell along the deep calm of the Potomac had brought her a measure of relief. Over the years, rowing morphed from an antidote to pain to a source of pleasure. At the boathouse one morning, Miles struck up a conversation and convinced Jackie to trade solitary rowing for dinghy sailing, at least for the day. On their third outing, Jackie learned that Miles had recently lost his father. She asked about him, about them. That day and during later sails they shared their stories, stories long enough for a slow, wide river, and their nascent friendship deepened.

Miles takes Jackie's hand and turns her wedding band. The tenderness of his thick, strong fingers makes her chest tighten.

"I'd love to go sailing," he says.

———

Late the following afternoon, Jackie scrounges in the freezer, hoping dinner will materialize. Miles is on the far side of the open-plan space, intent on a football game, a notebook in his lap and a bottle of IPA in his hand. Technically, this is work; he is studying strategy and taking notes on players, considering how his clients might fit into the roster. Miles is careful never to drink when he's courting young players and their parents, so the afternoon beer is an indulgence for home.

She pulls out a package of meat and holds it in the air. "Beef stew okay?"

Miles turns to her. "Delicious. Let me know if I can help."

"The Instant Pot and I have it covered."

Jackie places the meat in cold water to defrost and carries her Kindle, her phone, and a glass of iced tea upstairs to their office and her favorite reading chair. She and Miles have gravitated toward a more modern style, and the chair is shabby and not the least bit chic. Jackie sinks into it, opens her Kindle, shuts it again, and picks up her phone.

Just a bit of snooping, she tells herself, *the sort everyone does these days.* Just enough to confirm there is nothing to see. She hasn't breathed either Harlan's or Nasira's name since last night, but of course she has been thinking about them, replaying the moment when Harlan greeted her, before she knew who the mysterious friend was, and also the moment she recognized Nasira. If only Jackie had been able to catch sight of Harlan's face then. She would have seen something.

Jackie opens Instagram—the obvious choice for a millennial—types Nasira's name in the search bar, clicks through the handful of hits, and selects the only reasonable match. The avatar is a pineapple—*an ironic pineapple, perhaps?*—so Jackie scrolls through the feed and clicks on the first putative selfie. Despite the sunglasses and wide-brimmed hat, it's definitely her. That bone structure is hard to miss. Jackie scans the array of recent photos for anyone resembling Harlan but isn't really expecting to see him there. Nasira is savvy enough to know a postdoc-professor relationship is right at the edge of the ethical void. Most of her posts are of food and, recently, familiar sights in DC.

Jackie sips her iced tea and entertains the thought of reading her book, knowing she won't. She scrolls to the beginning of Nasira's feed and opens the most recent post, from 8:33 this morning. Jackie's heartbeat pulses in her throat as she examines the scene. Poached eggs on greens with avocado on a square white plate. To the side, croissants—enough for two—in a basket lined with slate-gray linen and a small pale-blue earthenware bowl filled with blueberries, a dollop of white on top. Whipped mascarpone, Jackie is certain. Everything is so familiar, it's as if she took the photo herself. She has eaten there, perhaps at that very table, dozens of times. The food is excellent at Stateside on M Street, but Adams is brimming with breakfast places for Nasira to choose among.

Jackie stares at the screen, pressure building at her temples. She knows something Nasira did not when she posted this shot. Harlan seldom goes out for breakfast, but when he does, it's there, and he always gets the poached eggs. When Harlan took Jackie to Stateside the first morning after she slept at his house, he recommended them. He was right, as he usually is.

They were delicious.

CHAPTER 3

HARLAN

I stand on the sidewalk in front of Stateside and watch Nasira leave. Her step is graceful and light, feline, her ponytail swishes. I'm thankful she went without protest or future commitment; I can't stand fussy goodbyes. She's lovely—and quiet, unlike Jackie. I am certain Nasira and I will see each other again. In fact, I'm counting on it.

She turns right on Franklin, toward her house presumably, and doesn't look back. Good girl.

The weather is pleasant enough, so I walk the mile and a half home. The round trip into town and back obviates the need for the cardio segment of my afternoon workout. When I reach my front steps, I notice the foundation plantings need attention and remind myself to email the landscape company. I punch the alarm code, step inside, and set about erasing Nasira's presence. Nothing personal; I must have order. I straighten the coasters on the end table, move a throw pillow two inches to the left, and proceed to the kitchen. As I load glasses into the dishwasher and wipe the marble counters, I mentally revisit last night's dinner.

The setting was perfect. Estrela is steeped in memories for Jackie and me, and never disappoints. The admixture of pleasure and pain I felt upon seeing her, touching her for the first time in nearly a year was exquisite. My attraction to her is visceral and relentless; only a fool discounts biology. When I kissed her cheek, I felt her wobble, so perhaps she loves me still. Or those ridiculous shoes might've been to blame. I did wonder why she chose them. It wasn't for me. She knows me better than that.

Then Jackie spotted my surprise guest—Nasira, pulled from the sleeve of Jackie's own coat. Jackie has never been one for masks, and her transparency leaves her vulnerable. Some might find it refreshing or endearing; I find it enlightening. In the moment before Jackie regrouped, each emotion was exposed—embarrassment, jealousy, anger—like a transparent model of the human body in which only the nervous system is shown: the brain and the facial nerves, the spinal cord, the sympathetic and parasympathetic networks, nerves running to the extremities and back again. Her limbic system was firing signal blasts to her prefrontal cortex, urgent, white-hot pleas for a logical response to the emotional bedlam Nasira's presence had incited.

Apologies for the shoptalk. Simply put, when Jackie recognized Nasira, I saw into Jackie. I always have.

She made a mistake in leaving me, in rejecting me despite everything I gave her. It was as much as I could give and have ever given, and had been enough for her. For years Jackie understood what we had together. Then she changed her mind, and now that she is married, she is smug. It's not a good look on her, and I find it insulting, to be honest, as if she has taught me something about who she is by marrying Miles. I know exactly who she is, what turns her head, what sparks her anger, what draws that insatiable curiosity of hers to the brightest, hottest flame.

I know because I love her.

CHAPTER 4

Jackie slows her car as she nears Harlan's house. Logan Street, west of campus, isn't on her way to work—or to anywhere—but she's only taking a quick peek. She pulls up to the curb beneath the boughs of an enormous oak. She isn't exactly hidden here, but it's not as if she's staying.

The house is typical of upmarket Adams: a handsome two-story brick Georgian with black shutters and white lintels. A long walk divides the deep front yard. Jackie can't hope to see in the windows, and she questions why she is even here. Unless Harlan and Nasira have the impulse to screw each other on the front lawn, this drive-by is pointless.

And disturbing, truth be told. What stable, happily married thirty-eight-year-old woman stalks her ex? If Miles knew she was here, he'd be appalled, and rightly so. *She* is appalled.

And yet here she is.

During the ten days since the Dinner, thoughts of Harlan and Nasira have bubbled up into Jackie's awareness on a steady boil. Yes, yes, it's disturbing and appalling—not to mention pathetic—and she has asked herself countless times why she cares. A neutral party would draw the obvious conclusion that she is still in love with Harlan. But love, in Jackie's view, is rarely the reason for anything, because it's not specific enough to have explanatory power. Jackie loves her husband, her sister, her brother-in-law, her nieces and nephews, and her mother, but the emotions each person evokes are unique. Including Harlan. She admires him and appreciates his humor and his candor. She is, despite her best suppressive efforts, attracted to him. Is that love? If it is, who cares?

The question is, why is she sitting in her car hoping to catch a glimpse of him with her postdoc? Curiosity, certainly. Prurient curiosity. And beneath that, the desire to know how much Harlan will grant Nasira. Jackie was so patient during their relationship, and in the end, after five years, Harlan denied her. Already she suspects he is moving faster with Nasira, and Jackie must know why.

Why her and not me?

Jackie winces at her own weakness. She checks the dashboard clock and drives away, glancing at the house one last time in her rearview mirror.

Belize Drake, a thirty-year-old law student, sits across the table from Jackie, holding her infant son in her lap. The boy has his mother's wide-set dark eyes and polished-bronze skin, but his dimpled knuckles are all his own. Jackie is always amazed at how much the babies change from when she first sees them at six months to when she sees them again at a year. This one-year-old, Xavier, is now his own person, solidly himself.

Gretchen, one of Jackie's graduate students, also sits facing Xavier and his mother, but off to the side. Both Jackie and Gretchen are using iPads to record the child's responses. The room is painted a sunny yellow and the floor is carpeted. Cabinets hold a vast selection of toys, plus playpens to confine children for certain tests. Video cameras and microphones record sessions, primarily for backup. The work is painstaking but Jackie is certain of its value. Finding the earliest signs of autism—at any point on the spectrum—is crucial in caring for these children and their families in the best way possible.

Jackie smiles at the boy. "How are you doing, Xavier? Ready to play some games?" He sticks his fist in his mouth. Jackie selects the rattle from the box on the seat beside her. She shakes the rattle in front of Xavier to get his attention, then moves it to her right. His eyes follow. Jackie moves the rattle back to the middle and over to the left side. Xavier tracks it all the way. "Bah," he says as she puts the toy away.

Jackie types a zero next to "Visual Tracking 1" on the form on the iPad, indicating that his response was typical. Later in the twenty-minute session, Jackie will again challenge Xavier to track an object. Gretchen also enters something on her form, but they won't compare the data until later.

The mother resettles her son. Jackie gets up and positions herself to the side of the Drakes. She waits until Xavier's attention is elsewhere, then says his name. He does not turn to her. Belize Drake casts a glance at Jackie over her son's head. Jackie nods to reassure her. Belize knows that Jackie will repeat the test, and how Xavier reacts to any one challenge is not crucial. When the Drakes signed up for the study, Jackie explained what all the assessments and procedures would entail. Today's test, the AOSI, or Autism Observation Scale for Infants, has been the gold standard in the field for ten years, using a standard set of objects, plus free-play sessions, to score the eighteen items that make up the scale. Some of the items are social, like smiling when the examiner smiles and sharing an emotion. The rest probe other behaviors relevant to a diagnosis of autism, like motor control, attention, and visual tracking—following the rattle.

But Jackie understands why Belize can't help but see any glitch in her child's performance as worrisome. Xavier's older brother, Charles, was diagnosed with autism spectrum disorder two years ago, at the age of three. In Jackie's study, that puts Xavier in the high-risk group, since he has about a 10 to 20 percent chance of getting the same diagnosis. Belize and the other parents who volunteer for the research are anxious to know as soon as possible how the die has been cast. So far, a diagnosis at six months has been impossible, and it's pretty unreliable at Xavier's age, too. But Jackie's work is all about searching for early, reliable signs, and given that she interacts every day with parents who do the same searching in an informal way, she feels nothing but sympathy for Belize's anxious monitoring.

"Why don't we play on the floor for a bit?" Jackie crosses the room and kneels on the floor.

Belize holds her son under the arms and stands him upright. He teeters toward Jackie.

"Look at you!" She stretches out her arms, but he falls onto his behind in front of her. He startles, sees Jackie's broad smile, and grins.

Jackie glances up at Belize in time to catch her smile.

After the session ends, Jackie digs her lunch out of the lab fridge and heads to her office. She clears away the stacks of papers and regards her kale salad dolefully. She ought to have chosen something that didn't require quite so much chewing to have a chance of finishing before the lab meeting. This semester, Mondays are doomed: a 9:00 a.m. developmental psych lecture, followed by a graduate seminar on social development, then a one-hour break, during which she squeezed in the session with Xavier. Next comes the lab meeting, several more study appointments, and today, as the second Monday of the month, the departmental talk at 5:00 p.m. She considered moving the lab meeting to a different day, but in her experience, it pays to get everyone pointed in the right direction at the start of the week. Graduate students are prone to drift.

She sorts through her emails—delete, delete, highlight, delete—and pauses on the reminder for Thursday's reception for new adjunct faculty, visiting professors, and postdocs. The word "postdoc" evokes Nasira, and Jackie struggles to dispel the image of Harlan and Nasira after the Dinner, walking away together in intimate conversation, and sharing breakfast at Stateside. As Jackie reads the details of the reception, however, thoughts of Nasira are replaced by those of herself at a similar reception ten years ago. Three recent faculty hires, including Jackie, were being honored.

She stood at the perimeter with a tepid glass of chardonnay, wondering if it was too soon to leave. The stacks of moving boxes occupying every room of her house called to her. Her lab and her classes held top priority, but living out of boxes wasn't her style.

Harlan entered the room, scanned the sea of heads, and caught her eye. He snaked through the tight crowd at the refreshment table, nodding at those who greeted him. Jackie had first met him when she interviewed for the position. Their conversation had been brief, and she had no memory of the topic. She remembered him, though: his eyes, his voice, and that smile, warm and edged in mischief.

When Harlan reached her, he smiled that smile and extended his hand. "Harlan Crispin. Congratulations."

"Thank you. I'm delighted."

"I hoped the search committee would put you forward. You were the best of the ones they brought in, but they don't always get it right."

Jackie sipped her wine while she unpacked Harlan's statement. No doubt it was complimentary, but it also suggested he didn't think highly of some of his colleagues, either those on the search committee or the allegedly ill-advised hires. She was tempted to ask Harlan whom he viewed as weak, but opted for diplomacy. Who knew which way the political winds blew in this department? "I'm flattered you think so, but from what I know, Josslyn Burnes and Hamid Kamar are first-rate."

He leveled his gaze at her. "You don't have to do that. Not with me, certainly."

"Do what?"

"Be evenhanded and thereby sell yourself short."

Jackie cast about for a quip to end this line of talk; she distrusted bold flattery. Harlan watched her, waiting, his eyes deep brown and inquisitive. He was striking rather than handsome, and something about him drew her closer, the temptation of a door left ajar.

A long moment passed. Harlan selected a cube of cheese from the table beside him and held it aloft by the toothpick buried in its center. He nodded once, signaling, she supposed, his approval that she had tacitly accepted his edict. He pulled the cheese from its skewer with his teeth and scanned the room as he chewed. She should ask a question, make small talk, but now that Harlan had made it clear he expected her to be brilliant, everything she thought of she discarded as trite.

He turned his attention back to her. She felt the heat of it in her face, in her chest. He gestured to the refreshments, inviting her to join in his assessment of the discount chardonnay and merlot, the perfectly symmetrical cookies that betrayed their supermarket origin, the unripe, outsize wedge of Brie, hacked by a translucent plastic knife. Jackie shrugged. The offerings were forlorn but predictable.

Harlan said, "I hope you don't judge us by this. Academics can be pointedly lowbrow in their aesthetics."

She laughed. "Our burning intellects must dull our other senses." She flashed on a conference she had attended in graduate school, where a female professor had warned her not to appear too put together if she wanted to be taken seriously. "You should look as though you selected your clothes at random because you were preoccupied with more important thoughts." The woman had only been half joking. It might be an anecdote Harlan would appreciate, Jackie mused, but she wasn't sure. She did surmise that, concerning Harlan, one ought to be absolutely sure.

He dipped his shoulder, poised to offer her a confidence. She could smell his cologne—grapefruit and something else, like turned earth. "You probably have a few people you need to check in with, per protocol, but after that, if you're not busy, we could find something palatable."

Jackie's standard response to flirtation was to pretend she didn't understand it for what it was, then make excuses. Men had to lay siege to her defenses before she would consider them head-on, and most men, thank God, didn't have the energy. She wasn't playing hard to get; she didn't want to be got, except on rare occasions, when she gave in to her craving for male company and intimate sex and lowered her drawbridge. During her junior year in college, Jeff Toshack had discovered her in such an unguarded state and pulled her close. A year and a half later, Jackie had retreated inside the fortress of her own making, and Jeff was three thousand miles away and, she assumed, bewildered.

She returned Harlan's gaze. Was he flirting or only being friendly? Either way, the reception was drab and, having skipped lunch to set up her office, she was ravenous—and intrigued.

She set down her glass. "Give me fifteen, okay? I'll find you."

"I won't be far."

A kiss on the second date—if the evening of the reception counted as the first—sex on the fourth, sleeping over at his house on the fifth because it was a Friday, all within three weeks. Jackie wouldn't call it a romance; there was no sense of losing her footing, of sliding or succumbing. If she had felt any of that, she would've turned on the sarcasm, stiffened her back, and drowned herself in work until the feeling passed and Harlan dissolved like the others. He was different, however. He was witty and interesting and interested, and, most important, did not appear to be either running away from or running toward her. It was as if they had both come to a standstill in mutual acceptance of their compatibility, although the idea of a perfect fit was itself too imbued with fate for her taste. She was certain Harlan held the same view. They would spend a few hours together and then return to their respective homes for sleep or chores or exercise, or to their labs to work.

As a new professor, Jackie put in long hours establishing her research program, developing curricula for classes, and mentoring graduate students. She had little spare time. As a full professor with an ever-expanding lab, Harlan had even less. Jackie and Harlan became a microcosm of two with limited scope and a predictable routine. They dated twice a week, usually Tuesdays and Fridays, with Fridays extending into Saturdays, though rarely past lunchtime. They never spoke of the relationship, only logistics, which gave Jackie permission to tell herself it wasn't really a relationship at all. Given her fitful history with men, denying the relationship was the only way she could continue. Love wasn't on the table; it wasn't even in the room.

What made Harlan the exception was his focus on her. The first time she had dinner with him after escaping the tedious reception, she was astounded at how she immediately felt at the center of his world. There was no place he would rather be than sitting across the table from her, nothing she could say that would fail to interest him, nothing she could do to lessen her appeal. It was heady stuff.

Her assessment was the same after every date, from the first to the second to the third and on to whatever number they logged years later. When they were together, Harlan's attention did not waver. In his light, she was smarter, funnier, and more fascinating than she had ever viewed herself. She was also sexier. He wanted her with a candid passion that rendered superfluous the need for lacy lingerie, fuck-me heels, or background music. The sex wasn't inventive, which suited her, but it was intense, and had the same clarity as all their interactions.

She accepted the version of herself he reflected back at her, and extended this acceptance more generally, viewing her life as he framed it. She was the best of the younger faculty, a rising star, a talented teacher, a writer of unusual lucidity. With his guidance, which he readily offered, she would win grant money, attract the most able students, gain tenure in record time.

And she did.

———

Now, in her lab office, Jackie takes a final bite of her salad and throws the rest into the trash. She closes her laptop, grabs her coffee mug and the pastry box she picked up from Sweet Somethings, the bakery near her house, and leaves her office. She actually has two offices: her official one on the same floor as the departmental offices and this smaller one in the suite of rooms that constitutes her lab. She prefers the lab office, especially when wolfing down a meal, because she is less likely to be interrupted. It is also quieter, except when experiments are ongoing and a child screams loudly enough to defy the triple soundproofing. Jackie doesn't mind the screaming; it reminds her that her work involves real people with real emotions and, often, troubled lives.

Jackie walks by the office space shared among the grad students—and her new postdoc, Nasira. The room is empty except for Kyle, her most senior student, hunched and tense over the computer, face inches from the spreadsheet displayed on the screen, long fingers poised above the keyboard, both legs hammering a silent rhythm under the bench. Jackie hesitates, reluctant to break his concentration, but the meetings aren't optional.

"Hey, Kyle. It's one."

He frowns, still glued to the screen, then breaks out in a grin. His fingers drop onto the keys, execute dozens of keystrokes in seconds. He hits save and scrapes back his chair. "That pivot table was a hairy mofo."

Jackie laughs and leads the way to the conference room, where the others wait: Gretchen and Tate, the other grad students; Rhiannon and Reese, the undergrads; and Nasira, seated to the left of Jackie's spot at the end of the table with the whiteboard behind it. Nasira wears an oversize white sweatshirt, and her hair is pulled back in an artfully messy bun. Jackie has attempted a messy bun, but hers turn out more frenetic than artful. Nasira looks up from her phone and smiles, her tiny reserved smile. Jackie is reminded of three weeks ago, when Nasira, as

27

a newcomer, presented her study plans to the group. Jackie and Nasira had a pleasant lunch together afterward, chatting about work and how Nasira was settling in. Jackie was optimistic about Nasira's potential contribution to the lab and felt confident in being cast as a role model for the young woman. They would learn from each other, Jackie thought. Nasira brought neurological expertise to the lab, broadening the scope. Jackie would serve as a mentor, but in a different way than for her graduate students, as was typical for postdoctoral appointments. Nasira would be more like a younger sister, Jackie thought. Women, even very intelligent, capable women, need a hand at their elbow in the male-dominated world of science.

Now she's not sure what to think. Nasira seems to have jumped right into the deep end with Harlan, possibly making Jackie superfluous as a mentor. Harlan is a much bigger fish than she is; his advice automatically trumps hers. In any case, Jackie isn't feeling quite as sisterly today.

Jackie takes a seat. "Hi, everyone. If your Monday is like mine, you're going to want one of these." She opens the bakery box and pushes it to the center of the table. "Cookies from Sweet Somethings." There's a buzz of appreciation, and everyone except Nasira takes one. Jackie scans the room, waiting for her students to settle again. "Okay, let's dive right in. Tate, you ready to tell us where we are with recruitment for the toddler study?"

Tate, pierced and tattooed and dressed in a vintage granny dress and combat boots, heads to the whiteboard, where she has already posted a summary. "Numbers are up from two weeks ago, but the new ad isn't boosting it as much as we need."

The team discusses recruitment strategies for several minutes; then Jackie moves on to confirming the research schedule. Nothing is more important than conducting the studies, and experience has taught her that students are more likely to show up to run the experiments if they commit to it at a meeting. What she would give to have a lab manager, like Harlan has, but she doesn't have the funding. Somehow autism isn't as sexy as lying. Most of her money comes from advocacy groups, and they are, quite rightfully, keen to ensure that every dollar is spent wisely. Research money from government agencies (like the FBI, in Harlan's case), tech companies, and the pharmaceutical industry flows more freely. Jackie doesn't resent a tight budget but does wish it came bundled with extra hours in the day.

After fifty minutes, the agenda is complete. "That's all I've got. You know where to find me with any questions." Jackie opens the Voice Memo app on her phone and records her action items as the meeting breaks up around her.

Gretchen comes around the far side of the table and confers with Nasira, who is typing on her phone.

Gretchen says, "You're working on the four-year study, right? I'm using the social part of the AOSI for my thesis and can't figure out how the cohorts are organized." When Gretchen was ready to choose her thesis topic, Jackie suggested she concentrate on one aspect of the AOSI scale.

"Sure. One sec." Nasira pulls up the file and angles away from Jackie, shifting her laptop so Gretchen can see the screen.

Nasira's phone is on the table; the screen displays a text exchange with someone named Rachel.

Jackie glances at Nasira, who is absorbed in her conversation with Gretchen. Jackie's heart beats faster, knowing she only has seconds before the screen goes dark. She drags the bakery box toward her until it rests between Nasira's laptop and her phone. Jackie rearranges the remaining cookies with one hand and, with the other, touches the back arrow to show the list of recent texts. "Harlan" pops out at her, and she opens the thread, horrified by her audacity, her unscrupulousness. She should close the thread and salvage her integrity (what's left of it), but now that the messages are right in front of her, she can't resist. If her conscience had shouted in outrage a few seconds earlier, she might have listened. Too late now.

Jackie reads while continuing to stack the cookies, blood rushing to her face.

Harlan: Maybe it's too soon, but the Blue Goose has a special on Tuesday night.

Nasira: Never too soon for geese.

Harlan: That's my thinking. Meet there at 7?

Nasira: Perfect. 👍

Harlan: 🏃

Tuesday. Tuesday and Friday. Date nights. Their date nights.

Jackie stifles a cry, hits the back arrow, and reopens Rachel's thread. Nasira swivels. Gretchen is leaving.

Jackie closes the bakery box, and wills Nasira's phone to turn off. Will she notice?

Gretchen speaks from the doorway. "See you later."

"Bye," Jackie and Nasira say simultaneously.

The phone's screen is black.

Nasira shuts her laptop, whisks the phone away. They are alone. Jackie feels Nasira's eyes on her, but she cannot, will not, meet her gaze. Jackie's face is flushed, she can feel it. Guilt rises inside her, leaving her nauseous.

Does Nasira know about Harlan's past with Jackie? For a moment Jackie thinks she might just tell Nasira that she was Harlan's girlfriend for five years, five of her best years, five years carved out of the heart of her life, like a cancer, an alien mass that was her and yet was not her, sliced out and discarded. There is something she needs to tell Nasira about Harlan, Jackie is sure of it, but she doesn't know precisely what to say, what the message should be. Perhaps "Don't do what I did." A cautionary tale? But it was Jackie who left; it is always Jackie who leaves. Maybe the cautionary tale is not to become Jackie. Talk about mentoring.

She hears her thoughts as spoken words and recognizes them as a thought salad. No, what she wants to tell Nasira is that she cannot bear to see her succeed with Harlan, but it would be madness to say such a thing. They've just started seeing each other, and Jackie hardly knows Nasira. She shouldn't concern herself with Harlan, either, especially his sex life. She's married to a wonderful man, and yet she's blowing up boundaries right and left and seriously contemplating giving unsolicited (and undercooked) relationship advice to her postdoc. What the hell is wrong with her?

Nasira gets up and studies Jackie. "Are you all right?"

"Yes, I'm fine." She says it too loudly, flustered. "Mondays . . ."

Nasira nods as she inserts her computer into her gray wool messenger bag. She ducks her head and slips on the shoulder strap.

Maybe Nasira will say something about Harlan, clear the air. Jackie waits, fiddling with her phone.

Nasira takes the long way around the table, her steps soundless, and leaves without another word.

Jackie sips her cold coffee. Her hand is trembling. What an unethical idiot she is, reading someone else's texts. She doesn't think Nasira saw her, but it was wrong regardless—and risky. And to what end? Now she knows they have plans for tomorrow, that the relationship is moving ahead full-bore. Did she expect Harlan to remain celibate to make it easier for her?

She closes the bakery box and thinks of Miles. Maybe she'll pick up something for him, his favorite, a lemon tart. Her conscience is urging her to correct her internal moral accounting, do something nice for the someone truly committed to her instead of becoming enmeshed in a relationship that has nothing to do with her. Well, almost nothing to do with her. After all, she and Harlan are friends, aren't they? And Nasira is her postdoc . . .

Jackie chastises herself for falling into the rabbit hole again.

Let it go. Be happy with what you have. Make amends.

31

Yes, a lemon tart for Miles. And tonight she won't do what she's done at every opportunity since the Dinner. She won't swing by Harlan's house or his favorite hangouts, hoping to spot him with Nasira. She won't go by Nasira's house, either, even though it's practically on the way home. It's humiliating, but satisfyingly so, the degradation of succumbing to jealousy, the weakness in being unable to control her curiosity—morbid as it is—and the desperate thrill of being a naughty snoop. She's vowed to stop a dozen times, but has thus far given in despite her mounting guilt over betraying Miles in doing so.

But today she crossed a bright line, reading Nasira's texts, and there is no justification for it, not even a self-serving one. Everything she learns only makes her feel more pain and more guilt. It's time to look away.

CHAPTER 5

Nine days later, Jackie finishes her office hours and heads to the faculty meeting. It's only Wednesday, and this is her third administrative meeting of the week. How is she supposed to accomplish anything? She takes a deep breath and resigns herself to the unavoidable.

Down the hallway, Ursula Kleinfelter is exiting her office. When she turns to close her door, she spots Jackie, waves, and waits for her. Jackie admires Ursula, a psycholinguist originally from Israel, for her take-no-prisoners attitude and would welcome a chance to socialize with her. Ursula splits her time with the Middle Eastern Studies Department and is intensely private besides, so Jackie has not yet found an inroad to friendship.

"Jackie! I never see you." Ursula touches Jackie's forearm in greeting. Ursula might be nearly sixty, but her brown eyes are bright behind her ultramodern glasses with emerald-green frames. Her outfit is on point, too—wide-legged trousers and an embroidered blouse—setting her yet further apart from her dowdy academic colleagues. Jackie pays attention to her clothes but never feels half as put together as Ursula.

"I was thinking that, too. Shame it takes a faculty meeting to bring us together."

"Everything about a faculty meeting is a damn shame."

Jackie laughs. As they set off together, she says, "Weren't you in Jordan this summer?"

Ursula nods. "Mostly. Also, Iraq—Mosul—and three weeks on vacation in Tel Aviv, although we're talking family, so 'vacation' is perhaps an exaggeration."

The hallway spills into a wider area, banked on one side by elevators and on the other by the glass-walled entrance to the Psychology Department offices.

"And what about you?" Ursula asks. "You were here, right? That big study?" She stops talking as her attention is drawn abruptly toward the office.

Jackie follows her gaze. Next to the reception desk, at the entrance to the mailroom, Nasira leans against the doorframe, a package in her arms. She's conversing with Harlan, who has his back to the entrance, but even from this vantage point Jackie notices they are practically touching. If it weren't for the package Nasira is holding, they could be slow dancing.

Ursula comes to a standstill. "Who is Harlan talking to? A grad student?" Her tone suggests she also notes their proximity.

"A postdoc."

"Oh, well, that's a bit different, I suppose." Ursula turns to Jackie. "Do you know her?"

"Nasira Amari. My postdoc."

Ursula arches one eyebrow. "I see."

Of course Ursula knows Jackie dated Harlan. The department is small, and five years is a long time, although in those five long years, Harlan never stood inside of Jackie's bubble in full view of anyone who might pass by. Not once. It was one of Harlan's rules. At this moment, Jackie cannot recall whether that was an explicit rule or an implicit one. It doesn't matter. What matters is that Harlan is flaunting a three-week relationship—one with questionable ethics—in their workplace. Since she peeked at Nasira's phone, Jackie has been trying to stuff her curiosity or jealousy or whatever it is back in the box it jumped out of. This PDA behind the glass wall is not helping.

Ursula is calmly regarding her, awaiting a response of some kind. Jackie shrugs. "I'll admit it is weird."

"Weird, yes, but perfectly understandable. He's a man, and she is, well, stunning."

Here's some salt, Ursula. Rub that into the wound while you're at it. Jackie looks at her watch. "We're going to be late."

As they start again for the conference room, Jackie thinks maybe Ursula wouldn't be such a great friend after all. She's a little too blunt.

———

The departmental chair is Amy Chen, a social psychologist with a strategic fervor more suited to Capitol Hill than a university. Successful faculty members—the ones who cause money and prestige to flow into the department—make her look good, so her favor shines more brightly on them. Not surprisingly, she adores Harlan and, provisionally, tolerates Jackie.

Chen opens the meeting with a detailed report of a university-wide technology initiative, the content of which was included in the email with the meeting agenda. Jackie skimmed it; there is nothing to vote on, and reviewing it now is a waste of time.

From her seat near the back of the room, Jackie sees Harlan enter. He opts to lean against the rear wall rather than take one of several empty chairs nearby. Jackie crosses her legs, angling away from him, and directs her attention to the tall windows on her right. Rain is falling in gray sheets, obscuring the view of the treetops and the science center that this sixth-floor room normally enjoys. A chill comes over Jackie, and the skin on her neck prickles. Her first thought is that Harlan is watching her, but given what she has just seen, that is unlikely. He has found someone far more captivating.

As Chen drones on, now about the ad hoc committee charged with assessing how space in Wolf Hall is allocated, Jackie conjures an image of herself, barely twenty-eight, lying in bed on a Saturday morning, Harlan's arm folded along her side, holding her firmly, his hand on her hip as if they were standing on the deck of a ship pitching in high seas and he meant to keep her from falling overboard.

Objectively, she wonders what drew her to him. Ursula's summation that men have license to ignore a woman's age is true enough, and Jackie has been aware of her ability to attract men since the age of twelve. No doubt Nasira is similarly aware. But this accounts only for Harlan's choice of her, not vice versa. Lying beside him ten years ago, his graying chest hairs were plain enough and consistent with the maturity evident in every aspect of his life: his remarkable career, of course; his spotless house, where clothes discarded in passion never lingered past noon; his manners, practiced and authentic; his wardrobe, displaying quality over quantity but curated to include T-shirts—notably ones featuring the Doors and a boutique Maryland brewery—to stop him from appearing stuffy. Did she have a daddy complex that placed a halo around Harlan's head, obscuring his silvery temples? Maybe, but she had no history of dating older men. Rather, she had a history of relationships that didn't last as long as her shampoo.

At first, Jackie didn't mind that most of her time with Harlan was spent on his turf and on his terms. She was new in town, so it made sense to follow his lead. He had excellent taste in restaurants, and they usually agreed on which movie to see. If she wanted to see a play or visit a museum, she could do it during the remaining four and a half days of the week—or never, given her schedule. Staying at his place made sense, too, because it was larger and in a better neighborhood.

Before Harlan, Jackie had accepted the cultural norm that relationships should go somewhere, progressing from less intimate to more, from dating to cohabiting to mating with purpose. The sense of stepping onto an escalator leading inevitably to a family (to becoming *her* family) was what kept Jackie from sticking with relationships. Jackie's father left when she was nine, and her mother, bitter to this day, instructed Jackie to not allow men to ruin her life. The lesson stuck; Jackie kneecapped relationships before they could go anywhere.

Jackie's feelings about having children were thus confounded. In her early twenties she thought she wanted them, but the relationship hurdle seemed insurmountable. She could imagine cradling a baby or holding the hands of a toddler learning to walk, and feel the promise of joy; she just couldn't imagine how to get there. When she chose developmental psychology as her concentration, Jackie told herself it was because she was fascinated by questions of nature versus nurture, but she was self-aware enough to recognize the sly hedge. Her career would place her adjacent to motherhood, where she could monitor the reality of it, knowing she could always, at some unspecified point in the future, decide to have a child outside the crapshoot of marriage.

The relationship hurdle was further complicated by the fact that she went to college in Maine, graduate school in Philadelphia, and did her postdoctoral work in Baltimore. She struggled to sustain her female friendships, let alone a committed relationship with a man. But when she took the job at Adams, Harlan appeared in her life and offered a novel path; he eschewed progression in favor of leaving well enough alone. Satisfactory, as a relationship grade, was an achievement. She became convinced she wanted what he did: dating for life. They were aligned, so why change? Just to do what others did, usually not successfully? Jackie had a friend from graduate school, Constance, who "had it all" and was stressed out of her mind, resenting the demands of her job one minute and the demands of her husband and children the next. Each day was scheduled with the precision of a NASA launch, and explosions on the launchpad were common. Constance criticized Jackie for being in a relationship without commitment. But she and Harlan didn't lack commitment; they were committed to a circumscribed relationship. All relationships were circumscribed in one way or another, she told herself; soul melding was claptrap. The only valid question was whether each person was getting what they wanted and needed, and for a time Jackie echoed Harlan's resounding "yes."

After two years of the Tuesday/Friday/Saturday morning routine, however, Jackie's relationship moxie grew. Maybe it was working with parents and children, witnessing daily how couples leveraged their love for each other to nurture the next generation, and often did so with grace. Maybe it was the radical notion that not all men were "useless bastards," to quote her mother. Jackie had attended three weddings during those two years: those of her sister and two friends from graduate school. If other intelligent, reasonably sane people were taking the plunge, why shouldn't she dip her toe in the water? She was happy with Harlan, warmed by the spotlight of his attention, awakened by his assurance in bed, lifted up by his respect for her work. If this much were possible, why not more? Her capacity for trust woke inside her like a small, blind, wingless creature.

During a Saturday brunch, Jackie threw out the question with all the insouciance she could muster. "How about we go away together for a few days?"

"As in a vacation? You know I don't see the point of them. I have no need to escape my life."

"Not escape. Variety." She almost used the word "adventure," but that would be abhorrent to him.

He'd been in a cheerful mood—that's why she'd chosen the moment—but now concern clouded his features. "Aren't you happy?"

"Very. But a jaunt could be fun." She resumed eating to show him how much it didn't matter.

"Wasn't last night fun?"

They had watched *Modern Family*, and she'd laughed so hard she had fallen off the bed. She smiled, thinking about it. "So fun. Big fun." He was right. Why change a winning strategy?

He grinned at her, eyes shining.

The key to happiness, she realized, was rejecting the impossible, glittering romantic quest and embracing satisfaction. To want more was foolishness, and Jackie was never foolish.

———

In Wolf Hall, Jackie stares out at the rain, lost in her reminiscences of her time with Harlan. She looks around the room at her colleagues and sees that her position among them is largely the result of accepting Harlan's vision of her authentic self, the person she was destined to become. He was the authority on her, writing her definitive biography as she stood before him and absorbed the glowing smile he gave only to her, mesmerized by his calm, rich voice. She acquiesced to him, to his schedule, to his plans for her. The only reason they are no longer together is that she found—inevitably, in retrospect—that she did want more.

Now she has Miles, who is nothing like Harlan, and she isn't at all certain this is the marriage she wants or needs. The uncertainty itself is familiar, even reassuring. It was ever thus. If she were blissful, she'd check herself into a hospital. Her doubt isn't about bliss; it's about having children, the next step in the progression that until now seemed beyond her grasp. Before they were married, literally days before, Miles said he was happy to consider having a child with her. She'd brought up the subject twice since, and while he hasn't said he's changed his mind, neither has he raced to the bathroom to flush her birth control down the toilet. Both times he was unequivocally equivocal, and she didn't push it. While he was away on one of his frequent trips, she'd resolve to talk to him about starting a family, but once he was home, she was loath to bring it up and spoil their time together. There was never a good time to talk, or maybe never a good time to hear the word "no."

Jackie watches rainwater spilling out of a clogged gutter and wonders whether, if she did a quick calculation, she might have averaged more time with Harlan than with Miles. She scolds herself for making the comparison and turns away from the window.

Miraculously, the faculty meeting adjourns, and Jackie shoots out the door before anyone can buttonhole her. She takes the stairs one flight down to her lab, hoping to complete a few more tasks before heading home for dinner with Miles. She lets herself in and pauses in the doorway of the shared office. Tate and Nasira seem to have just finished a conversation.

Tate smiles at Jackie. "Hey, Professor. Just getting back to coding." She spins the swivel chair back in front of the dual monitors and puts on a pair of large headphones. She hits a key and the video session resumes.

Nasira stands to the side collecting her belongings. "Hi, Jackie."

"Hi. Everything all right?"

"Sure. Tate was going to run through the four-year-study protocol with me on Friday, and I was seeing if we could reschedule."

"That's fine as long as you're up to speed soon. Study's filling up, thank goodness."

"I know. We're on for Tuesday. Such great news about the study."

Jackie is pleased with Nasira's enthusiasm for a project she's only tangentially involved with and decides she owes Nasira a more congenial attitude. Jackie hasn't been unfriendly to Nasira, only businesslike. "You heading out early for the weekend?"

"Yes, a quick trip."

Jackie remembers Nasira is from the Midwest somewhere—Ohio or Iowa maybe. "To see your family?"

Nasira zips her bag shut and places both hands on top, hesitating. "No, my parents are overseas. I need to make headway on the NIH grant, so I'm off on a retreat of sorts." She looks at the ceiling in thought. "A place called Greenfield, maybe?"

Jackie blinks at Nasira. "You mean Greenbrier."

Nasira smiles. "That's it." She takes a half step toward Jackie, a signal she wants Jackie to move aside so she can leave.

Jackie plants herself more firmly, as if Nasira might make a running tackle. "Greenbrier." Jackie shakes her head, perplexed that her brain is bothering to search for a different conclusion. There is none. Harlan avoids travel, but makes an exception for work weekends at Greenbrier Resort perhaps twice a year. Jackie had been dating him for two years before she received her first invitation.

Nasira stands patiently in front of Jackie. She doesn't shuffle her feet or play with her hair. She waits.

Jackie cannot hold back any longer. "With Professor Crispin?"

It's none of her business. She knows that. But if Nasira is flustered or offended by Jackie's intrusive question, she hides it beautifully. "I don't see how it matters."

"No. No, you wouldn't." Jackie is torn between wanting to clear the air, to find out what Nasira knows about her history with Harlan, and wanting to chase Nasira out of the building. Her curiosity wins out, per usual. "Nasira, I honestly didn't mean to pry. I couldn't have known you were going to Greenbrier."

Nasira purses her lips, the first signal that she is perturbed by Jackie's line of questioning.

Jackie is compelled to explain. "Maybe Harlan hasn't said, but he and I had a relationship. For five years." Jackie examines Nasira's expression, judging whether this is news and whether to say more. It's like conversing with a concrete slab. "Because of our history, I'm overly sensitive, I guess. I shouldn't be." She should stop right there—perhaps she's already said too much—but Nasira's stonewalling is provocative. Jackie fears she won't stop talking until Nasira opens up; the confusion and anger she's been harboring overwhelm her better angels. "It's been such a shock, starting with you as the surprise dinner guest . . ."

Nasira's face reddens slightly as she nods, not in assent, but with resolve. "And you with your husband." She allows that to sink in for a moment before stepping forward.

Jackie backs into the hall and turns away so Nasira cannot see her shame and regret. She exhales sharply, gathering herself, and turns back to wish Nasira a good weekend, but she is gone.

Jackie returns to her office. It's only five thirty, and she ought to get to work on revising a paper for the *Journal of Child Development*, but as soon as she opens the document, she knows she's too unsettled. Instead, she replays the conversation with Nasira and realizes the woman never confirmed she was going away with Harlan. He could have recommended Greenbrier to her, which is more plausible given his history. The more Jackie reflects, the more she sees how ridiculous it was to jump to the conclusion that Harlan would travel with Nasira so soon. Unfortunately, this revelation also makes Jackie look even more like a self-involved, jealous, meddling jackass.

Excellent work, Dr. Strelitz.

She packs up her laptop and tidies her desk. There's no point in beating herself up over her missteps. All she can do is vow to be more gracious, generous, and professional going forward. Right now what she wants most is to go home—to her husband.

———

Jackie dumps her bag by the front door and hurries into the kitchen. Miles is at the stove, stirring the contents of a pot. Jackie rises on her toes to give him a kiss.

"Yum," she says.

"Me or the risotto?"

"Both of you. What's going in it?" Risotto is Miles's signature dish. In fact, it's pretty much his only dish, with infinite variations. Jackie is not complaining.

"Lots of butter, lots of Parmesan, and roasted shrimp."

"I had all the kale in the world for lunch."

"This is the antidote."

She kisses him again, his cheek this time. "Thank you. Want me to take a turn stirring?"

"Not a chance." He twists his wrist to show his bracelet, a medical ID and fitness tracker combo. For his birthday last June, Jackie gave him this sleek platinum upgrade from the standard medical emergency bracelet that warned of his penicillin and sulfa drug allergies. "Vigorous stirring counts as steps."

Jackie laughs.

He tips his head toward an open bottle of red on the opposite counter. "Pour for us?"

"With great enthusiasm." She washes her hands, pours the wine, and hands Miles his. "To husbands at home."

He smiles, touches her glass, and sips. "If only the money would fly to me—or at least the clients."

"If only."

Miles is leaving again in the morning for a swing through North Carolina colleges, and Jackie wishes he could stay. Although she hasn't confessed to Miles that she's still entangled in the Harlan-Nasira business, he might be worried about just that. Maybe that's what the risotto is about, shoring up the marriage, reminding her how it feels to be loved and cared for. She tastes the sour pang of guilt at the back of her mouth and considers telling him how sorry she is, reassuring him that she'll detach herself from Harlan and Nasira and return her focus to their marriage. But bringing it up would only ruin this moment in which they are attuned to each other, and she decides to leave the apologies and promises for later.

They drink wine while Miles stirs. Jackie slips off her shoes and asks him about the upcoming weekend, about the clients he hopes to meet with and possibly sign. He's so animated in talking about his work, about his dreams for these talented young men, that she forgets about her postdoc and her ex. The fact that Miles is not an academic is consistently refreshing, and part of what drew her to him from the start. He respects her work and admires her intelligence and ambition, but appreciates the other worlds that exist beyond campus boundaries. After Harlan and his laser focus on her career, Jackie is grateful for Miles's ability to swing open the windows of her stuffy academic fortress, even for a view of the arena of professional sports. In Jackie's experience, universities are conservative—not in the political sense, but in their resistance to change—and it's easy to become insulated. Jackie loves so much about Miles, but perhaps his openness and broad-mindedness most of all. He can talk to anyone and is always the same person when he does.

After the meal, when the wine is finished, she puts the dishes in the sink and returns to the table. She slides onto his lap and wraps her arms around his neck.

"Fancy a tumble?" It's an old joke between them, the use of catch-phrases from each other's cultures.

He kisses her, slow and sweet, then touches her cheek. "Absolutely." His blue eyes sparkle. "More steps."

She smiles as a thread of warmth unravels down her spine. As she takes her husband's hand and leads him upstairs, she thinks, *Men. Women. Sometimes it really is this simple.*

CHAPTER 6

Jackie startles at the knock on her lab office door and looks up to see Vince Leeds, the departmental IT guy. She's been so engrossed in her work, she forgot he was installing new video cameras in the research rooms.

"Didn't mean to scare you, Jackie."

He yanks one sleeve down over his wrist, then the other, self-conscious about his eczema. Jackie can see he's having a flare-up from the sores on his neck.

"It's okay; I'm easily spooked. How's the work going?"

"You're all set. I tested all three. The configuration is virtually identical to your previous models, so you shouldn't have any trouble operating them, but let me know if you do."

Jackie smiles and wonders, not for the first time, if it weren't for the eczema, whether Vince would have pursued a different career or aimed for a higher rung. She's seen him at so many departmental lectures, sometimes she has to remind herself he's not on the faculty. "You're the best, Vince." She checks her watch: 5:45. "And sorry to keep you late."

"Not a problem. It's more important to me that your experiments run smoothly."

"Have we figured out a way to clone you yet?"

He blushes and pulls on his sleeves again. "Have a good evening, Jackie."

"You too."

Jackie listens to him collect his tools and exit the lab and returns to her work. She opens a new sheet in the Excel file and populates the cells with summary data copied from another sheet. She spent the last hour compiling the most recent data from a long-term study. The files are large, and she has to be careful to create backups as she works, leaving a trail of the data-crunching techniques she used. Anyone with a knowledge of behavioral analysis should be able to follow her process, but she's learned from experience that what seems straightforward when she is immersed in the work can be stupefying later on. She creates a graph, showing how the frequency of a child sharing an emotion with a parent changes over time in two groups: children who were eventually diagnosed with autism spectrum disorder and those who were not. Jackie verifies that the confidence intervals are set correctly and saves the file. She is labeling the graph when the door to the hallway clicks open. No one bothers to lock the door unless they are the last to leave. It's almost 7:00 p.m., but one of the graduate students might have forgotten something.

"Jackie?"

Harlan. Jackie pushes her chair back, straightens her shirt, fiddles with her hair. He rarely comes to her lab and never unannounced.

His footsteps echo on the tile floor, and a moment later he fills the doorway. He's wearing a leather jacket and carrying his computer bag, obviously on his way out, except her lab is not on his route.

"Hi, Harlan." She offers him a tentative smile. "What a surprise."

"Sorry if I caught you at a bad time. I had to see Greg one floor up. I should've texted first, but I was here by the time I thought of it."

"It's fine." It's weird. She gestures to a chair. "Have a seat, and give me just one sec." She saves her work and moves the laptop to one side.

"I really did interrupt."

"I'm meeting Miles soon, so I was just finishing. What's up?" A cloud of apprehension floats down on her. Maybe he's seen her driving by his house and he's come to tell her off for being nosy. Or maybe Nasira told him about the awkward Greenbrier conversation and he's going to chastise Jackie for being unprofessional. That conversation was two weeks ago, though, and she's turned over a new leaf since then, a saner one, so Jackie doubts that accounts for Harlan's visit.

He crosses his legs and leans forward. "I haven't seen you in so long. Thought I'd take a chance you were here and say hello."

"Hello." She smiles awkwardly, not believing him for a moment.

He returns her smile, gracious as always. "I guess I'll see you Sunday at the game, anyway. But like I said"—he swirls his hand to indicate the floor above—"I was in the neighborhood. Greg was telling me the funniest story about his neighbor. Apparently he has a parrot who's been using Alexa to order all sorts of things from Amazon."

"I'm sorry. What game? Miles hasn't mentioned it."

Harlan frowns. "That's odd. He's known for a while, and I explicitly invited both of you. And Antonio if he's interested."

He invited Miles's son, too? Must mean Nasira won't be coming, since he only has four seats. Jackie opens the calendar on her phone to confirm what she already knows. "My Sunday appears to be game-free."

"I'm sure I told Miles." His tone is pointed, as if she is accusing him of lying.

"Then he must have forgotten to tell me." At this, Harlan raises an eyebrow. Jackie is dumbfounded; why would he doubt that Miles simply forgot? "You know he's always on the road. Everyone forgets things."

Harlan nods, but his slight smirk indicates he's humoring her.

Jackie moves on. "But thanks for including me. You know how much I love football." She immediately regrets the comment; it's too intimate. Before they started dating, Jackie didn't know a first down from a touchdown—and she didn't care to learn. But Harlan gently brought her up to speed, made it fun for her, for them, and before long Jackie was buying Redskins spirit wear and commenting on the likelihood of a sack. That was the past, however. She's been to exactly three games during the five years since they broke up. Miles has an open invitation from Harlan and has attended every game he can squeeze in.

Harlan looks at his feet. "I do know that. Yes."

She's hit a nerve and keeps her voice neutral. "I'll ask Miles about it."

"Yes, do. They're playing the Cowboys." He pushes himself to standing. "Oh, one more thing. Some sort of plague is going through my lab. I've got two graduate students plus Marvin out sick and five MRIs scheduled in the next couple of days. Mind if I ask Nasira to lend a hand?"

Jackie stares at him. "Nasira?"

"Yes. Is it a problem?"

Nasira's dissertation research involved using an MRI to study the progression of Parkinson's disease. In Jackie's lab Nasira's goal is to spend a year getting up to speed on autism research and, at the same time, write a grant to fund her own MRI study with infants. Like Harlan's research on deception, the infant study would examine brain activity using functional MRI. For Jackie, the chance to expand the scope of her lab into neurological imaging was the main attraction of Nasira's application. Nasira works in Jackie's lab, but because she has her doctorate, she is more of a collaborator. Jackie doesn't own her, and Harlan knows it.

"Like most postdocs, Nasira manages her own time. I'm a little confused as to why you wouldn't simply ask her yourself."

He spreads his hands to indicate the answer is obvious. "I didn't want to overstep."

"I'm sorry?" Jackie is sure she misheard.

"I didn't want to overstep."

This is laughable, but Jackie isn't close to laughing—more like she's in the conversational equivalent of a fun-house mirror. Harlan knows damn well that his relationship with Nasira is no secret to Jackie, so why pretend otherwise? It's one thing not to address it head-on and quite another to act as though Nasira is a stranger to him. Jackie studies Harlan's face, his posture. Is he challenging her to say something, to admit to knowing more about his quasi-illicit fling than she ought?

Jackie glances at her watch, shuts and unplugs her laptop, and stands. It feels better to be on her feet, poised for action, rather than sit lamely and swipe at his ludicrous questions. She gives Harlan the most level gaze she can manage. "Please ask Nasira yourself. It's no problem on my end, of course."

"Great. I will." He gestures at her desk, her flurry of activity. "If you're leaving, we can walk out together."

For fuck's sake. *And then we will part ways,* Jackie thinks, *me to my husband and, because it's Friday, you to your new squeeze. How quaint.* "I've got to close up everything, so you go ahead."

He appears disappointed, hurt even. "Are you sure? I don't mind waiting." He points at the window. "It's getting dark already."

Jackie bursts out laughing, unable to edit herself any longer. As Harlan knows, she walks on campus by herself at all hours. It's perfectly safe. His protective gesture is misplaced and odd as hell. But when she sees his eyes darken, a splinter of fear slides into her chest and lodges there. She's seen that look of his twice before. It's unnerving as hell, and she quickly sobers, changes the subject, eager for him to leave. "I'll text you about the game after I talk to Miles."

"I'd appreciate that." He picks up his bag from where it leans against the chair. "Glad I caught you. I wish we saw each other more often."

"We should."

"Take care, Jackie."

He leaves, his long strides echoing down the hall. She hears the door latch click open.

"I will." She holds her breath until the door closes and the lab is silent.

"Take care" isn't a Harlan phrase, at least not as a pleasant wish, which is why when she replays it in her mind exactly as Harlan spoke it, without his presence making her ears buzz and her brain seize, it sounds more like a warning. Why on earth would he be warning her? Maybe her guilty conscience is affecting her perception. She should be warning him about *her*, given her crazy stalking.

Still, she is not misreading everything. She didn't invent that cold, dark look.

Jackie waits in her office, perched on the edge of her desk, to ensure Harlan has given up on her for the evening. Why did he bother to see her in person? He could have raised either issue easily via text—and the question about Nasira did not have to be raised at all. The only reason for him to drop by was to be able to judge her reaction to his oddly confrontational questions. She should have called him out, been more direct from the start. It's a bad habit of hers, letting Harlan drive the conversation, call the shots without any pushback.

Maybe it's because one of the few times she did push back, she learned her lesson.

———

In February 2010, Harlan's mother died unexpectedly of a stroke in her sleep at her home in Newton, Massachusetts. She was seventy-seven years old. Harlan received the news at home on a Saturday morning, so Jackie was there, as she had been for most Saturday mornings for nearly two years. Harlan took the call in the kitchen, where he was making coffee. Jackie was upstairs, drying off from a shower, and heard his hushed tones through the open bathroom door. In Jackie's experience, Harlan received few calls at home, which she attributed to his status as an only child and his preference for a clean separation between work and personal activities. She dressed, wrapped her hair in a fresh towel, and went downstairs.

He looked up, phone in hand, when she entered. Jackie noticed the coffee had finished brewing, but he hadn't poured it. The refrigerator door was ajar.

"Everything all right?" she asked, careful not to suggest she had any right to information.

"That was Miranda, the woman who helps care for my mother." His voice thickened. "She called to say that my mother died last night."

Jackie came to Harlan's side, slid her arm around his waist, and held him close. "I'm so sorry." She waited for him to lay the phone down or put his arms around her anyway, but he didn't move. She pulled back and studied his face. He stared over the top of her head. He was clearly in shock. Well, no surprise; it had been sudden.

"Miranda hopes to arrange the service for next weekend. She knows I have duties during the week. It was thoughtful of her." His voice was wooden.

Jackie had heard Miranda mentioned once or twice before. Harlan didn't talk much about his family, saying there wasn't much to talk about when one is the only child of two only children. Harlan's father, a physicist at Princeton, had died in a boating accident when Harlan was in college. His mother had moved back to her native Boston soon after.

Jackie reached up and laid her palm against Harlan's cheek. "Let me know if I can do anything, okay?"

He nodded, but she wasn't sure he was listening.

Jackie stepped around him, poured the coffee, and slid a mug over to him. She sipped hers and waited for Harlan to speak. She had questions but didn't want to bombard him.

Without a word, Harlan left the room. Jackie followed him to the foyer. He grabbed his wallet and keys from the hall table.

"Harlan?" Driving was probably not a good idea on the heels of such news.

He half turned. "I'm fine, Jackie. I just need some air."

She was about to offer to accompany him, but he was already out the door.

Jackie spent the next two hours tidying the bedroom, making breakfast, and researching flights to Boston. When Harlan returned, he was subdued, but not as closed down as previously.

"I've made something to eat." She gestured to the fruit salad, yogurt, and toasted bagels on the counter.

"Thanks, Jackie." He took a seat at the counter and spread cream cheese on a bagel. "I'll leave Thursday so I have time to take care of things there."

Jackie mentally ran through her schedule. "I can shuffle a couple of things and leave then, too."

He lowered the bagel onto his plate. "You don't need to come."

"I want to."

"Really, it's not necessary."

"This won't be easy. I want to be there for you."

"No, Jackie."

Jackie let it go—for the moment. But over the next two days, she became convinced she was right. Harlan was fiercely independent, but that didn't mean he had to bear his grief alone. It wasn't healthy, even if he wasn't close to his mother, visiting her only twice a year. Once he had described her as "ordinary and quite pretty," and there had been no hint of animosity. But Jackie knew that no one loses a parent without fallout, so on Tuesday evening she brought it up again, and again he refused her company. She dug in. Being in a relationship meant supporting each other in difficult times, even if that relationship had many rules. She and Harlan might not be on a track to marriage, but they cared for each other deeply. Faced with this tragedy, she would show him how much.

"Harlan. In this one instance, you are not the best judge of what you need. I'm not going to try to steer anything or judge how you're feeling in any way. I'm simply going to be there."

"Jackie, as I said before—"

She covered his hand with hers. "I'm going."

In the days running up to the Sunday service, Jackie was proved correct. Harlan seemed grateful for her company during lunch with Miranda and the minister and went so far as to ask her opinion on the choice of hymns. "I don't know why she asked for singing," Harlan said. "She hated church music."

"I'm with her. But the usual choices are popular for a good reason."

"Sensible."

As they traveled from the church to the cemetery, the winter sun glinting off the hood of the rental car, Jackie thought of how far she and Harlan had come in their relationship. Only nine months before, Harlan had adamantly refused to attend Jackie's sister's wedding. Jackie had been hurt, and worried it was a bellwether for his lack of conventional commitment to anything beyond regular date nights. But those were early days, and now he was allowing her to share in his mother's funeral—an order-of-magnitude change. She took Harlan's hand in hers, and he gave her a distracted smile. She imagined his stoicism as a wall behind which a beautiful and terrible loneliness swelled like a sea whipped by hurricane winds. She would gently dismantle the wall. He would allow her. Only her.

His mother's coffin was lowered into a hole lined with Astroturf. Harlan stepped out of the small gathering of mourners, most ancient, and bent to pick up a handful of dirt from the pile beside the hole. He dropped it in. The sound was large in the silence. He returned to his place next to Jackie, a hard knot in his jaw, his shoulders too square, as if he were propping himself up. He turned to her. She hadn't expected it and wasn't quick enough to adopt the neutral, calm attitude that had gotten her this far. Tears flooded her eyes; her pity for him was naked.

He absorbed it like a stench, his nostrils widening, eyes narrowing. She looked away. The wavering sight of the grave was more welcome than his stern disapproval.

The remainder of the day was filled with the business of death: a reception at his mother's house and a final meeting with the lawyer, which Jackie did not attend. She asked no questions on the plane trip home, choosing instead to wait out his anger or grief or embarrassment—whatever it was he was feeling. Like so many of her stances with Harlan, this patience went against her nature. She saw this as a good thing since her nature had not previously succeeded in placing her in a relationship in which she could stay.

Harlan ignored her. When they landed at National, she followed him out of the terminal—practically running to catch up—and stood beside him waiting for a taxi. The flight had been delayed by weather, and it was past midnight, all yellow lights and sooty shadows. She shivered, tired from the journey and the emotional jockeying.

Finally Harlan spoke. "Now you see why you should've stayed home."

"No, Harlan, I don't."

"I didn't want you there."

"Everyone needs support, and I—"

"Open your eyes, Jackie. I'm not like other people." His tone was harsh, his face lined and drawn. The wall was as high as ever, and it was costing him.

"I know that."

He laughed, a dismissive bark. "Then why are you still here?" He made a shooing motion with his hand and turned his back to her.

Jackie sucked in her breath. He had never been cruel. Insistent and exacting, but not cruel. This was his grief.

She said nothing—what was there to say? The taxi arrived and, twenty minutes of silence later, deposited Jackie at her house.

"Good night," she said from the sidewalk to the back-seat darkness. "Call me if you need anything at all." She shut the door before he could answer.

On Tuesday, her text to him suggesting dinner went unanswered. When he encountered her at work, he pretended not to see her, or spoke as if to a stranger. Jackie stayed the course. Grief was a process. Two weeks after her initial text, she texted him again. The following Tuesday, Harlan replied: Friday 7 pm Enoteca. She dressed carefully. He smiled when he saw her, a genuine smile. During dinner he was solicitous, if somewhat subdued. Still grieving, no doubt. After that night, they resumed their regular schedule and their regular level of fondness and intimacy, and Harlan's sense of humor returned. She never mentioned his mother again, accepting her pallid victory for what it was.

She takes a sip from the water bottle on her desk and thinks how during the short conversation with Harlan in her lab, she was perplexed, unable to tease out his motivation. Jackie has known him for a decade, and he just wriggled past her understanding of human behavior again. The problem in trying to understand Harlan, and therefore truly know him, is that he is, by turns, transparent and inscrutable. When he chooses, he slips behind a layer of gauze.

Jackie closes up the lab and leaves the building. Outside, the air is sharp, and the leaf-scented breeze clears her head. A group of students passes her, their conversation an excited tumble punctuated with laughter. Jackie walks more quickly, eager to see Miles and get his take on Harlan's behavior. Miles hasn't known him that long, but he's undoubtedly more objective than she is. Like standing too close to anything, it's hard to gain perspective.

And when it comes to Harlan, Jackie admits she has little perspective, only regrets and bruises.

CHAPTER 7

Miles is waiting at the bar, his back to the door, his head tipped back slightly, following the game on the screen. Thursday Night Football. Seeing him there moves her, the way his jacket strains across his back as he leans on the bar, an inch of blond hair over the collar of his shirt, the square of him. Her husband, especially when seated and viewed from behind, reminds Jackie of her father. There are other similarities: the deft movements Miles uses to fold back his shirt cuffs; the way he lowers himself into a boat as if sinking into a warm bath; how he grows still at the sight of sunlight spilled across water or a dogwood in bloom. Jackie didn't immediately recognize these parallels, but in retrospect they help account for why she felt drawn to him and is at ease in his company.

She winds through the bar tables, goes to him, places her hand on the nape of his neck. "Hey, handsome."

He swivels and smiles. Under his jacket he's wearing the teal shirt she loves so much. It's a fairy-tale color, the kind of perfect shade that's hard to find. Miles brought it home from one of his trips—San Francisco maybe.

"Hello, beautiful." He pulls out the neighboring stool for her. "Okay here? Or should we get a table?"

"Here's fine."

Miles lifts a discreet finger to the bartender, and Jackie orders a martini. Normally during the week she sticks to wine, but Harlan put her on edge. She touches Miles's arm. "How'd your trip go?"

"Good! I signed that quarterback this morning. Lucas Bell, the one who can run. And plays smart." Miles shakes his head. "What a rugby player he'd have made."

Jackie lifts her hand for a high five, which he gives, grinning. "Congratulations." Her drink arrives. "To Lucas."

Miles touches her glass lightly with his beer glass. "To Lucas. May his draft pick be high, his endorsements be numerous, and his career be long."

"What's his family situation?" Jackie has learned from Miles that nothing compromises a player's success—however defined—more often than family, whether it's desperation for money, conflicting dreams for the aspiring superstar, or, sometimes, absence of support.

"They seem solid to me. Invested but not overly attached."

Jackie bumps her shoulder against his. "Look who's picking up my shoptalk." She takes another sip of her martini. Feeling close to Miles, she's ready to get Harlan's visit off her chest. "Just before I left the lab, Harlan stopped by."

Miles has been tracking the game. He swivels to her. "How's he doing?"

"That's just it. The whole thing was weird."

"Weird how?"

"Well, the first thing he asked was whether I was going to the game on Sunday." Miles slides a finger down his glass, erasing the condensation. "I told him I didn't know anything about it." Jackie expects Miles to jump in and say he forgot, innocent mistake. Instead, he is thinking hard. "What's going on? Are you going with Antonio?"

"I was planning on it, yes, if he's not slammed with coursework." Antonio is a sophomore at Monroe University, a few miles away. "And it's not as though I didn't want you to come, too."

"Then why did I learn about it from Harlan?"

"I didn't want to get into it with you while I was away."

"Get into what?" She has raised her voice, drawing a look from a woman sitting a few stools away.

Miles straightens and finally meets her gaze. "Harlan told me some things. It made me think you might not want to go."

"What are you talking about?"

He exhales, takes a drink. "He called me two days ago and said he'd seen you drive by his house a couple of times."

Jackie swallows.

"Did you?"

"Maybe. I don't remember. Possibly on my way somewhere."

Miles nods, as if expecting this answer. "And he also mentioned that you've been interrogating Nasira."

"'Interrogating'? That's the word he used?"

"I think so. That was the message anyway."

"I didn't interrogate her." She thinks back to her conversation with Nasira about her weekend plans, and how to explain it to Miles. "It started off as a friendly conversation about her weekend. Then she mentioned Greenbrier, and that had Harlan all over it. We didn't go there until we'd been together for two years. They've only been dating a few weeks."

"I'm not seeing the crime here, Jackie."

"There's no crime. I didn't say there was. But Nasira was so cagey about it, unnecessarily."

"She has a right to her privacy, doesn't she?"

"Of course. I'm not the one who mentioned Greenbrier. It's like she wanted me to know, but then wouldn't cop to it."

Miles shakes his head. "Are you listening to yourself? You're not making any sense."

"Wait. Add that to this tidbit. Today, when Harlan comes by, he asks me if Nasira can help out with his MRI study." She takes a deep sip of her drink, watching for Miles to see her point.

"I don't get it."

"A postdoc isn't an indentured servant. He doesn't have to ask. He knows that. He was challenging me to say something about them."

"And did you?"

"No. He wanted me to confront him about Nasira. I didn't take the bait."

Miles pushes his stool back a few inches, as if she has become contagious. "Jackie, I'm worried about you. And, frankly, so is Harlan."

"Perfect. Let me get this straight. While you're away on business, Harlan's been talking to you about me, how I'm stalking him, how I'm harassing *L'enfant*."

He glances around the bar. "Maybe we should do this at home."

So now he's calling her hysterical, too. Fantastic. She downs the rest of her drink, lowers her voice. "Let me finish, Miles. Why, pray tell, didn't Harlan come to me about this? He was just in my office, literally minutes ago, and didn't mention a thing. And I know Nasira is of tender age, but she's definitely old enough to talk to me herself, not go through Harlan and then through you. It's like middle school." Jackie's stomach cramps from the hit of gin. She pushes her hair from her face; her forehead is damp.

Miles is facing the TV screen but doesn't seem to be watching the action. He scoots forward in his seat, places his hands flat on the bar. "While you and Harlan and Nasira are swirling around each other, how do you think I feel?"

Her husband rarely draws attention to himself, to his needs. He's the easy one who never causes a ripple. Jackie's chest tightens. "Shitty, I'd expect. Irrelevant. I'm sorry." She reaches for the truth. "I did drive by Harlan's a few times. He's right about that. And I promised you before that I'd let it go, and I have, for the most part. I've really tried. All the rest of it, though, that's not me." She leans forward, asking him to look at her. He does. "Harlan came to my lab, Miles. My workplace. He was really odd; I didn't imagine that. It unnerved me."

Miles weighs her words for a moment. "I can't think of a reason Harlan would want to unnerve you. He invited you to the game Sunday, remember? I'm not saying he can't be a little off sometimes—that's Harlan—but I don't want to focus on that. I want to focus on us, on why you are so wound up about another couple. You're married to me. I feel like I shouldn't have to remind you."

Jackie's nose burns with tears. She hates crying in public and regrets not leaving earlier. She takes Miles's hand in both of hers. The warmth and weight of it grounds her, and she has the urge to climb into his lap, to fold herself up there, feel his strong arms around her, stay like that for a very long time. Jackie looks into his eyes and tries to say that without speaking. If she speaks, she will cry. She hasn't meant to hurt him, although clearly she has.

"Hey," he says, adding his other hand and squeezing hers. "You're stressed. And probably hungry. Let's order burgers, watch the game, okay?"

Her throat is still choked, so she nods. Miles orders for both of them, and Jackie excuses herself and heads to the bathroom to regroup. She blots her forehead and cheeks with a paper towel, arranges her hair, applies lipstick. Maybe it's the fluorescent lighting, but she looks terrible—sallow and tired. Too much time indoors. She vows to go rowing at least once this weekend, maybe sail on Sunday with Miles. Ah, but on Sunday he'll be at the game. She won't. She wishes she hadn't made Miles insecure, but nothing he said has caused her to rethink her take on Harlan, or even Nasira.

Jackie adjusts the waistband of her skirt, returns her bag to her shoulder, and takes one last look in the mirror. She thinks again of what Harlan said to her after his mother's funeral.

Open your eyes.

———

Sunday morning on the Potomac. Rising sun lighting up the water, deepening the shadows along the banks. Between the boathouse and the bridge, in the center of the river, a puddle of mercury gives way to striations of silver and black. She climbs into the shell, stores her shoes, straps her feet into the boat shoes attached to the footboard, and gently pushes off the dock.

Another rower is upriver from her, a quarter mile away. She is otherwise alone. She reaches forward, knees to her chest, oars behind her, catches the water, and pushes her feet against the board. The seat slides back. As the shell slides in front of the oars, she leans back to complete the stroke, right hand over left against her stomach. Her back complains, and she ignores it. A small twist of her wrists and the blades are free of the water; Jackie reaches forward for the return, the blades skimming over the surface of the water, a breath of cold air on her face from her movement. The seat comes forward; her knees meet her chest. Her hip joints loosen a little, improving her reach. She dips the oars, catching the water. Push with the legs. Pull with the arms. Lean back. Return. Reach. Dip, push, pull, lean, return, reach. Again. Again. Again.

Jackie joined the crew team her freshman year at Bates. She'd never rowed before, in fact had never participated in school sports, preferring solo runs or long swims in the city pool. She wasn't a joiner. Her roommate, Camille, was a rower and convinced Jackie to try it out. The first two weeks were excruciating. She was so sore she could barely walk, and the early-morning workouts turned her into a zombie. But something stopped her from quitting, and as her body adapted, so did she. She began to love the dawn, the cool (sometimes frigid) air, the quiet water, the hushed, sacred tones of the other women. She had been rowing for nearly two months before she understood her subconscious had pointed her toward the sport because of her father and his canoe.

During summers when she was in grade school, her father would take her out on the Middle River north of Staunton, Virginia, their hometown. A modest, lazy body of water, it was rarely clear but easily navigable. Jackie's mother wouldn't dream of coming along; she didn't like boats, bugs, or, as it turned out, Jackie's father. Jackie's sister, Grace, four years younger, was too small. Samuel Strelitz worked long hours, but made time for the outings, packing Jackie into his Jeep a couple of mornings a month if the weather held. They brought sandwiches from home (strawberry jam for her, ham for him) and picked up lemonade at a tiny general store they passed on the drive. He let her pick out candy there, too, always saying it wasn't an every-time thing, but it was.

On their first trips, her father would lift her into the seat at the front of the canoe, the life preserver pushing up under her chin. The life preserver had a smell all its own, like rubber and moss and flies, and she remembered the first time she put it on herself and did up the straps, the satisfying sound of the buckles snapping in place. Once underway, her father would hover along the banks, whistling to himself, never catching much. Jackie peered into the water, hoping for a turtle or a fish to reveal itself like a magic trick, and she'd ask him questions about the houses they passed or the flowers or the sky.

"Why, I don't know," he'd always start out. But he did know, at least more than a small girl, and it made her feel the world could be understood, and she could learn to navigate it, the same way her father twisted his paddle and the bow pointed where he wanted them to go.

When Jackie was seven, her father left the family for the first time. Jackie and Grace had gone to bed listening to their mother slicing at him with words. She could be abrupt with her daughters, but there was a special edge and weight to how she fought with their father that made Jackie want to creep downstairs and take a look, make sure that it really was her mother, hard, angry, spitting. But fear froze Jackie in place at the top of the stairs, fear that it was her mother and fear that it might not be. As Jackie grew older, her mother told her that Samuel Strelitz made her crazy, and Jackie came to believe her father had the power to create monsters out of mothers. He seemed too quiet and ordinary for that, but the belief held.

The first night he left the house and didn't come back, she and Grace had already given in to sleep. He showed up two days later, and left again, coming and going for reasons Jackie never understood. When Jackie asked him why, he changed the subject, and, when she pressed, he said it was for the best. "How is it best?" she asked. He shook his head.

Her mother said Samuel Strelitz was lazy, and, later, a lazy, good-for-nothing drunk. The summer Jackie was nine he left for good. She woke up on a Saturday, light streaming through her window like it was a living thing, a perfect day for canoeing, only to find out he had gone. At the time she had no way of knowing it was final. She didn't know where he had gone, only that the canoe stayed behind. On perfect days for canoeing, or just okay ones, Jackie would venture out to the garage, where the canoe hung upside down from the rafters like the dried-out carcass of a giant fish. She'd imagine herself perched on the seat, her bare feet on the ribs, her father behind her, guiding them.

Sam Strelitz died soon after Jackie finished college. Rowing was the only thing she had left of him. That and her sister, Grace.

As the sun climbed up behind the sycamores lining the bank of the Potomac, Jackie touched upon the feeling of being with him in the canoe, of being safe in the bow, encased in a life preserver. She had been free to lean over the side to satisfy her curiosity then; as long as she did it slowly, he would balance her out. He powered them and steered, but now she moves across the plane of water under her own power and rows a straight line. Her questions today are as numerous as they had been as a child, but now she is the only one who can provide the answers.

———

Jackie is curled up on the couch, a book in her lap, an empty wineglass on the side table. She rowed farther than usual, striving to make herself too tired to give a damn about Harlan, Nasira, or anyone else in the universe, and she succeeded. In what was left of the morning she managed to plow through her errands, and, with the help of high-octane coffee, finish the edits of her paper for the *Journal of Child Development*. Miles left for the game at three to beat traffic, picking up Antonio at his apartment in Foggy Bottom on the way. Now it is ten, and if Miles doesn't come home in the next half hour, she'll drag herself to bed. She hates falling asleep on the couch but doesn't want to pass up a chance to catch up with Miles before he departs for the airport at zero dark thirty in the morning.

She rereads the last page of her book—a memoir about a single mother raising a severely autistic child—and hears voices on the landing. Not expecting anyone other than Miles, she puts the book aside and untangles herself from the throw. The door opens, and Miles spills in, practically carrying Antonio.

Jackie is on her feet. "What happened?" She scans the boy: no blood, no torn clothing.

Miles deposits his son on the couch with a grunt. Antonio's head lolls to one side, his long legs splayed. His eyes are closed.

Miles pulls off his beanie, unzips his jacket. "He's drunk."

"But—"

He puts a hand up to stop her. "I know. He's twenty."

Both of them know it's more than that. Antonio has ADHD, and when his prescribed medication isn't enough, he turns to alcohol and drugs. Beatrice (his mother), Miles, and, recently, Jackie have done everything they can to help him, but if he has made progress, it's never been a straight line. This summer Antonio spent a month in rehab in Alexandria and has been on a fairly even keel since. They all hoped he'd get through this semester without a relapse. Yet here he is.

Miles removes Antonio's baseball cap, and the boy's dark hair falls across his face. "Can you help me with his coat, Jackie? I don't want him to cook."

"Sure." She grasps Antonio's upper arm and moves him forward. Miles drags one sleeve off. "Did he take anything else?"

"I hope not."

"But you're not sure?"

Miles looks at her over the top of Antonio's head. "I wasn't watching him every second."

"I didn't—"

Antonio pitches toward Jackie, retches once, and, before she can react, vomits into her lap.

"Shit!" Her pants, the couch, and the rug are covered. She releases Antonio's arm, and he slips back against the couch, his eyes slits. "Well, if he did take something else, that helped."

"I'm really sorry, darling." Miles finishes removing his son's jacket and goes to the kitchen for paper towels.

Antonio revives a little, muttering, and lies down, his eyes closed. Jackie accepts a handful of towels from Miles and mops the worst off herself. Miles swabs the furnishings. They both sink into chairs and stare at the passed-out boy.

Jackie wishes she could rewind the evening to the point where she decided to stay up to talk with Miles instead of going to bed. Antonio would still be drunk, but at least she wouldn't be resenting him so much. It feels terrible to admit, but she is too tired to censure herself. She turns to Miles. "You've got no idea what happened?"

Miles sighs. "Harlan brought him his first beer while I was in the bathroom. By the time I got back, he'd drained it."

"How do you know Harlan only gave him one?"

"I wasn't gone very long."

Jackie shakes her head. Everyone, including Harlan, knows it takes no time at all to drain a beer.

Reading her thoughts, Miles says, "I told Harlan it wasn't right. He apologized. Then at halftime, Antonio disappeared. When he came back, he was out of his head."

"Harlan knows better. What was he thinking?"

"That one wouldn't matter. He didn't know Antonio would go off and get more."

Jackie shakes her head at Harlan's naivete. One does matter because it leads to this. And when Antonio wakes up with a hangover tomorrow morning, he'll be desperate for a quick fix for that. They've been through this before with him.

Jackie gets up, discards the paper towels in the kitchen trash, and retrieves the cleaning supplies from under the sink.

Miles calls to her. "I'll do that. You look beat."

She nods, places the cleaner on the counter, and heads for the stairs. "I'm going to shower and go to bed. Antonio can stay right there, can't he?"

"Sure." He hesitates before speaking again. "I have to leave at four."

She pauses with her foot on the tread.

"If I really have to, Jackie, I can reschedule the meetings."

A heaviness descends on her, a lead cloak. She does not want to deal with figuring out who is going to babysit Antonio tomorrow. She doesn't blame the kid, but she can't help but resent that because her schedule has more give, she is usually the one to deal with the fallout. If the world were just, Harlan would have to look after Antonio.

"I have to teach in the morning. Maybe he'll still be sleeping? I can't cancel my lectures. What about his roommate?"

"I can text him." Miles appears doubtful.

"I don't want Antonio to get hurt, either, Miles. It's just hard."

"It is. I'm sorry."

"It's okay. If he's up when I leave, I'll pour coffee into him and drag him with me."

Miles grins. "I'll leave him a note. Or text him. Or both."

"Both would be best."

Upstairs, she runs the shower and rinses out her yoga pants in the sink while she waits for the water to warm. Antonio is a good kid, through and through, and amiable like his father. His personality is difficult to reconcile with the damage he inflicts upon himself, as if he doesn't believe, on some level, that he is worth preserving. Antonio struggles and suffers, Miles endures and copes, and all of them feel powerless. In some ways, the upswings are the worst. When Antonio stays steady, out of trouble for weeks, a month, they warm themselves on the flame of hope that the worst is behind them. They hold their breath, knowing the absence of a crisis is as normal as it gets.

I'll take it, Jackie thinks, as she wrings out her pants and hangs them up. *I'll take false, temporary hope. Because if we don't have hope for Antonio, for each other, then why are we here together?*

The risk is, of course, that Antonio's history will repeat itself and vanquish hope.

Jackie bundles her hair in a knot on top of her head and catches her reflection in the mirror. The light is dim, her image blurred by the accumulating steam. She sees past the familiarity of her own features to what constitutes them: flesh, blood, sinew. Vulnerable, physical reality.

Her eyes fill.

We are frail, propped up by hope, leaning against each other like reeds.

———

The next morning, Jackie returns home from the university, shakes out her umbrella on the front porch, and unlocks the front door. It's tight, but if she stays no more than ten minutes, she should be on time to her next class. She slips off her boots but leaves her coat on.

Antonio is at the kitchen counter, hunched over a bagel and coffee. He swivels on his stool and gives her a wan smile. He favors his mother most ways, but his smile, hungover or not, is exactly Miles's.

Jackie's relieved to see that he's showered and changed his clothes; he's taking care of himself. "You found the coffee."

"The coffee found me. It lured me out." He gestures at the empty pot. "Want me to make more?"

She shakes her head. "I have to head back soon."

He nods. "Checking in."

"Checking in."

He wriggles his torso and shakes out his legs, the right, then the left, like his skin doesn't fit him correctly and he's trying to get comfortable inside it. He does it more frequently when he's stressed. Jackie wants to hold him, soothe him, but he's not keen on physical affection. She places a hand on the back of his stool instead.

"I'm sorry," he says, head down.

"I know."

He looks at her. "Erik—you know, one of my roommates? He's coming soon."

Jackie met Erik briefly when she and Miles moved Antonio in. He'd offered a timid handshake and returned to his room to study. "Sounds good." She lifts her phone from her pocket. "Call me anytime. It's not an issue." A notification pops up on her screen reminding her that HomeSafe is arriving at eleven to install a door camera. After three packages went missing in a single week, she and Miles decided it was prudent. She tells Antonio about the appointment. "If they come before you leave, you don't need to do anything."

"They know the system. Got it." He bites his lip, blinks. "Thanks, Jackie."

"As long as you're safe, Antonio." She lingers a moment, then goes to the door, starts putting on her boots. If she didn't have a job, she could stay with him, talk it through, or just pass the time, put hours between a fall from grace and a possible disaster. She turns to him. "Call me, okay? Keep me posted?"

"You bet." He waves to her and picks up his bagel.

She leaves, closing the door behind her, with equal measures of reluctance and relief.

CHAPTER 8

HARLAN

What a game. With seconds left, the Cowboys' kicker sends the ball through the uprights, snatching victory from the grasp of my beloved Redskins. But the play is called back for a snap violation; the guy holding the ball moved when he should have been frozen, drawing the Redskins defense over the neutral territory. That's what the referee saw, anyway, and a five-yard penalty brought the next field goal attempt to fifty-two yards. The ball bounced off the left upright. Victory was ours, snatched from the jaws of defeat—the best sort.

A pity, then, that Miles and Antonio missed most of the last quarter. I wonder how they were received at home, and whether, in the aftermath, Miles neglected to mention Nasira was at the game. Why should the ticket I'd reserved for Jackie go to waste when it could be used to entertain my new lover? No surprise that Nasira was initially reluctant to attend, but of course I convinced her. Miles, ever the gentleman, had the pleasure of explaining the game to her—in French, no less. She appeared to enjoy herself, at least until Antonio reappeared, having left most of his brain elsewhere. Miles was duly embarrassed by his son, and they were soon gone, leaving Nasira and me to the game. She cheered when the field goal was missed and kissed me. She's not demonstrative as a rule, which matches my own reserve, but also makes me long for Jackie and her bright flame. Who needs glowing embers when you can have fire?

On our way out of the stadium, I bought Nasira a Redskins jacket, the same style as Jackie's. Maybe she'll wear it to the lab one day soon.

As I said, what a game.

———

People are often surprised to learn of my interest in football. I am, after all, an erudite psychology professor, a recipient of a MacArthur Genius Grant. Shame on them for their elitism! I'm joking, but only a little. How can someone who studies the brain find pleasure in watching men smash their heads together? As with most choices, this one is the legacy of a screwed-up parent.

My father, Thomas Crispin, was a physics professor at Princeton. He couldn't distance himself far enough, socially speaking, from the church supper/linoleum flooring/ambrosia salad upbringing of his small Kansas hometown. He married Lucy Appleton, the spawn of Boston Brahmins, for her pedigree and unfathomable wealth. When I was a boy, my father was keen for me to take up golf, tennis, and, if I were to insist on a team sport, lacrosse. With his brains and ambition and her money and connections, the new Crispins (not the Chevy-driving Kansans) could choose from an array of highbrow delights. But my father never got it right. The Appletons boarded their private jet in Brooks Brothers button-downs with frayed collars, sleeves rolled up, the backs of their boat shoes crushed under bare heels. Thomas tried to ape their cool but couldn't pull it off.

As a boy, I despised the Appletons. Indifferent to everything— except their indifference, which they prized—they stood for nothing. If some of them worked in serious professions, it was with great irony.

I observed how my father lubricated himself from head to toe so he might insert himself into their uptight assholes, and that made me despise him, too.

Even after my father won the Nobel, he stood outside the Appleton clan. In fact, the prize only made things worse, evidence, as it was, of a seriousness the Appletons found distasteful. Ambition was unseemly unless it was applied to something whose outcome mattered not at all, like a game of croquet.

Winning the Nobel made my father insufferable, as if it conferred celebrity status. What rubbish. A Nobel is not an Oscar. The winners are mostly dull, graying men, indistinguishable from the VP of a bank or a first-rate accountant, and their expressions are not imbued with brilliance. I know; I've studied them. While their headshots were being taken, they were thinking about an experiment or an equation or about the mortgage on their lake cabin two hours' drive from the university.

Except my father. After he received the call from Sweden, he shoe-horned a mention of the prize into every conversation, reminding everyone that it was one thing to be smart and quite another to produce success, reward, and a brief mention in every major newspaper in the world. I was twelve at the time and wanted to kick him. Instead, I sneaked into his office, lifted the medal from the glass-fronted case, and spat on it. I did rub it off. A year or so later, after my father said something particularly insulting to me, I jerked off on Alfred's face and left it there. Perhaps the maid dealt with it.

Back to football. My father's view of the sophisticated life did not include it (did he not see the Kennedys tossing the pigskin in their loafers?), so, naturally, nothing else would do for me. We battled over football, over many things, but my mother sided with me. For all her money, she was ordinary. She believed in happiness and fresh air and family get-togethers with gin and sailing. If I wanted to play football, what harm? She saw only the good in me and sought to counterbalance my father, who, for all his intelligence and striving, liked to backhand his son like the good old Midwestern trash he was. I was taller than he was by the time I reached my teens and stronger and faster. He was outmatched and, being a coward and lacking financial control, could only sputter.

Tall, broad, and quick, I played tight end. I could've played in college, but by that time my father didn't care and neither did I. If I could've tolerated the pomposity of English or a similarly pointless major, I would've pursued it just to rankle him. Psychology was the compromise that became the perfect choice: scientific, if one chose the right specialty, but no possibility of a Nobel. And I have always had an interest in what makes people tick.

Some are complex, with a network of motivations not easily untangled. Jackie, for example. Perhaps Nasira, too, although I don't know her well enough yet. They are driven by more than one concern and, as a consequence, are pulled in different directions, making their behavior harder to predict. Others are more Cartesian: as in a game of billiards, the vectors are obvious, and one can predict how the balls will break. Ha!

Miles is simple like that. He is weak and will always avoid conflict. Although he's happier when the harmonious choice is also the morally correct one, harmony will win out. Don't get me wrong, I like Miles; he's my friend. We share interests (football, Jackie), he's reasonably intelligent, and, as I am arguing, easygoing. Not lazy—allergic to friction. His son is the same. Take him to a football game, offer him some beer, pretend you don't know what he's doing at halftime . . . eight ball in the corner pocket.

Poor Miles. Burdened by a defective son and, now, a wife obsessed with someone else's sex life. I wonder what Miles will do about that? Probably very little. He needs someone to give him a push, apply some steering.

And me? From the outside—which is to say, according to others—I am complex. I do hold myself back somewhat, creating a certain mystique, as Nasira does. I am charming when the situation calls for it and I'm in the mood and more businesslike at other times. Typically, I am positive and engaged, but also exacting; I think you've seen that. But that's on the outside.

On the inside? Well, let's just say I like a bit of friction.

Nasira's Story

~

I didn't sleep on the five-hour flight from London to Amman despite my exhaustion. I was too nervous. My father, on the other hand, shoved a pillow between his head and the window and dropped off before the landing gear was stored. He can sleep anywhere, anytime, a necessity, I suppose, for a doctor regularly working eighteen-hour shifts.

A driver met us in Amman, took our bags, and drove us out of the city into the deepening night. It was like driving off the face of the earth, the way the light bled from the sky until the horizon failed. The stars winked on, as did the smattering of lights from towns, making it even less clear where the surface met the sky. The windows had been open a crack for ventilation, but now the driver closed them, against either dust or cold or both. The sealed car did nothing to help my feelings of being in neither one place nor another, only hovering between.

We stayed the night at a simple hotel in Mafraq, a room for each of us. The next morning we rose at four and had tea and an abbreviated version of Syrian breakfast: pita, labneh, apricot jam, stuffed eggplant, olives, tomatoes, and cucumber. It was too early for me to eat, but it would've been rude to refuse. After breakfast, we climbed inside the car again. We drove west (I would only realize this later, as it was too dark to know then), and shortly I could see the white tents of the refugee camp glowing faintly in the dark.

"Zaatari," my father said, although I knew the name already. "We will return to Mafraq shortly, but I wanted you to see where the injured refugees will return to live." I knew this, too, as it had been discussed. My father likes to draw the lines around the day several times.

We passed through the administrative post and stopped at the clinic, which was only a larger tent. It was October, but the air was bitter, and I zipped my jacket to my neck. Inside the nurses' tent, we were given tea. My father asked about conditions, supplies, births, deaths, complications, and as he spoke the tent grew brighter, as if someone had a hand on a dial.

"Come now." The head nurse waved me to the door, ushered me through. "I'll show you around. Ten minutes." She'd obviously been given this job and was not enthusiastic. She'd also been told my Arabic was weak, because she spoke as if I had limited intelligence. In this place, it was true.

I won't describe everything I saw; you can imagine most of it since refugee camps are much the same. One white tent after another, row upon row upon row, each stamped with UNHCR, the United Nations Refugee Agency. Aside from water stations and the like, the entire camp was nothing more than a sea of white spreading to shelter the thousands who arrived each day.

"About forty thousand are here now," the nurse explained. "Eighty thousand is all we can take, so a new camp is already planned."

Where the tents ended, the desert began. Here was nothing. That was what I felt right away, that the refugees had fled war into nothingness. Who would not do the same? And yet I felt it was an evil bargain.

The camp was awakening. Children scampered out of tents. They wore clothes and shoes and were not obviously starving.

The nurse read my gaze. "They come mostly from Deraa, and their parents were shopkeepers, teachers, clerks, that sort of thing. They left with nothing, but they are not poor—or they hadn't been." She said it as if reading from a manual. I didn't judge her; she wanted to get to work, not be a tour guide for some doctor's daughter.

We circled back to the clinic. My father and I returned to Mafraq, to the hospital. No more scene setting—just work. He checked in at the office, put on his coat, washed his hands, and reminded me to follow him without comment. That, I thought at the time, was what he expected of me in general and why he had taken me on this trip. He wanted me to follow him into medicine, into caring for other Syrians. He wanted me to follow him into his life. My brother, Ramal, had been killed a year before. Since then, my father had devoted himself to saving Syrian lives in the most practical and direct way, and he made it clear that because I loved my brother and my family, I would do the same. The mantle was meant for my shoulders.

I already knew from my father that arriving refugees who were very ill or injured were brought directly to this hospital, then returned to the camp as soon as possible. The first patient my father saw was a boy of about seven. He was draped across the lap of a young woman who was introduced as his sister. The boy was awake and stared listlessly at the ceiling. One arm was missing; the stump was bound inches from the shoulder. The boy was coated with blood and dirt. The sister's expression held determination, but it was thin. She seemed a moment away from collapse.

My father spoke softly, reassuring them, promising to do his best with the arm, with the boy. The sister cried then and held her brother closer. The nurse soothed her, and after a moment she allowed my father to carry her brother away.

"Please. He's all I have. My parents, my aunts . . ."

Her sobs hung in the air. I trailed after my father, who was headed for a treatment room or surgery. I wasn't sure because I left the hospital through the first door I could find.

Much later my father found me on a bench in front of the building. The lines around his eyes had deepened and his shoulders sagged. He smelled of ointment, antiseptic, and sweat.

"I'm sorry," I said. And I was. What he expected of me was right and noble. I was honored to be seen as someone who could do what he did: not simply as a doctor, but a doctor who helped his own people in a time of extreme need, at great sacrifice to himself. He had been earning top dollar in the United States before signing up with Medicines Sans Frontiers.

"Don't be, Nasira, *habibti*. It takes getting used to."

I nodded then. I don't know why. I suppose I was a coward. I was absolutely certain I could not work there, or in any other place where families and children had been tossed into a void—broken, bleeding, bereft—but it wasn't until we were back in the States that I admitted it to my father. I could not tell him I could not work there—would not, in fact, become a doctor at all—not when, in the next moment, I'd be confronted with the misery of those camps, and feel the bright burn of shame.

I was ashamed of my decision, but I nurtured it in private. My father argued with me for a while, but I didn't budge, refused to even explain, and he stopped bringing it up. He treated me differently, though. He didn't call or text as much, and when we were together, the light that had always shone for me had left his eyes. Late one night in Evanston, a few years after my visit to Syria, I overheard my mother argue that he should be satisfied that I was getting my PhD, and would be using it to study children with disabilities and disorders.

As nice as it was of my mother to lobby on my behalf, especially given my refusal to do so, my father's response was entirely predictable: "Is she saving Syrian lives?"

When we said goodbye the next day, his embrace made it clear we had, in the most important ways, already parted. I stayed away more.

Ridiculous, isn't it, the words we carry inside us, how we allow them to shape how we feel about ourselves and the direction our lives take? I'm working on getting my father's words out of my head so I can feel good about the work I'm doing instead of ashamed about the work I'm not. Work defines us, whatever it entails, and I want to be defined by something important, something good, something that's mine.

It all goes back to my brother, I think, to his death, which none of us have spoken of in the years that have passed. We shared him when he was alive, but we carried our grief separately, protecting it as if it were a living thing we divided in three. I need to find a way to say to my parents that I cannot make up for his loss, because I have my own dreams and my own fears. But when I am with them, all I see are their broken hearts—for Ramal, for me—and words die on my tongue.

CHAPTER 9

The air has teeth, but Jackie is snug in her insulated jacket, and the double layer of blankets she's sitting on stops the cold rising from the ground. The sky is the cloudless electric blue peculiar to chilly autumn days and sets off the golden sycamores, orange sassafras, and purple sweetgum interspersed with the dark-green feathery branches of red cedar. Whoever designed this cemetery must have had autumn in mind.

The imposing, ornate statues and obelisks are arrayed behind her on the broad hill that slopes north toward the entrance. Here the markers are modest; her father's is a pale granite slab, three feet wide and two feet tall. She didn't have a hand in choosing it. Her father's brother, Jeremy, took care of it, albeit grudgingly. At the time his attitude barely registered with Jackie, as she was simply grateful not to have to cope with it herself. Her mother was deeply uninterested, and Samuel Strelitz had no other family nearby.

Jackie visits the grave every year on her father's birthday, November 3. Grace began joining her on the fourth visit, when Grace was twenty-two, the same age Jackie had been when their father died. Jackie never asked her sister if this was the reason; they never discussed the visits at all except to comment that every year, without fail, the weather was fine, like today. Jackie always brings blankets, a thermos of tea, and lunch. Grace brings as few of her children as possible.

A caretaker drives a small tractor along a nearby path. Jackie considers that she has been honoring this ritual for almost as long as she had a father. If she doesn't always find it comforting, it nevertheless feels right.

"Hey there, Jacks." Grace walks up, arms spread wide. She's wearing an enormous coat—probably belonging to her husband, Hector—which makes her appear smaller than she is. She's only a little shorter than Jackie, but finer-boned and packed with energy like a terrier.

Jackie scrambles to her feet and embraces her sister. She smells of almonds, as she has since she was a newborn, and banana, a consequence of having five children between the ages of one and seven. "No babies. How did you manage that?"

Grace tucks a windblown lock of auburn hair behind her ear. "Hector's sister to the rescue. I feel positively naked." She spins in a carefree circle, then frowns. "Probably shouldn't do that in a cemetery, huh?"

Jackie gestures to the headstones. "Lots of moms here who understand. Tea?"

"Please."

They sit cross-legged, drinking tea and eating ham sandwiches, their father's favorite. That tradition began after Grace asked, during their third annual visit, what their father liked to eat. The sisters did see their father after he left, but no more than two or three times a year, and never overnight. Their mother, Cheryl, remained in control, helped along by Samuel Strelitz's descent into alcoholism. Jackie is the repository of their father's memory, which she doles out to Grace, piece by piece, at his grave. They rarely speak of him outside these visits, either because their interest in him cannot be sustained or because they both tacitly acknowledge that Jackie's repository is not very deep and they would soon run out of stories. What then?

"I remembered something," Grace said, as she finished the last of her sandwich.

"Yeah?"

"Or I think I did."

Jackie nodded. Memories were slippery, but especially Grace's, since she'd been only five years old when their father moved out.

"The night he left, did he come into our room? To say goodbye? Because I think I remember that."

Jackie gives her sister a weak smile. They could not have known he wouldn't be coming back, so it was just another night to them, one like many others during which they listened at their bedroom door to their mother's serrated accusations and their father's unintelligible replies. If they had understood the importance of that night, the details would be cemented in their memories.

"Maybe," Jackie says. "I don't remember that, but maybe."

"I think he was looking for something, or said something." Grace pulls her knees to her chest and sips her tea. "Probably a dream, huh?"

"It makes sense, though. I imagine he wanted to say a lot of things he never did."

"Like what?"

They had this conversation during a previous visit. Jackie can't recall when, nor can she recall her answer. When your father is a ghost, it's hard to pin anything down, even the simplest things. "That he loved us. That he was sorry." Grace nods. "He probably didn't see the point in saying it because from his point of view he'd failed us already. He'd lost us and probably thought what he said or didn't say didn't matter."

Grace's eyes fill with tears. "That's too sad, Jacks."

"I know." Her throat tightens.

"He hadn't lost us at all."

"I know, Gracie." She pulls her sister into her arms. "That's why we're here."

They hold each other for a long while.

Jackie pulls back and adjusts her hat. "I remember when he walked me to the school bus, you rode on his shoulders every day."

"I remember that. Or maybe it's just from you telling me."

She shrugs. "Is there a difference?"

Grace's nose scrunches as it always does when she's thinking. "A little? But I think of it every time Hector gives a ride to one of ours. In the end, that's what matters."

Jackie smiles and busies herself refilling their mugs. She's happy that Grace can link an uncertain memory of their father to positive experiences in her own family. Jackie only wishes she knew how it felt.

———

Sometimes the grave site ritual lifts her up; other times, like today, it makes her pensive, even brooding. Miles texted her earlier to say he would be running errands this afternoon, so when Jackie arrives home, the house is empty. She leaves the lunch containers on the kitchen counter and goes directly upstairs to the extra bedroom, which serves as a home office. She carries a side chair into the walk-in closet, positions it in at the far end, and steps up. A small suitcase is stacked on top of a file box. The exterior is a muted-blue vinyl with ivory overstitching faded to yellow and worn at the corners and edges. Jackie pulls it down by the plastic handle, climbs off the chair, and brings it into the room.

She places the suitcase on the floor and kneels in front of it. The clasps are touched with rust, but when she presses the buttons with her thumbs, they open with a clean click. Jackie lifts the lid, and the distinctive smell hits her nostrils: starch, old cardboard, and a hint of lavender. The suitcase is lined with material the same shade as the exterior. An elasticized pocket runs the width of the lid. It is as empty as the day she appropriated it.

From her vigil at her bedroom door, Jackie heard her father leave the house after an argument with her mother. She heard the clink of the keys in his hand, the opening and closing of the front door, the creak of the door of his truck, the rumble of the truck's engine. Her mother was in the kitchen, running water. Jackie crept into her parents' room and, with only the dim light from the hallway to guide her, reached into the inky darkness under the bed and dragged the suitcase out. She carried it, bumping against her leg with every step, to her room, and hid it under her bed.

The next morning she relocated the suitcase to the far reaches of her closet. Later that day, her father returned, and she knew she'd done the smart thing. You can't really leave for anywhere without a suitcase. Everyone knew that.

Now Jackie runs her hand along the bottom of the suitcase, concentrating not on how she failed to prevent her father from leaving but rather on how proud she was of her tactical strike. She granted herself agency and created hope, when in truth she had rights to neither. She never felt foolish for trying, just not powerful enough.

She worries the lesson has been lost on her over the years. Maybe that is why she is kneeling in front of an empty suitcase, to remind herself to have faith in the power of action—her action. She stays a few moments longer, then returns the suitcase to the closet where no one questions its presence or its meaning.

———

Jackie grades papers until her eyes swim, then runs a bath—a rare event. She languishes in the tub and drifts behind the veil of sleep, dreaming of a blue suitcase that holds a piece of sky.

Miles calls out from below. She splashes water on her face to wake herself and listens to his footfalls up the stairs and along the corridor. He knocks on the bathroom door.

"Come on in. I'm all bubbles."

His head appears. "Hey, beautiful. We're leaving in thirty minutes, right?"

"What? It can't be four already."

"It is indeed."

They have a wedding reception to attend, the children of two of her colleagues: Amy Chen's daughter, Juliet, and Isaac Sorenson's son, Leo. The dress is black tie, which means she has to pull out all the stops in precious little time. She yanks the drain plug, grabs the towel from the floor, and calls to Miles, "Do you need to shower? Because it's going to be a NASCAR pit in here."

He laughs. "I can use the guest bath. What are you wearing?"

"You pick! Extra points for accessories!" She owns only two dresses that would be appropriate, given the occasion and the season, maybe three, so the choice isn't burdensome.

She dries off, throws on a robe, and sets to work. As she blow-dries her hair, she thanks her mother for teaching her how to create a chignon and tries to whip up enthusiasm for the evening. She doesn't socialize with the parents and only knows Leo from a summer he spent as an intern in her lab six years ago. No one would miss her. When the invitation arrived, she intended to decline, but shortly afterward she ran into Leo at Wolf Hall. He had returned from California with Juliet to make wedding arrangements and made her promise to attend. His appeal was so sincere—he is nothing if not sincere—that she readily agreed.

At a quarter after six, the ceremony, wonderfully brief and ecumenical, is over, and the throng of guests has dispersed across the atrium of the Celestine Grill. Jackie accepts a glass of white wine from a roving waiter. The decor is old-world elegance; the marble floors, vaulted ceiling, and white columns are softened by potted palms and diffuse lighting. The tiers of the central fountain are arrayed with glass-covered candles, and the flower arrangements—dusky green, ivory, and blue-gray—are artful yet understated.

Ursula Kleinfelter appears at her elbow, wrapped in a flowing gold silk pajama-like outfit. On her, it works. "I see you silently tallying the cost."

Jackie touches her glass to Ursula's. "Touché. They seem so in love, though, don't you think?"

"If not on their wedding day, when else?"

"Good point." She sips her wine.

Ursula scans the crowd surrounding them. "Is Miles here?"

"Somewhere. When word gets around that he signs sports talent, he becomes instantly popular."

"In this crowd?"

Jackie laughs. "Don't be a snob, Ursula. You should know by now that Americans take their sports seriously, even those with Ivy League ambitions. Perhaps especially those."

"I keep forgetting." She snags a salmon and caviar canape from a passing tray. "So few quarterbacks from the Middle East."

They chat for a few minutes before Ursula excuses herself. "I'm off to see Dodie, make sure she's holding up." Dodie is Isaac Sorenson's wife and the mother of the groom. Ursula and Dodie are close, close enough that Ursula shepherded her friend through radiation treatment for breast cancer this past summer.

"Of course. See you later, Ursula."

Jackie exchanges pleasantries with a couple of other acquaintances, the last of whom mentions the view from the rooftop bar, open only during private events. Dinner will be served soon, Jackie surmises, so she scans the room for Miles and, failing to spot him, heads to the elevator and the roof, figuring they'll spend the rest of the evening together. Who knows? With a few drinks in him, he might even be up for a dance.

Jackie steps out onto the roof deck. The nighttime air shocks her bare arms and shoulders like a splash of ice water, but as she takes in the scene before her, she forgets the chill. The perimeter is adorned with a string of fairy lights along the railing and another above, with more crisscrossing the space and along the bar itself. Her gaze travels beyond the roof, across the top of the Treasury Building to the White House, its facade aglow, then beyond to the Washington Monument, a solitary spike against a velvet background. She moves between clusters of wedding guests to a spot at the railing. The obelisk is familiar, of course, but from this angle, in darkness, it's as if she is seeing it for the first time. The sight fills her with reverence and awe.

"I wondered if you'd come."

Jackie startles. That voice. She takes a breath before turning to face him. "Hi, Harlan. I didn't hear you sneak up."

He smiles and points to his shoes, gleaming black patent. "Leather soles. And you were entranced by the view, understandably."

"It's remarkable." She glances at the monument, as if confirming her assessment, and surreptitiously takes in his suit: midnight blue with satin lapels. Unquestionably new. Miles opted for the classic black dinner suit he has owned for years, a three-piece style, which, he rightly argues, outlasts every trend. Jackie can't imagine why Harlan would have invested in such an outfit. He eschews weddings, and formal occasions in general. Perhaps this has something to do with his new interest in portraiture and twenty-seven-year-olds. Jackie quickly surveys the guests clustered around them for Nasira and returns her attention to Harlan.

His smile contains great patience.

She regroups. "I was speculating about why you were here, but remembered that Amy and Landon are your neighbors." *And Amy Chen is an ardent fan*, but she didn't voice that.

"Yes, it would've been awkward to refuse." A server nears. Harlan motions her over and takes two glasses of wine from the tray, handing one to Jackie. "To the promise of young love."

It's not like Harlan to recite Hallmark verse, but there's not a hint of a smirk on his face. "Yes. Cheers."

They drink. Harlan leans back, and his eyes roam over her body—appraising, but not lascivious—then return to her face, her lips, and settle on her eyes. Her first impulse is to throw her drink at him, but this is a wedding, and the roof is crowded. Plus, he's giving her that look, the one that twists her, creating an ache she would rather not admit to.

"Don't squirm," he says softly. "You look extraordinarily beautiful. That dress on you . . . I can't take my eyes off you."

Her cheeks flame.

He grins. "That's not helping."

She escapes by turning to the view and sips her wine. Miles chose this strapless burgundy silk sheath. "To show off what rowing does for shoulders," he said when she found it on the bed earlier. She was pleased then. Now she feels exposed. How dare Harlan play with her this way? She's married; he should make no claim on her. Jackie's anger flares, but the admonishments sitting on her tongue remain there. Her thoughts blur in confusion. She's been obsessing over Nasira, and all along Harlan has remained attracted to her? Is he serious? The idea that he might be triggers a warm surge of—what? Desire?

No.

Her body is treacherous to respond to this man, here, now. Harlan had his chance. She loves her husband.

She feels the impulse to flee, and the muscles in her legs tense. But he has frozen her. She is going nowhere. His claim on her is fresh, real.

Damn him.

"Jackie. Please look at me."

She takes a half step back, creating a buffer. She's aware of other people nearby, talking, laughing; she can't imagine what they are saying. She is numb, confused, ashamed.

"Jackie."

She lifts her eyes. The air separating her from Harlan is made of crystal.

"I can't—" His voice falters, but his eyes are certain. He is in pain. His pain is for her.

She sees it. He allows her to.

Jackie grabs hold of the railing, unsteady. She squeezes. The hard, cold metal ushers a signal up her arm, breaking the spell.

She drains her wine, sets the glass on a bar table behind her. "It's freezing up here." She rubs her arms, erasing gooseflesh, to show it is true. Jackie steals a glance at Harlan, but he is now surveying the people behind her, casually, as if the two of them are both somewhat bored with their small talk and are ready to move on.

"You go in," he says, mild as a June morning.

Jackie hesitates. A moment before, he was bare to her, utterly. According to a moral calculus she cannot explain, it seems wrong to leave him like this. "Aren't you going down to dinner?"

He glares at her, his irises fusing with his pupils, black as sin. A rushing sound fills her ears. He places his drink on the railing, shoots his cuffs as if he wears black tie every night, and walks away.

CHAPTER 10

Last year, Jackie and Miles were late to Thanksgiving dinner at her sister's in Staunton, caught behind a big rig crash on Interstate 66 out of DC. So this year they leave at eight o'clock, armed with coffee and muffins for the road, plus citrus sweet potatoes, pecan pie, several bottles of wine, and a bouquet of yellow roses—Grace's favorite. The drive is only two hours, but Jackie figures they can help Grace and Hector with the dinner and kids. With five, adults are always in short supply.

Miles is driving and singing along with Adele on the radio, his voice soft but perfectly tuned. Jackie smiles. For several weeks she's successfully reined in her preoccupation with Harlan and Nasira, and although Miles has been away five days of the week, their time together has been nearly conflict-free. Antonio is teetering on the verge of needing to be checked into rehab again, but he's resisted—with Miles's acquiescence. Jackie wants to see Antonio complete the semester, too, but his health should take priority. She's only the stepmother, though. Antonio's mother, according to Miles, has never taken their son's problems as seriously as she should, so it is down to Miles to work things out with him.

"You're lost in space," Miles says.

"I was wishing Antonio could have come this year. I know his mother flew in for the break, but I would've loved to have him be with my family." Jackie paused. "Other than my mom."

"Your mom's not so bad."

"Compared to whom? Hannibal Lecter?"

He laughs. "When is she arriving at your sister's?"

"After the kids are asleep."

He glances at her. "You're joking."

"Only slightly. I mean, my sister's house *is* the embodiment of chaos. I get that."

"But as a grandmother, she should be tolerant."

"Or delighted. Many grandmothers are delighted with five healthy, adorable grandkids. I'm only an aunt and I'm delighted."

They exit I-81 and head west into Staunton, passing the old brick buildings of the state asylum on the hill to the left. The next exit off the interstate offers a slightly more direct route to Grace's house, but Miles knows that Jackie likes to swing through her hometown. Not much changes, but Jackie keeps tabs. It's a game.

At the next stoplight, Jackie points down the next block. "Look, Miles. That's the third restaurant in that building in two years. Think it will stick?"

He cranes his neck to see the sign. "Trapeza. Greek for 'table.'"

"Who knows that?"

"Every English schoolboy." He turns left onto Middlebrook Road. "Drive by?"

"Yes, please."

A left on West Hampton and left again on Winthrop. The houses on this tree-lined street are nearly all the same: two stories high, two rooms wide, and three rooms deep, with full-width front porches, modestly adorned with decorative spindles, sidelights around the doors, and brackets at the top of the porch supports. Each house is painted a different color. Jackie's childhood home, her mother's house, is white with red shutters, with the front door on the left, between a blue house and a pale-green one. Farther up the street, where Miles will turn around, are a few older, more stately brick buildings. Jackie's mother always coveted one. It was a sore spot, the brick houses so near yet out of reach. The blame went to Jackie's father.

Miles slows down in front of the house.

"Okay," Jackie says. She knows Miles doesn't think there's anything to see but is too polite to say so. Jackie is compelled to visit the house (but not her mother) whenever she is nearby. The house adds heft to her memories and reattaches her to her sister. *We lived here, inside these walls, Grace and I. We slept under that roof, learned to walk in that backyard, took baths together in the tub with the chipped enamel, and when our father left, he went out that front door.* From this distance, the house still belongs to Jackie. As soon as she steps inside, it is her mother's house, every inch of it. She is a visitor, and visitors don't belong.

Miles points across the street to a peeling gray house; the front lawn has become a field. "I still don't understand why that's not on the market."

"The kids can't agree on what to do with it. It'll fall down first."

"That's tragic."

"It is." But Jackie hasn't been looking at the gray house. Her eyes are fixed on her house, picturing herself at twelve.

———

Jackie stood on the porch counting to one hundred so she wouldn't turn around and watch Matthew King leaving. She could hear his skateboard rumbling down the sidewalk. But was he looking back at her? That was the question. Jackie didn't check. She played it cool.

As she opened the front door, her mother pounced on her. "You're thinking about kissing that boy, aren't you?"

"What boy?"

"Don't be smart. The one practically on top of you on the porch."

Jackie focused on her mother's right earring and thought of the most boring thing she could—reciting the states in alphabetical order—and was glad she had counted to a hundred earlier, dropping her pulse. She sighed hugely. "Oh, you mean Matthew? He's just a friend."

Her mother scoffed and jabbed the air with the eyeglasses she was holding. "That's how it starts. I suppose he's funny, too. Remember what I told you about men and their senses of humor. Get you laughing and you'll forget you were once an intelligent, independent person without the slightest desire to do the bidding of a man-child."

"He's not that funny." Actually, he was.

"They have other methods, Jackie."

"So you've said."

Her mother glared at her for a long minute, weighing the necessity of repeating the lesson she'd been drilling into Jackie for three years since her father left—or was forced to leave. She went back and forth on which it was, and mostly it didn't matter because it was her mother she had to deal with. Jackie did like Matthew quite a lot. He was goofy and smart and hadn't been put off by her pretending for the longest time he didn't exist. He'd broken through her mother's training, and now every time she saw him, her stomach was full of squirrels. It had to mean something.

Her mother released her death stare, satisfied for the moment that her daughter would not fail her and fall stupidly in love. "Grace is at Natalie's, and I'm working through dinnertime, so just order whatever sounds good, okay?"

"Got it."

Jackie ditched her backpack, grabbed a snack, then went upstairs to do her homework. At seven fifteen she ordered pad thai from her favorite place and watched a *Saved by the Bell* rerun while waiting for it to arrive. The episode was one of many featuring Kelly getting her heart crushed by a guy, a funny guy (are they always funny?), a seemingly nice guy. He even looked a bit like Matthew. Jackie skipped what she knew would be a happy ending; why bother? Kelly would find a different boy, a better one. It would be romantic, but not realistic. There aren't that many funny, nice guys. Her mother was right. If you get your heart broken, it's your own stupid fault.

The next morning Matthew found Jackie in the hallway outside her English class.

"Hey." He stood close, but not too close, and smelled like soap and peanut butter. He smiled, and his dimples showed, setting off that jumpy feeling in her stomach.

"Hey."

"I've got a skateboard thing tonight at the park. A competition." He spun his cap on his index finger. Prowess. "Want to come?"

He cared enough to ask her, but everything else about him—the way he stood, hands loose at his sides, the way he didn't notice the kids having to go around him to get inside the classroom—said he might not care about her answer, or that he was determined to give that impression. Jackie pictured herself at the park, elbows propped on the railing with the other girls, each claiming a skater or hoping to, not paying attention to the tricks or even the falls, only the possibility of a boy—a look, a kiss, a feel—like catching a wave and riding, just because it's there, riding it to . . . nowhere.

"Not really," Jackie said.

"How come?"

She shrugged one shoulder. Matthew seemed perplexed. He must've thought everything had been going so well. He'd scratched her surface and discovered she wasn't all that shy, and now he wanted a reward, she could see that. He wasn't getting one.

The bell rang. The clusters of kids around them shifted and broke.

Jackie tilted her head at the classroom door. "I gotta go."

He stuck his hands in his pockets. "It'll be fun. Starts at seven thirty, but you could come whenever." He smiled again, another dose of dimples.

Jackie's heart squeezed but she ignored it. "I don't actually like skating. Watching people skate."

His eyebrows went up, then knit together in a frown. "Okaaaaaay . . ."

"But good luck." A bone. Jackie didn't want to be mean. She was just being realistic. Adults were always saying twelve (or eleven or thirteen or whatever) was too young for dating, but for Jackie, twelve already felt too old.

Matthew stood waiting for her to change her mind. She could see that he expected her to want what he wanted, to adore him at the skate park, to kiss him back when he wanted to kiss her. This must be what her mother had been getting at. Jackie wasn't positive, but thinking about it made her tired, and she had a class to get to.

"Bye, Matthew." She said it a little like she was dismissing him. Which she was.

He actually pouted. Then he turned away and walked slowly down the empty hall.

Jackie felt a surge, like clean, cool water in her veins. She'd made the choice. She'd made him leave. Her mom would be proud.

Jackie squared her shoulders and followed the other kids into the classroom, feeling like she'd already learned the most important lesson of the day, or maybe even her whole life.

———

Miles drives up Winthrop to the top of the hill, turns around, and rejoins Middlebrook Road. Jackie is quiet. The businesses thin out and are replaced with fields and farms. The sky is clear and a shade of blue she never sees in DC. Miles gives up on the radio, having lost the only decent station. Twenty minutes out of Staunton, they veer onto a gravel road and wind along a slope bordered by woods on the right and open pasture on the left. The road bends, and an old brick farmhouse appears, with scattered outbuildings that seem to multiply between visits. In the summer, towering walnuts and silver maples shade the house; now they are bare-branched sentinels. Grace and Hector bought the property six years ago when they had only Daniel. Hector, a professional builder, recognized the bargain and has been renovating since.

They pull up alongside Hector's black F-250.

Now that they've arrived, Jackie's mood brightens. She can't wait to see her sister, Hector, each of the children. Jackie gets out and opens the rear door to retrieve the food. "You haven't been here since July, right?"

"Right." Miles unfolds himself from the car, stretches his arms above his head, casts his gaze over the house and the view of the fields running golden and russet over the near hills.

"Wait until you see the new kitchen."

"I remember we had to use the outdoor grill to cook everything. Like camping."

Jackie laughs. Miles does not camp.

He retrieves the wine, shuts the door, and catches Jackie's eye over the roof of the car. "You look beautiful, by the way. I've been looking forward to cooler weather just so I can see you in that coat."

The coat, made of deep-green felt with intricate hand stitching, was a gift from Miles last Christmas. "You're sweet. And you have excellent taste."

Jackie leads the way along the curved walk and up the front steps. The porch serves as a mudroom; a dozen pairs of boots and shoes in all sizes are scattered on either side of the door.

Miles holds open the glass storm door for Jackie.

"Brace yourself," she says.

Miles shrugs and smiles. "It's a party."

"Every day's a party here. And sometimes the guests get put in time-out."

"Praying it's not me."

She opens the door. A jubilant sea of children and dogs crushes into the hallway.

Grace wades through, arms outstretched. Her hair has mostly fallen from its clip, and her T-shirt has stains where little hands have pulled at it. Jackie gets a lump in her throat as Grace hugs her around the box of food she's carrying.

"Happy Thanksgiving, you two!" She kisses Jackie's cheek and wipes the spot even though she's not wearing lipstick. "I'm going to change later. Don't worry."

"You look great."

"Liar. Go put that food down somewhere." She gently pulls one of the five-year-old twins away from Miles's leg. "Mommy's turn, Maria." She hugs and kisses Miles. "God, you're cute."

"I have wine."

"Even cuter."

As they proceed down the hall, Jackie and Miles greet the kids, the dogs, and, in the kitchen, Hector, holding the youngest, Edith, on his hip and rinsing green beans in a colander with his free hand. He's an Antonio Banderas look-alike. All the children inherited his olive skin and dark hair in varying degrees except Edith, who sports the same red hair and freckles Grace had as a baby.

"Hi, Hector!" Jackie places the food on the counter and kisses her brother-in-law on the cheek. Edith kisses the air and laughs. Jackie reaches for her, and the baby hides her face in her father's neck. "Maybe later, huh?" At fifteen months, Edith is the right age for separation anxiety.

Miles shakes Hector's hand and clamps him on the shoulder. "Good to see you, Hector."

"You too. The kids have been so excited to see you guys."

Roberta toddles into the kitchen, trips herself up, and bangs her head on the counter. She wails.

Grace scoops her up. "How about we divide and conquer?"

Ten minutes later, the four older children are outside with Miles and Hector. Edith sits on the kitchen floor playing with Tupperware while Jackie and Grace organize the kitchen.

"Everything okay?" Grace asks. "You sounded pretty stressed on the phone the other day."

Jackie weighs whether to say anything about Harlan and Nasira. She's put them out of her mind, more or less, and her stalking is under control. Her sister's stance on Jackie and Harlan's relationship had been that as long as Jackie was happy, Grace was happy. But when Jackie broke it off, Grace admitted she'd never been crazy about Harlan. "A bit too smooth," her sister said, adding, "at least for my taste," which for Grace was tantamount to a damnation. Jackie is certain Grace would not approve of the new twist on her interest in Harlan—who would?—and decides to jump past it.

"Did I? I guess I'm worried about this long-term study. So much is riding on convincing the foundation it's worthwhile."

"You mean funding?"

"Yes. They want results, understandably. Four years is a long time." Jackie covers the potatoes with water and places the pan on a back-burner to cook later. "Good thing is, the results look solid so far."

Edith pulls herself up on her mother's pant leg and lifts her arms. Grace picks her up. "I'm proud of you, Jacks. Every time I think of your work, I count my blessings with these rascals." She blows a raspberry on Edith's palm, and the baby smiles. "Did I tell you I'm thinking of homeschooling?"

"Why am I not surprised? You'll be great at it."

"Thanks. Most people say I'm a lunatic to consider it."

Jackie smiles at her sister. "They must not know you very well."

———

At midday, Grace and Hector give the kids lunch even though the turkey dinner is scheduled for three.

Grace pokes the last spoonful of mashed carrot into Edith's mouth. "Low blood sugar will have them snapping at your ankles."

Hector lifts Edith from the high chair and rinses off her face and hands in the sink. "Nap time. Miles, can you grab Roberta?"

"Absolutely. We're good friends now."

Jackie watches as Miles wipes off the little girl's hands and gently lifts her to his chest. Roberta sends her mother a worried look, which Grace answers with a smile and a wave. Roberta lays her head on Miles's shoulder. His hand spans the width of the girl's back. Jackie's chest tightens. As Miles follows Hector to the stairs, Jackie fights back tears.

Grace reads Jackie's expression and reaches for her sister's hand. "Oh, sweetie." She waits until the men are out of earshot. "Have you guys talked about this recently?"

"Not really."

"No time like the present."

"Today?" Jackie gathers dishes and takes them to the sink.

Grace joins her. "What's Thanksgiving without family strife?"

"Miles doesn't do strife. It's one of his most endearing qualities."

Grace lifts the lid on a pot and tests a potato with a knife. "Almost." She replaces the lid. "Jacks, just talk to him. He's your husband."

Michael runs in from the den, red-faced, his twin sister on his heels. "It's my turn to choose the game, and she won't let me."

Maria scowls. "Your games are stupid."

"Are not."

"Are too."

Grace says, "Who wants to set the table?" The twins look at each other and head back to the den. Grace turns to Jackie. "The key to diplomacy is misdirection."

Jackie laughs. "I'll set the table and take care of the potatoes."

"Thanks. I'm off to change before Mom gets here." Grace stops at the entrance to the den. "You can watch your movie until Grandma comes, okay?" She disappears up the stairs.

Other than the sounds from the movie, the house is quiet. Jackie finds a pale-yellow tablecloth in the sideboard and shakes it onto the table. It's creased but no one will mind. She brings plates and flatware from the kitchen, and wonders which kids she should set places for. All but Edith, she decides.

Miles appears in the doorway. "Can I help?"

"Sure." She points to the plates and flatware. "You can do these, and I'll figure out glasses." She retrieves five wineglasses from a high cabinet. "Did Roberta go to sleep for you?"

"Out in seconds. She wore herself out chasing after the others outside."

"You haven't lost your touch." Jackie rummages in the sideboard for cloth napkins and finds the purple dahlia ones she gave Grace ages ago. There's a little yellow in the design, so Jackie calls it a match and circles the table, laying one at each place. She observes Miles arranging the flatware precisely. "You probably know what I'm going to say."

His hands still.

"That predictable?"

He looks up. His expression is full of sympathy. "You know I love kids, Jackie."

"I do."

"But it's hard. I've spent twenty years putting out fires around Antonio. I know every child is different, but it makes me leery. We've talked about this."

Jackie selects water glasses from a cupboard and carries them to the table. "I understand, Miles, but we could have a very different experience. Plus Antonio is a great kid; he just has challenges right now."

He runs a hand through his hair. "Do we even have time for a baby? Look at us. We barely have time for each other."

"We can change that. We can decide to." She hears herself pleading and wishes she didn't have to. When she first met Miles, she was thirty-four. Antonio was sixteen and living with his mother in Italy. Everything was possible then, including a family. Miles was receptive to having children and, after Harlan, that itself seemed like a gift. Doors reopened, and she no longer felt as though she'd missed out. They got married. Now she's thirty-eight and the opportunity to have a child is dwindling.

Miles's tone becomes more adamant. "We are already deciding we don't have time—with our schedules."

"I've got some flexibility in my schedule, but not a ton. Could you cut back on travel if we had a baby?" The last time they spoke about a baby was a year ago—last Thanksgiving. Miles had just left Athletes First to strike out on his own and wanted to devote his energy to the new venture. What he didn't say, and perhaps didn't anticipate, was that he would spend the next twelve months on the road.

Jackie stands with two water glasses in her hands, holding her breath.

He shoves his hands in his pockets. "I don't know. Right now, the travel is essential to what I'm building. So right now, no."

She should have anticipated this response, but hearing him state it so definitively rattles her. She doesn't have much time beyond right now, so what he is saying is bigger than it seems, maybe even to him. He has Antonio after all.

He comes around the table and touches her cheek.

She ought to tell him it doesn't matter, that he is enough.

She can't.

"I'm sorry," he whispers. "Let's talk about it more when we're alone, when we have time."

"Okay," she says, and sinks into his arms.

It feels like the end of a conversation, not the beginning of one. Maybe he's right. Maybe it's too late for them to reshape their lives to accommodate a child. Maybe what Jackie feels is wistfulness, an ache for something she can never have. The reason she can't have it isn't because of schedules or because of Miles. It's because of Harlan. She made the decision to hang in for so long with him, first refusing to acknowledge what she truly desired, then kidding herself that he would change. The years slid by, passing unnoticed behind the opacity of her self-understanding, years she can never retrieve.

CHAPTER 11

On the family room couch, Jackie is wedged between Daniel and Maria on one side and Michael on the other, leafing through their baby albums and making up captions for each photo. Michael points to his twin sister in the bath and quacks. The others join in, including Jackie, and their quacking dissolves into helpless laughter. The kids fall into Jackie's lap and spill onto the floor. Roberta waddles in from the kitchen and pats Michael on the head. "Good duck." They howl.

With each laugh, Jackie is aware of the hard ball of disappointment in her chest, but she is determined not to let it spoil her time with her nieces and nephews. Maybe the reason she brought it up again was to banish the uncertainty once and for all. What, then, accounts for her palpable disappointment? Hope is a pain in the ass.

A blur of movement snaps Jackie back to reality. Roberta lunges to tackle Maria and misses, and Jackie catches the toddler just before her head collides with the coffee table.

"Goodness gracious."

Jackie's mother stands in the doorway. Her chin-length deep-brown hair looks freshly cut, and her navy peacoat sets off her pale skin. She's wearing lipstick, which is unusual, a lively shade of berry that matches her nails. This, Jackie surmises, is related to the elderly man hovering behind her.

Jackie picks her way over the sea of children to greet her mother. Grace approaches from the kitchen, and Jackie catches her eye. Grace's shrug, which anyone other than Jackie would miss, signals her ignorance of Cheryl's companion.

"Hi, Mom," Jackie and Grace say simultaneously, drawing it out into a brief chorus as they have done since they were teens. If their mother is amused, she doesn't show it. They take turns kissing her cheek.

"Girls," Cheryl says. "This is my friend Martin Rhodes."

Jackie knows nothing about her mother's social life, and Cheryl has never brought a date to a family gathering before. Cheryl is sixty-one. Judging by his wrinkles, Martin is in his midseventies. He's pulled together, though, with a neatly trimmed beard and a well-tailored jacket. He extends his hand, first to Grace, then Jackie, and Jackie notes the Patek Phillippe watch. Money. Cheryl's holy grail.

Grace rounds up the children, reminds them to greet their grandmother, and introduces them to Martin.

Cheryl holds a stale smile on her face. "So lively. Isn't there one more somewhere?"

"Edith will be up soon."

"Wonderful."

Grace herds the kids into the den. "A little more movie until turkey time, okay?"

Martin Rhodes smiles broadly at Cheryl and tips his head toward the den, then to Jackie. "Well, I must say, Cheryl, you are truly blessed."

She takes this as her due and moves on. "I didn't want to come in carrying everything and risk an accident. Martin, would you mind getting the packages from the back seat?"

"I won't be a minute." Martin leaves. His brisk, efficient response makes Jackie think he might have been in the military.

As soon as the door closes, Jackie says, "I guess we'll need another place at the table."

Their mother appears taken aback by Jackie's tone.

Grace says, "It's not a problem, Mom. We've got plenty."

"I would've mentioned it earlier, but I just asked him yesterday."

Grace scrunches her face in confusion. "How long have you been seeing each other?"

Cheryl waves her hand. "A few months."

"He didn't have plans?" Jackie says.

"Oh, he did." Cheryl unbuttons her coat and hands it to Jackie, who takes it automatically. "But he changed them. That's how it is."

Jackie glances at Grace, but she is bewildered, too. "How what is?"

Their mother sighs. "He'll be back in a minute, but the short of it is I've told Martin that because I'm a feminist, he must maintain flexibility. I won't have anything to do with a man who can't respect my wishes, even if they are last minute."

"Mom," Jackie says, "I'm pretty sure being a feminist isn't the same as being an autocrat."

Cheryl walks past Jackie into the kitchen.

"I think what Jackie means," Grace says, "is that you could've asked him earlier."

"Why make things easy for him? Did any man ever do that for me?" She looks from one daughter to the other.

Jackie says, "I assume that was rhetorical."

"I wouldn't bother with them at all, except I've discovered I enjoy sex, now that it's not with Samuel Strelitz." Cheryl makes a point of referring to their father by his full name, as if he were a distant relative or a name on a business card. She scans the covered dishes on the counters and the stove. "Looks like you girls have everything under control. Jackie, have you opened a bottle of wine?"

There was crying from upstairs.

"That's Edith," Grace says. "Back in a flash."

Jackie is tempted to follow her to be spared more intimate commentary on her dead father. Instead, she finds the wine Miles stashed in the pantry and pulls out a bottle. On this, and little else, she and her mother can agree.

She pours them each a glass of pinot noir—her mother's favorite because the good bottles don't come cheap. Cheryl has worked in the registrar's office at Mary Baldwin University in Staunton since Samuel Strelitz moved out. With steady pay increases, she earns enough to live in comfort, but not splendor. "Happy Thanksgiving, Mom."

They touch glasses. Her mother's smile is warm. "And to you, dear."

Martin Rhodes is back, along with Hector and Miles, who appear to have met Martin on their way back from Hector's workshop.

Hector checks his watch. "Game time, friends. Miles, can you get everyone a drink, open another bottle for the table, and get out the apple cider for the kids?" He guides Martin to the island where the turkey is under foil. "If you would carve the bird for us, I'd be honored. We just do it in the kitchen. No Norman Rockwell moments for us."

Martin gives a solemn nod. "I'm your fellow."

Jackie brings her glass to the stove. "Gravy duty here."

Her mother leaves her perch on the stool. "I'll just put the bread and relish on the table."

"Awesome." Hector knows Cheryl doesn't like taking orders, but she's not lazy.

And that's the thing about her mother. Jackie may not like her, but she can't help respecting her. Cheryl raised her daughters to be independent, to value their intelligence and capacity for work, to set goals and stick to them. After Cheryl managed to push Samuel Strelitz out of their marriage, she was unapologetic and unafraid, setting an example of how well the world could function without men. Within months, and without any prior history of office work, she secured the job at Mary Baldwin. Jackie was in third grade and Grace had started kindergarten. After school, the girls would go next door to the Trumbulls, who were retired. The arrangement lasted until Jackie was eleven, old enough to take care of herself and her sister, given that the Trumbulls were still next door and her mother a phone call away. Jackie remembers that time as more settled than her earlier childhood; the calm and predictability were like warm milk. Jackie missed her father, but the rare visits she and Grace had with him were disruptive and strange. He was too polite with them and would comment on how nice she and Grace looked, as if he had forgotten that they were older, and didn't have jelly stains on their shirts anymore or tangled braids.

Jackie learned her mother's lessons: Have self-respect and self-reliance, but do not be selfish. Watch over your sister. Be thoughtful of your mother. And, most of all, beware of men.

And Grace? Grace smiled and nodded and ultimately followed her own heart. She didn't remember when her parents had been together and so avoided the emotional branding that framed the cautionary tale. Grace listened to her mother politely and attentively, absorbing what resonated with her and discarding the rest. How Grace knew what to accept and what to reject mystifies Jackie to this day.

———

Jackie pours the gravy into the ceramic boat and places it beside the platter of turkey, the slices evenly carved and neatly arrayed. She smiles at Martin, acknowledging his skill and care. *Run while you can*, she wants to shout, but instead refills his glass.

Grace and Hector fill up four plates for the older children and a bowl for Edith, tiny piles from each dish.

Michael hovers at Grace's elbow. "I can eat twenty zillion times more mashed potato than that!"

"After you try the rest." She distributes plates, tucks in napkins, butters rolls, adjusts chairs.

Hector sits with Edith on his lap. She strains against his arm and sticks her fingers in her sweet potatoes. "Anyone care if the kids start? No? Wonderful!"

Cheryl stands next to Miles, making small talk, Jackie assumes. When Jackie first introduced Miles to her mother upon their return from their Vegas wedding, Cheryl offered brief congratulations, then made a feeble excuse to Miles and pulled Jackie aside. "What was wrong with Harlan? Tell me again why you broke up? It seemed like the perfect arrangement to me."

"I can set you two up." Jackie's intention was to wound her mother for her pointless posthumous opinion; she had no other ready response. To talk of love would only cause her mother to sigh with impatience. To enumerate Miles's good qualities—his kindness, his generosity, his steadiness—would only cause her mother to shake her head at Jackie's gullibility and neediness. What was the point? Anxious to duck the burden of her mother's disapproval, Jackie said nothing more and cut the visit short.

Jackie's routine sarcastic jokes about her mother, then and now, are deflections from the sad and obvious truth that Jackie has not moved beyond pleasing Cheryl. Grace has disappointed their mother in choosing to be a stay-at-home mom with five children; that Grace is happy is a detail Cheryl dismisses, and Grace ignores their mother's disapproval. No wonder Jackie never told her mother why she acquiesced to Miles's snap proposal in Las Vegas, why she didn't mind the instant wedding. Miles had agreed to have a child—or to consider having one, which seemed awfully close—and that, along with their undeniable compatibility, made it seem like the right decision. They been dating two and a half years, plenty long enough given the time she'd wasted on Harlan. She had in front of her a man who, instead of freezing time, wished to accompany her on a journey. How could she anticipate that he would sleep most nights in distant cities, that their sex life would be at the mercy of his schedule rather than mutual desire? How could she predict that Antonio's problems would worsen and blight Miles's enthusiasm for parenting?

Now, in Grace's kitchen, Miles has left Cheryl's side and stands in front of Jackie. His eyes are tinged with sadness, whether for him, for her, or for them, she can't tell. Perhaps all three.

"You ready to sit? Everything looks delicious."

She doesn't want to blame him, not today. The day is about giving thanks. "It really does. Lead the way."

She stops at the table to set down her wineglass. Daniel peers up at her, his dark eyes glittering, and points to the empty seat beside him. "You're next to me, Aunt Jackie!"

"Oh, lucky me!" She returns to the island and picks up the last plate. Yes, lucky in many ways, with much to be thankful for, starting with a roomful of people who love her. Everyone has unfulfilled dreams, buried hopes, misgivings, and regrets. She must adjust her sights.

Jackie takes her place at the table. Miles is conversing with Martin, making the most of whatever common ground he can find. Hector smiles down the length of the table at Grace, who is transferring her mashed potatoes onto Daniel's plate so she doesn't have to get up yet again. Their mother is across from Grace, smiling slightly at no one in particular, content (for the moment) in her well-made dress, with her willing but temporary man. She is not adjusting her sights. She bends the world.

Jackie's bind is this: she can accept what she already has, what her mother schooled her to value—her work, her independence—or she can convince Miles they should have a child, now. The decision is in the spirit of her mother's edict, if not the letter of it. If Jackie truly wished to honor her mother's courage, she would have the child anyway. But Jackie could never unilaterally bring a child—however conceived—into the marriage without Miles's blessing, and so has painted herself into a corner over a man yet again.

If Cheryl could read her daughter's thoughts, she would be appalled.

Jackie drains her wine and gets up to retrieve another bottle. Grace's eyes follow her as she pours herself a glass and passes the bottle to Miles to pour for the others.

Grace leans toward her. "Did you talk to Miles? I can't read you guys."

"I did."

"How'd it go?"

"Like this." Jackie picks up her glass and drains it. Grace's concern is etched on her face. "Don't worry. Miles is driving."

CHAPTER 12

Late afternoon on the Wednesday following Thanksgiving, Jackie strides down Q Street, mapping out errands in her head. First, the dry cleaners, then CVS and the liquor store. The return trip to the car will count as weight training. With the busiest part of her week behind her, she's in no hurry. She used the long weekend to catch up on absolutely everything and feels in control and organized. Miles is away until Friday night—Florida, if she remembers correctly—so her plans for the evening are a bowl of popcorn, a bottle of wine, and a movie. Bliss.

She passes the shoe repair store and makes a mental note to drop off her favorite Italian boots to be reheeled. Next door is Bean There, the window tables jammed with students hunkered over laptops. Jackie stops and looks more closely at the woman seated at the corner table, staring out at the street, her hands cupped around a mug. Nasira. Jackie hasn't seen her since before the holiday; Nasira wasn't present at the lab meeting on Monday and didn't show for her one-on-one with Jackie yesterday afternoon. Wary of appearing to meddle in her postdoc's personal business, Jackie decided to let another day pass before reaching out. But now that Nasira is right there—and obviously not severely ill—Jackie's curiosity is piqued.

Nasira meets Jackie's gaze and lifts a hand in greeting. Jackie smiles and walks inside as if it were her original intention. It might very well have been; she lives a few blocks away, as does Nasira now that she thinks about it, albeit in the other direction. She orders a chai latte, fiddles with her phone until the drink is ready, and approaches Nasira's table.

"Hi, Nasira. I don't mean to intrude."

"It's okay." She doesn't offer a smile, subdued beyond her usual cool demeanor and perhaps anxious as well.

"Are you all right? I haven't seen you—"

"I'm sorry about missing our meeting. I should've let you know." She straightens, tucks a lock of hair behind her ear, and gestures to the empty seat across from her.

Jackie drapes her coat over the back of the chair and sits. The situation is odd. They haven't met outside the lab since the Dinner. Jackie wants to know what's going on, but there isn't a way to ask. She crosses her legs, sips her chai, and burns her mouth. "Ow!" Before Nasira can say anything, Jackie holds up her hand. "I'm fine."

Nasira lets out a long breath. "My apartment was broken into over the weekend."

"Oh no! You weren't there when it happened, were you?"

"No. They tossed it, but only took a couple of things."

Jackie pictures her own living room, her bedroom, upended by a stranger, and shivers. "I hope it wasn't anything you can't replace."

"No, just electronics." She sips her drink, relaxes a little. "They broke in through the French doors at the back."

"That's really frightening, Nasira." Jackie doesn't remember discussing Nasira's Thanksgiving plans with her. After the Greenbrier incident, she's avoided that sort of inquiry. "Had you been away? I mean, might you have been home when they broke in?"

"Oh, no. I was visiting my parents. The police are pretty sure the burglars knew I was away. The people upstairs from me were gone, too. They weren't broken into, but they also weren't home to hear anything."

"I'm really sorry. I can't imagine." Jackie senses Nasira hasn't finished what she wants to say. "Why didn't you let me know what happened? I noticed you weren't at the lab, but never imagined this was the reason."

Nasira's gaze grows more intent. "What did you imagine?"

"I don't know exactly—"

"I couldn't stay at my apartment. The landlord was away, too. He does all the repairs himself. Plus I'm not staying there again without a security system."

"Totally understandable." Nasira is openly staring at her now, and Jackie realizes they are sailing toward the reason Nasira raised this topic. Jackie can damn well guess what it is. Her face burns, and a trickle of sweat runs down her spine. She should excuse herself, leave, but she won't. Having decided to see this through, she wades straight in. "You must've found somewhere to stay already, but Miles and I have an extra room in our house if that's any help to you."

The offer ought to be received with a touch of gratitude. A smile would do. Nasira has seen through Jackie, however—it's clear from her expression—and she's not playing nice. Jackie pulls back from the table, in anticipation of the blow.

"Oh, I'm all set," Nasira says. "On Sunday, when I discovered the break-in, I was supposed to go to a movie with Harlan, so he knew about it right away. He has plenty of room, too." She is tracing the rim of her mug with one delicate finger. The nail is perfect, shell pink. "It's easier, in a way, since I'm working on that grant every evening, and he's been such a huge help. It's coming along really well."

Jackie is transfixed by the bald admission that they are living together. In what world is that acceptable? Surely Nasira is not blind to the impropriety of dating Jackie's colleague (her ex!) or the yawning chasm of their age gap. The only sign of Nasira's discomfort is the length of her speech. Jackie has never heard her string so many words together in casual conversation.

"It's just convenient," Nasira adds.

"Wow."

"Wow?"

"Yes. Wow." Jackie's jealousy catches fire. She wants to take a bite out of this woman. "I feel like that word should be an acronym. Maybe it stands for Wow Oh Wow."

Nasira arranges her hands in her lap and frowns. "Harlan warned me about this."

"This?"

"You."

"Me."

"Yes. He said you wouldn't take it well."

"I said 'wow' and now I'm not taking it well?"

"You're obviously upset."

Jackie lifts her mug slowly and takes a long sip, demonstrating her absolute control. It takes more effort than she anticipated. The thought of Harlan coaching Nasira on Jackie's reaction is maddening all by itself. Like she's some lunatic who has to be managed. "I'll admit I'm surprised."

"And upset." She pauses, scanning Jackie's face, her posture. "Seems like Harlan was right."

Jackie laughs, a bitter, metallic sound even to her own ears. "Harlan is always right. Look, Nasira, the fact that Harlan is worried about my reaction tells you a lot about the situation you've gotten yourself into. He knows it's inappropriate."

Nasira's eyes flash in anger. "Your behavior and your comments are what's inappropriate. Harlan told me about the stalking, you know. Lucky for you that was after the police asked me if I had problems with anyone recently."

"You can't be serious." Her scalp is sweating, and she resists the urge to adjust her hair. Instead, she pushes her mug away.

"They asked. Some burglaries are personal apparently."

"And Harlan has you convinced you should have mentioned me to the police?" Jackie is incredulous. Driving by someone's house, however embarrassing and lamentable, is not in the same league as burglary.

Nasira purses her lips. "I don't think we should keep talking about this."

"Probably not." Jackie stands. She regrets having approached Nasira at all. The young woman is naive and will believe whatever Harlan tells her. It pains Jackie to admit she had been exactly the same only a few years ago. She feels a surge of empathy for her younger self—and Nasira. "Just be careful."

"That's ironic, Jackie." Nasira has boxed in her anger and returned to her prim Disney-princess persona, lifting her chin slightly, widening her eyes. "Because that's exactly what Harlan said to me about you."

Jackie hurries out of the café and pulls her phone from her coat pocket as she race-walks toward the dry cleaners. She pecks the screen, calls Harlan. The sidewalk is jammed with holiday shoppers, and Jackie weaves through them, her blood pressure rising as the phone rings again and again and again. He's avoiding her, the coward. The call goes to voice mail; his recorded message is slick and precise and infuriating.

Beep.

Jackie stops at a lamppost to let the foot traffic flow by her. "It's Jackie. Listen, Harlan, I don't know what you think you're doing, but Nasira is my postdoc. I work with her, and I can't have you telling her I'm dangerous or whatever nonsense you put in her head." Her heart is pounding, but she's not finished. "Same goes for Miles. He might be your friend, but he's my husband first, so stop whispering in his ear. Stop interfering in my life." She closes the call and stuffs her phone in her pocket.

She ought to feel better for having told him off, but she doesn't. As she pushes open the door of the dry cleaners, she imagines him listening to her indignation and hearing it, recognizing it, as defensive.

———

Jackie arrives home and leaves her bags inside the door. She carries the dry cleaning upstairs, hangs up the knit dress she wore to work, and slips on pajama pants, thick socks, and her favorite sweatshirt. Her plans for the evening no longer seem simple and relaxing; they seem pathetic. If only Miles were home. She thinks about calling him, but remembers his meetings with the players and their coaches will run until nine or later.

She microwaves some leftovers, and curls up on the couch with her food, a glass of wine, and the remote. She scrolls through the offerings and finishes her dinner before finding anything worth watching. Giving up on TV, she retrieves her Kindle from the bedroom, makes popcorn, refills her wine, and settles on the couch once again. She's halfway through a suspense novel about a missing husband. The wife is uncovering some ugly truths that leave her torn about whether she actually wants to find the bastard. Jackie is becoming increasingly impatient with the wife's vacillation and hopes it turns out that when she does find him, she exacts revenge. She reads a few pages and puts the Kindle aside.

So easy to talk tough about a hypothetical situation in a book, Jackie thinks. Distance—and perspective—are everything, which is why she started her career studying theory of mind.

A huge cognitive milestone for a child is the ability to take someone else's perspective, to imagine herself in another person's shoes. Before the age of four or five, a child can't differentiate between what she knows and what someone else knows, and she can't generalize from her own internal experience (her mind) to that of others. A three-year-old will hide himself by covering his eyes because he hasn't figured out that just because he can't see doesn't mean everyone else is also in the dark. He doesn't know that different minds can see the world differently (literally and figuratively) and have different information.

But once children develop a theory of mind, once they get that not everybody sees and knows what they do, their horizons explode. Hide-and-seek works because they don't leave bits of themselves sticking out. Secrets become possible. Telling the truth becomes optional. And emotions get complicated. The moment you see yourself as others see you, you become self-conscious. Welcome to embarrassment. And shame.

And empathy. There is a bright side.

Jackie feels empathy for the fictional woman whose missing husband may not be worth finding. But the woman is caught up in the quest, is desperate to find the truth, and Jackie understands that, too. It parallels her own situation, after all. If only Jackie's frustration with herself were enough to change her behavior, to make her stop caring about what Harlan feels for Nasira. She wants to get inside Harlan's mind and know, really know, what he thinks of Nasira, and of her. Jackie's only clues are his behavior, and lately none of it makes sense. When Harlan was hers, she understood him, and trusted his view of her. She was certain of his perspective. She saw clearly through his eyes, and what she saw made her happy.

Isn't that what love is, the belief that you exist in the private world of someone else's mind as a beautiful, cherished being? Perhaps that's the problem with love: it's unverifiable.

She gets up, pours another glass of wine, and checks the time on her phone. Almost ten. She calls Miles, and it goes straight to voice mail. She texts him, asking if he is still working. While she waits for his reply, she empties the dishwasher. Still no text. She goes back to the couch and her book, willing her attention to stick. The next time she checks her phone, it is eleven, and Miles hasn't responded.

She imagines Miles with his arms around another woman, a faceless other. The knifepoint of jealousy pierces her.

Jackie pours the wine remaining in her glass down the sink, checks the front door is locked, and heads to bed. She is foolish to make anything out of an unanswered text or of the slight but undeniable increase in the distance between her and Miles since Thanksgiving. Still, she cannot deny her loneliness. She never expected to be isolated inside her marriage. The point of marriage is to have a partner, to belong. Her husband has become her roommate, an occasional one at that.

As she brushes her teeth, she parses her emotions, teasing jealousy apart from regret, love apart from nostalgia, pain apart from self-pity, all with limited success. The wine has not obliterated her encounter with Nasira, only deepened how shitty she feels. She takes an Ambien and puts her faith in pharmaceutical sleep. Until it arrives, she lies in bed, facing the empty space where Miles ought to be. She cannot possibly sleep facing away from this void, but tonight confronting it is just as bad.

While she is alone and medicated, Harlan and Nasira are enjoying a drink together, relaxing on Harlan's low-slung tweed couch. He's talking about how well the grant is coming along, how strong her writing is, or a more intimate topic, how beautiful she looks. While Jackie stares into the empty room, not bothering to close her eyes to help bring sleep, Nasira moves closer to Harlan, tucking her feet neatly beneath her like a cat wrapping its tail along its leg, conforming her body to the space he makes for her against his side, under his arm. While Jackie hates herself for her dissatisfaction and selfishness, for her inability to release the past, for her thoughts that will not unhook from the happy couple, the happy couple is thinking of nothing other than each other, and pleasure.

CHAPTER 13

October 2010

Jackie gave Harlan an ultimatum, overdue by at least a year by her reckoning. Seeing each other two and a half days per week for two years was reasonable, allowing for their busy schedules. Allowing for Harlan, she waited another year. They were out for dinner celebrating their third anniversary when Jackie brought up the subject of living together.

"Why?" he asked. "Are you unhappy?"

"No. Not at all. I'd like more happiness."

He smiled. "Ah, but if you try to maximize 'happiness,' you might inadvertently decrease something else."

"Like what?"

"The need for solitude. Autonomy." He paused and wiped his mouth with his napkin. "The ability to tolerate the foibles or even the unsavory qualities of the other person."

"You have unsavory qualities?" She was sure he was joking and played along.

"We all do. And not being totally enmeshed with another person keeps them submerged."

Jackie laughed. "You sound like you're talking about Mr. Hyde."

His tone was pleasant but he didn't laugh. "Only a little."

In rehearsing this discussion, Jackie had resolved to not be deflected. Harlan was an expert at deflection. "I'm serious, Harlan. We've been together for three years."

He reached for her hand and held it gently. "You're right. Three perfect years." He brought her hand to his lips, kissed her fingers, never taking his eyes off hers, then released her. "We should celebrate with more than dinner. How about a trip?"

She ignored the heat in her cheeks. "A trip is not cohabitation."

"Indeed. And neither you nor I are ordinary people. Let's do what suits us, not what is supposed to come next."

He spoke with assurance, and it was flattering to be categorized as extraordinary, so Jackie let it go. Or, rather, she stepped to the side of her own proposal. She was happy with him as they were. Why change a winning strategy? Besides, in three years she'd be up for tenure, so she only had two years to complete the studies and write the papers the department would evaluate. Once that hurdle was cleared, she could breathe and think about making bigger changes. She was only thirty after all.

Harlan noticed the shift in her and smiled, lighting his eyes. "So, my dear Jackie. Where would you like to go?"

In May 2013, at the end of her sixth year at Adams, Jackie received the email from the department chair informing her she had been awarded tenure. She treated Harlan to an elaborate dinner at Chopin to thank him for everything he'd done to support her over the previous five years. It had been considerable, beyond what any colleague or friend would have done. He had supported her every step of the way, never overstepping or intruding on her process or her decisions, but always there with a hand at her elbow, and a word of encouragement or a morsel of advice in her ear. He read drafts of her papers and grant proposals, spitballed study design ideas with her, walked her through the proce-dures for submitting her studies to the Institutional Review Board, the university committee that oversaw the ethical conduct of experiments. When Jackie had been a new assistant professor, Harlan had sketched the interpersonal dynamics of the department for her. "We are a large family, and dysfunctional like all the others," he said, smiling. He was correct, of course, and Jackie's insider knowledge of the faculty—their sensitivities and peccadilloes—gave her a leg up.

Jackie wondered at times whether she would have made tenure without Harlan. Perhaps it was only impostor syndrome, so common as to be banal, but nevertheless, Jackie did wonder.

Across the table at Chopin, Harlan listened as Jackie thanked him. He looked very handsome that night, softened by the indirect lighting, the polite hush of the room, the glittering crystal filled with deep-red wine. He had shaved carefully and wore a new shirt in navy, his best color.

"I'm rambling," Jackie said, as she lifted her glass. "Thank you, Harlan. For everything."

He smiled, and she thought, in that moment, her life had never shone brighter. They touched glasses and drank.

Harlan reached under his chair and presented her with a wrapped box, a four-inch cube. For a split second, she thought it might be a ring. Her heart lurched, then recovered. Of course it was not a ring. This was Harlan and Jackie, not a rom-com.

"But this dinner is for you."

"In that case, you can wait to open it." He grinned with mischief; her impatience was legendary.

"If you insist—"

"I did nothing of the kind."

She snatched the box from him and untied the ribbon. "Too late. I've started now." She removed the wrapping and opened the box stamped with Bell & Ross in gold. Inside was a rose-gold watch with a black face and a black alligator band. "It's stunning." Tears filled her eyes. He'd given her beautiful gifts before, but nothing as magnificent as this. She came around the table and kissed him, a long, full kiss. "Thank you."

"You're welcome. If it's not exactly your taste, feel free to exchange it. I won't mind."

"I wouldn't dream of it."

Six weeks later she would leave the watch at his house and not return. She would also leave the toiletries she kept in a drawer in his bathroom and the bathrobe in his closet. The pathos contained in those few items—that there were so few—was enormous. She removed the watch as she backed out the door, venomous with anger, eyes flooded with tears, and threw it in the bird's-eye maple bowl in which Harlan stashed his keys. The watch no longer represented the achievement of tenure or Harlan's pride in her but everything she had given up to arrive at that moment, everything she would never get back.

———

Grace gave birth to the twins, Michael and Maria, on June 1, two weeks after Harlan gave Jackie the watch. Hector was behind on a project for an important client, and with Daniel barely two years old, Grace needed help. Their mother, Cheryl, clucked in sympathy, but offered nothing more.

The timing was perfect for Jackie. Classes were over, and her research was in a slow part of the cycle, but Jackie would've made time regardless. She packed a bag and her laptop and moved in to care for her niece and nephews and her sister. Michael, the smaller of the twins, developed digestive problems, Daniel was acting out from having to share his mother, and Grace was a zombie. Jackie stayed three weeks.

Harlan was not amused. After the first week, he called Jackie to announce he had tickets for a new play at the Woolly Mammoth the next night.

"I'm here, Harlan. Until I'm not needed."

"I see."

"I'm glad you understand." Jackie moved her phone to the other ear, away from the squalling Maria. "You're welcome to visit. It's not far."

"I'd prefer to see you here."

"Up to you."

He called every few days, seeking to entice her with restaurants, movies, even a trip to Chesapeake Bay. This last offer signaled desperation.

"I miss you, too, Harlan." Jackie wasn't sure if that was honest; she was too exhausted to miss anything other than sleep. "Drive down and I'll make some time for you."

A long quiet moment passed. "Let me check my schedule."

He drove up to the house at noon on a Friday. Jackie was outside playing ball with Daniel. He had gotten bored with rolling it back and forth, and was now kicking it. The sight of Harlan's car distracted him midkick, and he stumbled over the ball, landing hard. Before he could start crying, Jackie scooped him up. "You're fine, big guy." She smoothed back her hair, which she had styled for the first time in two weeks, and she was fairly confident her shirt was still clean.

Harlan met her on the walk and kissed her. "Wonderful to see you finally, Jackie."

"You too." He smelled delicious. "Let's go in and you can meet the babies and say hi to Grace."

"Sure, for a bit. I was hoping to take you out to lunch."

He hadn't mentioned this before. "Sounds good, but I'll have to see how everyone's faring."

She opened the screen door and set Daniel down. He toddled over to his mother, who was swaddling one of the babies on the couch, probably Maria. Jackie had a vague memory of putting that yellow onesie on her earlier. The baby was kicking and red-faced. Daniel made a grab for the blanket, but Grace deflected him with a tickle to his belly.

"Hey, Harlan." Grace lifted the cocooned Maria onto her shoulder. The baby closed her eyes, peaceful.

"Hello, Grace. Congratulations." He stood rooted in the entryway. Jackie followed his gaze as he took in the blizzard of toys, diapers, dishes. She had tidied the room before she'd gone outside with Daniel, but in a house with small children, entropy is queen.

"Thanks. You guys going to grab lunch somewhere?"

"Only if you can spare me." Jackie collected the dishes and carried them to the sink. "Can I make you something, Grace? A sandwich?"

"I'm fine. I just finished that breakfast burrito you made. Scrumptious, by the way."

A mewling came from the den, where the newborns slept in bassinets during the day. Or not.

"I'll change him and then sneak out," Jackie said.

"Great. I'm putting this one down and grabbing a quick shower."

"I've got her, Grace." Jackie took Maria from her sister and rubbed her back.

Grace spoke to Daniel, who was stacking blocks into the bed of a toy truck on the living room floor. "You be good for Uncle Harlan for a little bit, okay?" She smiled at Harlan, who nodded, and went upstairs.

The cries from the den grew louder. Jackie said to Harlan, "Five minutes, ten tops."

"I'll be here."

He smiled at her, but his impatience—or was it discomfort?—was obvious. Whenever they'd visited Grace and Hector, there had always been four adults and one child—Daniel. Jackie noticed Harlan didn't go out of his way to interact with the boy, but many men had little interest in babies or small children. Given that Harlan didn't spend time with children, it was hardly surprising that two newborns and a toddler might be excessive.

Jackie carried Maria into the den, placed her in the empty bassinet, and picked up Michael, who was howling. Jackie swayed and rubbed his back, but he would not be soothed. Afraid he might wake his sister, Jackie grabbed a couple of diapers and the wipes from the changing table and went out into the hallway. The baby quieted, probably from the change of scenery.

"Okay, okay, my little man," Jackie whispered in his ear. She planned to change him in the downstairs bathroom, but as she passed the opening to the living room, she paused to check on Harlan and Daniel.

Harlan sat on the couch, in profile to Jackie, his phone in his hand, scrolling. He hadn't noticed her. Daniel stood two feet from Harlan's knees holding a blue plastic square in one hand and a yellow box with different-shaped openings on each side, only one of which would accommodate the blue square.

"Help," Daniel said as he pushed the square against the wrong hole. "Go in. Go in."

Harlan glanced at Daniel and returned his attention to his phone.

"Help." Daniel hit the square against the yellow box. "Please!"

Harlan ignored him. The boy stepped closer and gently placed the box on Harlan's knee.

Jackie held her breath.

Harlan fixed Daniel with a look that made Jackie's blood run cold. The box fell from Harlan's knee with a clatter. Jackie took a step back in the hallway, her heart beating in her ears. What had she just witnessed?

Michael squirmed in her arms. She talked to him, loudly enough for Harlan to hear. "It's okay, Mikey. I'm going to change you now." She passed behind the couch on her way to the bathroom and called to Daniel. "Everything okay, Daniel?"

The boy gave Harlan a sidelong glance. "Hungry."

Harlan picked up the box from the floor and held it in front of Daniel. "Why don't you give it another try?" He swiveled to face Jackie and winked. *Just Uncle Harlan bonding with little Daniel.*

Jackie strode to the bathroom. After she'd changed the baby, she left him swaddled on the rug at her feet and washed her hands. She stared at her reflection in the mirror, challenging herself to deny what she had seen. Her vantage point hadn't been straight on, but the feeling his look conveyed was obvious to her: hostility. To a child.

If Harlan wanted to have lunch with her, she decided, he'd have to share her with Daniel.

Back in the living room, she proposed this to Harlan. "It's easier for Grace, too."

"I came all this way, Jackie." He stood and came closer.

"I know." Jackie cupped the baby's head in her hand. It just fit.

He gestured to the upstairs. "Can't Grace cope for an hour or two?"

The image of Daniel standing in front of Harlan flashed in her mind. "The question is, Harlan, why can't you?"

"Really, Jackie. I wouldn't have thought it of you." And he left.

That day was the beginning of the end. When Jackie returned home and was no longer distracted by babies, she and Harlan returned to their usual routine, during which he gave her the usual attention. But something had changed for her. During an unguarded moment, she had seen how he felt about Daniel and, by extension, about children generally. What else was hiding beneath his impeccable exterior? She had excused his faults, allowed his perspective to dominate, but now a crack had appeared, and every insignificant and monumental issue that had bothered her pushed through to the surface. Jackie didn't berate him, but whenever he acted, well, like his worst self—controlling and exacting and overly assured—she called him on it. He was not amused.

One night at his house, she confronted him about living together, whether he would ever seriously consider it. He tried to deflect, but she volleyed the question back at him, coated with frustration. "You won't give me a straight answer, will you?"

"Jackie, calm down. Please."

"I'm fucking sick of being calm!"

"Don't be a child."

"Answer the damn question!"

"Jackie—"

She stormed to the door, and grabbed her bag. Her eyes went to the watch on her wrist. She clawed open the clasp, pulled it off, and threw it into the dish on the hall table.

Harlan was behind her. "Jackie!"

His tone was admonishing, chiding. She turned to shout at him again, but as they locked eyes, her heart stopped.

His face was steel. His eyes empty.

She backed up, her knees giving way, her stomach slick. *Go! Go!* Her mind overruled.

She yanked open the door and fled into pelting rain to her car.

"Jackie!" He shouted from the porch, in the dry.

She was hardly aware of the drive home. She entered her house, went to her bedroom, stripped off her soaking clothes, and got into bed. She lay there sobbing, her phone ringing again and again. What seemed like hours passed. She got up, put on pajamas, drank three glasses of water, and sank down on the floor beside her bed.

Her phone rang. She answered it.

"Jackie. I've been so worried."

She couldn't answer. Her throat was sealed shut.

"Why do you want to ruin what we have? Why do you insist on it?"

She began crying again, her face raw, her head pounding.

"I'll come to your house tomorrow at one o'clock. You're free until three, right?"

She didn't have to answer. He knew her schedule. If she had had other plans, he knew those, too. He also knew she was sitting on the floor with snot running down her chin, eviscerated by regret, and wouldn't be doing anything else for a very long time other than asking herself why she'd fallen in love with this man, while at the same time wondering how she could live without him.

"I'm hanging up now, Jackie. I hope you feel better."

She felt as if she had the stomach flu, something that made you retch, something that emptied you, but only for a day or two.

The doorbell rang at precisely one o'clock the next day. Jackie was still in her room, on the floor, and did not answer.

CHAPTER 14

Jackie is reviewing patient consent forms for a new study and drinking her third cup of coffee. She hasn't had a decent night's sleep in the two weeks since Miles's Thanksgiving pronouncement. Several times each day Jackie recites a mantra about being grateful for what she has. It isn't working. Losing her hope of becoming a mother has left a void that gratitude for other things cannot fill. It might be easier if she could blame Miles, but she can't; they both bear responsibility for not addressing the issue sooner and more thoroughly. Jackie is left with a jagged sadness that slices into her repeatedly and unexpectedly.

Learning that Nasira moved in with Harlan has not helped. Every morning Jackie vows to put it out of her mind, to ignore how wasting time on Harlan dashed her hopes for a family, and every day, as soon as she sees Nasira, she fails. (Between the mantras and the vows, she could start her own religion.) By the time evening rolls around, Jackie convinces herself Nasira must have returned to her own apartment by now, so she checks, just a quick drive-by on her way home. She chastises herself for giving in to morbid curiosity, especially since Harlan and Nasira have called her out on it, but it doesn't stop her. Driving by a house doesn't seem like a major moral transgression, or so she rationalizes.

Only two windows of Nasira's apartment face the street, and when Jackie cruises by, they are always dark. Nasira's car is usually there, but that doesn't mean anything. From Harlan's house, the Metro is more convenient for most destinations, and the university is within walking distance. Nasira might have moved in because of the burglary, but she is staying for other reasons. And Harlan is allowing it—after dating for less than three months. Three years in—*years*—all Jackie got was a weekend in Asheville.

Jackie's stomach sours from all the coffee, and she sets her mug aside. Harlan must be madly in love with Nasira, so much more than he ever loved Jackie. What other explanation is there? That he is getting old and becoming afraid of living out the rest of his life alone? If so, why didn't he come to that revelation earlier? Are men really so deeply in denial about aging?

Jackie forces her attention back to the monitor. She strives to make the consent forms simple for her subjects to understand while still accurately portraying the details of the study. Her procedures are not invasive and carry minimal risk, but parents are more relaxed when they know exactly what to expect and what not to. Her research isn't designed to provide a diagnosis or solve behavioral problems.

"Jackie?" Tate, one of Jackie's graduate students, stands in the doorway, her laptop balanced on her forearm. She wears a knitted beanie and a quizzical expression. "Do you have a few minutes?"

"Right now?" Jackie glances at the computer clock and clicks on the calendar icon. "Yes, another forty-five minutes or so. What's up?"

"Something weird's going on." Tate comes around the desk, pulls up a chair, and clicks open an Excel spreadsheet. "I've been going over the analysis of the eye-tracking data from the four-year study."

"Yes. I'm presenting the interim data to the board at Autism America tomorrow. I already sent the director the slide deck." Jackie asked Tate to rerun the data analysis, mostly to give her practice.

"So, on this spreadsheet are the numbers that I used for the analysis." Tate points to the screen. "I copied them from the spreadsheet below it, the one with the formulas that compile the raw data."

"Okay." It's all familiar to Jackie—she's been working with this structure for years—and she wonders why Tate is being so deliberate in her explanation.

Tate looks at Jackie, her brow creased. "The results you got aren't coming up. I mean, your results are saved on another spreadsheet, but when I run the analysis of variance, I get something different."

Jackie zeroes in on the numbers, an array of cells, four by thirty-four. The study has a total of fifty-eight children, each of whom is tested every six months starting at six months of age, but so far only thirty-four have reached the two-year mark. They fall into two groups: low-risk, those with no family history of autism spectrum disorder, and high-risk, those with an older sibling diagnosed with ASD. The table shows only one eye-tracking measure; for each behavior, they recorded results in one table like this. The study will be over in about two and a half years, when all the children turn four, but the foundation wants a snapshot of the study's progress.

"Are you running the analysis with the Excel add-on or SPSS?" The lab has always used SPSS for statistical analysis, but the Excel programs are improving. The two programs run the same test, so the results should be the same. But using SPSS means exporting the data from Excel, a possible source of error.

"I did both. They agree with each other and don't match yours."

"That's odd."

"Right?" Tate is perplexed but also distressed. She knows how crucial this experiment is.

"Tate, we've got all sorts of backups. It's just a matter of figuring out what happened."

Tate nods. "That's what I've been doing. I've checked the table I used for the analysis, and it looks solid. I thought maybe some stuff was accidentally deleted, but there are no missing cells or anything obvious like that."

Jackie is tracking Tate's logic. The young woman is unusually methodical and thorough; Jackie trusts her completely, but everyone makes mistakes.

"Okay, so it's not the stat program, and it's not a problem in the compiled data, at least as far as you could tell. So either I messed up completely, or something else has been changed lower down."

"That's where I got to. I didn't want to go scrambling around in the formulas, though. It's password protected for a reason, right? And the only other thing to check is the raw data, and those files scare me."

Jackie smiles. "I can see why. But, again, we've got backups." Something in Tate's expression gives Jackie pause. "Tate, about the changes in the results. Was it anything important or just slightly different numbers?"

Tate rubs the bird of paradise tattoo on her arm. "You know how your results were really encouraging?"

"Sure. Having significant results at this stage is exciting. Especially the eye-tracking data."

"Well, it's gone."

"What?"

"Look." She clicks to a sheet with two line graphs, the old results and the new ones. Each data point is bracketed by the confidence intervals, making the shift in the results obvious.

Jackie stares at the screen, unbelieving. "How is this possible?"

"I have no idea." Tate picks at the skin on her knuckle. "I'm worried I did something."

"Please don't worry. We'll figure it out." Jackie forces confidence into her voice. In truth, she's alarmed. She has a presentation to give tomorrow, and her data might be corrupted. "I'll take it from here, Tate. I appreciate you bringing this to me. As soon as I know what happened, you'll be the first to know."

"Okay, Jackie." Tate closes her laptop and goes to the door.

"Oh—and I'm going to talk to everyone as soon as I can—but do you happen to know who might've been in that spreadsheet since my analysis, since last Thursday?" Because lab assistants and grad students come and go, everyone in the lab except Jackie uses a shared log-in instead of having separate accounts, so it's not easy to know who logged in.

Tate thinks a minute. "Kyle probably wasn't, since he's up to his ass with his own study. Sorry. Language."

"It's fine. I guess Rhiannon and Reese aren't around much, either, because they have finals coming up."

"Haven't seen them at all. So Gretchen. And Nasira has been learning how to upload the raw data from the iPads, so she might have been in there? Or maybe she's using a separate spreadsheet to practice?"

"Thanks. That helps."

Tate gives Jackie a thumbs-up as she disappears down the hall.

Nasira. It's almost as though Jackie were expecting it. Although it makes no sense whatsoever.

She has no time to think about Nasira. On her computer, she mouses over to OneDrive, where all the files are stored, enters her log-in information, and opens the spreadsheet Tate was showing her. Her nerves jangled, she reviews the eye-tracking analysis and also the other results she is due to present tomorrow, comparing them to the information in her PowerPoint presentation. To her chagrin, everything Tate said is correct. Jackie copies the compiled data into a new file and runs the analysis in Excel. Same result as Tate's. An unpleasant tingling sensation runs up her limbs. Either the formulas that compile the data have changed, or the original data that feeds into them has. Neither is good news. And who knows how widespread the problem is or how long ago it started? She might have to audit every single study—a nightmare scenario. The thought that she might have published results based on faulty data makes her nauseous. It won't just tarnish her reputation; it could end her career.

A notification pops up on her phone. Time to leave for class. She packs her laptop, puts on her coat, and leaves the building. The air is frigid and the sky a gunmetal gray.

Think, Jackie. What's the plan?

All the data files, the Excel spreadsheets, are on OneDrive, which keeps every version that is saved. Once a day, everything on OneDrive is automatically backed up on the university's network. There has to be some way to figure out what was changed and when. Vince Leeds is her go-to IT guy, and with any luck he'll have a clever trick to deploy. Pinpointing the nature and the date of the changes should help her figure out how it happened. Beyond that, she can't guess what will transpire.

The sleuthing will take time, which she does not have. Without confidence in her results—already in the hands of Deirdre Calhoun, the foundation director—she cannot give the presentation tomorrow. She's tempted to plead illness, but rejects the idea. Her professional integrity is sacred.

Jackie pulls out her phone and calls Calhoun, who picks up on the second ring. Knowing the director appreciates efficiency, Jackie gets right to the point.

"I'm calling with some unfortunate news. I reviewed one of the analyses I was planning on presenting, and there's a glitch in the data."

"A glitch?"

"Yes. Everything is backed up, so it's not a serious problem, but until I find out what happened, I cannot share any results."

"I see." A long pause. "This casts something of a pall over your work, Dr. Strelitz. Especially since the results you sent seemed so encouraging."

A pall? "I take data management very seriously." Jackie avoids the term "data security." "I'll let you know immediately once I understand what the issue is. It's my top priority."

"I'll notify the board." Another long pause as the director deliberates Jackie's transgression. "We've been enthusiastic about supporting your work, but might have to take a closer look at further funding."

"I understand and will be in touch. And please communicate my regrets to the board."

"I will."

Jackie closes the call. *That went well.* Undoubtedly Calhoun suspects she fudged the data to grease the wheels for her upcoming grant submission. Jackie hates the idea of her reputation slipping in the eyes of the foundation, but the call was unavoidable.

At the building entrance, a student jogs past her. Jackie's late. She hurries into the lecture hall, her heart beating too fast, her stomach in knots. She sheds her coat, attaches her laptop to the projector, and clicks open the file for today's lecture. The students tuck their phones away (for now—they always come out eventually). Jackie takes a sip from the water bottle she carries in her bag and wills herself to calm down. Luckily, she has taught Methods for Behavioral Science several times and, unlike other classes, the course content only changes if Jackie updates the examples.

Jackie looks out at the sea of heads. "Good afternoon, everyone." She glances behind her to ensure the image is focused properly. The slide is of a road sign, with arrows labeled "Right" and "Wrong" pointing in opposite directions, and a third arrow in the middle, "It Depends." In her distress, she'd completely forgotten today's lecture topic: ethics.

———

Vince Leeds arrives at the lab conference room at seven thirty the next morning, his hair still wet from showering. Rosy patches of eczema stand out on his pale skin. He's wearing an ironed button-down shirt instead of his usual plain long-sleeve T-shirt, and Jackie wonders if this is for her.

"Good morning, Vince. I can't tell you how grateful I am to you for helping me with this—especially so early."

"Hello, Jackie." He pulls at the cuffs of his shirt. "I'm always happy to help you if I can."

Jackie gestures at the coffee and muffins on the table. "Fuel."

"Thanks."

He takes a coffee, pours in three sugars, and sits beside her, perching on the edge of the chair. He's nervous, more than usual, but Jackie doesn't dwell on it. She has limited time to get him up to speed. The spreadsheet in question is open on her computer. She shows him the graph with the discrepant results and gives the dates that she and Tate ran their analyses.

Vince frowns. "I know a little about your methods from your talks, but can you walk me through how the data are handled?"

"For this study or generally?"

"Generally first, I think. You don't know how big a problem you have, right?"

"Right. So, during a session, the observer captures the behavior in real time using a form on an iPad. Usually we have more than one observer. For some studies we rely only on video, like for tracking eye movement, and code the data later."

"You use Access to create the data entry form for the iPad, right?"

"Yes. We customize it for every study, but the basics haven't changed for years. We also record all the sessions on video as backup." Jackie clicks back to the screen that shows all the lab's files on OneDrive. "The next step is uploading the data from the iPad into a file here. Each study has its own file, an Excel spreadsheet, but they are all set up the same way."

She selects one of the files. Three tabs are at the bottom: Raw Data, Compiled, Analysis. She clicks open the Raw Data tab. A security prompt pops up, and she enters the password. "The data from the iPads are uploaded here." She clicks the Compiled tab, and another sheet opens. Again, she enters a password—a different one—at the prompt. "The raw data feed into this sheet, which does the number crunching." She right-clicks on one of the cells in the table. "For instance, this cell averages the three observations of vertical eye movements in one session for one child. All of these cells contain formulas; they don't store data per se, because whenever the Raw Data sheet is updated, the numbers flow through here and change."

"But the formulas don't."

"Which is why this sheet is locked, so no one can change it by mistake, and also password protected, restricting who can lock or unlock it. We don't want anyone changing the formulas by mistake."

"Makes sense. Who has the passwords?"

Jackie sighs. "Everyone we've trained to upload the data. The password is only there to get people to pause."

Vince sits back in the chair. "If you don't mind me saying, that's not much of a firewall."

"No, it isn't. But I never thought I needed one."

"We'll see, right?" He straightens his collar, probably because his neck itches. "What's next in the chain?"

Jackie selects the Analysis tab. "The formulas shoot the numbers into this sheet. From here we use a statistical program to run the analyses, either the one built into Excel or we export it to SPSS." She lifts her hands. "That's it."

Vince sips his coffee and drums his fingers on the table. "You've probably already figured out that we can use the daily backups to the network to retrieve previous versions of this file."

"Yes, but how do we know if it's the raw data file or the formulas that have been changed? And won't it take forever to find the changes? Maybe not for one study, but for all of them?" Jackie hears the desperation in her voice. In her mind, the vast quantity of data files she has amassed over ten years is a stack about to fall and bury her.

"Here's an idea. I'll make a dummy data set with random numbers, run it through each day's version of the sheet with the formulas, and compare the output. I can do that just by subtracting one day's output from the next, like using one set of results as a filter for the next. If there's a change, it will pop out."

Jackie grabs his arm. "That's brilliant."

His face flushes. "Not really."

"It really is." Jackie tears off a corner of her muffin. She hasn't eaten since yesterday, and a little good news revives her appetite. "What about the raw data file?"

Vince shakes his head. "Harder, I think. But let's blow up that bridge when we get to it."

Jackie pushes back her chair. "I can't thank you enough, Vince."

"I know it's important, but I probably won't get to it until next week."

"That's fine. Today's Friday, after all. And thank you."

"I haven't done anything yet."

"Yes, you have. You've given me hope."

After Vince leaves, Jackie closes the conference room door so she can think without interruption. Tate has already narrowed down who might have altered the spreadsheet to Gretchen and Nasira. Jackie assumes the changes were made by accident—why would anyone alter her data?—but is wary of asking her postdoc questions that might be taken the wrong way, especially given their last personal conversation. Nasira has been polite but cool to Jackie, and it's clear to Jackie that the other members of the lab, especially Tate and Kyle, who have been with her the longest, are picking up on the tension. Whatever Jackie says to Nasira has to be phrased carefully. Given Jackie's lack of sleep and her stress level, she might need a teleprompter to pull it off.

If only Nasira were Jackie's sole worry. Harlan and Nasira have obviously been talking about Jackie's mental state and erratic behavior, so why wouldn't Nasira bring home the juicy tidbit about the data problems? Jackie could question Nasira with kid gloves, and Nasira might still share the news. Jackie's not sure why that bothers her, but it does.

She finishes the muffin and reprimands herself for yet again being too wrapped up in how Harlan and Nasira might react. Her priority has to be discovering the nature and extent of the data problem. If Nasira was rooting around in that spreadsheet, Jackie has to know. It's her lab, and the data are her responsibility. If Harlan wants to make something of it, let him. She's got nothing to hide.

———

Jackie returns to the lab after a seminar and sticks her head into the shared office where Kyle, Gretchen, and Nasira are eating lunch and working. Jackie was hoping as much.

"Hey, gang. Mind if I grab my lunch and join you?"

Kyle speaks around a bite of sandwich. "Sure thing, boss. I wanted to run something by you anyway."

Jackie doesn't wait for a consensus. She drops her bag in her office, retrieves her lunch from the fridge in the hallway, and pulls a chair from the corner of the shared office. Gretchen smiles at her and scoots over to make room. Jackie lets the small talk drift around the room while she opens her salad container (more kale) and squirts on the dressing from the packet.

A lull in the conversation gives Jackie her opening. "Tate came to see me yesterday about a discrepancy in the interim two-year data analysis. We're both scratching our heads over it."

"What sort of discrepancy?" Gretchen asks.

Jackie keeps it vague. "Just a difference in her analysis and one I did a week before. We've got backups, of course, and Vince Leeds is looking into it, but it might be helpful to know if any of you were in there." Jackie reaches for her iced tea and takes a long sip, trying to appear casual.

Gretchen tilts her head. "That's the four-year study, isn't it?"

"Uh-huh," Kyle says.

"Then no. Not since, what?" She glances at Kyle. "Maybe the beginning of the summer?"

Kyle nods. "Yeah, we were looking at the eighteen-month data." He stretches his long legs in front of him. "I haven't been in there since then, either. Because *dissertation*." His intonation suggests the narrator of a horror film. Everyone laughs and nods in sympathy.

Jackie pokes around in her salad as if she's being picky about what to eat next. Without raising her head, she says, "What about you, Nasira?" and stabs a chunk of feta.

"I don't remember the exact day, but yes. I've been looking at which behaviors seem to change the most from six to twelve months, and that's one of the data sets I was reviewing."

Nasira doesn't seem bothered by the question, so Jackie probes deeper. "Were you in the formula sheets?"

Nasira puts down her sandwich. "No. I just wanted the analyzed data." She thinks a moment. "Were the formulas changed?"

"Not sure."

"Why would anyone do that?"

Jackie shrugs. "I really can't guess."

"By mistake?" Gretchen says.

"It's got separate password protection." Nasira folds the wrapping around her sandwich. "I've got a meeting at the medical center. Jackie, I hope you find out what's going on with your data."

"I'm sure I will. Maybe you could reflect on it, and let me know which day you accessed that spreadsheet."

Kyle scrapes his chair back to allow Nasira to pass. As he does, he sends Jackie a quizzical and somewhat worried look.

"Bye, everyone." Nasira slips out.

From her seat near the door, Jackie watches her postdoc retreat down the hall without a sound. Kyle and Gretchen are getting ready to return to work. Jackie carries her chair back to its place, and the meaning behind Kyle's look dawns on her.

Nasira wouldn't know the formula sheet was password protected unless she attempted to access it. Maybe she clicked on it by mistake. Maybe not.

CHAPTER 15

A week later, Jackie is holding extended office hours in honor of the end-of-the-semester crunch. She didn't count, but guesses she answered questions for (and held the hands of) more than two dozen undergraduates.

She ushers the last student out the door. "Good luck on the exam." Jackie forgives herself for having forgotten his name as there are more than a hundred students in the class.

The tall young man waves as he lopes down the hall. "Thank you, Dr. Strelitz."

Jackie's phone pings, and a notification appears on the screen: Endowed Chairs Reception, Dabner House, 5:30 p.m.

"Crap."

She completely forgot. The stress of waiting to hear from Vince Leeds about the source and scope of the data problem is turning her mind into a colander. She was eager to get home. Miles flew in from Houston earlier, and she hoped they could relax together—or bitch and moan together—anything other than continue to dance their strained minuet. But one of the visiting professors at the reception is Lindsay Michener, a disabilities activist and expert on developmental disorders. Jackie is eager to talk with her, even if only to set up a time for a more in-depth conversation. The Dabner House is on her way to her car; she'll stop by briefly.

She checks her outfit, a camel-colored sweaterdress and brown suede boots, and deems it spiffy enough for a glass of wine with academics.

———

The Dabner House is a Gothic outlier on a campus dominated by Georgian stateliness and glass-and-steel modernity. Dwarfed by the surrounding buildings, it has an otherworldly aura, as if the university sprang up unexpectedly around it, its original purpose forgotten. Jackie knows Dabner House is not the oldest building on campus, but the feeling sticks.

A man emerges and holds open the thick wooden door with black strap hinges.

"Thanks." Jackie unbuttons her coat and hangs it on the rack in the foyer.

The main room is vaulted, but the walnut paneling and oversize paintings bring the walls in close. On the far wall, the fireplace—roomy enough to cook a steer in—is ablaze, rendering the air stifling. Jackie scans the people nearest to her for Dr. Michener, whom she knows only from her headshot, then proceeds to a table in the corner where, judging from the clot of bodies, drinks are being served.

A chilled glass of sauvignon blanc in hand, Jackie greets faculty she knows, keeping a lookout for Dr. Michener. Perhaps she decided to skip the reception.

"Jackie."

She startles. Harlan is at her elbow, along with a man, somewhat younger than Harlan, sporting a tweed blazer and a neatly trimmed mustache.

"Hello, Harlan." She offers a terse smile, unable to completely mask the tension he evokes. Two weeks ago, she left him the stay-out-of-my-life message, and she's only seen him in passing since.

"Let me introduce Peter Durbin. He's visiting from Nottingham as the McIntyre chair in English. We met a week or so ago at the president's house—something Chen asked me to attend. Boring as hell save for Peter."

Jackie shakes hands with Durbin. His smile is warm but he keeps his chin elevated. Jackie never cares about being a woman of average height except when men look down at her like this. She doesn't judge him for it, though. For some it's habitual.

"Welcome. Although by now you must have settled in."

"I have indeed." His accent is pure BBC. "The students are quite refreshing."

Jackie smiles. Before she can speak again, Harlan does.

"I wanted you to meet Peter because we've discovered the most extraordinary coincidence."

The twinkle in Harlan's eyes is captivating, as ever, but Jackie is wary. Something is afoot. "Really?"

"Yes. It turns out that Peter went to prep school—public school, I guess you'd call it, Peter—with Miles."

Jackie looks from Harlan to Peter. "You knew Miles at Felsted?"

"I did."

"That really is a coincidence." Jackie sips her wine, calculating the probabilities. "How did you two happen to uncover it?"

Peter shrugs. "At the previous function we wandered into the topic of American football, and I mentioned the structural similarities to rugby, wondering if Harlan here was familiar with it."

Harlan eagerly picks up the story. "Naturally, I am quite familiar. In explaining how, I mentioned Miles by name." He grins broadly, looking from Jackie to Peter and back to Jackie. "Remarkable, isn't it?"

Jackie puzzles over why Harlan is so gleeful. "Such a small world."

"Indeed." Peter is staring at her, still smiling, examining her while pretending not to do so. Jackie is confused and a little unnerved. "And you and Miles are married, I hear."

"Yes, two years in February. I'm sure Harlan would have said."

"He did, of course."

"I might be mistaken, but you sound surprised." Jackie is sure of the latent message in his tone and is annoyed enough to confront him, albeit politely.

"Do I? Well, I—"

"He was married before. Perhaps Harlan mentioned that as well. And he has a son." Jackie realizes she sounds snappy and steps back. "I'm happy to let Miles know you're in town. Were you close?"

"Friends, but, no, not close."

"Either way, I'm sure he'd be pleased to see you."

Harlan says, "I suggested that, too." He spreads his hands. "We could all go out."

Peter nods and sips his beer. "I'm game."

"Wonderful." Jackie smiles and hopes it looks sincere. She can't honestly say why she feels at a disadvantage in this conversation, but she does. It reminds her of the evening Harlan came into her lab to ask about borrowing Nasira for his project. The words made sense, but she was missing something, not in on the joke. "If you'll excuse me, I need to find someone, then head home. Peter, I'll be sure to tell Miles I met you. Enjoy yourselves."

She smiles again and winnows her way through the crowd, keeping one eye out for Dr. Michener. Her trajectory is toward the door, however, and home.

Jackie steps into the warmth of her house, deposits her coat and bag on the bench by the door, and pulls off her boots.

She calls out to Miles on her way to the kitchen. "It's me."

He's cutting tomatoes for the salad at his elbow. "Hi, beautiful. Two seconds." He scrapes the tomatoes from the cutting board into the bowl, rinses and dries his hands, and comes out from behind the counter, opening his arms.

"So good to see you." He hugs her and plants a kiss on her cheek. Not her mouth, she notes.

"You smell good." A new cologne? She doesn't want to say in case she is wrong. Nothing says "estranged" like forgetting what your spouse smells like.

"It's the risotto. Chicken and fontina."

"Sounds amazing." She peeks over his shoulder. "Has it been ready long?"

He shakes his head. "No, your timing is perfect." He returns to the stove and stirs. "Any news from your IT guy?"

Over the phone last night, Jackie told him the essentials of the data problem without indicating how serious it might be, either in its cause or scope. No point in being an alarmist. But he must have read the concern in her voice, since he remembered to ask her about it.

"Not yet. He's working on it, but he has to deal with emergencies first, like computer crashes."

"Right."

"Did you finally meet with that player?" Miles is home a day later than scheduled because a key player had a family emergency.

Miles stops stirring, then resumes. "Oh, yes. Yes, I did. Walter LeFebvre. Looks as though he might sign. I'll know for certain in a couple of days." He points at the open bottle on the counter. "Wine?"

"Uh, no. Not this second." Why did he seem thrown by her question? He couldn't have forgotten having to change his flight. Then again, their transition to being together is always somewhat awkward, especially lately. Jackie has been assuming it's her fault, but perhaps that's reflexive on her part. She can't remember the last time he initiated sex—or the last time they had sex, now that she thinks about it. Definitely not since the Thanksgiving baby discussion three weeks ago. Talk about voting with your feet—or your whatever.

Miles is recounting his meeting with Walter LeFebvre. Jackie retrieves bowls, salad plates, and flatware. She tosses the salad, arranges a portion on each plate, and carries them to the table.

"Anyway," Miles says, as he spoons risotto into the bowls, "I'm hopeful. He's an incredible athlete."

"Fingers crossed." Jackie decides on wine after all and crosses to the table with her glass. "I dropped in at a reception just before I came home. Harlan was there."

Miles sets the bowls on the table and sits. "Oh? How is he? I haven't talked to him in a while."

"Fine. Harlan is Harlan." She tastes her risotto. "This is delicious, Miles. Anyway, he introduced me to someone who knows you—from Felsted."

"Really?" Miles picks up his wineglass, by the stem as always, and pauses before taking a sip. "Who was it?"

"Peter Durbin." Jackie continues eating, but also watches her husband. "Do you remember him?"

Miles concentrates on his food and waves his hand vaguely. "I didn't know him well."

"He remembered you, obviously, although he did mention you weren't close."

Miles meets her gaze. "Funny sort of cocktail-party conversation."

"Not really. He struck me as somewhat arrogant." She searched for the right phrasing. "And bemused by you, or by his memory of you, I suppose."

"Bemused? Why?"

Jackie shrugs. "Got me." She is about to add that, if she had to guess, Peter and Harlan shared a secret, but Miles will dismiss it as preposterous, given that the men hardly know each other. She has learned to refrain from sharing her thoughts about Harlan with her husband.

"How odd." Miles had stopped eating, but now picks up his fork. "How very odd."

"That's what I thought." She sips her wine. "He wants to see you."

"Who? Durbin?"

Jackie laughs. "Yes. Who else? Harlan suggested we all go out."

"Well, I suppose . . ." He still hasn't resumed eating.

"Are you okay? You seem a little weirded out."

"Do I?" He takes a bite of the risotto and chews thoughtfully. "This is actually really tasty. I'll have to save the recipe."

"It's excellent." Jackie gets up and retrieves the wine bottle. "More?" Miles nods, and she pours. "Peter Durbin is in the English Department. In case you want to contact him."

"I suppose he was wearing tweed."

Jackie is perplexed by her husband's response to Durbin. Jackie didn't like the guy, but Miles said he hardly knew him, so why isn't he more curious about the man?

Her phone vibrates on the kitchen counter. She pushes back her chair. "Do you mind? It might be IT." She normally wouldn't answer during meals, but she told Vince Leeds to call her with any news.

"Of course not."

Jackie picks up her phone, sees that it's Vince. She raises a finger to signal Miles and heads to the guest room. "Hi, Vince." She leans the door closed.

"Hi, Jackie. Is this an okay time?"

"Yes. It's fine."

"I'm sorry to keep you on tenterhooks, but it's been a crazy end to the week."

"I understand." She sits on the easy chair, and stands up again, agitated. "What did you find?"

He lets out a long breath. "It's like we thought. The formulas were changed on Saturday the first. Or, more precisely, sometime between two a.m. Saturday and two a.m. Sunday. Two is when OneDrive is backed up."

Jackie paces the room. "Okay. Were you able to tell how extensive the change was?"

"I know where you're going. If it's just one cell, it could be a mistake. If it's several changes, more likely it's foul play." He pauses. "Five changes in that spreadsheet, the one we looked at."

Jackie's head feels like a balloon. She reaches behind her for the chair and lowers herself into it.

"You there, Jackie? You all right?"

"Yes, I'm here, Vince. But holy crap."

"That's the technical term for it." A rustling sound, like he's squirming in his chair. "Sorry. Trying to lighten the message."

"I know. Don't worry." That's what she told Tate. But now she is worried. Very worried. She has managed to cut off every rabbit trail of disaster her mind has wanted to follow during the last six days. Now her thoughts are a pack of wild rabbits scurrying down every single one. Who would do this? And why?

Vince clears his throat. "I did find something else."

Jackie pulls herself out of her dark thoughts. "What do you mean?"

"I took the liberty of sampling a couple of your other recent data files. This wasn't the only one with a problem. I found another formula change in a file labeled AIOS17, from more than three weeks ago."

"Which day?"

"November twentieth. Why? Is that day significant?"

It is. Tate met with Jackie about her independent research that day. It stuck in Jackie's mind because it was Tate's birthday, and Jackie brought a cake from Sweet Somethings for the lab to share at lunchtime. Tate was really touched. After they finished, the others left for a seminar, except for Tate, who stayed to help Nasira learn how to upload the data from the AIOS assessments. There was no reason for Tate or Nasira to monkey with the Compiled spreadsheets—the ones with the formulas—no reason whatsoever. But she doesn't want to get into that with Vince, at least not tonight.

"Sorry, Vince. I think I've had about all the news I can handle tonight. Can we talk again tomorrow—or whenever you have time?"

"Sure, Jackie. I understand. I'll be touch tomorrow."

"Have a good evening. And thanks again."

"No problem." His voice softens. "We'll figure it out. Nothing is lost."

"You're right. Good night, Vince."

She closes the call. *Nothing is lost.* Sure doesn't feel that way. And without knowing how deep or wide the problem is, it's impossible to say what has already been lost, including her reputation. Vince meant to convey that the data can always be recovered; there is a safety net. But Jackie isn't certain of anything anymore. She doesn't know whom to talk to, whom to trust. Even Miles, always trustworthy and transparent, has become enigmatic, and Harlan, who has always been crystal clear in his motives, now operates in the shadows.

And Nasira. Jackie wishes she could peer inside the woman's head and gain a sliver of insight into what makes her tick. It's been more than two weeks since their testy confrontation in the café, and since then, Jackie has done her utmost to keep personal matters out of the lab and normalize their interactions. But the data breach *is* lab business. What motivation could Nasira have to meddle with the data files? Jackie is stumped, but since nothing else makes sense, either, Nasira's motivation is simply one more open loop trailing in the swirl.

Her data, those reliable specks of reality, can be recovered, but there is much more wrong in her world than jumbled formulas. It's as if she has been thrown out of a plane in the night.

She can tell herself there is a net below, but that doesn't stop it from feeling like a free fall.

Nothing is lost.

Nothing except her grip.

CHAPTER 16

Another night of crappy sleep. At a campus coffee shop Jackie orders an extra shot of espresso for her latte to go and hurries to her office, wishing she'd remembered her gloves. It's well below freezing, and the wind is biting at her fingers. Within minutes her face is numb, and it's possible her nose is running, but she can't feel it. Students and faculty rush past, wrapped in bulky scarves, hats pulled tight over their ears. The second week in December is never this cold.

Jackie pulls open the door to Wolf Hall. Amy Chen, the chair of the department, arrives from the other direction, and Jackie props the door open with her boot.

Amy hustles inside, and Jackie follows her in. "Jackie! Good morning."

"Good morning, Amy. Isn't it awful out?" She stamps her feet to bring the feeling back.

She smiles. "You forget I went to school in Syracuse."

"Right. Just another balmy day for you."

They set off toward the elevator. If they keep walking together, Amy Chen will ask about her classes, her work. She always does, not so much out of friendliness, but as a way of keeping her fingers on the departmental pulse. Jackie doesn't want to say anything about the data security mess in her lab, nor does she want to pretend nothing is going on. If there is fraud, she'll be obligated to tell Chen about it, and she doesn't want her to remember this conversation as one where she said everything was fine.

"You know what, Amy?" Jackie slows to a stop and Chen does, too. "My feet are so numb, I'm going to take the stairs and hope that warms them up."

"Sure, sure." She is already moving off. "Let's catch up soon, though."

"Definitely."

Jackie hates taking the stairs—the building is old, and the stairwell is dingy and neglected—but the exercise does thaw her toes and force her to breathe deeply. Her nerves are frayed, and her stomach is turned inside out. Today she must confront Nasira, and it fills her with dread. Last night, after Jackie spoke with Vince, she texted Nasira, asking to meet at eight this morning, but has not yet received a reply. Jackie really wants to get this little chat out of the way so it doesn't hang over her all day.

She lets herself into the lab and stops by the shared office. It's empty except for Kyle, who is surrounded by takeout containers, candy wrappers, and coffee cups.

"Morning, Kyle."

"Hi, Jackie." He rubs his cheeks with his hands.

"Did you go home at all?"

"Yeah. But only because you won't let me set up a cot in here." He gives her a crooked smile.

Jackie realizes how much she'll miss him when he leaves next year. He was her first post-Harlan student—in other words, the first one she selected without his input. "Do me a favor? If Nasira comes in, let her know I'm here."

Kyle raises one eyebrow. "Is this about the data problem?"

For him to reach that conclusion, Jackie must have failed to keep her tone neutral. "Yes. I didn't want to say anything until I knew what was what."

"Because you knew I'd worry about my study?"

"In part. And don't worry."

"Hey, these days I schedule all my worrying, and it's tight. Right now the only thing I'm worried about is running out of coffee." He lifts his cup in a toast and turns back to his computer.

In her office, Jackie distracts herself with mindless tasks: sorting through emails, updating the study schedule, making a to-do list for the weekend. She usually looks forward to Fridays; with no classes and no regular meetings, she can catch up and head into the weekend with her desk clear. Working every weekend is a must when classes are in session, and empty Fridays keep her sane.

Except today.

By midmorning, Jackie's anxiety is shifting toward anger. Why hasn't Nasira at least texted her back? Jackie picks up her phone and considers calling her, but she really doesn't want to have this conversation on the phone. Instead, she takes her coat and scarf from the back of the door, resolving to pace outside in the cold until she regains her equilibrium.

A rap on the door. "Jackie?"

Nasira. Jackie yanks open the door and steps back.

Nasira's eyes widen in surprise. "Oh!" Her cheeks are rosy, and she's wearing a white cable-knit scarf over a black shirt. She's obviously just arrived. Her eyes go to Jackie's coat. "Were you going out? I can come back later."

"No. Stay." She takes a breath. "Please. Have a seat." She hangs up her coat, closes the door behind Nasira, and sits at her desk. Her palms are sweating, but she's fairly certain her demeanor projects calm.

Nasira unwinds her scarf. "I'm sorry I didn't answer your text. I wasn't sure of my schedule."

Nasira falls silent, her gaze drifting, and Jackie wonders if something is amiss. She can't ask, of course. "Well, you're here now." She considers where to begin. "I heard back from Vince about the problems with the spreadsheet for the four-year study. As we guessed, the formulas were altered. Vince was able to figure out when it happened." Nasira nods. Jackie is hoping to see some sign of guilt or discomfort, but the woman maintains her usual equanimity. "It was Saturday the first."

"Okay. Does that help somehow?"

"Were you working in the spreadsheet that day?"

"I don't remember exactly—"

"I did ask you to try to recall."

She straightens. "If I had, I would've told you. Isn't this just a mistake?"

Jackie leans forward and rests her forearms on the desk. "Apparently not. Several formulas were changed."

Nasira frowns.

"I've asked the others, and no one else was in there that day."

"So you're accusing me?"

"I'm not accusing you. I'm asking you. I'm trying to figure out what happened to my data." Jackie strives to keep her tone level; she's acted like a whackjob with her postdoc often enough.

Nasira twists and extracts her phone from her rear pocket. "Let me check, okay? I don't make notes on everything I do, but maybe there's something here." She scrolls and pecks and swipes. "Oh, right." She crosses her legs and swings her foot. The slider on her insulated boots hits the zipper with each upswing. Click, click, click.

Jackie leans toward her. "What?"

Nasira looks up from her phone. "I remember now. The night before, Friday, Harlan's router stopped working. He ordered a new one, but it wasn't going to arrive until Monday. Neither of us had anything planned, so we took the train to New York—without our laptops." She slips her phone back in her pocket and resettles. "Looks like I'm in the clear."

Jackie is struck dumb by the news of this jaunt, which serves both as an alibi for the data fraud and as a dagger in her foolish, jealous heart. "Listen, Nasira—"

"What reason would I have to tamper with your results? I want to work here, remember?" She gets to her feet. "Honestly, Jackie, I don't know what to think about you anymore." Indignant a moment before, now she appears genuinely wounded.

Jackie, perplexed and distraught, searches for words, but her thoughts won't link up. She wipes her sweaty palms on her jeans.

Nasira moves to the door, her hand on the handle. "Working here has become stressful. I'm committed to the research, but the subtext of your questions—plus everything else—is a bit much."

Whatever is going on with the data, the woman's distress feels honest. "I don't want you stressed, Nasira. That's not my goal at all. Please try to understand the situation from my point of view. I'm asking everyone the same questions, and there are only so many people with access to the files."

Nasira pauses, her posture softening a fraction. "Do you honestly think any of your students would try to sabotage your research? They worship you, Jackie. Don't you see that?"

Jackie blinks at Nasira, a lump forming in her throat.

"I'm going to think hard about this, Jackie." She leaves, closing the door softly behind her.

The room is quiet. Jackie's temples throb and she's desperately thirsty, but her limbs are leaden and she can't seem to move. If nothing made sense before, it makes even less sense now. She is no closer to knowing who manipulated her data, and now her postdoc is claiming a hostile work environment. Jackie is so stressed herself she forgot to ask Nasira about the other spreadsheet Vince said had been altered. It's not like Jackie to be derailed, but the mounting problems and lack of sleep are taking a cumulative toll. She closes her eyes and tries to calm her mind, but she's always been a failure at calming techniques of any kind and more inclined to reach for the wine bottle than the yoga mat.

Jackie is touched by Nasira's assertion that her students worship her. True or not, they depend on her, especially the graduate students, and until she knows what happened to her data, she must rely on reason, not emotion. How many of the people working in her lab are sloppy about leaving their laptops where others can access them, store their passwords somewhere obvious, like on their phones, or give access to lab files for other reasons? If she had to hazard a guess, she'd say most if not all of them.

Again she considers Nasira, whose defense is that she wants to work in Jackie's lab. But the truth is that if Nasira is successful in obtaining a grant for her MRI research, she can take the money anywhere with a machine and a source of subjects—in other words, almost any larger university or medical center. She only needs Jackie now to gain experience to be credible as an expert on autism. Once that has been established, Jackie and her lab are expendable.

The gap, however, between expendable and worthy of sabotage is enormous. Could Nasira be angry enough about Jackie's snooping and meddling to attempt to torpedo Jackie's career? It seems unlikely, a wildly disproportionate response, especially given the risk of getting caught. Meanwhile, Jackie has further estranged her; she resolves once again to take the target off Nasira's back.

Her head is pounding now. She digs in her bag for ibuprofen and finds none. She checks her phone for messages and is surprised it's almost one o'clock. She skipped breakfast so no wonder her head hurts. Having organized her work for the weekend before Nasira showed up, Jackie decides she'll head home and pick up food on the way. It's only going to get colder anyway.

She packs her bag and slips out of the lab without stopping by the shared office. Ten minutes later she's at the counter at Sweet Somethings. The room is warm and smells so good she wants to curl up in the pastry case, eat her way through the contents, and fall asleep forever. She orders and carries a sticky bun and tea to a window seat while they make her sandwich. The blue-and-yellow French Provençal tablecloth is so cheerful, her eyes well with tears.

Just eat, Jackie. Eat, and drink your tea.

The sticky bun is heaven, the brown sugar and butter and cinnamon melding in her mouth, sparking associations with childhood treats and holidays and happiness. The sensation smooths her a little, like a stroke across ruffled fur. As she eats, she looks out the window at the people walking by, mummified in their coats and scarves. Despite the cold, people are out getting ready for the holidays. Jackie wonders why she doesn't do this more often: drink tea from a porcelain cup, people watch, eat wicked pastry. The answer, she knows, is that she works too much. But still.

"Hello, Jackie." Harlan looms over the table. She startles, and her cup clatters against the saucer. Before she can gather her thoughts, he's pulling out the opposite chair. "Mind if I sit? We didn't get a chance to catch up last night."

Why does he keep sneaking up on her like this? She wipes her mouth with her napkin, pushes her plate to the side. "Actually, I was just leaving." Her moment of calm ruined, all she wants is to go home.

He gestures to her half-finished bun and steaming teacup. "You'll get a headache if you skip meals." His brow is knitted with concern. He was always watchful of her erratic eating habits, and his reference to them now is both disconcerting and reassuringly familiar.

She sighs and takes a drink of tea. She'll go when her sandwich is ready. There's no point in making a scene.

Harlan settles into the seat. "All ready for your talk next week?"

Neutral topic. What a relief. She's giving one of the Gottfried lectures on Monday night, part of a series open to the public. She provided the title months ago—"What Theory of Mind Teaches Us about Autism"—but beyond that she hasn't given it any thought. She hasn't had the bandwidth. "It's on my agenda for the weekend." She almost adds, *Unless another disaster strikes,* but stops herself. "It's always hard to know how to pitch a talk to such a broad audience."

He laughs gently. "You mean, when not everyone is a psychologist?"

"Exactly. I don't know anymore what's lingo and what's true language."

"Test it out on Miles. He's your perfect lay audience."

The reference to Miles has the effect of drawing a circle around her and Harlan, leaving Miles on the outside. Did Harlan do this on purpose? She's been avoiding his gaze, but now she looks directly at him, judging his intent.

He smiles, and his eyes grow soft. "I can see you're upset, Jackie. If something's wrong—and it clearly is—you can tell me."

She shakes her head. No way she's going to spill about the data breach and her heated interchange with Nasira.

He leans closer, lowers his voice. "Is it Miles?"

"What?"

"I just thought perhaps . . ." He frowns, pulls back a little. "It's nothing. I shouldn't have said anything."

"Said nothing about what?" Her heart rate kicks up a notch. "Did Miles tell you something?"

"Well we *are* friends. We do talk." Harlan spreads his hands. "I only mentioned Miles because I assumed that was what is upsetting you."

A weakness comes over Jackie. She stares at Harlan, willing him to tell her everything and hoping to God he doesn't say a word more.

"I am sorry, Jackie. I shouldn't have said anything."

She leans toward him. "Please tell me." She winces at the rawness of her plea, but she's too desperate and exhausted to filter.

He shakes his head, shrugs. "I suppose I'm projecting because Nasira's been somewhat distant lately."

"Nasira's distant? What's that got to do with anything?" Harlan shakes his head again. "Did Miles actually tell you something or didn't he?" Her mind is a storm.

He holds up his hands. "I've already said too much. Triangles make for unhealthy relationships." He smiles, his eyes shining with sympathy.

"You have to learn things yourself, Jackie, even if it's hard. It's the only way."

More prevarication and riddles. Her frustration erupts. "Learn what?" Her voice is too loud, and people at the other tables turn to stare. Let them.

"You're tired." Harlan pushes back his chair. "Let's leave so you can go home."

"What am I supposed to learn?" Distress grabs hold of Jackie with a metal fist, rattling her. "What?"

He's getting up, putting on his jacket. The room feels too close suddenly, the sweet smells now cloying.

She's had enough. She throws on her coat, grabs her bag, pushes past Harlan, and nearly collides with the waitress proffering a white paper bag.

"Here's your sandwich. Sorry for the wait."

Jackie accepts the bag, thanks her, and hurries out the door. Harlan's behind her, she can feel it, but she ignores him and strides toward her car, her scarf trailing in her hand.

At her car, she digs in her purse for her keys, and Harlan catches up to her. "You all right to drive?"

She beeps open the car, hands trembling. "I'm fine."

"I'll text you later."

"Don't bother."

She gets inside, shuts the door. Her breath comes out in rapid white puffs. Harlan hasn't moved. He's waiting for her to leave, a concerned look on his face.

She resists the urge to give him the finger. She starts the car, backs up a few feet, and pulls away.

She'll drive home and talk to Miles, ask him the questions that even now are stacking themselves in her mind.

CHAPTER 17

HARLAN

Jackie is always beautiful to me, but never more so than when she is on the knife-edge between distress and anger. I realize I'm supposed to find her at her best when she is laughing and playful or when she is calm and studious or even when she is asleep, although I never understood the attraction of the last. When a person sleeps they are entirely mysterious, and there is nothing beautiful about that, at least to me. She could be dreaming about anything or anyone, finding pleasure and satisfaction in another man's (or woman's) arms, rowing a boat across a swamp filled with snapping crocodiles, or climbing an endless set of stairs to escape the monster whose breath is hot on the back of her legs. If I can't know what is in her dreams, then how could I possibly love her best then? Dreams are mere by-products of the daily housekeeping our brains must undertake, but that doesn't rob them of their emotional significance, only of their meaning. So, no, Jackie asleep is beautiful, but that is not how I prefer to think of her.

When she is distressed and that distress is colored by indignation or frustration, Jackie is simultaneously the epitome of fierce strength and vulnerability. She could explode or implode; all bets are off, unless you know her like I do, and even I have judged wrongly which way she would fall. Today, for example, she was there, on the precipice, but too exhausted to give in to the anger, to allow it to ignite her so she could then extinguish it with a flood of her own tears. I brought her to that perfect point once, the day she left me. Ironic, yes, but it was nearly worth losing her. Today confusion and exhaustion muddled her emotion and kept her from telling me her problems and her secrets, or what she believes are her secrets. They are, in truth, already mine.

It's nice to share something even if she isn't aware of it.

Jackie mistrusts Nasira. I've helped it along but it's a natural impulse. Women point the finger at other women whenever they can, even when a man is a more worthy target. So much for female solidarity. I assume there is something biological in this tendency, an assumption, perhaps, that men are hapless victims of a woman's power to bewitch. Another way to put it would be that men follow their dicks and can't be held responsible. The woman who entranced him, however, can. It's all hopelessly sexist and outdated, as all good biological imperatives are, but they don't call them imperatives for nothing.

Jackie blames Nasira for another reason: Nasira is taciturn and allows people to write motivations all over that perfect blank face of hers. Jackie also has more interactions with Nasira than with me, so I can stay safely in the background with my faultless dick and let the ladies tear each other to pieces. I could see it in Jackie's eyes today, the itch to trust me, to believe I have answers, not just riddles. I have never openly betrayed her trust, you see, but she's simply unsteady enough at the moment to be confused about that, too. Granted, she doesn't know what Nasira has told me. I almost forget, myself, at times.

No matter, because I've benched Nasira. She's hurt, which is sweet, but I don't have time for her emotions, not since fortune brought me Peter Durbin, Miles's prep school chum. He's a real type, Durbin, shaking my hand and right away digging around for who we knew in common, as if influence and success could be calculated using the dynamics of a LinkedIn network. What a fool. I saw through him immediately, with his falsely jocular, regimental-tie-and-family-shield sensibility. A bit like my father.

Durbin's social ferreting did lead to our mutual connection with Miles, and to what I have long suspected about my friend. It was all very English—nudge-nudge, wink-wink—and Durbin held me to the understanding that Miles was only a boy at the time. Boys will be boys! I don't believe that for a minute. People are born as they are and only get into trouble if they deny their true natures.

Miles, my dear, sweet friend. Jackie miscalculated—again. If only she had listened to me, stayed with me.

I was amused when she started dating Miles, never thinking for a moment she would marry him. Their Vegas wedding stunned me; my beautiful Jackie in a quickie wedding in the crassest city in the world. Well, Atlantic City might have been worse. The news enraged me, and I feared I would lose control and, in doing so, lose everything. It was touch and go, but the damage was confined to my house. I decided that same day to take my overdue sabbatical, to drop through a trapdoor and regroup in private, where I didn't risk running into Jackie and exposing myself.

I went to Madison and grew a shell. And from inside of that new carapace, I took control once more.

And here I am.

CHAPTER 18

Jackie ascends the porch steps. Music is blaring from inside, the screech of electric guitar and the thrum of a bass. Miles's taste runs more to R&B, and in any case, it's not like him to play it so loudly. The nape of her neck prickles, and she wonders if she should go in.

Honestly, she thinks, *whoever it is can just do me the favor and shoot me.*

She unlocks the door, pushes it open, and shouts over the noise. "Hello?" The hall is empty, as are the portions of the dining area and kitchen she can see. A pizza box lies open on the counter. It would be unusual for a burglar to order in. She closes the door behind her and proceeds down the hall. "Hello?"

Sprawled on the living room couch is Antonio. He's gaming and hasn't noticed her entering. She walks in front of the set and points to her ears. He nods, grabs the remote, and turns down the volume.

"Hi, Jackie."

"Hi, Antonio." If Miles said anything about his son coming over today, she's forgotten, although it seems unlikely. "I wasn't expecting you."

He shrugs and shuffles his feet. "Something came up and I couldn't stay at my place."

"Something came up?" Her head is throbbing. She doesn't want to play twenty questions.

"Yeah. My dad knows." His tone suggests telling his father fulfilled his obligation to keep parents informed.

"I see." Jackie sighs. "How're your classes going?"

"I was just taking a study break."

Jackie spreads her arms. "Innocent question." She nods at the pizza box. "Do you want anything else to eat? A sandwich?"

He shakes his head. "I'm good."

"Do you happen to know where your dad is?" She has questions, terrible questions.

"He went to get some stuff for dinner."

"Okay. Listen, can you use the headphones?" She flinches at the piercing sensation behind her eyes. "Actually, can you use the TV in the guest room?"

Antonio sighs. "This one is so much better."

She can't do it. She can't argue with him. The thin piece of string that has been holding her together all day is frayed and about to break. Without a word, she hurries into the kitchen, grabs a bottle of wine from the rack under the counter and a glass from the cabinet, and heads upstairs. She will draw herself a scalding bath and barricade herself in the bathroom with her wine. It won't fix anything, except perhaps her headache, but right now she doesn't give a damn.

———

Jackie sits cross-legged on the bath mat in her fleece bathrobe, having given up on the bath when the water became tepid. The wine, at least, has not failed her in this way, though only a glass or so remains. The three ibuprofen she swallowed as she waited for the bath to fill have her headache on the run. She does not, however, feel better, just numb to whatever she might feel. This is excellent news, but no way will it last.

Miles knocked on the door a while ago. She ignored him until he said he was worried about her. She said she was fine, a lie of course, but he did go away. She is just so fundamentally sick of everyone, especially husbands who might be cheating. What else could Harlan have been alluding to? And why did he bring up Nasira in the same breath? The idea that Miles is having an affair with Nasira is outlandish, but, as Jackie is learning, that's no reason to reject an idea.

She pours herself the last glass of wine, congratulating herself on not spilling any on her robe. She wants to stay in here, but when the wine runs out, seclusion will be the room's only attraction. The bath mat is damp and not that comfortable. She would like to be in her bed now, but it's Miles's bed, too. Her desire to be alone is powerful, and she imagines staying the night (or two or a week or forever) in a hotel. She could stay in her robe, throw a coat over it, call an Uber. The plan is taking shape but her phone is elsewhere. Downstairs maybe. What she would truly like is to close her eyes and wake up in a hotel bed. The pizza box would be left behind, as would the laundry. In the hotel, there is room service.

Jackie finishes the wine and stands to stretch her legs. She looks in the mirror, at her too-red cheeks and her wild, damp hair, and the spell is broken. There will be no hotel, no room service. There will, in all likelihood, be more of the same: many, many questions, all with unsatisfying answers. Riddles.

She opens the door. The air in the hall is cool and dry. Antonio's voice drifts up from below; he's talking on the phone. Jackie pads to the bedroom—the door is ajar—and goes in. She is clean and warm and tipsy and, underneath that, frustrated and quite possibly furious.

Miles is sitting on the bed, fully dressed, leaning against the pillows, his legs angled so his feet are not touching the covers even though his shoes are off. He's holding his phone, but his gaze is toward the window, which faces the backyard but is dark now except for the neighbors' lights. Jackie has no idea what time it is.

He turns to her and sits up. "Are you all right?"

"I guess so." She comes to the end of the bed. "I drank a bottle of wine and should probably eat something."

He frowns. "There's dinner downstairs."

"Antonio was a surprise."

"I texted you. Didn't you get it?"

"I haven't looked at my phone. But wasn't he here already when you texted me? I mean, was it a question?"

He rearranges himself on the bed, pulling one leg up. "There was a problem with his sublet, and he had to leave his place. I couldn't just turn him away."

Jackie is dizzy, but doesn't want to sit, so she steps forward and presses her thighs against the bed. "I have another question. Have you done something that would upset me?"

His eyebrows shoot up. "What are you talking about?"

"I wish I knew. Harlan seems to think that if I'm upset or troubled or frustrated or losing my mind—and all of those things are true—that you must be the reason."

Miles frowns so deeply it's almost comical. She can't read his expression, though; is he worried about her or about himself? "Harlan said that? That's ridiculous."

"Well, he started to say that. Got my attention, that's for sure, then he said he didn't want to meddle."

Miles spreads his hands. "I have no idea what he could have meant."

"He mentioned Nasira."

"In connection to me? I hardly know her."

"Hardly?" As far as Jackie knows, Miles's only contact with her was at the Dinner.

"From the dinner we all had. From the football game. From once when she was at Harlan's."

"She was at the football game?" Jackie doesn't know why this bothers her, but it does.

"Yes."

"The one you forgot to invite me to."

"Really, Jackie? If I didn't mention Nasira was there, it probably had something to do with Antonio getting absolutely plastered and me having other things on my mind."

Jackie blinks at him, remembering the scene—and getting vomited on. She and Miles had been pulling in the same direction then. It feels like eons ago.

Miles is watching her. From his expression, he's likely having the same thoughts. "What difference does it make, Jackie, if I've talked to Nasira a few times? You are making too much of this." The anger in him fizzles; he is never successful at holding on to it for very long. He comes over to her, holds her arms. He waits for her to lean into him before he pulls her into an embrace. His warmth, his strong arms melt the top layer of her resistance.

Miles lays his cheek on her head. "You're fatally tired, darling. You're seeing problems everywhere."

Was she? She decides to apply Occam's razor, the centuries-old guidance for deciding between competing explanations. If you can't decide based on evidence, then choose the simplest one. That Harlan is causing trouble—or meant something else entirely—is a simpler explanation than that Miles and Nasira are having an affair. Nasira is living at Harlan's by her own admission. It would be bad form to be sleeping with Miles, too, especially given that the men are friends. Jackie is the one who's a mess lately, not Miles.

Jackie squeezes him and kisses his neck, embarrassed that it took so much thought to decide he is blameless. He's her husband, after all, and he's never given her reason to doubt him.

"I'm sorry," she says, and lets go of him. "I'll put on some clothes and be down to eat in a second."

She retreats to the closet and slips on flannel pajama pants, a sweatshirt, and her sheepskin slippers. As she hangs up her robe and throws her work clothes in the hamper, she thinks again of the hotel, the simplicity of it, the anonymity. Over the last three months, her relationships with Miles, Harlan, Nasira, even Antonio, have had the quality of a rickety roller-coaster ride. It's as if she doesn't know these people, or they have somehow changed, and she can't focus on what's happening because she's being thrown all over the place. The hotel fantasy appeals to her because she can disconnect and do as she pleases instead of being yanked around by forces she cannot see much less control.

Jackie leaves the bedroom, walks down the hall, and pauses halfway to the stairs.

The hotel fantasy is about becoming her mother. She sees that now, and, surprisingly, the realization does not spoil the fantasy.

———

The morning breaks clear. Without waking Miles, Jackie dresses in a thermal base layer, leggings, a wool vest, a zip-front top, gloves, and a wool hat and leaves the house with a travel mug of coffee. She drives to the boathouse to administer the antidote to too much wine: a long session of rowing on the Potomac. Her phone tells her the temperature is thirty-eight, warmer than yesterday but not by much.

Jackie sets the shell in the water, latches the oars into the gates, and climbs in. She stores her running shoes, slips her feet into the shoes on the footboard, and gently nudges the shell away from the dock. The shell slides out in a whisper. Jackie points it away from the sun and sets up a rhythm, dipping the oars for the catch, stretching her back muscles for the full stroke, skimming the blades an inch above the surface on the return. The self-made breeze steals her breath, leaving white clouds in front of her. Her hands warm.

Jackie rows until the pain in her thighs overwhelms her. Back at the dock, her legs tremble as she climbs out of the shell. She rests for a long while. When her sweat turns cold, she lifts the shell onto her shoulder, carries it across the dock, and stores it in the boathouse. It occurs to her that a river is much more useful to her than any hotel.

———

On Sunday morning, Miles is packing for a few days in San Francisco—his last business trip before the holiday break. Jackie is cross-legged on the bed, working on her speech for tomorrow evening. It's partially recycled from one she gave at a cognitive psychology conference last year, so she should be able to finish it this morning, then do something else this afternoon—like see a movie or read a book or go Christmas shopping. Something normal. She might even find out if Grace is free and get a dose of her nieces and nephews, or steal Grace away for an hour.

Miles stacks his shirts into the roller bag on the bed. He could pack for work in his sleep—and sometimes does. "Antonio says he's found another place but can't move in till next weekend. Is that going to work for you?"

"I guess so. I can't supervise him, though." Jackie never got the whole story of what happened with Antonio and his roommates. Miles told her it was a subletting mix-up, that the guy whose room Antonio was renting promised he could have it for the whole semester, but then reneged and wanted it back sooner. Jackie thought it odd that a college student would want to move during finals—and right before the holidays—and said so. Miles shrugged and said he could only relate what he'd been told.

"He's got three finals to go. That's the hurdle, so anything you can do to help him would be fantastic."

"You could lock up the remotes." She is only half joking. If Antonio is studying, he's doing it on the sly.

Miles smiles and shakes his head. "He's twenty and has ADHD. He needs to be able to take breaks."

"I'll do what I can. But please text and call him yourself, too. Let him know you're there."

"Will do." He zips up the bag, sets it on its rollers, and comes over to give Jackie a kiss. "Good luck with your talk."

"Piece of cake."

"Only for you, smarty-pants." He smiles to signal he means it in the nicest way and heads for the door.

"See you Friday."

Miles pauses in the doorway.

"Forget something?" Jackie scans the bed—nothing there—and returns her gaze to her husband.

He smiles again. "Don't think so. Friday, then."

"Safe travels." Jackie watches him go, wondering why he hesitated. He probably feels bad about leaving her with the responsibility of Antonio. Fair enough. She wonders, too, if she ought to feel a pang at his departure. They haven't yet been married two years. Maybe it's because Miles leaves so often, and she has become inured. Maybe it's because they aren't exactly young. Life isn't a movie, her mother used to say, at least not one on the Hallmark channel. This must be what she meant.

Jackie turns her attention back to her talk. Once she starts recalling her mother's droll commentary on relationships, it's best to move to safer ground.

———

At one o'clock Jackie closes her laptop. Her talk is ready. She calls Grace, hoping to meet up with her this afternoon, but it's the twins' turn to have the stomach bug. Since Thanksgiving, the whole family has been ill at least twice, first with the flu, now this. "I haven't seen this much vomit since that Sigma Chi party freshman year," Grace tells Jackie.

"Can I help?"

"Nooooo. Stay far, far away."

"Well, call me if it gets uglier."

"It's a twenty-four-hour thing. What's today?"

"Sunday."

"I knew that. Okay, I figure by Tuesday we're done. If I can get a sitter, can we do something Wednesday? Something adults do?"

"Hang on." Jackie consults her calendar. "My afternoon is officially yours. I'll make a plan and let you know."

"You're the best, Jacks."

Jackie's urge to hold her sister is so acute, tears of frustration sting her nose. "I love you, too, Gracie."

She ends the call, and daydreams about stealing a few peaceful hours with Grace. Outside the bedroom window, rain is falling in sheets. With an empty afternoon ahead of her, she decides to lose herself in a movie. Jackie checks the showtimes on her phone, grabs a raincoat, and heads downstairs. Antonio's door is closed, and there's no sign he's been up. She texts him her plans and drives toward the Uptown Loews theaters.

An accident on Connecticut slows her progress, and by the time she gets to the theater, the show is sold out. Wandering through stores on her own doesn't appeal to her. She is seeking escape from thoughts of Antonio's potential instability, news about the data fraud, and further disturbing encounters with Nasira. Nothing in the mall can promise that. Jackie gets back in her car and drives home, envisioning a prosaic afternoon with a book and a pot of tea by the window in her room.

She parks in the drive. Rain is hammering down. She prepares her umbrella and dashes to the front door, which opens just as she reaches the bottom step. A tall, heavyset man in a black windbreaker with the hood up is in the doorway, turning to speak to someone inside. Antonio presumably. She can't see because the man is blocking her view.

Jackie takes the next step. The man still has not seen her. He extends his hand to Antonio. Jackie is expecting a handshake, but the man's palm is up. It closes over whatever Antonio has given him, a practiced move, as smooth as the delivery of the item into his pants pocket. Antonio is closing the door.

The man turns and sees Jackie. The cap he's wearing under the hood shades his eyes. His cheeks are pockmarked, and his neck is heavily tattooed. Jackie steps back and feels an adrenaline surge.

"Oh. Hey." His tone is calm and his posture relaxed.

Behind him, the door opens again. Antonio must have heard the man speak. When the boy spots Jackie, his eyes shoot open in surprise. "I thought you went to a movie."

The man shuffles past her. "Later."

Antonio retreats inside. Jackie watches the man until he is no longer in sight; her heart rate slows. She shakes out her umbrella and walks inside, impatient to find out what the hell is going on. Jackie finds Antonio in the living room, sitting in near darkness. She turns on the lights, her irritation growing. Antonio doesn't look up and Jackie's suspicions bloom.

She takes a seat across from him. "Who was that?"

"A friend."

"Antonio, look at me."

He gets up and starts toward his room.

Jackie jumps up and intercepts him at the kitchen. "I saw you give him something. Was it money?"

He doesn't say anything, keeps his head down.

"Did you take something?"

"Like what?"

"Like drugs. Like pills."

"No." He glances at her. His eyes seem normal, but that's not definitive.

"Are you about to?"

He throws his hands up. "Could you quit with the third degree?"

"No, I can't. It looked to me like that guy was here, in my house, selling drugs to you. I'm not going to let that go." She searches for the right thing to say. He's safer here than anywhere else other than a rehab facility, but she can't tolerate drug deals under her nose. "I'm worried about you. You've got finals this week."

"Hey, I'm aware."

"Will you empty your pockets, let me search your room?"

He pulls back. "What? No." He wriggles his torso, shakes out one leg, then the other. "Just let me go to my room, okay?"

Jackie doesn't like the idea of physically blocking him, but neither does she want to let him lock himself inside his room and do God knows what. She steps aside. "You have to leave the door open."

He storms past. "No way." He goes inside and slams the door.

Jackie retrieves her phone from her bag and calls Miles, but he doesn't pick up. She texts him, saying she thinks Antonio has drugs. She fills a glass with water from the tap, drinks it. What is she supposed to do now? Call the police? What would they do? She resolves to give Antonio a few minutes, then talk to him again, maybe invite him to go out, have dinner with her. She can't remember the last time the two of them did something normal together. No wonder he wasn't very responsive to her. She always felt she was on good terms with Antonio, but when dealing with problems this daunting, nothing is more valuable than a deep reservoir of goodwill.

She calls Miles again and leaves a voice mail. It's Sunday evening—wasn't he supposed to be free?

A door opens down the hall, and Antonio lopes by, a bag slung over his shoulder.

"Where are you going?" He walks to the front door and puts on his boots, lacing them. Jackie follows him. "Please don't go. Let's talk."

He straightens, adjusts the bag. "Listen, Jackie. I know you're trying to do the right thing, but I can't stay here." He wiggles his shoulders, an abbreviation of his tic. "I'm crashing at a friend's."

"Can you wait until finals are over? You're so close."

Antonio groans. "Did I say I was skipping out on them? Did I say that?"

He's keyed up now, bouncing on his toes. Jackie wants to hug him, gather him together. He's like a flywheel inside, about to let go, spin free, and he has no clue what to do about it. If he were a small boy, she could help him with this. She could hold him, ground him. But she doesn't dare touch him, not when he's so agitated. What choice does she have but to let him go? At least he doesn't have a car. That's a plus.

"Will you tell me who your friend is, just so I know where you are?"

He eyes her, considering. "I'll text you later."

She figures he won't. "Please stay. I'll make you something to eat." Be honest. Be real. "I've been having a really shitty time lately, and I'd love to just hang out with you and not think about it." Jackie hears the pleading tone in her voice. Okay, so she's pleading.

His face darkens. "That's so fake, Jackie. You wanting to be my mom so you can make up for the fact that my dad is never around." He takes a step toward the door, pauses with his back to her, before swiveling to face her. "I don't know how you can stand this. I don't know what you tell yourself this is"—he gestures to the walls, the house—"but it isn't what you think, and I can't stand to be around it anymore."

Jackie stares at Antonio in confusion. "Stand what? What are you talking about?"

He shakes his head. "I know I've got issues, and it's a pain in the ass, but at least I'm not lying to myself." He opens the door, and a blast of wet, cold air fills the entry. "See you later, Jackie."

She grabs the door, her head buzzing with confusion. "Wait!" He's already bounding down the walk in the rain, pulling up his hood, hunching over. "Wait!" She's on the porch. The wind drives the spray into her face. She wants him to stay with her, to be safe. She'll let him be secretive and sullen. She won't mother him. She'll know he's there, and when Miles finally calls her, she can tell him everything is fine. Everything is perfectly fine.

Jackie wants Antonio to come back, explain what he meant, but realizes as she wipes the rain from her eyes and hugs herself, shivering, that she's not fine, and yet she was prepared to lie. Antonio meant more by what he said, she is sure, but that's the start of it, because maybe it's true after all that the worst lies are the ones you tell yourself.

Miles's Story

~

Essex, England, 1987

I didn't want to leave my school in France for a new one in England. Probably no kid ever wants to change schools, especially not at thirteen, but my father was transferred to Cambridge by his company, so that was that. His boss suggested Felsted for me, a four-hundred-year-old public school an hour away from our new house. It wasn't Eton, but then, I wasn't exactly Eton material.

It was all the same to me. I didn't mind studying—it came fairly easily—but I lived for rugby. Felsted had a respectable team, so I was as happy as I could be, with my Dutch-French-accented English and my feet as big as canoes. Having yet to grow into my own body, I tripped myself up regularly, but never on the pitch.

The boys at the school were like boys anywhere: full of piss and vinegar, afraid to admit when they were scared, and always ready to settle any conflict with their fists. If I'd entered Felsted when they had, at age eight, I'd have fit right in. As it was, I knew from the outset I would have to see which way things fell, whether I would find a slot I could be content with and perhaps be a part of something, a group, or whether I would suffer as an outsider.

Two things worked in my favor. Rugby is a fall sport, and I made the second team easily, giving me teammates if not friends. Second, I had a knack for languages; I coasted in French and Greek. The Greek, in particular, set me apart, although I was careful not to be too capable; nobody likes the kid with all the answers.

Greek 4 was a small class, only ten of us, and since we shared other classes, too, I got to know those boys quickly—at least the ones who acknowledged me. Tim Grantham and Quincy Rodd were on my floor in Gebb's House, and after my first week they invited me to study with them. Grantham, a quick-witted, chummy boy, seemed to know absolutely everyone. Friday night of my first full weekend, we were just finishing eating when Grantham grabbed the jacket of a boy passing our table and made him sit. I scooted over to make room.

"Miles! Meet my mate Ryan Underwood. He's all right when he's not being a wanker."

Ryan smirked at Grantham and punched him in the shoulder. They grappled for a moment, but with subtlety, to stay under the radar of the masters at the high table. Ryan let go first. He pushed back the hair that had fallen into his eyes, shook his jacket straight, and turned to me, extending his hand.

"Miles. Sorry about that."

I must have shaken his hand, but I don't remember it. All I remember are those eyes of his, a blue like the sea beyond the breakers. I felt dizzy and a bit unwell, as if a hole had suddenly appeared at my feet and I was on the verge of falling in. He must've read my expression, or understood something, because one corner of his mouth lifted in a cockeyed grin. My dizziness eased, and in its place I felt extraordinary happiness, that first-day-of-summer feeling. I thought I was going mad. Who knows what my face betrayed, but Ryan just grinned wider.

"Have you got a surname, my new friend Miles?"

"De Haas." And I stupidly added, "I'm Dutch."

"Better than French."

Grantham chimed in. "I figured you for Greek the way you can bloody decline."

They all laughed. By the time it died down, Grantham was telling a story to someone at the far end of the table. I fiddled with the treacle pudding on my tray—disgusting stuff if you're used to crème brûlée—and tried to think of something to say. I could feel Ryan looking at me, which was making my thoughts jump around in my head like fleas.

He nudged me. "Chin up, my new friend Miles."

I turned partway toward him, staying away from those eyes.

"Tomorrow's Games Day. Should be a bit of fun." He stood and jumped backward over the bench. He smiled again, and I felt it in my knees. "I'll find you."

"All right. See you."

After he left, I was relieved—and sorry he'd gone.

I didn't know what to do with myself. It was like the world had been shaken and reordered, and I was the only one who noticed. I couldn't fall asleep that night, just lay there staring at the ceiling beams, listening to the other boys turn in their beds and murmur in their dreams.

Ryan didn't touch me that weekend or even the one after that. It wasn't like that. Okay, maybe in part. For me, it was bigger than that. I was happy around him, and when I wasn't, I was half-miserable and half-happy just to be able to think about him. I felt like a fool around him, and probably was, and also as if I had a light around me only he could see. That was the heart of it. I'd fooled around some with girls, making out, a grope or two, but I'd never felt like this. The touching, the kissing—I'm not going to pretend I didn't want it, or he didn't want it, but he was as beautiful to me walking toward me on a footpath, unaware of me, as when I held him.

And that, rather than the physical part, was what other boys noticed. Boys fooled around at Felsted like at any other school. It wasn't a secret, but neither was it discussed. There was an unspoken hierarchy; for instance, Year 9 boys blew Year 10s and older, never the reverse. But mooning over someone? That was disastrous. Mooning was for girls.

"Millie! Hey, Millie! I think I see Ryan coming!" they would screech. Once it started, it was relentless. I was new. I was foreign. I was a girl. Me, not Ryan, because he was there first, part of their tribe, and maybe he didn't look at me the way I looked at him. It was hard for me to know for certain and still is. They called me other names, too—the predictable ones—and that shocked me. I wasn't queer or a faggot or whatever else. I didn't like boys or men. I liked Ryan. He ignored the taunts, reminding me of how my mother would pretend not to hear my little brother's whining. Maybe it was an effective strategy, but it also felt like a betrayal. The idea of Ryan betraying me was also confusing. I was confused about everything, it seems.

One evening in November, I waited for him outside the gym where he fenced. The fencing group was small and didn't include any of our mates, plus it would be dark when he emerged. It was a safe place to meet, and I needed to talk to him.

He saw me straightaway and peeled off from the group. We kept a distance between us and went to the back of the building.

"Why the ambush?" His tone was light.

"I'm getting a lot of flak. You know, because of you."

"I know. And I'm sorry." He reached a hand toward me, but thought better of it.

"They're your friends mostly. Can't you talk to them?"

"Those fellows. Might work better if I beat the crap out of them. Or if you did."

I studied Ryan's face in the dim light. "You serious?"

He shrugged, looked away.

"I don't want to beat up anyone."

"I know. So there's not much we can do." He scuffed his feet. "Except stop."

I swallowed hard. "Stop?"

"Yeah." He finally looked at me.

Up until that moment, the worst I had felt was frustration and anger at not being able to be with Ryan without getting shit from our mates—plus being in a muddle over exactly what I was feeling. Now I felt shame. It took Ryan's doubt to bring it forward. Once that happened, shame threw its dank cloak over me, over both of us. The weight and the stink of it never left me.

I retreated from Ryan and everything he meant to me, or could come to mean—I had a sense of that, even then. The shame overwhelmed everything. I didn't know where to put it, so I lived with it or, rather, under it. After a while, it was simply part of who I was, a part I kept far away from other people. On the outside, I was a man who liked rugby and women, who got married and had a son and got divorced and remarried, as many men do. On the outside, I had nothing to be ashamed of.

Except that's not how powerful emotions work. The shame affected me no matter how deeply I thought I had buried it. It made me shy away from conflict or confrontation of any kind. I was quick to admit wrong, to apologize, or take the high road, walk away. I was already stained inside; what difference would it make? I wasn't worth standing up for. I was fundamentally screwed up. I was dirty.

If I've done good things in my life, it has been for others, a kind of penance that also brings me happiness at times. I did things for Beatrice, my ex-wife, supporting her and giving her a son, and now I do things for my son. (Don't get me wrong. I love Antonio more than anything, but I never would've given myself the gift of fatherhood, and I don't think I'm much of a success.)

If you are stained and dirty, it's fiendishly hard to care about yourself. That's why I smoke, more than anyone knows. That's why I work so hard, travel so much. (I do love sports, I won't pretend I don't, but the travel is handy for avoidance, isn't it?) That's why I have, albeit rarely, slept with men I did not know and probably would not like if I did. That's why I failed Beatrice and will likely fail Jackie.

Yes, it's fatalistic. I'm not strong enough to maintain a pristine exterior. The stains show through.

CHAPTER 19

Jackie keeps the usual Monday lab meeting as short as possible. Vince texted her a few minutes ago, saying he needed to speak with her, and for now the data issue has priority. It is obvious to Jackie from the low-lying awkwardness in the room that everyone now knows about the problem, but she isn't going to say a word until she has more information. She isn't in the mood to cope with all the concerns and questions, either, given how she has not been able to sleep and then didn't wake until almost nine. So far the day has been a frantic game of catch-up, and she is losing.

"Okay, gang. Everything we didn't get to today we'll cover next week. If it's urgent, shoot me an email or catch me after Wednesday. Thanks for understanding." She makes a point of looking around the table to assure her students that although she is coming unglued, it is slowly, and they all might survive it. When Jackie's gaze falls on Nasira, she is already getting up from the table. Fine.

Jackie collects her laptop and paperwork and beelines into her office. A bagged lunch waits on her desk. She can't even recall what she chose in her mad dash through campus this morning, but she has to eat. And have more coffee. She'll pick some up after she meets with Vince. As she unwraps what is apparently a turkey sandwich, she recalls her phone call with Miles last night. He called as she was getting into bed, and he wasn't happy to learn Antonio had left.

"He didn't text you the friend's info?"

"As I already said, no."

"And have you searched his room yet?"

"No. And I don't plan to." She exhaled and tried to remember how hard it is for Miles to be away when there is a crisis with his son. He's working; it isn't his fault. "If Antonio wants drugs, he will find them. It's terrible to know that guy who came to the house might've been a dealer, but honestly, there isn't much we can do if Antonio can't control this."

"We can't just throw up our hands."

That stung. "I'm doing my best, Miles, I really am. And I'm open to suggestions. Always."

Silence on the other end. Jackie was expecting an apology, or at least some recognition of her efforts. But Miles was thinking about his son, not her; again, she could hardly blame him. Miles signed off, saying he was going to call Antonio's friends to ask if they'd seen him. After the phone call she spent hours trying to fall asleep, but her mind would not calm. She was beset with snippets of crazed scenarios involving data and infidelity and overdose and failed speeches and jealousy involving every significant person in her life. When she finally succumbed to exhaustion, she fell asleep with her head under a layer of pillows and bedclothes and slept through her alarm.

Now, as Jackie chews her sandwich, a wave of sadness washes over her. Having married late, her expectations were realistic—or so she thought. The space inside her marriage had felt comfortable and smooth, but lately she can barely turn around without bumping into something, or someone, impinging on what should be hers and Miles's alone. There is nothing lonelier than being alone inside a marriage.

Vince Leeds appears in her doorway.

Jackie waves him in. "Hi, Vince. Please close the door."

He's more jittery than usual, pulling on his cuffs repeatedly as soon as he's seated. He doesn't have a laptop or any paperwork with him. "I have a little information for you. I figured any information is better than none."

"True. And I appreciate it." Jackie pushes her sandwich away, no longer hungry.

Vince runs a finger across his lips. "Okay. So your lab has a shared log-in, which means we can't see who accessed the files, but I did have a quick look at the IP addresses."

"Each computer has its own, right?"

"Sort of. We know the addresses of your lab computers because we installed them in our network. Which is why I can say for certain that whoever accessed your files on December first didn't use those machines."

"That's helpful, I guess." Jackie reminds herself to be patient. Vince's text implied real news, and this isn't it.

He nods. "I also looked at the histories for IP addresses that had frequent log-ins, like the one from your home network."

"You can see that?"

Vince smiles a little. "You use Outlook, so the IP address is in every email you send."

"That's a little creepy."

"And the reason Gmail is better from a security point of view." He scratches the back of his hand. "Anyway, you did log in that day."

Jackie closes her eyes. It would've been nice to have been excluded.

Vince continues. "And there was one other log-in from an address I didn't recognize, which means next to nothing. If one of your grad students accesses the files from the same Starbucks every single night, I can't tell because their Wi-Fi recycles a bunch of addresses. Same with hotels and libraries."

"So all we know for certain is that the formulas weren't changed from my lab."

"Yes."

"Which only leaves the rest of the world."

"Specifically, the parts with connectivity." Vince offers her a tentative smile. "I know this must be stressful, Jackie, but we'll straighten it out."

Jackie wishes she had his confidence. Every time she hears this assurance, even out of her own mouth, it feels less true. She is left wondering why Vince didn't share this fairly innocuous information with her over email or in a text.

Vince leans forward in his chair. "Do you want me to come to the meeting with Dr. Chen? I can make time."

"Dr. Chen?" Even in her frazzled state, Jackie would not forget a meeting with the department chair.

Vince blinks at her. "Have you checked your email this morning?"

"Not since I first got in. What's going on?" But she knows. It has to be about the data issues. Who the hell told Chen?

"It's better if you read them yourself, I think." Vince pauses. "I can leave, if you'd rather."

"No, it's fine." Her hands are clammy as she clicks open her email. There are a dozen unread messages, including one from Amy Chen and, directly below it, one from Deirdre Calhoun, director of Autism America. Jackie's throat constricts as she opens Calhoun's email.

From: dcalhoun@autismamerica.com
To: jstrelitz@adamsuniv.edu
Cc: achen@adamsuniv.edu
Re: Study mismanagement

Dear Dr. Strelitz,
On December 6, you informed me via phone that you could not provide an interim report for the four-year study funded by our organization due to discrepancies in the data. You assured me at the

time that discovering the source of the problem was your highest priority; however, in the intervening eleven days I have not had an update from you. I remind you that providing interim reports to the board is a requirement specified in your contract with us. We are extremely concerned that study mismanagement may have affected not only the results you were poised to report, but also previous research. As a consequence, the board is requesting a complete audit of data collected under your supervision during the last three years. Until the audit report is presented to the board, we will not be able to consider the grant proposal you submitted on August 28, 2018. Current research may continue until we have a clearer picture of what has transpired. Your Institutional Review Board should be notified immediately so they can assess whether recruitment of new subjects is advisable.

These developments are highly regrettable. We trust you understand that we must act to protect the integrity of our foundation and the trust instilled in us by our donors.

Yours,
Deirdre Calhoun
Autism America Foundation

Jackie's mouth is dry. She clicks opens the email from the department chair, which was forwarded from Calhoun's.

From: achen@adamsuniv.edu
To: jstrelitz@adamsuniv.edu

Cc: vleeds@admasuniv.edu
Re: Study mismanagement

Jackie,
Please call Martha for the first available time to
see me, and bring Vince if he can make it.

Amy

Jackie checks the time of Amy Chen's email: 10:37 a.m. It's now
12:23. Shit.

Vince clears his throat. "You okay?"

"Definitely not."

"If you ask me, it's an overreaction."

Jackie lets out a long breath. "It might be." Vince is regarding her
with pity. Her nose stings with tears. She reaches for her water bottle,
takes a drink. "Chen won't help me, you know, although I shouldn't
say that to you." Vince nods like he already knows all about Chen. Of
course he does. The IT people know pretty much everything. "Chen
will do what she has to in order to look good."

"I know," Vince says. He places his hands on his knees, pushes to
his feet. "Let me know when the meeting is. I'll be there."

Jackie picks up her phone, desperate to get the meeting scheduled
and over with. Then Vince's pledge registers, and she sets the phone
down and looks him in the eye. "Thanks, Vince. I don't know what I
would do without you."

He reddens, opens the door, and speaks over his shoulder. "Anytime,
Jackie."

———

The lecture hall at the Women's Faculty Building is standing room only. Jackie is at the podium. A student AV aide adjusts the microphone on her jacket. Underneath it, Jackie's shirt is damp, but it's better to be too warm in a dark jacket than to risk visible stains on the shirt.

"You're all set." The student smiles at her. "Good luck."

"Thanks." A little luck would be a godsend. In the restroom a few minutes ago, Jackie applied concealer to hide the bags under her eyes, but nevertheless she looks like ten pounds of shit in a five-pound bag. Perhaps the audience will assume she is habitually overworked rather than embattled, emotionally frayed, and sleep deprived. All stress appears the same.

The meeting with Chen went as she thought it would. Jackie, with Vince's help, briefed her on what they knew so far. Chen suggested she keep the foundation in the loop rather than wait until all the answers had been obtained.

"If you'd done that, you might have avoided the audit," Chen said. "And if you'd told me about it, I'd have advised exactly that."

Jackie apologized, but Vince jumped in to say Jackie didn't know it was anything more than an isolated error until Thursday night. "Given that today is Monday, Dr. Strelitz is hardly dragging her feet."

Chen leveled a stare at him that made Jackie cringe, but Vince was not cowed. *He's got cojones,* Jackie thought.

Chen then addressed Jackie. "Just get it cleaned up—and fast. We don't need money rushing out the door." She dismissed them in a tone befitting a headmistress. Jackie might have been offended at being treated this way by a colleague, but she was too preoccupied with the prospect of the audit and the possibility of widespread data corruption. Her sensibilities would have to take a back seat, at least until she had a nervous breakdown.

Ironically, as Jackie waits to begin her talk, she is calmer than any-time recently, not counting her sessions on the river. Her speech is ready, she's confident in her ability to deliver it well, and the audience seems friendly and eager. A forty-minute performance followed by questions, her favorite part. As long as no one asks her about the integrity of her data, where her stepson might be, or whether it was really she who had been driving by Dr. Crispin's house again and again, she can handle it. Game on.

Jackie sits with her ankles crossed and her hands folded neatly in her lap while the organizer thumps the microphone, issues a detailed if overly flattering introduction, and welcomes Jackie to the podium. Jackie clicks on her first slide, and the part of her brain that contains the drama of the last months goes quietly to sleep in a corner. She sails through the talk, covering all the points she planned and sprinkling them with anecdotes and a couple of lines that are meant to draw laughs, which they do. She finishes to applause and broad smiles, feeling satisfied for the first time in too long.

The organizer invites questions. Although Jackie has answered variations on all of them in previous talks, the exercise isn't rote for her. Education is central to what she does.

"I thought about my dog during your description of the theory of mind experiments, and I'm sure he would pass. This has been proven in animals, right?"

"Do you ever think it might be better for parents not to have an early diagnosis?"

"My two-year-old grandson is definitely on the spectrum, but his parents are in denial. How do I get through to them?"

"Do children ever recover from autism?"

This last question always gives her pause because it is both technical and potentially emotional. What parent wouldn't hold out hope for a change in diagnosis? "If you've learned anything from me today, I hope it's that the science of autism is rapidly evolving. Every day we are finding out more, which sometimes means finding out that we were wrong. About ten percent of children diagnosed with autism eventually 'lose' the diagnosis, meaning they no longer meet the criteria. Some then receive a different diagnosis, often ADHD because many of the symptoms overlap. Do children who lose the autism diagnosis 'recover'? It's hard to say. One of the special challenges in my research is that early diagnoses are the ones most likely to change. I'm trying to find the best reliable predictors. We want to be as certain as we can as early as possible, but it's tricky."

The woman who asked the question nods and smiles.

As the organizer scans the crowd for the next question, Jackie's gaze snags on a man sitting behind the woman who asked the last question. He's familiar, but it takes her a moment to place him. When she does, her heart skips and her face warms. Jeffrey Toshack. Jeff. Her college boyfriend.

"Dr. Strelitz?"

The organizer smiles at her with the patience of a kindergarten teacher. Jackie has missed a question.

"I'm sorry. Could you please repeat that?"

Jackie avoids looking at Jeff until the Q&A comes to an end. The organizer effuses over her performance; Jackie thanks her for the invitation to speak and for the compliment, takes a long drink of water, and stashes her laptop away. A few attendees gather at the podium, the ones too shy to ask questions in front of the audience. Off to the side is Jeff, weight on one hip, hands in his pockets. The same catastrophically good looks in the vein of Hugh Jackman, looks with longevity. Jeff's jaw is squarer now, and he's grown a trim beard, which suits him. He isn't as skinny as he was at twenty-two, a little padding now on his athletic frame, but his quiet smile slays her still. What is he doing here? She hasn't seen him since they broke up, and the last time she heard about him from a mutual friend, he was living in Portland.

She lifts a finger to let him know she'll be a minute. She answers questions, hands out her card to a woman whose daughter has expressed interest in a study, and offers a referral of Autism America's list of doctors to a man concerned about his three-year-old. When the last person shakes her hand and turns to go, Jeff steps forward. Jackie isn't sure of the protocol. Should she hug the man she dumped sixteen years ago or shake his hand? He solves the dilemma, taking her gently by the shoulders and kissing her cheek. He smells the same—of woods, citrus, salt. Like California, where they were supposed to join their lives.

He holds her at arm's length and smiles. "Jackie. So great to see you."

"You too. Though I couldn't be more surprised."

"Didn't mean to blindside you. I'm here for a business meeting. Before I left, I happened to see the announcement for your talk in the information from the university. I messaged you on Facebook, but I'm guessing you don't go on there much."

"Hardly ever."

He nods. "I get it. When I got here yesterday I left a message at the Psychology Department, but still managed to surprise you." He shrugs in apology. "I had to come say hello."

"I'm glad you did." She is being polite. Jackie isn't at all sure how she feels about Jeff's appearance.

"I worried I might throw you off your game, but you're obviously a pro."

Jackie laughs. "Is that a nice way of saying I was always good at talking?"

"Yup." His smile is confiding and a little sly. Jackie worries that she shouldn't have referenced their past without knowing what his situation is. Too late. "Hey, I don't suppose you have some free time? Coffee? Or something stronger?"

"Now?" What an idiot. He's not talking about next week.

"If you can. I've got no plans."

Jackie sorts through a list of reasons she should beg off. She's sleep deprived. She has work to do and has to find time to get her lab straightened out. Her life is an unmitigated disaster, and she hardly needs any possible further complication.

Jeff is watching her, his quizzical expression making it plain that it should not take this long to figure out whether she has time for a drink. He doesn't say anything, though. He was always patient.

"To be honest, you've arrived in the middle of a shitstorm."

"Let me distract you from it, then."

Suddenly it seems like exactly what she needs, a short break with someone she knows—or used to. "Would you, please?" She pulls on her coat and picks up her bag. "But I'm buying. As I'm sure you remember, I dumped you, so I owe you." She flashes him a smile to let him know she is aware the debt will not be so easily repaid.

"If you insist. Where's a good bar?"

"If by 'good' you mean 'nearest,' the University Hotel is a ten-minute walk."

"How convenient." He grins. "That's where I'm staying."

He's not flirting, Jackie tells herself. *He's just being factual.*

CHAPTER 20

June 2002

Jackie had sold or given away everything she owned except what could fit in the back seat of Jeff's Subaru Forester. His stuff was in the back, with his bicycle and ski gear taking up most of the space. They were spending their last night in Lewiston on the sofa bed he was leaving behind for the next tenant. Jackie sat on the bare floor, hugging her knees and drinking cheap cabernet while Jeff patched the last of the picture-hook holes.

He held the can of Spackle in one hand and pointed to his handiwork. "It's the thought that counts, right?"

"Absolutely."

Jeff came over, his steps echoing in the empty room, and bent to kiss her. The taste of him was one part of her billowing happiness, a sensation that had been growing, becoming rounder and larger inside her as the day of their departure for California approached. If she weren't tethered to Jeff, she might float away on the feeling, like a kite tugging at the hands of a child. She felt good, like she had goodness in her and around her, like goodness was at her back and in front of her. She'd never experienced this before. They, she and Jeff, were traveling together into their future—he straight into a tech start-up and she into grad school. They'd managed the hard part, finagling the next steps in their careers in the same city. It was all working out. Ever since she'd realized she trusted Jeff, Jackie had been terrified she'd lose him. Earlier on, she'd tried to sabotage their relationship, being casually cruel to him, testing him for all the faults her mother had assured her were endemic to men. He had been hurt, but he had persevered. He saw something in her, he had said.

"What?" she asked.

"You," he said. "The real Jackie, not the bullshit one."

Now he lowered himself to sit beside her, shoulders touching. She passed him the jelly jar serving as a wineglass.

He raised it. "Cheers."

She thought they'd make love soon, their last time in Maine, at least for now.

Her phone warbled on the sofa bed. She scrambled onto her knees and checked the screen.

Jackie turned to Jeff. "It's my mom. I'll make it quick, okay?"

He nodded. His parents were the steadiest, most normal people in the continental United States, and sometimes he had a hard time understanding why she often didn't want to speak to hers.

"Jackie. It's your mother."

Her mother never had a singsong voice, but it was dead serious now. Jackie sat on the bed. "Is everything okay?"

"I'm afraid I have unfortunate news. Your father has had a stroke—a serious one."

The bottom fell out of Jackie's stomach. "Serious? How serious?"

"You should go see him, dear. He's at Augusta Health."

"What about Grace? Did you call her?"

"She's on her way there. Don't call her while she's driving."

Jeff had moved onto the bed and reached for her hand.

"Where are you, Mom?"

"Me? Oh, I'm at home. I'll be right here if you need me." She paused. "He did this to himself, you know."

Jackie was so awash in emotion that she hardly registered the comment. Later, however, she would recall how her mother valued blame above all else.

———

Jeff's new job gave him no leeway, so he drove across the country without her. Jackie moved in with her mother and Grace, living out of the suitcase she had hurriedly stuffed with a random assortment of belongings from the back seat of Jeff's car. She visited her father every day, taking the bus if her mother needed the car. Grace came most days, too, despite working sixty hours a week as a nanny. It was more time than Jackie had spent with her father since he had moved out so many years before. He lay unresponsive in the bed, the tan on his forearms fading by the day, the skin on his upper arms almost transparent, as if the layer that kept him whole was disappearing. The breathing tube attached to his face seemed like a parasite, sucking out each breath rather than making each one possible. Keep talking to him, the nurses said. And she did sometimes, just to do the right thing. Grace read to him from the newspaper, adding commentary as if they were across the breakfast table from each other, making their way through a platter of pancakes. None of it would matter, Jackie knew. Grace knew, too, although they did not discuss it. The father who had left was really leaving this time. It was hard to know what to make of the pain. The flavor of it was so familiar, and yet distinct, because it meant to stay. At night, when the house was quiet, Jackie saw the pain for what it was: the dousing of the tiny flame of hope she had not known she was carrying.

Her mother was incensed by her daughters' attention to their father. "You don't have to go every day, Jackie. He doesn't know you're there."

"How do you know? Besides, I don't have much else to do." She hated herself for putting it this way, but her mother wouldn't relent otherwise. Her mother needed confirmation that Samuel Strelitz didn't matter, not just to her, but to everyone.

Days passed, then a week, two. Jackie's mother dropped reminders of the shortcomings of Samuel Strelitz like a child might drop a LEGO piece that ends up underfoot. Jackie couldn't avoid them. She couldn't move out—she had no money—and much of what her mother said was true. Her father had failed all of them, abundantly and repeatedly. He was not going to be romanticized, not if Cheryl had any say in the matter.

Jackie came home from a hospital visit. Two weeks and no change in his condition.

Cheryl gave her a hug and stroked her hair. "You'll miss him less if you remember him accurately."

Jackie could not argue the point. She began to think she should book a flight to California, although she wasn't required to start graduate school for another six weeks. Jeff was hard to reach. She was used to talking to him whenever she felt like it; now, between his work and the time difference, she was lucky to catch him once every few days.

One day her call rolled to voice mail and a panic built inside her. Finally he picked up.

"Where have you been?" She didn't care if she sounded accusatory. He was supposed to want to talk to her.

"Work and more work. Everyone's putting in killer days."

"You don't have time for a phone call?"

An enormous sigh. "Honestly, sometimes I don't have the energy for it. I want to talk to you, but I'm just wrecked."

"I hate this."

"Me too. How's your dad?"

She wished he hadn't put it that way, so casually. She wasn't sure how he should put it, but not like that. "The same."

"You sound bored."

"Bored and stressed. It's perfect."

There was no joy in this conversation, or other recent ones, and Jackie wondered if Jeff was morphing into someone else, or if she had been mistaken about him, or about them, their happiness. Maybe happiness wasn't durable or portable. Maybe it was something you could have in only one place, at one time, of fixed duration. Her chest ached as her thoughts turned in this direction. Jeff was her guy, the one she had finally let in close. How could such a short separation make her question it?

She was fickle; it was her fault. Or his. How could she know? She was singularly ill equipped.

"Jackie? Are you still there?"

"Yeah, I'm here."

"What's going on?"

"Nothing." It was too much to explain on the phone, even if the phone was all they had. "I should let you go. It's late out there."

"Sorry I'm not better company."

"You're fine. I'm not much better. Good night, Jeff."

"Good night, sweet girl. I really am sorry."

After she hung up, Jackie let the tears fall. Her mother had told her too many times about men who say they are sorry. It's the cheapest deal they can make, costing them exactly nothing, and they'll make it again and again and again. "The only question," Cheryl would say with her eyebrows raised, "is how long you're dumb enough to believe it."

Jackie didn't resolve to break up with Jeff that night. The next time they spoke she told a funny story about a nurse, and Jeff's laughter reminded her of her fondness for him. The phone call after that was short, perfunctory, and then they didn't speak again for three days, during which time Jackie stopped going to the hospital and spent all her time in her room, pretending to her mother and sister she was ill.

She did feel ill. She had been infected, yet again, by the idea that men were faithless and therefore useless. She fought it as best she could, writing out lists of her father's and Jeff's positive qualities. The lists bore certain similarities—both men were gentle and soft-spoken, manly in unassuming ways—and this worried her anew. Her mother had, after all, once loved her father enough to marry him. Here Jackie was at twenty-two, poised to fly across the country and move in with Jeff. What did she know about living together? What did he? They'd never discussed it; it was the next natural step in the progression of their relationship. They could hardly move to California and not live together. Even if they could afford it, what would that say?

On her childhood bed with the white ruffled coverlet, Jackie allowed one day to lapse into the next and came to recognize everything she lacked to make her relationship with Jeff work. She lacked the courage to act without dwelling on each potential pitfall. She lacked the strength to be different from her mother. Most of all, she lacked faith in her partner and in partnership generally.

When the blood vessel in her father's brain exploded, neurons died en masse, starved of oxygen. The blood spread and pooled and congealed, poisoning more brain cells, too many to compensate for, too many to regrow. He would remain as he was, silently awaiting complications that might never kill him. Regardless of the endgame, the damage was done.

Jackie couldn't predict whether she would ever acquire what she needed to make a relationship work. If she had to bet, she'd put the odds at three to one against. But her mother was alive, vibrant even, and her father lay unfeeling, awaiting complications. As she had throughout her teens, Jackie threw her lot in with her mother. She allowed things to cool off with Jeff and, as busy as he was, she could assign a portion of the blame to him. Jackie contacted Stanford University, explained about her father, and said she had been in touch with the University of Pennsylvania, her second-choice school and much closer to home. They understood. Everyone understood.

In the hotel bar, Jeff leans his elbows on the small table and gestures with his hands, telling Jackie about his company, an innovator in 3-D printing based in Seattle. She sips her martini, thinking how every promise he showed as a young man was fulfilled, in his professional life anyway. He isn't wearing a wedding ring, which tells her exactly nothing about her personal life. She isn't going to ask, at least not yet. Listening to him talk and feeling the gin melt the kinks in her neck is plenty.

"I'm boring you."

"Not a chance. I love hearing what you're doing. And you had to listen to me for a full forty minutes."

He smiles. "You should be very proud of what you do."

His comment catches her off guard, and she takes another sip of her drink to ease the clog in her throat. It's been weeks since she felt anything about her work other than panic. "Thank you," she manages.

They sit in silence for a few moments. Jeff points to her left hand. "I see you're married."

"Almost two years." She tells him about Miles and asks Jeff if he is married.

"Divorced five years ago."

"I'm sorry."

"Yeah." He strokes his beard, and his voice takes on a somber tone. "We lost our daughter when she was four. She had a rare leukemia. We couldn't get past it."

"Oh, Jeff." Without thinking, Jackie reaches for his hand, but he has leaned back in his chair, and her hand dangles in the air. She returns it to her lap. "I can't imagine."

He had looked away, but now meets her gaze. "It truly is the worst." He finishes the last of his bourbon. "I'm up for another one. Join me?"

"You bet. But let's get some food, too, okay?"

They order another round of drinks plus calamari and sliders. The conversation takes a lighter turn to the disposition of mutual friends, movies (they are both longtime film buffs), and what life is like in DC under the current administration.

"Everyone is drinking *Mad Men*–style," Jackie says, sipping her martini.

They stay for another hour. Jackie pays, as promised, and they say goodbye in the lobby. Jeff enters Jackie's number into his phone.

"You're here till Friday?" she asks.

"Yeah, then up to Connecticut to see my folks until after Christmas."

When they were dating, Jackie visited the Toshacks' home near Storrs several times. She visualizes snow falling around the beautiful old farmhouse, the blue spruce in front lit with old-fashioned bulbs, a candle shining in each window. Regret rises inside her, a sickening ache, and she pushes it down. "I'll bet they're thrilled. Please tell them hello from me."

"I will. But I'm hoping we'll see each other before then."

"I can't promise, but I'll try."

"I get it. The shitstorm."

Jackie smiles. "Yes. The shitstorm."

He slides his phone into his jacket pocket. His face is pensive. "Can I ask you something?"

"Sure."

"Is your husband part of it, the shitstorm?" Jackie blinks at him. "It's okay. I shouldn't have asked."

"No, it's fine." A man enters the lobby, and a chilling breeze sweeps in. She adjusts her bag on her shoulder. "It's complicated." She gives him a lighthearted grin that she hopes will end his questions. Drinks with Jeff was a welcome reprieve from her problems, and the last thing she wants to discuss with him is her marriage.

He studies her, uncertain what to say, then hugs her briefly. "I'll text you."

"Bye, Jeff. I'm glad you came to my talk."

He nods as he backs away. "Me too."

Jackie buttons the collar of her coat and waves to him as she exits the building. As she heads to her car, she checks for messages. A missed call and a text from Miles, the text from an hour ago. Antonio's staying with Larry in Foggy Bottom. Took two finals today. One more Thu. Sounds ok. xx M.

Great news, Jackie texts back. Call me later? 😊

She doesn't expect to hear from him soon, given he's in California, where it's just past five, but she's relieved that concerns about Antonio won't dominate their conversation. As Jackie arrives at her car and gets inside, she wonders if she should say anything to Miles about the chance appearance of Jeff. He knows about Jeff—an abbreviated version, anyway—and their relationship ended so long ago it's unlikely Miles would feel threatened, not that he is the jealous sort. But Jackie's attention to—okay, obsession with—Harlan's love life has altered the dynamic. For that she is sorry, because secrets really aren't her thing. Right now, however, she has to admit that Jeff is a tiny bright spot in an otherwise bleak time. She doesn't want their innocent encounter to be tainted by recent events, even if some of those have been of her own making.

She won't lie to Miles about Jeff, and she won't avoid telling him if it comes up, but she can't think of a reason to throw more fuel on the bonfire of her life. Not a single one.

CHAPTER 21

HARLAN

Jackie didn't notice me, but I attended the second half of her public lecture. I stood just outside the doors at the back, hoping to gauge how she was holding up. The answer: well enough to deliver a coherent story and deftly handle the inane questions that inevitably follow. I thought about approaching her, inviting her for drinks or even dinner, but as I winnowed through the crowd filing out, I saw I had been usurped. From Jackie's body language I surmised she knew this strikingly handsome man. He wasn't familiar and that concerned me.

With a conference on campus, plus the usual holiday uptick in drinking, the bar at the University Hotel was packed. I stayed out of view, but given how enthralled she seemed with Mystery Man, I needn't have bothered. She downed two martinis—near her limit—and I was relieved to see she left the hotel on her own. I couldn't know how long Mystery Man would be in town, so I'd have to keep tabs on Jackie until the rest of the dominoes fell. On the off chance there was something between them, I had to know. The complication perturbed but did not derail me. I toyed with the idea of hiring a private investigator to tail her, but by the time I parked in my driveway I had come up with a better, cleaner plan.

In my home office, I log on to Maitre'D using Jackie's email address and password. With Christmas approaching, Jackie and her Mystery Man will need a reservation if they want to eat anywhere decent in DC. Jackie, like everyone else, ignores security on sites like this, and hasn't changed her password since she was with me: !Rowurboat*. It's the same for all her low-level accounts. I'm not surprised to find there is no reservation yet, but I'll check back.

Later that evening, I find myself with time on my hands. The teaching assistants in my classes have taken care of all the grading, and the lab is effectively closed until after the new year. I have goals for the break—writing two papers—but there is no rush. I admit, I am distracted.

I compensate by figuring out how to make Jackie's data problems worse. I originally decided to change the formulas because it seemed the least detectable. Jackie has Vince Leeds involved, as I knew she would. That revolting little man has a crush on her and would jump at any chance to scratch himself in her presence. He's no fool, however, not when it comes to IT, and it's only a matter of time before they narrow down the possibilities.

But my new idea is sneakier, and I'm eager to move forward with it. When I try to log in, however, I'm denied access. That weasel Vince. I'd like to wring his red, flaking neck. Unfortunately, that's not practical, so I resolve to circulate a rumor that Vince is the source of the data fraud. It won't be hard; graduate students love to gossip, especially when the story involves one of their professors. A graduate student of Jackie's, Gretchen, is dating one of mine, so I predict the rumor will get back to Jackie within forty-eight hours. As a bonus, perhaps Vince will get fired.

He is a minor annoyance, however. My focus is and always will be Jackie. She must recognize the full extent of her error.

———

You undoubtedly think I'm a monster. Maybe I am. If a monster behaves without compassion or even consideration for life, I guess you could make the case. But no one has been flayed or eaten alive by the monster, have they?

I act according to my own wishes, driven by my needs. You are no different. My tactics are more ruthless than most, I grant you that, but if you had my cunning, would you not try to do what I did, exact revenge on someone who injured you? If you could get back at someone who wronged you—and get away with it—wouldn't you jump at the chance?

Before you argue otherwise, let's be clear about one thing: Jackie did wrong me.

I love her and only her. It's not an easy thing for me to admit. If my mother weren't already dead, I would throw her off a bridge for Jackie, and I have nothing against my mother, strictly speaking. Here's the other thing: Jackie will never have anyone love her more than I do. The tragedy of our mutual loss pains me, and the pain sparks anger. It didn't have to be this way, but she forced my hand.

We were together for five years, five long, happy years. She's never denied her happiness, because she's not a liar. After she was tenured, which I was instrumental in helping her achieve, she decided she wanted to change everything. She wanted to have what everyone has. She wanted to have it all.

Here's the world's worst-kept secret: no one has it all. I'm speaking strictly about women, of course, and only about women with ambition—intellectual, artistic, entrepreneurial, whatever—any female with a dollop of passion for something beyond getting her nails done and waiting for pumpkin-pie-spice season to roll around again. Those women, which is to say most women, do not have it all, unless what you mean by that is all the conflict, all the disappointment, and all the anxiety. Work demands too much or it is not sufficiently satisfying. Children demand too much or . . . ha! There is no "or." Children are, by their nature, demanding.

Then there is marriage. In theory, it should be the answer to a woman's work-children conflict. In practice, it's just another problem. Or, I should say, he's just another problem. He wants to have it all, too. Plus time for running or golf or fiddling with cars and also a man cave, unlimited gaming, and porn viewing. Think I'm exaggerating? Seventy-five percent of men watch porn regularly. Do seventy-five percent of men do half the household chores—or half of anything unpleasant? Even when the woman earns more money, the man refuses to take up the slack. It's laughable, really, the idea of marriage as partnership. A man who wants simply takes.

I'm not saying anything revolutionary here. I'm just saying it bluntly.

Jackie, as a modern woman, has the right to choose. But marriage and children are not an add-on configuration to work. It's a zero-sum game. The circle of time and energy is finite; slice the pie however you wish, but something gets smaller as something else gets bigger. In pushing me to agree to living together, which would then progress to pushing me to having children with her, the pie would undergo massive reorganization. Perhaps I sound selfish, but look at it this way: Jackie loved the attention I lavished on her during the time we were together. How could I possibly continue to do that as the pie wedge of children squeezed us out? She would miss my attention or resent the children. The struggle for balance would be constant, and she would never be satisfied that she got it right. There is no winning, only settling for the mediocre.

I think Jackie sees that now—and Miles will, too—how difficult it is to focus on someone and also share them. You lose so much more than you gain.

CHAPTER 22

Grace points at a display of white poinsettias. "Is it just me, or are those more Halloween than Christmas?"

Jackie laughs. "Personally, I think the pink ones are worse. What do you say, a dozen of the red?"

Grace's eyes widen. "Steady, Martha. I don't live at Turkey Hill Farm."

Jackie ignores her and transfers the plants to a large cart. Other than putting up a tree right after Thanksgiving, Grace has had no time to decorate because of the illnesses plaguing her family, so Jackie suggested they spend their afternoon together on a shopping spree at the White Horse Nursery in Waynesboro.

Jackie points to a wreath display on a nearby wall. "Next stop."

"Those are gorgeous. I wish I had more doors."

"You can put them wherever you want."

Grace wheels the cart over. "Don't you want one?"

"Me?" Jackie ordered gifts for her nieces and nephews a while ago, but she hasn't given a thought to decorating the house. She hasn't had the bandwidth or the requisite cheer.

Grace is reading her thoughts. "You going to tell me what's bugging you, or do I have to wheedle it out of you?"

"You've been in the trenches, Gracie."

"And now I'm out, so spill."

They load up Grace's minivan with their purchases and order lunch at the adjacent diner. Sitting in a booth across from Grace, Jackie feels the weight of her secrets. "I'm sorry I haven't told you all this. There was always a reason, at first because it was embarrassing, then at Thanksgiving the stuff with Miles took over, then the kids were sick—"

"It's okay. I mean, if it was too embarrassing to tell me, it must've been bad."

"Is. It's still bad."

Grace picks up Jackie's hand and holds it in hers. "Tell me everything."

Jackie does, through lunch and dessert and coffee. Grace asks few questions, letting Jackie reel out the troubling and peculiar story of the last three months. When Jackie relates her encounter with the strange man at her house Sunday night and the encounter with Antonio that followed, Grace puts up her hands.

"Wait. He said what?"

"That I was living a lie. He was probably high on something; that's all I can figure." She didn't believe it, but after hearing herself talk about Harlan and Nasira and Miles and Antonio and have little of it make sense, she allows herself a minor defensive dismissal.

Grace sighs and leans back in her chair. "First, you are a batshit crazy stalker. Seriously, Jacks." She locks eyes with Jackie. "But you're done blowing past boundaries now, right?"

Jackie nods, her shame as familiar and stifling as being wrapped in an old comforter on a sweltering day.

"Hey, for what it's worth, I wouldn't have thought you had that in you, so kudos for keeping it fresh." She smiles, and just like that, Jackie is forgiven. Grace goes on. "As far as the data stuff goes, I've got nothing. It could be anybody, right? It's the world we live in now."

"True, but I have to assume it's not random. My lab was the target, or I was."

Grace frowns. "I don't like the sound of that—any of this."

"I wish I'd told you sooner."

"To be honest I'm not sure I could've taken this blow-by-blow. The executive summary is working for me." Grace pauses and lets out a long breath. "Okay, so Harlan. You know I never had the warm fuzzies for him, but I'm trying to look at all this objectively. I don't know why he's so inconsistent with you, why he's normal friends one minute and weird and cagey the next. I don't know why he'd openly drool over you at that wedding, except you're gorgeous, so there's that." She grins at Jackie, who rolls her eyes. Grace points to Jackie's chocolate ice cream. "You finished with that?"

Jackie pushes the bowl toward her sister. "Have at it."

"If you ask me, Jacks, you'll find yourself strapped to a table zonked on trazodone before you figure him out." She takes a bite of ice cream and wiggles her spoon between her fingers, lost in thought. "But what about Nasira?"

"What about her?"

"Have you tried talking to her?"

"I've tried a few times. I told you." Jackie wonders if Grace was really listening.

"No, not that. Really talking to her. Like you just did with me. Leave out some of the Miles and Antonio stuff, but tell her everything."

"Why?"

"Because you don't know what's going on with her, and she doesn't know what's going on with you. Nothing you told me made it seem like she was hiding anything or acting bizarre or nasty. Aloof, maybe, but that's not a crime."

Jackie stares into the middle distance, imagining the conversation with Nasira.

"What have you got to lose, Jacks?"

On the drive back to DC, Jackie realizes she forgot to tell Grace about Jeff Toshack. She considers texting her but decides it's only a curiosity. It can wait.

———

The next day is Thursday, the last day of finals, and the campus has a funeral quality not helped by the dull gray skies. Jackie takes her time walking to the lab; she has a call later with the Autism America director and is mentally drafting her replies to what she knows will be pointed questions. Be transparent but emphasize the positive. The data are intact. Significant findings at this stage are unlikely, but the results show promise. Recruitment to the study is strong, so getting adequate data won't be an issue. And, yes, she is instituting new security measures.

And, no, Ms. Calhoun, we don't yet know who was at fault. Me, yes. I'm at fault.

Jackie is getting used to saying that, but it still feels terrible. It is her responsibility, but the level of security she had is typical for behavioral research. Her findings shouldn't require a security clearance. How could she possibly have known someone was out to get her?

The question pinballs around her mind again and again, and the answer seems just beyond her grasp. If she could shut down the rest of her life and concentrate on this one question, the answer would come to her, she is sure.

She arrives at her lab and lets herself in. Even though no subjects are scheduled this morning, the silence is unusual. She proceeds down the hall, stopping at the shared office. Nasira is seated in front of a monitor and turns to Jackie.

"Good morning." Nasira's face is drawn and her lips are pale. Her posture, normally regal, is slumped.

"Good morning. Are you feeling all right?"

She pauses. "Not exactly."

Jackie is pinned on the horns of a dilemma. Her experience with personal conversations with Nasira is that they lead to strife and misunderstanding, so Jackie's first impulse is to express her regret and skedaddle to her office. But Grace's words are fresh in her mind and, along with them, the possibility of clearing the air, and more.

"Would you like to talk?"

Nasira eyes her warily. "I don't know."

"I don't blame you. I haven't given you much reason to trust me, and I'm sorry." Jackie gestures to her office. "How about some tea? Black, right?"

"Sure. Tea sounds good."

A few minutes later, Nasira sits across the desk from Jackie with a mug in her hands.

Jackie leaves her laptop in her bag and pries the lid off her coffee. "Do you feel like telling me why you're upset? You don't have to."

Nasira shuts her eyes for a moment, then opens them again. "I don't know where to start. Everything is such a mess."

"Professionally? Personally?"

"Yes."

Jackie smiles slightly. "See? We have much in common." She said it as a joke, but it rings true. "Look. I must be part of the problem, so let me start with an apology. I didn't take it well that you were seeing Harlan. In fact, I was obsessed with it. Maybe I still am." Nasira is listening closely, her forehead creasing slightly. Jackie barrels ahead. Somehow regurgitating the whole story to Grace yesterday makes it easier to get to the point today. "You are so beautiful and smart—and young—that part is hard, I admit. Harlan is obviously smitten with you, and I took it badly. I'm sorry."

She nods and sits quietly for moment, considering. "If he was smitten before, he's over it now."

Jackie is about to sip her coffee and sets it down again. "How so?"

"Are you sure you want me to talk about this?"

"No."

The women look at each other. Outside the lab, a door closes. Jackie breaks the eye contact and sips her coffee, worried the next thing she says will spin the conversation out of control, as before.

Be honest. Be more honest than you think you can be.

"Nasira, you feel like everything is a mess, and so do I. And neither of us quite knows what the hell is going on, except that we can't help but blame each other, at least for some of it. Is that about right?"

"Yes."

Jackie places her hands flat on the desk. "Then let's talk—really talk. If it's me, it's me. If it's you, it's you. But this dance isn't doing either of us any good."

Nasira shrugs one shoulder. "We can try, I suppose."

Jackie hesitates, not from uncertainty, but because she is afraid Nasira will throw up a wall or accuse Jackie of something. She takes a deep breath and begins. "I have no idea how much you know about Harlan and me, but we dated for five years, starting when I was twenty-seven. We saw each other twice a week, always at his place. He helped me, like he's helping you, but the similarities end there, which is why I've been so jealous. It took over *two* years before he agreed to go away for a weekend." Nasira raises her eyebrows but says nothing. "And he wouldn't agree to moving in together. Ever. He wanted two dates a week for the rest of our lives. Eventually, I realized it wasn't enough."

Nasira leans back in her chair. "And with me he was doing all that right away, before I even asked."

Jackie nods. She's thought about it so many times, it has finally lost its sting. "Not to be rude, but why the change? The first rule of human behavior is that people don't change."

"I don't know why. But he's ignoring me now, shutting me out completely, acting as though I've done something to offend him. I have no idea what." Her face crumples, and it seems she might cry.

"Oh, Nasira . . ."

She rubs her nose. "It's not just about him. Two weeks ago, my parents came to see me and arrived early. They saw Harlan kissing me goodbye and completely lost their minds." She stares at the ceiling, as if the right words were written there. "My parents are strict, especially my father. I was supposed to marry a Syrian man from a family my parents know. He's a nice guy, the nicest really, and I thought I could go along with it." She shrugs. "I'd already disappointed my father by leaving med school, so I tried not to break his heart again."

"But you didn't want this other guy."

Her face is pensive. "It wasn't about him, exactly. It was about making my own decisions. Anyway, they were just getting over it, just starting to treat me like their daughter again, and then they see me with Harlan." She spreads her hands, indicating the obvious.

"He's too old."

"Yes. And too non-Syrian."

Jackie gives her a half smile. No wonder Nasira is troubled. "Does Harlan know about this?"

She shakes her head. "Right after it happened, we went to New York. I tried to put it out of my mind, have fun."

"The New York trip after his router broke."

"Yeah."

Jackie studies Nasira, judging whether it's time to touch the third rail. It is. "That was the day the formulas were changed."

"So you told me." Nasira's gaze intensifies. "I did not go into that spreadsheet that day."

Jackie's heart tells her this is the truth. "I believe you."

"You should. It's the truth."

Jackie nods. "But someone was responsible, clearly. Where do you keep the log-in info?"

"On my phone." A sheepish look.

"I'm sure you're not the only one." She opens her desk drawer and pulls out a sticky note. "Here's my top-secret system for dealing with the mandatory password updates."

Nasira's face relaxes in relief. "I'm glad you believe me. I've wanted to work with you since the first day Harlan told me about your work and mentioned you had an opening for a postdoc."

"Wait." Jackie is flabbergasted. "You learned about the position from Harlan?"

"Yes, in Chicago. Last June."

"I thought you were in Boston."

"I had been in med school at Tufts, but after I left, I was living with my parents. They're in Evanston, outside of Chicago. I went to the University of Chicago to hear Harlan talk, just out of interest."

"I assumed you met here. I'm feeling a bit blindsided, honestly."

Nasira sighs. "I'm sorry. I wasn't hiding the information; it just never came up, and I didn't want to mention Harlan to give me an edge. If he wanted to say something, that's different. Of course, given what I know now, it might've been more of a negative."

Jackie exhales slowly. The mess they are attempting to straighten out is only getting worse. And it's damn odd that Harlan would not have mentioned Nasira at all. Why didn't he put in a good word for her? "Can I ask when you started dating?"

"Oh, after I moved here. I honestly didn't have much contact with him through the summer. Madison's a ways from Chicago, but I did meet him again there at a regional conference." She recrosses her legs, bounces her foot. "As soon as I got here, though, he was so attentive. So, I don't know, eager. It was a bit overwhelming—and also flattering."

"I know exactly what you mean."

"But now I'm—" She makes a fluttering motion with her hand.

They both sip their drinks, retreating into their private thoughts. Jackie digests the news that Harlan was responsible for Nasira applying for the postdoc position, but initially didn't show any sexual interest. Then, as soon as Nasira was here, he swooped in.

Since talking with Grace yesterday, a thought has been lurking in the back of Jackie's mind, like a tip-of-the-tongue memory. It breaks into the daylight. "Nasira? I don't quite know how to say this, but do you get the feeling both of us are being played?"

"By?"

"Harlan."

She opens her mouth, presumably to protest, but frowns instead. "Tell me what you're thinking."

Off the high dive and straight into the deep end. "I'm just going to relate the facts, okay? Harlan meets you in June, tells you about the postdoc, but doesn't do the obvious thing, which is tell me about you, put in a good word, or at least a mention. He doesn't show any interest in you until you get here, but then right away invites you to a dinner with me and my husband, texting me that he's bringing a friend, but not saying it's you."

"I didn't know that. I mean, you seemed surprised that night, but I never thought much of it."

"Right. Then Harlan starts seeing you on the exact schedule we had when we were dating."

"Why does that mean anything?"

"It doesn't necessarily. I'm just laying everything out."

"Okay." Nasira thinks a moment. "How do you even know that?"

"I was stalking you, remember?" Nasira's eyes turn a shade darker. "We promised to be honest here, so that's what I'm doing."

"Okay." She sounds doubtful.

Jackie can't blame her; the honesty is new and Jackie's credibility sucks. She pushes away her embarrassment at the reminder of her stalking, and lines up the events in her mind. "Did you go to Greenbrier with Harlan?"

"Yes. Is that significant?"

"Like I said, I wasn't granted vacations for two years, so maybe."

Nasira sips her tea. "Where is this going?"

Jackie isn't sure, but the facts are aligning in perfect order, a set of fallen dominoes, one leaning on top of the next. She saw them fall, but did not discern how they were connected. Even now, as she speaks to Nasira, she can't see the whole picture. She needs to watch each domino fall or she might miss something. "Let's just keep going. So, what, a month, no, six weeks go by, and your apartment is broken into. You move in with him."

"Right. I was really spooked."

Are Harlan and Nasira, in fact, still living together even though Harlan has soured on her? Jackie suspects Harlan is treating Nasira the way he treated her after his mother's funeral, but exploring that now would derail them. So would asking whether Nasira has sublet her apartment. The woman is twenty-seven, not seventeen, and Jackie is trying to tread carefully. She pulls up the next logical question. "Did they ever find the burglar?"

"No. I don't think they looked very hard to be honest." Nasira's gaze has been elsewhere, unfocused, but now she stares at Jackie and leans forward. "You don't think that Harlan—"

Jackie spreads her hands. "I don't know what to think. All I know is that every one of my personal nightmares is coming true. After all those years with Harlan, he knows what I wanted from him, for us, and he's serving it all to you."

Nasira sits up straight, sets her jaw, clearly angered by the suggestion. "I'm just a pawn? He doesn't actually feel anything for me?"

"I didn't say that, and I can't know the answer. I'm just looking at what's in front of me, and asking you to help me figure it out." She pauses, hoping Nasira will lower her defenses. "Think about it. After you move in, what's the very next thing that happens?"

She shakes her head, disbelieving. "The data."

"The data. The only thing as precious to me as my jealous pride is, apparently, my integrity."

"But how could he have altered the data?"

"Vince Leeds tells me 'how' is easy." Jackie waits for the next domino to fall. She hopes Nasira gets there on her own.

"You thought it was me."

"I did. I'm sorry."

"Because of the timing of the breaches."

"Yes. And only the other people in the lab knew what you were working on, unless the hacking was deeper than that."

Nasira shifts in her seat. "Harlan knew. He always asked what I was working on. He's interested, and not just superficially."

"I know." Harlan's interest is like stepping out of an air-conditioned building into the warmth of the sun. Jackie can feel it now, the way it made her pause to soak it in, made her want to stay in his golden circle forever.

She is definitely outside it now.

"Listen, Nasira. I don't even know if I believe all the crazy things I'm suggesting." Nasira's shoulders relax an inch. "Just think about it."

"I will."

Nasira is now more subdued than defensive, and Jackie wonders if she's wondering how it will feel to walk into Harlan's house this evening.

Perhaps she won't. To Jackie's surprise, she feels no victory in this. If Harlan is as twisted as her theory proposes, then Nasira—and every other woman on the planet—is better off elsewhere. "I appreciate you giving me a chance to talk it through. See you tomorrow, Nasira."

After her postdoc leaves, Jackie considers the biggest revelation of their conversation: that Harlan was instrumental in placing Nasira in her lab. Everything that falls from that is logical if Harlan's goal is to push Jackie to the edge. But why? It's been years since they broke up, plus Harlan had been away for a year before this semester started.

The sabbatical. Jackie recalls being surprised when he told her he was taking a year in Madison. When had that conversation taken place? She vaguely remembers they had been walking together across campus, and the sun had a warmth it never had during winter. March perhaps?

Jackie had asked Harlan where he had taken sabbaticals before.

"I haven't. You know how I prefer to be at home."

"Why now, then?"

He stopped walking and looked at her with an expression she could see even now and still did not understand. "I don't want to be utterly predictable, I suppose."

They talked a little about people they knew or knew about in the University of Wisconsin Psychology Department, then changed the subject.

But today, sitting in her office, Jackie questions Harlan's account of his motivation. He decided to do something new and unexpected only a few weeks after she had also done something new and unexpected: she had gotten married. Would he have fled to a different university because of it? She and Miles had been seeing each other for two and a half years before they married. Had Harlan held out hope that she would come to her senses, drop Miles, and return to him? She cannot imagine why he would believe that. She has given him no reason to hope. She is careful not to flirt with him or talk about their past in a sentimental way. She has tried to remain a friend, but never a confidant. Miles is closer to him than she is.

Jackie drinks her coffee, but it does nothing to stop the cold chill settling along her spine. If her theory is correct, Harlan has gone to great lengths to unsettle her emotionally and threaten her career. What else is he planning? What is his endgame? The events of the last three months might have brought out her worst self, but they have also made her fight for everything she has achieved. What is left?

She needs an ally and is disheartened to know it is probably not Miles, not at the moment. How much of her suspicion can she convey via FaceTime? It's too convoluted. She closes her eyes against the pain of what this says about her marriage. While she accepts a large portion of the blame for their current distance, Miles hasn't exactly made it easy for her to be transparent. He has been adamant that she stay out of Harlan's affairs. What sort of reception will she get if she tries to convince him that Harlan is really and truly out to get her?

CHAPTER 23

Jackie and Jeff are at a corner table at the Festive Hen. Jeff texted her in the morning to say he had no dinner plans, and she couldn't think of a reason not to accept. She had been considering going out on her own to celebrate having survived a tense phone conversation with Deirdre Calhoun. The director listened without comment to Jackie's account of the timeline of her investigation and the updated security measures. At the close of the call, Calhoun reiterated the necessity of an audit, and Jackie replied that she would find someone from outside the lab to conduct it at her expense.

"Plug the dike, Jackie, and plug it fast," Calhoun said.

With monumental restraint, Jackie did not utter one of several pointed comebacks that rushed toward her tongue.

Jackie has said nothing to Jeff, yearning to put Calhoun and the entire mess behind her.

The waiter approaches and arranges a wedge of ricotta cheesecake topped with dried fruit compote, two forks, and two glasses of sauterne in front of them.

"Enjoy."

They lift glasses.

"To old friends," Jeff says.

"I'm not toasting the old part, but cheers."

Jeff smiles, sips his wine, and nods in approval. "You seem less tense tonight. Is the shitstorm clearing?"

"Maybe a little? I had some problems with my research and the foundation that funds it. It's not solved, but it's likely it will be."

"That's great. You do important work."

"I try. Some days—like the last hundred of them—I start thinking about doing something simpler."

"Like?"

She imagines her sister, Grace, at home with her children, then remembers about Jeff's child. "Oh, an accountant or an Uber driver."

He laughs.

They finish their meal and walk back to the university lot where Jackie left her car. The air is much warmer than it has been recently, and both their coats are unbuttoned. Jeff was easy company at dinner; it was as if they were friends who caught up every year or so. Jackie breathes in deeply, savoring the unusual sensation of relaxation. If she could stay in this moment for a while longer, she might be able to cope with all the rest. How do you make a reprieve last? Maybe she should scrap the idea of becoming an accountant and become a monk, living in the moment.

She fishes in her bag for her keys and clicks open her car. "Sure I can't give you a lift?"

"I'm sure. I've been imprisoned in meetings all day and need to walk."

"By the river is nice."

"That was my thought." He sighs and spreads his hands. "I'd be lying if I didn't say that I'm sorry I'm leaving tomorrow."

"It's been so wonderful to see you."

An awkward space fills up between them. Jeff reaches out and pulls her to him. He holds her tightly and she can feel his muscles through layers of clothing, and it makes her a little dizzy. He kisses her ear. "Stay in touch, Jackie," he says softly.

"I will. I promise." Her voice catches. Before she knows what's happening, his lips meet hers. Warmth spreads through her veins, and she catches herself midfall and pulls back. Drinks and dinner and conversation are one thing; kissing is another. She's married. Whatever problems she and Miles have won't be solved this way. "I can't. I'm sorry."

He lets go of her. "No, I'm the one who's sorry. I shouldn't have."

Jackie takes a half step back for good measure before meeting his gaze, which is full of concern.

"It's okay. Really." She wants to touch his cheek but stops herself. No more contact. She opens her car door and slides in. "Bye, Jeff."

"Bye, Jackie." He stands there a moment, a wistful expression on his face. As he walks away, he extracts his phone from his pocket, presumably to pull up directions. He reaches the corner of the science building and is gone.

Movement to the right catches her attention. A figure stands near the covered entrance to Wolf Hall, fifty feet away, in the shadows between the entry and the streetlight.

She inserts the key in the ignition and waits a moment, sure whoever it is will step forward into the light. It's a strange place to wait, in the dark. She looks around for another person, someone approaching the shadowed figure, or a waiting car, but there is no one. Nothing.

Fingers trembling, she starts the engine, backs up, and swings the car onto the road. Her hands grip the wheel. She checks in the rearview mirror, half expecting whoever it is to be running headlong toward her.

The figure is gone. And for some reason she cannot pinpoint, this is worse.

———

Ten minutes later she is inside her house, taking off her jacket, kicking off her shoes. Her hands are trembling. She checks the dead bolt and tells herself not to be paranoid. Whoever it was couldn't possibly have followed her home.

She proceeds to the kitchen, contemplating another glass of wine, but decides against it. Exhaustion spills over her like a mudflow. It's only nine thirty, but maybe, just maybe, if she goes to bed now she will get several hours of sleep. Six uninterrupted hours would be wonderful. No appointments tomorrow, none whatsoever; dare she hope for eight hours? The thought of the oblivion of sleep fills her with such longing her eyes well with tears. This must be how the babies in her lab feel when the world is too much for them, and they howl and howl in their desperation to close it out and sleep. Jackie is even too tired to howl.

She mounts the stairs and goes directly to the bedroom, foregoing any preparations other than undressing in the dark. If she pauses to brush her teeth or wash her face, this trance might vanish. She climbs under the covers, her eyes already closed, and succumbs.

———

She awakens from a dream that runs away from her consciousness in an instant. Her arm is pinned underneath her, numb and tingling, and she turns onto her back to free it. A weak light seeps around the edges of the curtains. Rising on her elbow, she reads the bedside clock: 7:15.

Good Lord.

She throws off the covers, pads to the bathroom. Her limbs are leaden, her mind stuffed with cotton. She runs the shower and tidies the clothes she discarded last night while she waits for the water to get hot.

Fifteen minutes later Jackie is downstairs, dressed in leggings, a T-shirt, and a fleece, starting the coffee. The house is unusually still, as if it, too, were struggling to rouse from a deep sleep. Outside the kitchen window, the clouds are steely. A blue jay lands on a fence post, fluffs its feathers, picks up one foot, then the other, and flies off.

Miles is coming home this evening, which means he is probably at the airport in San Francisco, or at least preparing to go. She can't remember exactly what time he was due in, but can check his calendar on her phone. Jackie looks around for her bag and finds it by the front door. She searches the external pocket for the phone, but it's not there, nor is it in the main compartment. Recently she's been misplacing her phone, a behavior she attributes to stress. She checks the pockets of the coat she was wearing last night and pulls out the phone.

"Gotcha."

She turns it on, but the battery is dead, so she plugs it into the charger in the kitchen and pours coffee into a mug. How long has it been flat? The last time she remembers using her phone was to text Antonio to say she hoped his last exam went well. She sent it shortly before she left the office to have dinner with Jeff. Jackie leans against the counter and sips her coffee, her alertness ratcheting up in response to the anticipated caffeine hit. The phone screen lights up.

Oh crap.

Three missed calls from Miles, all from last night, the first at 11:35. A series of texts from Miles.

Antonio is at the Adams jail. Drinking charge. Can you pick him up so he doesn't have to sleep there?

Where are you?

FFS Jackie, this is important.

FYI Harlan got him and took him to his friend's house.

Jackie's thoughts are darting too fast for her to pin them down. She takes a long drink from her mug and reads the texts again.

Antonio knew his father was out of town but called him first anyway, probably because of the last scene she had with him. Antonio expected her to come, once summoned by Miles, and she would've, had she known. Why didn't she check her phone last night? Was she trying to stay under the radar while she was seeing Jeff again? Her own motivation is muddy to her, but what does it matter now?

In any event, Harlan stepped in to save the day. How totally unsurprising.

Miles will be furious, but delaying will only make things worse, so Jackie takes a deep breath and calls him.

Five interminable rings before he picks up. "Jackie." His tone is hard and flat.

She starts to pace into the living room, and the cord pulls out of the wall. "Shit. Hold on." She plugs it back in. "Sorry. Are you still at the hotel?"

"I got out of the shower to get your call. Did you get my texts?"

"Just now. My phone died."

He pauses, as if weighing this excuse. "That's not like you. Were you home last night?"

Here we go. She winces at the bite of guilt. "I had dinner with Jeff and was home at nine thirty. I was completely shattered and went straight to bed."

"Jeff? Do I know Jeff?"

"I've told you about him. I dated him in college. He's in town on business and happened to come to my talk."

"Your talk was Monday."

"Miles, this feels like the third degree." Also totally justified; she'd do the same—and had when she questioned him about Harlan's insinuations.

A short huff. "Does it? You were going to look after Antonio this week."

"Meeting an old friend and looking after Antonio are unrelated. Antonio was staying with a friend because I objected to drug deals at our house. How am I supposed to keep track of him?"

"You aren't. That's not what I mean. But when he ends up in jail, I would've hoped you would help him."

Jackie closes her eyes to quell the frustration rising in her chest. "I would've helped him. You know that."

"Luckily I was able to get a hold of Harlan. I felt bad about asking him to go so late."

"He's a night owl. And it wouldn't have been the end of the world if Antonio had to spend one night in jail. It might have taught him something." Immediately she wants to take back these words. She stands by them, but it's not what Miles needs to hear, not right now.

He drops his voice. "I'm surprised at you, Jackie. I thought you understood something about what he's going through. I thought you cared about him."

Jackie bends forward, absorbing the blow. "I thought you knew me well enough not to question that." Silence hums on the line. "Have a good flight and I'll see you later."

Miles ends the call without another word.

———

Somehow getting adequate sleep has left Jackie more aware of the emotional bruising she's sustained. She wants to crawl back into bed, but knows she will lie there tormented by an endless loop of negative thoughts about her career, her integrity, and her marriage. Instead, she occupies herself with mindless, long-neglected tasks. First she attacks the laundry. She strips the bed, collects the soiled clothes and towels, and starts the first load. The cleaning service comes every two weeks and is due in three days, but she gives the bathroom a quick scrub, replaces the towels, and puts fresh sheets on the bed.

The fact that she is making progress toward something, even if it is menial, settles her nerves. She vacuums upstairs, then takes a break to eat some yogurt and an apple. Noticing that the refrigerator contents are 90 percent condiments, she makes a mental note to stop at the market on her way back from the lab. After she vacuums the downstairs and straightens the living room, she tackles the kitchen. Finally, Jackie takes stock of the guest room in case Antonio returns. By midday, the house is in order. It's all superficial, but it's better than ruminating.

She downs a quick lunch of crackers and cheese, changes into jeans and a blouse, and drives to work. Tate is setting up one of the research rooms for the first subjects.

"Hi, Tate. Thanks for coming in right before break." Tate is from Falls Church, so she doesn't have far to go to for the holidays, but she never complains about being the last one released from duties.

Tate places the iPad she was checking on the table. "It's fine. Too much time at home isn't advisable." She sticks her hands into the pockets of her skirt, a full 1950s style in yellow-and-white gingham. "Can I ask you something? About the data problem?"

"Sure."

"Rumors are swirling that it wasn't a mistake, that someone meant to screw things up."

Jackie sighs. "It looks that way. I haven't wanted to advertise it."

She tilts her head. "Do you know who it was?"

"No."

"Do you have an idea?"

Jackie hesitates. "It would be wrong of me to share that without being sure. You can see that, right?"

"Yeah. I'm sorry."

Tate is shuffling her feet, and Jackie realizes why she's asking. "What are people saying, Tate? Can you tell me?"

"That it's Vince Leeds. That he did it for attention." Her gaze has been lowered, but now she studies Jackie, measuring her reaction. "Like a nonmedical Munchausen by proxy."

Jackie laughs. Vince? Seriously? Where did that rumor start?

Tate is watching her, her brow furrowed.

"I honestly don't know who it was, Tate. But the data are secure; that's the important thing." Jackie orients toward a knock at the main door, then turns back to Tate. "The Ramirezes. Early as usual. I'll get them."

As she enters her office to leave her things, Jackie admits she was only mollifying Tate. The data matter a great deal, but not as much as reputations and careers, which, once damaged, are unlikely to recover. Vince is an easy target. If Harlan is really behind her life unraveling, who else is in his way?

CHAPTER 24

At six o'clock that evening Jackie transfers the grocery bags to one hand, unlocks the front door, and makes her way to the kitchen. Muffled music emanates from the guest room, the living room is in disarray, and takeout containers litter the kitchen counter. Antonio is here, and probably Miles since his flight landed at National two hours ago. Jackie begins to put away the groceries. Her stomach growls; she hasn't eaten much today. She's dreading seeing Miles and isn't too crazy about Antonio right now, either. What she wouldn't give to return to early this morning when she awoke from her impossibly long sleep.

Miles is descending the stairs and stops halfway between the kitchen and the living room, pointedly not approaching her for a hug or a kiss.

"Hi, Jackie."

"Hi. How was your flight?" The soft pitch of small talk.

"Fine." He nods toward the guest room. "I collected Antonio from his friend's on my way back from the airport. You might've thought to do that."

Wow. That was fast. "He chose to go there, remember?"

"Yes, but he obviously needs supervision."

"I begged him to stay, Miles. I don't know why you don't believe me." Her head feels like giant hands are squeezing it. Low blood sugar, stress, anger.

Miles steps closer. "Did you even check in with him all week?"

"Yes, by text—"

"Once."

"I don't remember exactly—" She picks up her phone from the counter to check, then changes her mind. Miles is staring at her; he is indignant and angry. "This is absurd!"

"Is it?" He paces into the living room and back again. Jackie can't remember ever seeing him so agitated, and it scares her. "You've been too distracted to fulfill your promise to me about Antonio because you've reconnected with your old boyfriend."

"We had drinks and a dinner. Like I told you." And a kiss, which Miles knowing about will help exactly nothing. Of course she feels guilty that it happened and is glad she threw cold water on the situation.

Miles shakes his head, disbelieving. He might have seen a flash of doubt on her face. In any case, he's not buying it. Or he's simply too angry.

Jackie's head is throbbing. She opens a bag of almonds she left on the counter, tosses a handful in her mouth. "You know, I've had a lot going on at the lab, pretty disastrous stuff, and you've totally ignored that."

"You haven't filled me in."

"When? While you're yelling at me about your son?" She pulls a bottle of white from the fridge, one with a screw top because today is like that, and gets two glasses from the cabinet, out of habit, not charity.

"I've been in California, Jackie. Working." Miles runs a hand through his hair. "What happened at the lab?"

Jackie knocks back half the glass she poured. Where does she begin? "The foundation is pissed, and so is Chen, the department chair. And Nasira . . ." Jackie hesitates. She wants to be forthright with her husband, and he did ask, but every conversation they've had about Nasira or Harlan has gone sideways.

He places both hands on the counter. "What about Nasira?"

"She told me some things about Harlan that, together with what I know, paint a pretty concerning picture."

"A 'concerning picture'? What does that mean?"

Jackie bites her lip. "I think he might be behind it, Miles. Behind all of it."

He jerks back. "What? I suppose Nasira is in on it, too."

"I don't—"

"Really, Jackie. You've gone around the bend."

The guest room door opens, and Antonio appears, rubbing his face as he approaches them. His hair is rumpled, he's unshaven, and his pants look like they're about to fall off his hips. "Heard you guys fighting—over my music, which is something. I'm trying to get some rest."

Miles holds up his hands. "Don't worry. We're done. I'm leaving."

Jackie says, "Leaving to go where? You just got here."

"And it's been a lovely reception from both of you." He stalks to the front door, grabs his jacket and his keys.

"Bye, Dad." Antonio lifts one hand. "Sorry I'm such a fuckup."

Miles stands there for a moment, his chest rising and falling with the heat of his emotion. Jackie wants to run to him, calm him, hold him, but he's so foreign to her right now, she cannot bring herself to do it. The gathering sense that nothing is what she thinks it is, that everything is being toppled over by forces she does not know and cannot understand, frightens her. She is not simply alone in her marriage. She is a stranger in her own life.

Without a word, Miles opens the door and is gone.

———

Three hours later, Jackie is sitting on the couch with her feet on the coffee table, finalizing grades for the methodology class. Each student's numerical grade is calculated based on their performance on tests, quizzes, and projects, but Jackie takes other factors into account, such as improvement over the semester or special circumstances. And an average of 89.5 is always an A minus.

The doorbell chimes, and she startles. She saves her work, sets aside the computer, and goes to the door, pausing to glance in the entryway mirror to ensure that she is marginally presentable. She touches the door-cam screen and an image appears.

A uniformed police officer, male, white, and heavyset, and another man, lanky and black, wearing wire-rims and in plain clothes.

She twists the dead bolt and opens the door, dread rising inside her.

"Good evening," the policeman says. "I'm Officer Goodyear and this is Detective Cash." The detective flashes his badge. "Are you Jacqueline Strelitz?"

"Yes." *Something has happened to Miles. He was upset. He was in a car crash.*

"Mind if we come in?"

"No, no." She steps aside and gestures down the hall. "The living room is just here."

The policeman leads the way, scanning. "Anyone else home, Ms. Strelitz?"

"Doctor. I mean Jackie." What is she saying? Her brain is fogging over. "No one right now, but my stepson is due back soon. He went out to eat."

"Name?"

"Antonio de Haas. With two *a*'s."

"How old is Antonio?"

"Twenty. Is this about him?"

The detective raises his eyebrows. "Let's sit down, okay?"

"Sure."

Jackie takes the seat where she left her laptop, and the men sit in the chairs angled toward her. The detective unbuttons his coat and extracts a small notepad from his jacket. His fingers are long, graceful.

He seems to be moving in slow motion, and her own movements drag, too. Her hands are clammy, and she rubs them on her thighs before clasping them in her lap.

The detective says, "Do you know Jeffrey Toshack?"

Jeff? This is about Jeff? "Yes. Why?"

"How do you know him?"

"He's an old friend. We had dinner last night."

Detective Cash holds her gaze. "Mr. Toshack was found dead earlier today."

"What?" Her hand flies to her mouth. "No. No, that's not possible." She looks at the officer, whose expression has not changed, then back to the detective. Her heart is in her throat. "What happened?"

"We're still piecing it together. When exactly did you last see Mr. Toshack?"

"After dinner. It was around nine fifteen." Jackie pictures Jeffrey standing in front of her, smiling. Tears sting behind her eyes and she fights them back. "We walked back to my car from the Festive Hen. I was parked on campus, outside Wolf Hall. I offered him a ride to his hotel, but he said he wanted to walk."

The detective is taking notes. "And what did you do after you left?"

"I drove home."

"Straight home?"

"Yes."

"Did you leave the house again?"

"No. I went to bed early."

"Did you have any other contact with Mr. Toshack after that? A phone call, maybe?"

"I sent him a text this morning, wishing him a safe trip. He was going to see his parents in Connecticut." Her voice catches. "Oh God. Those poor people."

Detective Cash adjusts his glasses. "I'm sorry, ma'am."

Jackie nods.

"Does Antonio's father live here?"

"Miles? Yes. Why?"

Officer Goodyear leans forward, elbows on his knees. "And where might he be now?"

"I'm not sure." The room swirls at the edges. Jeff is dead, and they are asking about where she was, and now about Miles. Jeff isn't simply dead; they think he was murdered. Jackie closes her eyes a moment, opens them again. "We had an argument earlier and he left. I don't know where he went."

The policeman glances at Cash, who is nodding. Cash says, "Do you know where he was last night?"

"In San Francisco. He didn't come home until this evening." Jackie pauses, collecting her stampeding thoughts. "Did someone kill Jeff?"

The detective dodges her question. "So your husband was away when you had dinner with Mr. Toshack. Is that what you argued about?"

Jackie's mouth feels like parchment. She stands. "I need some water."

The policeman gets up, blocking her. The man is huge. "If you don't mind, I'll get it for you."

"What? Why?"

"Just being careful, ma'am." He heads to the kitchen.

Jackie watches his back as he opens cabinets, searching for a glass. The edges of everything are bright, shimmering. She's struggling to assimilate what's going on: the sudden intrusion, the news about Jeff, the questions about her movements, about Miles. It is surreal.

Focus, Jackie.

She addresses Detective Cash. "Did someone kill Jeff? Do I need a lawyer?"

"Please sit down." He sighs. "You can have a lawyer present, but then we'd need to take you to the station." He spreads his hands in a gesture of innocence, which she doesn't buy for one minute. "Up to you."

The officer hands her the glass. She takes a long drink, tells herself she's done nothing wrong and has no reason to be defensive. "Look," Jackie says, as she sits down. "Last night I came home after dinner and went to bed. My husband was in California. I didn't check my phone after I came home, but in the morning I found out Miles was trying to get hold of me last night because Antonio had been arrested for drinking." Both men shift in their seats. "He'd just finished his finals." Jackie hears how lame that sounds—as if completing a term always leads to an arrest—but she presses on. "So I told Miles I'd been to dinner with Jeff, and he was upset because I wasn't available to pick up Antonio from jail. We argued about it briefly on the phone, and when we saw each other again a few hours ago, we picked up where we left off."

"Dr. Strelitz," Detective Cash begins, "were you having an affair with Mr. Toshack?"

"No."

"But your husband was jealous that you had dinner with him."

"Miles was upset about his son."

"Sure. And also jealous?"

Was he jealous? In talking to Miles, Jackie deflected his probes about Jeff, determined to keep the focus on Antonio. Miles was definitely miffed that Jackie was socializing, but there is an infinite distance between that and murder. "The implication is ludicrous. Miles isn't capable of hurting anyone."

Cash nods, politely acknowledging the defense, as predictable as it is. "Did you and Mr. Toshack see each other on another occasion before the dinner?"

With each question, Jackie increasingly feels she should stop talking and insist on a lawyer. But each question is so straightforward, it seems silly not to answer. She has nothing to hide and wants to help. "We had drinks on Monday. He came to a public lecture I gave, and we went out for drinks after. Before that, we hadn't had any contact since college."

Cash scratches on his pad. "Old friends catching up."

"Yes." Jackie takes another drink of water. Her hand shakes, and the glass hits the end table with a thud. The reality that Jeff is dead is sinking in, as is the likelihood that it wasn't an accident. "Where did you find him?"

Cash and Goodyear exchange glances.

"In the river," Cash says.

The room is still. Jackie sees Jeff floating facedown, ghostly. Bile rises in her throat.

The front door opens and closes. Cash and Goodyear get to their feet, move toward the hall.

Jackie follows them. "Antonio?"

Antonio startles at the sight of the policemen. "What the—" He spins and lunges at the door, throws it open.

"Stop!" The officer, quick for his size, sprints the few steps to the doorway, makes a grab for the boy.

Antonio ducks and flies outside onto the porch.

"Antonio!" Jackie shouts. "Don't run! It's okay!"

Three strides and Officer Goodyear has Antonio by the jacket. The boy flails. "Don't fight me!" He yanks Antonio closer, grabs his arm. "Simmer down. We just want to talk."

Cash is there, takes hold of Antonio's other arm. The men turn him around, move him into the house.

Antonio's eyes are wild. "What's going on?"

Cash sighs and shakes his head. "That's a good question to ask before you run from the police." He shuts the door behind them.

Jackie's heart squeezes, and she places her hand on Antonio's arm. "It's not about you." She addresses Cash. "He has ADHD. Thinking first isn't his strong suit."

Cash lets go of the boy. "Why don't you go sit down, Antonio?"

He does as he's told. On the couch, with his hands between his knees, he looks like a small boy.

She moves to join him, but Goodyear intercepts her. "Dr. Strelitz, can you give us a minute?"

"What? Why?" Now they think Antonio is involved? Or maybe they want to check her story against his. Everything is moving too fast. She can't keep up and feels unbalanced, like she might knock something over—her life, for example.

Detective Cash says, "We just want to ask Antonio a few questions. It'll only take a moment." His tone is level, patient, as if it's perfectly normal to ask someone to vacate their living room for questioning about a murder.

Murder. A wave of nausea rises in her throat. "I'll be upstairs," she manages. She sidles by the men, runs up the stairs, the fact of Jeff's death catching her by the heels. She rushes into the bathroom, kicking the door closed behind her. She flips up the toilet seat and vomits. Breathing hard, she steadies herself against the cabinet, waiting for another heave. It doesn't come. She flushes the toilet and splashes cold water on her face. She rinses her mouth, dries her hands and face, and crosses the hall to her bedroom. Voices drift up from below, but she can't make out the conversation.

She retrieves her phone from her pocket and calls Miles. It goes to voice mail. She texts him, asking him to call. She needs to tell him about Jeff, that Antonio is being questioned, that he himself might be a suspect. That she might be. Oh God.

Someone killed Jeff. The reality of it is settling black and gritty over her skittering thoughts.

After pacing the room a dozen times, she texts Miles again, saying she is sorry. She doesn't say for what, because she doesn't know. Sorry for everything. Sorry for her jealousy. Sorry for sparking his. Sorry for not being a better stepmother. Sorry for not running after him when he left. Sorry that her old boyfriend is dead and the police are here and Antonio is being questioned.

Sorry for everything that has not yet happened.

The certainty that the worst is still in front of her, in front of them, strikes fear in her heart.

She calls Miles again. No answer.

"Dr. Strelitz?" The detective is at the bottom of the stairs.

Jackie passes Antonio on his way to his room, touches his arm, searches his face. Nothing remarkable. If anything, he seems bored, but maybe that's a cover. Antonio walks on and Jackie meets the policemen in the kitchen.

"One more thing before we go," Cash says. "Do you happen to have the flight info for your husband?"

Miles again. Why Miles? Because a man is the percentage guess? Or do they know something she doesn't? The thought that Miles might have secrets and darknesses she has no knowledge of floors her. Was her defense of him based on reality, or was it naive?

"Dr. Strelitz."

"Sorry. Yes, I think I do." Jackie pulls up the calendar on her phone. Cash is ready with his notebook. "Alaska 1001, leaving SFO at seven twenty a.m., arriving at National at three thirty p.m."

"Thanks. If you hear from your husband or find out where he is, I'd appreciate a call."

"Okay. I want to help if I can."

"We'll be in touch if we have more questions."

She sees them to the door and throws the dead bolt behind them. If only that action could separate her from what she just learned. Her head is pounding, and she leans her forehead against the door and rubs the rock-hard muscles at the back of her neck.

More questions. Like what? She was at home, asleep. Miles was in California, and Antonio was out drinking or in jail or at his friend's, depending on the time. Jackie feels a surge of sympathy for Antonio for getting dragged into this after what was undoubtedly an upsetting night already. She goes to find him.

When she reaches the kitchen, Antonio is approaching from his room and reads her anxious expression. "It was no big deal. They just asked about last night, what I was doing, what I knew about where everybody was, whether I knew the guy."

"That makes sense." She wants to know about his night, about the drinking, being arrested, to see how he's dealing with it, but doesn't want to interrogate him. The police took care of that. "You sure you're okay?"

He nods and reaches into the fridge for a soda. "Want one?"

"No thanks." She watches him unscrew the cap, take a long drink, Adam's apple bobbing. The little boy she saw earlier is gone; she wonders if this is how Miles feels constantly.

"They did ask me, though, why after Harlan picked me up from jail, he didn't just bring me here instead of Larry's. Since I have a key."

She fights with everyone in her family, that's why. She couldn't get her stepson to stay. The shame of it sickens her. "What did you say? I hope you told them the truth."

"I told them I had my stuff at Larry's."

She nods. He wouldn't have divulged they'd been fighting about a dealer coming to the house, but he could've said they had a fight about something else. He opted for a simpler partial truth. Oh, the practice it takes to become a full-fledged adult.

"I'm sorry the police frightened you when you came home, Antonio."

He shrugs, takes another drink, then meets her eye. "And I'm sorry about your friend."

"Thank you. I can't believe it."

He leans a hip against the counter. "Were you guys close?"

"Yes," Jackie says, as she brushes the tears from her cheeks. "Yes, we were."

CHAPTER 25

Jackie tosses and turns all night, checking her phone between bouts of half sleep to see if Miles has responded. He hasn't. Before she went to bed she asked Antonio to contact his father. He said he would and promised to let her know if he heard anything. At midnight Jackie texts Harlan in desperation, asking if he's seen Miles, but that text remains unanswered as well.

At seven in the morning she finally gives up on sleep and goes downstairs in her robe to make coffee. As it brews, she considers a session of rowing to release her nervous energy but wants to be able to answer her phone when Miles finally surfaces. Maybe the police have already located him. The thought of the river triggers the image of Jeff's body, cold and lifeless, and a wave of sadness hits her. How could he have wound up dead? She's been turning this question over in her mind all night. If he had a heart attack or an accident, the police would presumably know that already. Why would anyone want to murder him? As the last person known to have seen Jeff, Jackie is more than a little worried that she's the prime suspect, with no alibi and no defense other than her innocence. Detective Cash focused on Miles as the putative jealous husband, but Jackie can't see how he could be involved. Miles a murderer? Antonio didn't seem to be in their sights at all, thank goodness, but there's no way she could know for sure. One thing she does know is that whatever happened to Jeff wouldn't be affecting her family if she hadn't agreed to have dinner with him, and the knowledge weighs on her.

Jackie checks the local news on her phone. Thus far they've only reported that a body was found midday yesterday by a kayaker and that the identity of the man and all other specifics are being withheld pending the investigation. Jackie thinks again of his parents and of his ex-wife, suffering now from another untimely loss.

By the time she finishes her coffee, she knows she cannot stay cooped up in the house all day. She pulls up the forecast—a high of fifty-two and clear—and decides to try to eat something and go for a walk. She makes toast, eats one slice, and gives up.

Her phone warbles. Nasira, at 8:00 a.m. on a Saturday? Worry gnaws at Jackie as she accepts the call.

"Hello?"

"Jackie, it's Nasira. I'm sorry to call so early. I hope I'm not disturbing you, especially right before Christmas."

Christmas. If only decorating a tree and preparing a meal were her biggest problems.

"No, it's fine. Really. Is everything okay?"

"Sort of? I thought about our conversation, about Harlan, and decided the best course of action was to put some distance between us."

Jackie is surprised but relieved. If her suspicions about Harlan are correct, he cannot be trusted. She and Nasira have been at odds for a long while, but now it seems both are arriving at the conclusion that their enmity was a mistake, if not a setup. "It can't hurt, even if you decide later you want to continue."

"Yeah, that was my reasoning, too. So yesterday around five, I texted him that I was coming over to get a couple things." She hesitates, and the tension is palpable. "He wanted to know why. I tried to make excuses—I should have planned what to say—but honestly he'd been ignoring me recently, so I thought he wouldn't care. I could just grab my stuff and go."

Jackie doesn't like the sound of this at all. For Nasira to be this frank with her, to trust her with details of her relationship with Harlan, could only mean he had crossed a line. Given the manipulation Jackie suspected him of, Nasira was a vulnerable pawn. "Did he confront you?"

"Not exactly. He answered the door and handed me my stuff. He'd collected everything, which I hadn't expected. Usually I can mask my emotions, but I guess he could see I was wary of him. He didn't do or say anything terrible, but, oh my God, Jackie, the way he looked at me."

Jackie knows what Nasira is about to describe. She feels it blow across her like freezing rain. "I know," she manages.

"Do you? I can't stop seeing it, his face, his eyes—"

Jackie is rushing toward the door, furious. She tears off her watch, tosses it.

"—his eyes were completely blank. Like he was dead."

He calls her name. She turns, sees his face.

Jackie moves to the kitchen window, stares out at the yard to dispel the image. She hasn't thought about Harlan's reaction to her leaving for years. Had she suppressed it to make friendship possible? What else has she stuffed into a dark corner to convince herself there need be no hard feelings? Is she still desperately hungry for his approbation?

"Jackie? Are you there?"

"Yes. Sorry. That sounds so frightening."

"I'm okay now. I might go somewhere, though, for a couple days."

Jackie remembers Nasira's parents are not speaking to her. The family probably doesn't celebrate Christmas, but it's still a hard time to be alone. "Do you have friends you can stay with?"

"Maybe. It's awkward on short notice."

Jackie's heart goes out to her, and she regrets her role in isolating Nasira via her jealousy and mistrust. "Call me anytime, Nasira."

"Thanks." She pauses. "Everything okay with you?"

It's not a cursory question; she obviously heard the strain in Jackie's voice. Jackie searches for what to say, where to begin, and gives up. "Sure, I'm fine. Just the usual holiday madness."

After Jackie ends the call, she wonders what it would be like to be honest with everyone, truly honest.

Probably disastrous—in other words, no different than her current situation.

———

Upstairs in the walk-in closet, Jackie changes into jeans, a long-sleeved T-shirt, and running shoes. As she layers on a fleece jacket, her gaze snags on Miles's carry-on bag lying open at the far end of the closet. A navy sport coat and pale-blue scarf are tossed on top, presumably what he was wearing on the trip home. He was probably about to unpack when she came home and interrupted him.

Jackie grabs a hanger and picks up the coat. As she places it on the hanger, she notices a piece of paper in the inside breast pocket and lifts it out. His boarding pass. She finishes hanging the jacket, and takes the boarding pass with her to recycle downstairs on her way out.

In the kitchen, she pulls open the drawer and is about to drop the card inside when she remembers the police asking about Miles's flight. Does that make the boarding pass evidence?

Jackie holds it in her hand, uncertain, and her attention shifts to the flight information in the upper right corner: SFO —>DCA, and below that, DEPARTING 20 DECEMBER 2018.

That's not correct, she thinks. Today is the twenty-second, she's sure, but confirms it on her phone. Miles flew home yesterday, not Thursday.

Or not.

She places the boarding pass on the counter, staring at it, as if it were in her power to make the printing align with the facts, or what she believes are the facts. Her heart rate increases as she realizes that when she spoke on the phone with Miles yesterday morning, he wasn't in California. He obviously wasn't at home, either. So where the hell was he—and why did he lie about it? Her sweet, loyal Miles.

The next realization hits her: on Thursday evening when Antonio was arrested, Miles was here, in DC. Her stomach clenches. Miles took the call from his son while he was, in all likelihood, near enough to help Antonio himself. Instead, he relied on Harlan to save Antonio from a night in jail, then berated her mercilessly for having slept through it all. Her Miles, the conniving liar.

Whatever he is hiding, he doesn't want Antonio to know about it, either.

Maybe this isn't Miles's first lie. Maybe when he said he barely knew Nasira, that was a lie, too. Nasira. Jackie decided to take a chance and trust her postdoc, open up to her. If it turns out Miles came back from California to be with Nasira, the bottom will drop out of Jackie's world. She closes her eyes, tells herself to breathe, to think. Jackie can't wrap her head around the possibility that her husband had a hand in Jeff's death; she told the police Miles was innocent. Does she still believe that? She wants to—she loves him—and despite the evidence that Miles has deceived her, she doesn't know a goddamn thing.

Jackie swipes the boarding pass from the counter, folds it in half, and slides it into her back pocket. She yanks her phone from the charger, grabs her keys and wallet from her bag at the entry, and flies out the door. She needs to figure this out, this unholy mess. All the pieces are almost certainly right in front of her if she can work out how they fit together. She'll call the police, let them know about the boarding pass, but not right now. For all she knows, they already have the information from the airline. Either way, she needs to walk and she needs to think.

She heads west and south on Thirty-Third, not thinking about where she is going, just breathing in the cold air, working her legs to free her mind. It's early on a holiday weekend. The only people out are a couple of runners and people clutching their bathrobes closed while collecting their newspapers. Jackie wants out of this neighborhood, out of the sight of red bows on streetlights, tasteful twinkling reindeer skeletons, and the couple on the street corner ahead, warming their hands on take-out coffee. She breaks into a jog and turns west onto the university campus, the only sound the jingle of her keys in her jacket pocket.

Jackie arrives at Wolf Hall. Of course her brain would take her here, along the most well-worn trajectory—and where she last saw Jeff. She strides over to the spot where she parked her car, stares at the piece of old and pitted pavement where they stood, where he hugged and kissed her. Jackie brushes the hair from her face and feels a sharp ache in her chest.

Jeff walked there, down that path.

Immediately afterward she saw someone in front of the building. Which means absolutely nothing, since she has no idea who it might have been. A man, she had that impression, larger than average. In other words, no help.

She follows the path Jeff took past the science building and makes her way down to the river, along what feels like the route someone unfamiliar with the area would take. The wind has picked up, and she zips up her jacket. She turns left down Prospect and right down the alley steps to Canal Street. She waits for the walk light and jogs across Canal Street, past the Francis Scott Key Memorial, and down to the towpath. Jackie has a sense now of being pulled along, as if she knows where to go, not by guessing, but because she is being led there.

She arrives at a footbridge over the canal and hesitates. She wouldn't go out here at night, even as safe as Adams is, but Jeff would've. He was the kind of guy who'd go for a run at midnight, figuring he could outrun just about anyone. Jackie crosses the bridge, and the sense of inevitability grows, and with it, her dread.

She walks faster, past a small park with shade trees. An old man sits on a bench with a bulldog at his feet. Up ahead, tucked under the first arch of Key Bridge, is the Potomac boatyard. Jackie breaks into a run, passing a block of abandoned three-story buildings with broken windows. The overpass shadows the path. At the boathouse entrance she pulls up short, sweat trickling down her back, her breath coming in gasps. A set of steps leads to the main dock, where colorful kayaks are stacked on racks. To the left of the steps is the boathouse, flanked by the repair shed. She walks slowly toward the buildings, gravel crunching underfoot, then halts. The alley between them is cordoned off with caution tape. She sucks in a sharp breath.

The boathouse where she rows. Where she and Miles met.

Jackie is suspicious of coincidences. Especially this one, so rife with meaning. Her thoughts swirl, one blending into the next, fact and conjecture mixing in a nonsensical slurry: Jeff, Miles, Harlan, Nasira. A kiss, a lie, a series of attacks, a pawn. So many coincidences, or apparent ones. She is a fly in a web. The more she twists and turns to see her predicament, to guess from which direction the spider might ambush her, the more entangled she becomes.

She extracts her phone from her pocket and takes a photo of the alley without questioning her motivation. She doesn't go up to the tape to see more, though. There might be blood.

Her phone vibrates, startling her. A text notification appears on the screen.

Harlan.

Miles is at my house and in a bad state. Please come.

It's so damned perfect. Harlan is delivering her to Miles. Every single shitty thing that has happened to her since September leads to goddamn Harlan.

Static fills Jackie's head and she sways, dizzy. She closes her eyes to level herself. No choice; she has to go to Miles.

On my way. She presses send.

———

Harlan's house is about a mile away, on Logan Street west of campus. Jackie checks for an Uber, but the closest one won't come for seven minutes. She can't possibly wait here that long, so she pockets her phone and retraces her route along the towpath, running along the flat and crossing under Canal Road into Jackson Valley Park. Out of breath, she climbs the hill as quickly as she can and resumes running after it levels out. A few runners pass her on the dirt path, and a woman pushing a stroller calls out, "Good morning!" Jackie is gasping and doesn't respond.

She reaches Pierson Road, turns left, and slows to a walk. Whatever is wrong with Miles, she needs to be as composed as possible. She wipes the sweat from her forehead with her sleeve. Logan is the next right; she's almost there.

Jackie scans the street for Miles's car but doesn't see it. As she starts up the long front walk, her mouth is dry and her breath ragged. Sweat is pouring off her, and she unzips her jacket partway.

The front door is ajar. Music is playing, some R&B she doesn't recognize, loudly enough that there is no point in knocking. This strikes Jackie as odd. Who blasts music in the middle of a crisis?

She texts Harlan. I'm at your door. Waits.

Nothing.

With no alternative, she lets herself in.

"Hello?" Her greeting is lost.

The stairs are in front of her. The original paneled wainscoting along the hall and stairwell gleams. The room to the left had been the parlor and is now Harlan's study. The door is shut. To the right is an arched casing into the living room. The plantation shutters are closed, but sunlight leaks along the margins, bathing the dove-gray room in gentle light. The music is coming, she now realizes, from the kitchen, at the back of the house, and grows louder as she proceeds through the living room, passing the low-slung gray tweed couches, the wood-slat and black metal end tables, all spotless, nothing out of place.

The dining room is in front of her. She pauses at the table, an expanse of stainless steel. Miles's jacket is draped over the back of a chair.

"Hello?" She'd have to shout at the top of her lungs to be heard, but feels compelled to announce herself.

The harlequin flooring of the kitchen extends before her, the only element to break with the industrial styling. The kitchen table, a rough-hewn wood slab surrounded by black Lucite chairs, sits empty in the corner of the room. The kitchen proper is to her right. She turns. Sunlight streams through the transoms above the shuttered French doors.

Miles is standing between the central island and the counter extending into the room. He has his back to her and is shirtless. It's so odd, she thinks, to see him this way, half-naked, from a distance. She wonders if perhaps he has been swimming, but Harlan has no pool. A recent shower, then.

Her brain is amassing the information, formulating scenarios, sorting possibilities.

Make it fit. Make it sensible.

For a half second, Jackie looks but she does not see. Then she does.

An arm across Miles's back, holding him tightly, stroking his flesh. A hand on the back of Miles's head, which is tipped sideways, accommodating a kiss.

The kiss ends.

Over Miles's shoulder, smiling at her, is Harlan.

CHAPTER 26

Jackie stares at Harlan, at Miles. Miles untangles himself from Harlan, swivels to face her.

The floor falls away from beneath Jackie's feet. She throws her arms out to catch hold of something, to steady herself. Her phone flies out of her left hand, skids across the floor.

"Jackie!" Miles calls from above her somewhere, like he's shouting down an elevator shaft. Her right hip hits the ground, followed by her shoulder. She pushes up to sitting, the black-and-white geometry of the floor dazzles her, swirling.

A shadow across the tiles, the pattern resolving. A hand on her arm.

"Jackie! Are you all right?" Miles's face is in front of her.

She closes her eyes, smells sweat, salt, heat. She breathes in through her mouth and her lungs expand. She opens her eyes; her vision clears. Miles. She pulls her arm free. "Get away from me!" Scrambling to her knees, she spots her phone by the breakfast table, crabs over to retrieve it.

Miles follows her, reaches for her. She lunges back, hits a chair. It topples, clattering.

"Jackie, please stop. Jackie, please."

Out. Away. She gets to her feet, glances to her left, at Harlan. He hasn't moved, his grin now a satisfied sneer. His mask is off. He did this to punish her. The horror of who Harlan is beneath his cool, polished exterior sends shards of ice into her veins.

Miles moves in front of her. She won't look at his face. Whatever is there holds nothing for her.

"Get away from me!" Jackie pushes past him, runs blindly through the house, throws the door open, flies down the steps. The cold air hits her, and her chest constricts. Gasping, she bends over, hands on her knees. Her stomach heaves.

After a few moments, her gasping eases. She straightens and jogs down the walk, wiping her eyes with her sleeve.

She reaches the street, turns right, and breaks into a panicked run.

The campus is deserted. At Wolf Hall she tries to insert her key in the door, but it jumps around the opening. Jackie groans with frustration, shakes out her hands, and tries again. The key goes in, turns. She calls the elevator, takes it to her lab. Cold sweat coats the nape of her neck and runs down the small of her back. She shivers.

She unlocks the lab door. The hall light is on, and the door to the shared lab is open.

Tears flow down her cheeks. She cannot go home. This is her refuge. Her space.

She rushes toward her office, slips inside. As she is closing the door, Nasira appears in the hall, a startled look on her face.

Jackie slams her office door shut, leans against it. She fights against the sobs mushrooming in her chest, but cannot hold them back, and doubles over.

"Jackie! What's wrong?"

Jackie slides down the door and hugs her knees. Closing her eyes, she wishes that was all it took to disappear. The bliss of oblivion. Lights out.

"Can you tell me what's wrong?" Nasira's tone is softer. "At least open the door?"

Silence, except for the ragged sounds of her own breathing. A knife blade is lodged behind her sternum.

"Jackie? I have some water for you."

Water. She attempts to swallow but has no saliva. So much running, and now so many tears.

Jackie pushes herself to her feet, opens the door. She can't bear any more emotion, regardless of whose it is, and moves slowly around her desk and lowers herself into the chair.

Nasira places the glass in front of her. Jackie drains it, wipes her mouth with her sleeve. Keeps her eyes trained on the surface of her desk.

Nasira says, "Should I call Miles?"

Jackie spits out a laugh. The release brings on another bout of tears. Nasira leaves the office and returns with more water. She takes a seat opposite Jackie.

Finally, Jackie looks up at Nasira and remembers their conversation two days ago, during which she resolved to be honest, to listen to Nasira's side of the story and let go of her jealous obsession. Because of that fragile trust, she and Nasira were able to discern a pattern. Harlan's hand appeared to be at the controls of the disasters befalling Jackie—and Nasira. Nasira had reached out to Jackie just this morning to relate her upsetting encounter with Harlan, mirroring the trust Jackie had offered her. Jackie can't think of a reason not to open up to Nasira now, especially since the odds of Nasira and Miles having an affair just lengthened considerably. Jackie shakes her head ruefully.

Nasira says, "When I called you this morning, something was wrong then."

Jackie reaches for the tissues on the shelf behind her and blows her nose. "Yes. The problem is, I can't think straight right now. My head is filled with sludge."

"Maybe if you tell me, I can think for you."

"Maybe," Jackie says, but the truth is she wants to curl up in the dark and let the world spin without her for a while, for however long it takes for her to forget what she just saw at Harlan's house, to forget what happened to Jeff. But she doesn't have the luxury of oblivion; she has to figure out what to do. She faces Nasira and takes a deep breath. It rattles in her chest. "My college boyfriend came to my lecture on Monday, totally unexpected. We had drinks after, and dinner on Thursday evening. On Friday, yesterday, he was supposed to go to his parents for Christmas—they're in Connecticut . . ." She stares at the ceiling, collecting herself. "He's dead."

"What?"

"The police came to my house last night. They asked about Miles, of course, assuming a jealous husband, but I said he was in California."

"You said? You mean he wasn't?"

"I thought he was, until this morning, when I found this." She sits forward and extracts the boarding pass from her back pocket. She unfolds it and lays it on the desk. "Apparently he came back Thursday."

Nasira's brow is furrowed. "Why would he lie to you?"

"Exactly. Why? And that same night, Thursday, Antonio was arrested for drinking. Miles tried to get hold of me to pick him up, only I was already asleep."

Nasira cocks her head. "So Antonio is in jail?"

"No, Harlan went to get him and dropped him at his friend's house." Jackie sits up straighter. Laying out the sequence of events is sharpening her mind. She drinks more water and returns her attention to Nasira. "I've tried again and again to contact Miles since then. He didn't answer. I should've just gone to the police first thing this morning with the boarding pass. After all, I'm the one that gave them the mistaken flight information."

"But you wanted to give Miles a chance to explain."

"Right." Jackie fingers the boarding pass. "And now I know why he lied about his flight."

Nasira looks confused. "You found Miles?"

"I sure did." Jackie's thoughts pull up short. Thus far she has been caught up in the implications for her own marriage in seeing Harlan and Miles in a passionate embrace. She hasn't thought of the impact on Nasira. She hesitates, thinking of what to say, and how. "Harlan lured me to his house with a text saying Miles needed me. I was down at the river, looking for the spot where they found Jeff. I didn't want to wait for an Uber—the text sounded urgent—so I ran to Harlan's." She shakes her head at her gullibility. "When I got there, I found them together."

"Together? What do you mean?"

Jackie's throat closes. "They were holding each other, kissing."

Nasira covers her mouth with her fingers. "Oh my God." She stays like that for a long moment, then returns her hand to her lap. "What did you do?"

"I ran out the door and didn't stop until I got here." She bites her lip. It tastes of salt. "My life is destroyed, but at least today's workout is taken care of."

Tears well in Nasira's eyes. "Jackie . . ."

The women stare at each other for a few moments, each in her separate pain, each considering the other's. For the first time, Jackie appreciates Nasira's reticence. Most people would launch into a series of questions. God knows Jackie has quite a few herself: How long has this been going on? Has Miles had other men? Has Harlan—even when he was with her? And why did Harlan orchestrate her arrival on the scene?

The answer to this last question, at least, seems straightforward. He intended to injure her, to deal a blow engineered to level her.

He nearly succeeded.

Jackie's eyes are trained on Miles's boarding pass. Presumably her husband returned to DC Thursday night to be with Harlan. He couldn't pick up Antonio because he was supposed to be in California, not rendezvousing with his lover. Jackie's heart lurches. Had Miles been duping her all along? The idea that her marriage is a sham seems preposterous, but that, as it happens, is no criteria for rejecting an idea. Not if recent events are any indication.

Her thoughts of Antonio spark a recollection of the words he tossed at her the night she encountered the dealer at the house, the phrase Grace wondered about and for which Jackie had no explanation. About lying to herself, about her life not being what she thought it was. No, not her life, she sees now, but her marriage. Antonio knew. Is that why Miles divorced Antonio's mother?

Nasira gets up, takes a tissue, and dabs at her eyes.

"I'm sorry," Jackie says.

"I guess he fooled us both."

Jackie nods. Harlan played Nasira to get at Jackie and deceived Jackie into thinking he was over her, that they had segued into friendship. But none of that matters at the moment.

She pulls her phone from her pocket. She's fairly certain that Miles's deception about his return flight had to do with wanting to see Harlan and nothing to do with Jeff. Still, she doesn't have all the facts, precious few, in fact.

"Who are you calling?" Nasira asks.

"The police."

———

Detective Cash ushers her into a small conference room. Abandoned coffee cups litter the table, and the fluorescent fixture overhead pulses sporadically. He gestures to a chair and sits across from her, taps his pen on the legal pad in front of him. Over the phone, Jackie told him she had seen her husband at Harlan's house. She didn't go into detail about what she witnessed—she wasn't sure it was relevant—but she mentioned the boarding pass. Jackie places it in front of the detective, and takes a seat.

Cash uses his pen to drag it closer and examines it briefly. "Thanks for bringing this, Dr. Strelitz. I've sent a cruiser to Harlan Crispin's house."

Jackie frowns, torn over whether to volunteer information about Harlan and Miles. The encounter (or relationship or whatever it is) does go partway toward exonerating Miles. Wouldn't he be less likely to act out of jealousy while having an affair himself? She decides not to bring it up for now. "You just want Miles for questioning, right?"

"I can't answer that." He leans back, gives her a long look, tapping his pen absently. "Is there something else you want to tell me?"

"Yes. No." Jackie's temples are throbbing. She rubs them with the heels of her hands, then returns her attention to the detective. His expression is impassive. Jackie opts for transparency. Everything else takes too much energy. "Listen, Detective Cash. I'm sleep deprived and frazzled. I don't know what's relevant to you. I don't know what to say or do or who to believe. I'll tell you everything I know, but don't expect it to make any sense."

He nods, but there's little apparent sympathy. He has no real reason to believe her. "Let's focus on what might be related to the death of Jeffrey Toshack."

"As I said yesterday, my husband can't be responsible."

Cash leans his forearms on the table, hands clasped. "So how did you happen to find your husband?"

"I received a text from Harlan, saying I should come to his house because Miles was in a bad state." Cash scribbles on his pad. "Do you want to see the text?"

"No, just forward it to me, please. So then you drove to Dr. Crispin's?"

She shook her head. "I was at the river, on foot. I'd been retracing where Jeff might've walked."

Cash raises his eyebrows but says nothing.

"When I got the text, I ran to Harlan's, through the park." She explains about the door, the music, the embrace, running away.

The silence in the room is leaden.

Cash runs a hand over his chin. "You had a shock, I can see that. And maybe this changes the way we look at things." He puts down his pen. "And maybe it doesn't."

Jackie is oddly relieved by this—that what is monumental to her personally might have nothing to do with what happened to Jeff, or, more simply, that Detective Cash is as confounded by the events as she is. "Isn't it possible the person who killed Jeff had nothing to do with me?"

"Sure. We're pursuing every lead we've got. We just don't have many, and 'random killer' is an explanation of last resort. There's almost always a reason, and it's usually close to home."

Jackie nods. *Close to home.* But how close?

CHAPTER 27

Jackie leaves the station and checks her phone. A missed call from Miles, which she has no intention of returning. She gets in her car, a hot ball of anger establishing itself in her gut. As she drives home, the image of Miles and Harlan embracing flashes in her mind again and again, dry kindling to the fury building inside her. She grabs the wheel more tightly, focuses on the traffic, the stoplights, the crosswalks, anything other than the heat building behind her eyes like a fever. Good thing it's a short drive.

She enters the house—their house—and drops her bag at her feet. The first thing she sees is Miles's umbrella, his fucking British umbrella that opens to the size of a carport. She takes it in both hands, lifts it overhead, and brings it crashing down on the hall table, scattering the pile of mail she's ignored for a week. She raises the umbrella and brings it down again.

"Goddamn you!"

Electricity courses through her limbs. Still clutching the umbrella, she strides into the living room and up the stairs. She flings open the door to their bedroom, crosses to the far side of the bed—Miles's side— and swings the umbrella across the night table, sending books and all his other crap flying. The tip of the umbrella catches in the drapes. Jackie gives it a yank, then lets it fall to the floor. She storms out of the room, kicking a tissue box and an alarm clock out of her way.

"Goddamn you, Miles!"

In the hallway, she pauses, panting. She's wearing her coat, her boots, her scarf. Sweat breaks out on her back, on the nape of her neck. She unwraps the scarf, takes off the coat. The white-hot energy is gone, burned through. Her legs wobble as she returns downstairs and to the front door, where she pulls off her boots, abandoning them among the mail.

She thinks of Antonio for the first time. Her eyes go to his bedroom door, which is closed. If he were home, he'd have heard her and come out. Something small to be thankful for.

Jackie hangs up her coat and picks up the mail. As she's stacking it on the table, the specter of Harlan's face appears before her, grinning at her over her husband's shoulder. Jackie holds on to the coatrack to stop herself from getting in her car, driving over to his house, and burning the goddamn place to the ground. She wants to do this with every cell in her body. She wants to destroy him. If she thought she could get away with it, she would.

———

Jackie binge-watches *House of Cards* and, when she's dizzy with hunger, scrounges for what she can eat without effort: crackers, olives, the ends of cheese, more crackers. She glances out the window to assess the time of day, drinks a bottle of wine. Antonio comes, Antonio goes. She barely talks to him, unwilling to delve into anything meaningful and equally unwilling to pretend nothing is wrong. He doesn't press her. Avoidance is his strategy, too.

She falls asleep, wakes, watches TV. The day passes, and the night, time slipping under her feet like a treadmill.

It is Christmas Eve morning. Not that she gives a shit.

Grace might call in advance of Christmas morning, and Jackie would not want to worry her, so she turns on her phone. Jackie is supposed to be there tomorrow, although it seems unfathomable that she would be able to accomplish everything necessary, mentally and physically, to arrive in another town to celebrate anything. So much excitement and joy. So many smiling, cheerful people. Impossible that seven people she is related to could be so cheerful. (She is not counting her mother.)

Jackie is out of crackers. The house is close, and the air, which she had not noticed at all, now feels toxic. The furniture, the windows, the walls, appear coated in film. She is coated in film. She drags herself to the shower, runs it scalding. When she is clean and dry, she rummages for a clean pair of jeans, a T-shirt, a sweater.

The shower has exhausted her, the hot water and steam have melted her tendons. She stumbles as she pulls on socks, slips on her winter boots. It's cold out, she reminds herself. Winter. Christmas.

Her coat is by the door, her keys, her wallet. The frigid air slams her in the face. The feeling of it is exquisite. She thinks of rowing, long pulls of the oars, again and again, until her thighs bite in pain, but the thought holds for only a second. The river. Jeff.

Her hair is damp and she has no hat. She pulls up her hood and walks to the shops. She wants the bakery, but even as a possibility, it is too reminiscent of happiness. She desires only the cold air, the shock of it, and something that isn't crackers and opts for the corner grocery store, which contains the miracle of having everything despite its size.

This miracle she can manage.

At home again, her phone warbles. Miles.

By the fifth ring, Jackie realizes she can't avoid him forever. Well, she could avoid him forever, but she has things she wants to say, and questions she wants answered.

"Hi, Jackie." His voice breaks. "I'm so sorry. I—"

"Let's not start with that, okay?"

"Okay, you're right."

"Where are you?"

"At the Courtyard on State Street."

Not at Harlan's? It doesn't matter to her one way or the other. The damage is done. Jackie pictures the hotel room, the drab furnishings, the patterned carpet, the reminder cards on every surface, the windows that don't open. She does not feel sorry for him.

"What happened with the police?" She keeps her questions neutral. There is no point in asking if he did it.

"They asked a lot of questions but didn't charge me with anything. My lawyer—Rory McMaster, the guy I used for Antonio—says they can't build a murder case with zero evidence." He pauses. "They kept asking me about the boathouse."

The mention of their shared activity, the one that brought them together, stops the conversation. The silence enlarges until it compresses the air around Jackie and she struggles to breathe. She gasps, half filling her lungs, then coughs.

"Jackie? Are you all right?"

The weight of her losses, the extent of her foolishness and gullibility, hits her once more. The rickety scaffolding from which she launched her feeble attempt at a full life has collapsed. No, she is very much the opposite of all right, and Miles damn well knows it.

Miles says, "You don't really think I could do that, do you? To your friend?"

His naked presumption pulls her upright, as if she has an obligation to consider him in a good light, to be fair with him. "You know what, Miles? I honestly don't know who the hell you are or what you're capable of."

"Darling." His voice is pillow-talk soft. "I know you're angry, but can we do this in person? Just talk?"

"Fuck off, Miles."

She punches her screen with her finger and ends the call.

How is it possible to feel furious and devastated at the same time? Oh, and humiliated and heartbroken and gullible, too. With so much emotion coursing through her veins—her cortisol levels must be through the roof—it's like she doesn't have skin or muscle, just nerve ends and neurons and hormones, pure emotional juice.

In the bathroom she splashes her face with cold water. She avoids scrutinizing herself in the mirror, hurriedly pulls her hair into a pony-tail, then, desperate to burn off energy, scrubs the kitchen counters even though they aren't dirty. If she keeps busy, she won't implode.

The kitchen is as antiseptic as an operating room when the doorbell rings. She wipes her hands as she goes to the door, checks the door cam.

Miles.

She yanks open the door. "Why are you here?"

"To talk. Can we please talk?"

Jackie turns away without answering, leaving the door open. Why not talk to him? She does have questions, although she can't guarantee she won't pummel him before he answers. At least he didn't just waltz in as if he weren't a cheating bastard who destroyed their marriage. It's the little things, she thinks, as she dumps the towel on the kitchen counter, punch-drunk on adrenaline and grief.

Miles stops at the end of the hallway. He looks terrible—bags under his eyes, lines around his mouth that age him ten years, a sadness in his eyes she's never seen.

Good.

Jackie moves into the living room, keeping her distance. "Antonio's in his room if you want to say hello." She knows her casualness is cruel and doesn't care.

Miles follows her, shucking off his coat on the way. "I texted him before I left the hotel, saying I'd take him out to eat in a while."

Jackie picks up the throw from the couch and folds it to have some-thing to do with her hands. It's as though Miles doesn't belong in this house already, like he's a guest. Their marriage is a fresh corpse he steps over with exaggerated politeness, not looking down.

She sits, the tension in her limbs now apparent. Her neck is encased in a steel collar, and her heartbeat is kicking up.

Hello, anger. Welcome back.

Miles lowers himself into the chair across from her. He looks at her, and she meets his gaze. A long moment ticks by, and Jackie has the sensation of viewing the two of them from above, with the marriage corpse between them.

He leans forward. "I'm so sorry, Jackie." He waits for her to speak, then continues. "I'm sorry about your friend. I had nothing to do with his death. You know that, don't you?"

Jackie is surprised to hear herself speak; the voice seems to come from elsewhere. "Many things I was certain of are apparently false."

Miles winces. "I know. I get it. But I didn't kill anyone."

She has felt the truth of this since she heard of Jeff's death, but she doesn't trust her judgment anymore. Change of subject. "Tell me about the men."

He pulls back, as if she struck him, but then nods and resettles in the chair, resigned. He had to have thought of what to say. "I've struggled with it, really struggled. I guess you'd call it denial." He's been studying his shoes, but glances at her briefly. "I had an affair with a man when I was married before. Beatrice and I tried to work through it, but failed."

"Antonio knew."

Miles sighs and spreads his hands. "She was adamant about being open with him. I wasn't so sure."

Jackie imagines Antonio as a young teen, learning about his father's sexuality, the implications for his parents' marriage. And here he is again. She wonders if she and Antonio might have become closer if this secret hadn't been wedged between them.

Miles is watching her. "I know what a mess I made. Believe me, I know."

"What about since then?"

"Rarely. Because of my denial. Because of my job."

His job? It hasn't occurred to her, she hasn't had time to think that far, but Miles is probably right that young football players and their families might not put their trust in a gay man as readily as one married to a woman. "Is that why you proposed to me?"

"What? No, Jackie. Of course not." She has no faith in his denial. He leans toward her, his elbows on his knees, clasps his hands. His eyes are pleading. "I haven't had an affair since I've been with you. Never." His voice breaks. "Not until . . ."

Jackie's throat closes. He can't even say Harlan's name.

"Please believe me." He searches her face, then gives up. "Why did you come to Harlan's, anyway? He said he had no idea."

Jackie shakes her head at Harlan's duplicity, the layers of it. "He sent me a text, Miles. He wanted me there. He staged the whole thing. Why else send me a text, saying you were in a bad state, saying I should come?"

Miles looks incredulous, and his expression reminds her of Nasira's when Jackie tried to convince her of Harlan's ulterior motive. Sure, it's not easy to accept that you're a pawn, and Harlan is so convincing, so slippery. But Jackie is weary of being the one who now sees through his facade, the one whose job it is to open everyone's eyes. Let Miles figure it out himself. "When did it start with Harlan?"

"Recently, as in a couple of weeks ago. I'm telling you, it was like he suddenly noticed me, like a sign lit up on my forehead that said, 'Men Wanted.'" He shakes his head in disbelief. "I was so fucking helpless. So fucking helpless." He swipes at his eyes with the back of his hand. "I'm truly sorry." His shoulders heave as he tries to hold himself together.

Jackie cannot bear to witness this, and yet her anger and pain won't allow her to go to him. That her best feelings toward him should be thwarted by his transgression makes her anger hotter, but the impulse to comfort him is still there.

She gets up. "Do you want something to drink?"

"Yes. Please."

"I've got coffee."

"Okay. Coffee."

In the kitchen, twenty feet distant from her husband, Jackie forces herself to take deep breaths. She prepares their coffees—how many times has she executed this small domestic routine?—and turns over what Miles has shared. Her stomach sours at the thought of him with someone else, and her mind skitters away from the details. Being held by someone else, wanting them, giving to them, that's where the knife goes in.

And Harlan. Not just some other man. Harlan. She knows all too well what it is like when he fixes you in his sights. You freeze, as prey do, forgetting even to cry out in surrender. She and Miles share this now.

Jackie returns to the living room and hands Miles his mug.

"Thanks."

The way he takes the mug, the familiarity of the movement, the cadence of his voice over that one word. She resents knowing how soft his fine blond hair is, the way his dimples appear when he's delighted, the weight of his hand in hers. She moves away, bends a leg under herself, and sits, cradling her mug in her hands. "Have you heard from Harlan?"

"No. Not since Friday."

"The police must've interviewed him."

"I assume so, since I was at his house when Jeff died."

Jackie sets down her glass. Again she considers telling Miles everything she suspects about Harlan, the whole theory. But she doesn't have the energy to lay it all out, try to convince him, but she can at least warn him. Miles might be more than a pawn in Harlan's scheme; he might be a target. "I know you didn't believe me when I said Harlan was acting strange, but you should think about it now, think about how he might not be acting in your best interests. Who knows what the police know about Jeff's death that we don't? Who knows what Harlan said to the police? This is serious, Miles, more serious than an affair." Miles is doubtful, but Jackie presses on. "Tell me what happened that night, what you told the police."

"It's pretty simple. I went to his house from the airport, with an Uber. I got there about four thirty." He drops his gaze. "We had drinks, several, and . . . got involved. I don't know exactly when, but at some point Harlan said he was going downstairs to his office to work. I fell asleep."

Jackie pushes away the image of her husband sleeping peacefully in a tangle of sheets on Harlan's bed. "Then what?"

"Antonio called at around half past eleven. Then I called you."

"Where was Harlan?"

"There, asleep. I mean, he woke up when Antonio called."

"So he could've been anywhere, then."

"I suppose so."

"You know what I'm worried about? The possibility that Harlan told the cops he couldn't account for where you were between whenever you said you went to sleep and eleven thirty. You could've left without him knowing."

"I don't have a key."

"You could've left the front door unlocked or taken a key. You could've gone in and out a million ways."

Miles scowls. "What are you saying? I thought you believed me."

"I'm trying to believe you, Miles, but it's hard." She wields her doubt as a weapon, but does not own it. "You did just deceive me." Miles closes his eyes, as if to hide from her, as a child would. "Anyway, it's the police you have to convince. And I doubt your friend Harlan is going to help you with that."

Miles's expression is skeptical as he reaches for his mug. The cuff of his shirt slips back, exposing his allergy and fitness bracelet. He never removes it. Jackie's thoughts spark.

She gets up and places her mug in the kitchen sink, eager for Miles to leave. "Antonio's probably hungry."

Miles follows her partway into the kitchen and shoves his hands in his pockets. "Thanks, Jackie."

She notes he did not call her "darling" or "beautiful" as he has always done. She misses it already, and the ache in her chest expands. "Thanks for what?"

"For not being as angry as you have every right to be."

"I could get angry, and I probably will be again soon. But right now I'm sad, and that's a lot harder."

His face falls. "Can I hold you?"

"No."

He stands there, unwilling to give up.

"Go out with Antonio, Miles. I'm sure he's worried about you."

"Okay, Jackie. I will." He looks at her a moment longer, then walks down the hall to knock on Antonio's door.

———

After they leave, Jackie retrieves her laptop from her computer bag and opens it on the kitchen counter. She finds the MedFit page and logs in. Before she gave Miles the bracelet, she set up the account for him so he could start using it immediately. He appreciates technology but prefers his experience to be turnkey.

Jackie hasn't been on the site since she established the account, so it takes her a few clicks to navigate to the fitness data and find the right date: December 22. She sets the time frame for 3:00 p.m. to 2:00 a.m. and selects the graph icon. A line graph appears. The heart rate line is red, the activity line blue. Jackie follows the blue line with her cursor, evaluating whether it corresponds to what Miles told her about that evening. From four to four thirty-five, when Miles said he was in an Uber, the activity is near zero. For the next two hours, it undulates between zero and low activity, consistent with having drinks with Harlan, moving about the house, probably going out to the patio for a smoke. At about six thirty, the pattern changes abruptly; the heart rate line shoots up like a flare, and the activity line ratchets higher.

Jackie's stomach clenches. She slams the laptop closed and paces from the kitchen to the living room and back again. She can't bear to examine the data anymore—it's torture—and why should she care whether she can corroborate Miles's story? Jeff is dead. Her marriage is over. What power does the truth hold when her world is in ruins?

She pours herself a glass of water and drains it. She stares at her laptop as if it is rigged to explode.

It's not just about Miles, she tells herself. It's about Jeff.

It's about Harlan.

Jackie takes several deep breaths and opens the laptop. The screen lights up, and she follows the timeline past the period during which Miles and Harlan were presumably having sex. The red line drops down to eighty, seventy, sixty-five beats per minute. The blue activity line falls to zero.

At 8:00 p.m. Miles was asleep. And he stayed that way until eleven thirty, exactly when he said Antonio called him.

Everything he told her is corroborated. Because he never left Harlan's house, he had nothing to do with Jeff's death.

Jackie moves to the window overlooking the backyard. Wet clods of leaves cover the central path, huddle under shrubs. Bare tree branches twitch in the wind. Above, clouds skitter across the dull sky. Stress has left ragged snippets of thought clogging her reasoning, but as she absorbs this barren scene, her mind clears, a patch of blue, and she remembers saying goodbye to Jeff, getting in her car. She remembers the figure.

Was it Harlan? He would've seen Jeff hold her. Kiss her.

Leave.

He could have followed Jeff, killed him, tossed him in the river. Returned home.

Slipped into bed.

A chill starts on the back of her neck and spreads down her spine. Jackie turns from the window and goes to the back door to check the dead bolt, then to the front to do the same, and checks the door cam.

What is she doing? This is madness, the idea that Harlan could have murdered Jeff. Harlan might be more controlling and vindictive than Jackie could have imagined, but murder is an order of magnitude more serious than inciting her jealousy, tampering with her data, or even seducing her husband. She was right to warn Nasira and Miles, but the idea that Harlan, a man she dated for five years, would attack and kill Jeff because of a kiss strains the bounds of credulity.

Stick with the facts, Jackie.

She retrieves her phone from the kitchen counter, scrolls to find Detective Cash's number. She'll let him know about the MedFit data, but there's no point in telling him about a shadow.

CHAPTER 28

Four o'clock and still Christmas Eve. Detective Cash didn't pick up when Jackie called, so she left a message about the MedFit data and texted him a screenshot of the graph.

Jackie opens a bottle of red—a very good rioja she and Miles had been saving for the holidays. It *is* the holidays, so why the hell not? She swirls her glass, a concession to lacking the energy to decant it, and breathes it in. Earth and berries—blackberries, maybe. And alcohol, that's the main thing. She takes a sip. It's so damn good.

Too anxious to sit, she goes to the window. The light is draining from the sky, and indigo shadows pool in the corners, under trees. A flash of red in the shrub below the window snags her attention. A cardinal. It's only three feet from her, and she can discern each overlapping feather, the perfectly drawn black mask encircling a shining black eye. Tears flood her eyes.

Jackie raises her glass to her lips, and the cardinal flies off.

Her phone vibrates on the counter. Jackie thinks it might be her sister. Grace called yesterday and left a message about plans for Christmas day, but Jackie couldn't imagine relating the news about Miles and Harlan, about Jeff, over the phone. Not to Grace.

Jackie crosses the room, reads the notification on her phone screen. Nasira. Apprehension coils inside her; if it's bad news, she can't cope with it.

"Hi, Nasira."

"Hi, Jackie. Am I disturbing you?"

"Not at all. Is everything all right?"

A pause. "Yeah. No." Another pause. "I was just thinking about you."

"That's kind of you."

"Thought I'd check in. You probably have plans—friends or whatever."

Jackie regards the wine bottle on the counter. "Only if you count my good buddy rioja." Nasira laughs. "Christmas is always at my sister's in Staunton, but Christmas Eve, Miles and I, we, I mean, I—" She swallows around the lump in her throat. "Definitely no plans. None whatsoever."

"In that case, do you want to come over? Because it's a party over here." Her voice is strained with manufactured cheer.

Tears clog Jackie's throat. One kind gesture and she's unglued. "I'd love to. I'll bring rioja and another friend of his."

"Perfect. I'm at 645 Randall, first floor."

Jackie cringes as she recalls the countless times she drove by the place. "See you soon."

"Great." Nasira's voice drops. "You'll get through this, Jackie."

What choice do I have? "Thanks, Nasira."

Jackie pockets her phone, corks the wine, puts it in a wine carrier with another bottle, then fills a tote bag with an assortment of finger food: cheese, olives, artichoke hearts, chocolate. She contemplates changing into something more festive than the pilled navy sweater she has on, but worries her burst of energy might not last. The thunderhead of grief looming overhead will follow her to Nasira's house, she is certain, but if she pauses here, where Miles's presence is palpable, the cloud will envelop and suffocate her.

As she zips up her jacket, her phone trembles in her pocket. She pulls it out, figuring it's Nasira or her sister, and is surprised to see it's Detective Cash. "Hello?"

"I'm sorry to trouble you, Dr. Strelitz."

"It's okay. You got my message?"

"Yes, and it's useful information for us."

"I thought it might be."

"And I appreciate you sharing it."

"Sure." The tenor of the conversation feels surreal. They are talking about exonerating evidence in a murder case involving her husband and her ex-boyfriend, but judging by the tone, they could be swapping turkey roasting tips.

A rustling sound, like he's moving papers. "I also wanted to tell you that unless something changes, we no longer consider you a suspect. And before you ask, I can't say why just yet."

"Oh, that's good news." The knowledge of her own innocence had partially shielded her from anxiety over being a suspect. Now she's relieved. After all, people go down for crimes they don't commit. "Thanks for telling me." She catches her reflection in the mirror over the entry table and tucks her hair inside her coat collar. "Well, merry Christmas, Detective Cash. If you're celebrating."

"Aaron."

"Aaron. But then it's Jackie."

He laughs softly, an easy, rolling laugh. "Okay, Jackie, merry Christmas." She's about to end the call when he speaks again. "One last thing. I could be wrong, but I get the feeling you're holding back on telling me something."

Given how little they've spoken, this intuition surprises her. She's tempted to deny it, but the truth will, at worst, embarrass her. At this point, that doesn't even rate. "Nothing factual, nothing you'd consider evidence, or that would make sense to anyone else. It barely makes sense to me."

"Well, I'd like to hear about it. You never know. Call me next week and we'll set a time."

"Sure. I'm around."

"Great. Try to have a nice Christmas, Jackie."

"I will. You too."

———

Nasira lets Jackie in, and they share an embrace limited by the bags Jackie is carrying. Her postdoc is wearing sweatpants and a plaid flannel shirt, and Jackie is glad she didn't change.

Nasira relieves Jackie of the tote bag. "I'm glad you're here. I was worried you wouldn't come." The vulnerability in her expression makes her seem younger than she is, almost childlike. Although what Jackie herself is going through is momentous, Nasira is suffering under the weight of her own troubles. It's a mistake, Jackie thinks, to compare your interior world with someone else's exterior.

"I need a friend, too."

Nasira smiles, her eyes shining. "Well, welcome to my very humble home."

She leads the way through the living room to the galley kitchen, which opens onto it. The place is a perfect reflection of its tenant: elegant and enigmatic. It isn't clear whether the minimalistic styling is due to lack of time to decorate or a preferred look. Either way, Nasira seems to have few belongings, but what she has is carefully chosen. The living room is furnished with only a long saddle-brown leather ottoman, two red sling-back chairs, and a deep-pile oatmeal rug begging for bare feet. The walls are bare except for a large hanging, a mosaic of richly colored fabrics, mostly in blue, green, and teal, embellished with beads and sequins.

Nasira follows Jackie's gaze. "It's made of wedding saris."

"Stunning." Jackie unpacks the wine carrier. "But saris are not your culture, right?"

"No, they aren't. I got it on eBay."

Jackie shows Nasira the opened bottle. "Okay to start with this? I can vouch for it."

"Looks delicious." She transfers wineglasses from the other counter, and Jackie fills them. The women raise their glasses.

Jackie says, "What do we toast? Do you celebrate Christmas?"

"My family is Muslim, not extremely devout, but certainly more than I am—hence the wine." Nasira pauses. "Let's forget all that for now, anyway."

Jackie nods and touches her glass to Nasira's. "Cheers, then."

Nasira smiles. "Cheers." They sip the wine. "Wow, this is tasty."

While Nasira retrieves food from the refrigerator, Jackie wanders through an arched opening into the dining area, which has windows on two sides and a set of French doors. The roller shades are drawn on the windows, and a white linen curtain covers the doors. Jackie notices the double dead bolts and remembers this is where the burglar entered— Harlan, if her hunch is correct. She'll mention it to Detective Cash when she sees him, along with all her other suspicions.

Nasira says, "Mind if I put out your food with what I've got?"

"Go ahead. Let me help you." She crosses the room and stops to inspect a photo on a small side table. A younger Nasira, perhaps sixteen, standing beside a handsome man a head taller and several years older. The man has his arm across Nasira's shoulders, and they are tipping their heads together. The family resemblance is strong.

Nasira enters the dining room. "I've got a platter in here some-where—" She spots Jackie viewing the photo.

"I didn't mean to snoop," Jackie says.

Nasira is still. "It's okay. That's Ramal, my brother. He died eight years ago, in Syria."

"Oh, I'm so sorry."

She stares at the far window, at the blank shade. "The war had only just started. There was no way to know the danger. He was on his way to class at the university when the artillery fire started."

Nasira stands in profile, utterly fragile in that moment, an exquisite, crazed piece of glass. One misplaced touch and she will shatter.

The pain we carry, Jackie thinks. *Everything we do not say, everything we bury deep, shapes and controls us, in the best and the worst ways.*

She reaches out, places her fingertips on Nasira's arm. "That's so terrible, Nasira. You must miss him."

"I do. For my family, the loss is so large, sometimes it seems like all we have." Nasira meets Jackie's gaze, and Jackie sees how hollowed out her cheeks are, how thin she's become. "I don't mean to be morose."

"You're not. Don't worry." Jackie tips her head toward the food on the counter. "We both should eat. I can't remember my last decent meal."

In the kitchen, Nasira hands Jackie a plate. "I made the hummus, but everything else is from Whole Foods."

"I forgive you."

They fill their plates, carry them to the living room, and chat about food—favorite appetizers, Trader Joe's finds, and their most impressive ten-minute meals. Jackie laughs, and the sound surprises her. They finish the wine, and Jackie makes a trip to the kitchen to open another. With the shades drawn against the world, she feels safer and more whole than she has in too long. Maybe she should ask Nasira if she can sleep on the fuzzy rug tonight—or forever.

Jackie refills their glasses, noting that color has returned to Nasira's cheeks.

Nasira leans back in the sling chair and crosses her legs. "Can I ask what's going with the investigation into your friend's death? Or don't you want to talk about it?"

Jackie notes this is a back door into a conversation about Miles, and again she appreciates Nasira's delicacy. "There's not too much to report. I think I've helped exonerate Miles, though I'm not sure why I'm being so generous."

"Because you love him."

"Yes. Because of that." Whatever love is, it's hard to undo. She can't cleave off the part of herself that feels for Miles, despite her anger and humiliation. She relates the outlines of her conversation with Miles and her discovery of the MedFit data.

Nasira is rapt. "That's incredible. I mean, it must've been excruciating to review it, but how lucky for Miles."

"I'm not sure either of us feels lucky quite yet." Jackie takes a long sip of her wine, and a thought drops. "I just realized I haven't told him about it yet. About the MedFit data. I told the detective, but not Miles."

"Do you want to call him?"

"I really should." Jackie looks at Nasira, grateful to have her company this evening, to be invited into her home. With everything that's transpired with Miles, Harlan, Antonio, and Jeff, Nasira's companionship is a refuge. "Listen, I have an idea. How about you come to my sister's tomorrow morning? I guarantee it will be a distraction."

"That's so kind, but it's your family time. I wouldn't want to intrude."

Jackie waves her hand. "We're not like that, I promise." She pushes herself to standing. "I'm going to call Miles before I'm completely trashed, then let Grace know you're coming. I haven't told her about Miles—I couldn't face it—so this gives me the push I need."

Nasira smiles and points across the room. "My bedroom's through that door if you want some privacy."

"I'll just be a minute. I've been eyeing that chocolate torte."

———

Her call to Miles goes directly to voice mail. It's just after seven, so he's probably in the middle of dinner with Antonio. She leaves him a message, telling him about the MedFit data and suggesting that if he needs to pick up some things, anytime between eight and four tomorrow would work. She ends the call, impressed with how decent and businesslike she sounded, wondering how long it can possibly last.

She calls Grace.

"Hey, Jacks! Hold on a sec while I detach this parasite." Muffled words between Grace and Hector, and a short squawk of protest from, Jackie assumes, Edith. A door closes. "I'm here." She exhales loudly. "You should call more often so I can skip out like this."

"I know. I'm sorry I didn't call you back."

"You sound weird."

"I'm sorry."

"Stop saying sorry and tell me what's up. You're coming tomorrow, right?"

"Wouldn't miss it." This simple statement is so deeply true that Jackie's throat closes. "Listen, Grace. Miles isn't coming."

"Is he sick? Oh, wait. *This* is why you sound weird?"

"Yes. I can't tell you about it, not over the phone. I promise I will tomorrow. But it's over with Miles." Jackie hasn't said it out loud before and winces at the stab of pain just below her sternum. The stab becomes an ache and lodges there.

"Oh, Jacks . . ."

"It's okay."

"I call bullshit."

Jackie nods. "Yeah, okay."

"Is it about kids? Is that it?"

"I can't do this now. I really can't. It's too raw."

"Aw, Jacks. I'm hugging you right now. You know I am."

Jackie wipes the tears from her cheeks. "I do know."

"No Antonio, then? He's with Miles, I'm guessing."

"That's right." Jackie assumes they'll be together, but in truth, she doesn't know. Miles and Antonio were supposed to go skiing in Vermont for a few days before New Year's, so maybe they'll head up there early. As accustomed as she is to being privy to their plans, she can't spare the energy to consider anything other than simply getting to Staunton tomorrow.

Grace's voice is soft. "You still there?"

"Yeah."

"I love you so much."

"I love you, too." Jackie pulls the phone from her ear, wipes the screen dry with her sleeve. "Is it okay if I bring a friend?"

"A *guy*?"

Jackie laughs, then hiccups. "No. My postdoc, Nasira."

"You talked to her!"

"I did. Is it okay if she comes?"

"Bring the whole damn lab. You know we don't care."

"We'll be there by ten. With pie." Only because she'd ordered them two weeks ago. Sweet Somethings might be the only thing standing between her and a complete breakdown.

"Promise to call me if you get more weird."

"Promise."

CHAPTER 29

Jackie is up before the sun. Her sleep was punctuated by disturbing dreams of being chased by Harlan, who, as he gained ground on her, turned out to be Miles. She never puts much stock in dreams, but the emotions revealed in them are undeniable, and long before the sky brightens, she relinquishes the bed and puts her faith in coffee. She makes it strong.

The house is quiet, and because it is Christmas and she will spend the day with family, she chooses to feel peace in this morning rather than loneliness or despair. She cannot guarantee she can sustain this cognitive bootstrapping—it might not last the hour—but here it is.

An hour and a half remain before she is due to pick up Nasira. She drinks her coffee, checks her phone. No messages from Miles. The weather app is confident the day will break dry and bright. That's all she needs to know.

Upstairs in the bathroom, she clips and files her nails, cleans up her eyebrows, and applies a face mask. Nothing says you have your shit together like small pores. While the emulsion is cinching her skin, she chooses her outfit. Something festive but not gaudy. No black. She settles on a wine-red sweaterdress and brown boots. As she's carrying them out, her eye lands on the green coat she wore at Thanksgiving, the one Miles loves on her, and the bottom falls out of her stomach. Jackie pushes the coat aside and grabs a black wool one, throws the coat and the dress on the bed, and exchanges the brown boots for black ones. Underwear, bra, tights, and a white, gold, and dark-red plaid scarf.

She tosses it all on the bed and sits, exhausted.

Shower. Do it.

Forty minutes later, Jackie looks a hundred percent better than she feels. The effort hasn't made her feel worse, which she counts as a win. She makes scrambled eggs, drinks more coffee, cleans up, places the pies in a tote bag. She ordered the gifts for her family shortly after Thanksgiving and had them shipped to her sister's directly. Her presents for Miles and Antonio are in a bag at the foot of the bed. If Miles comes today to collect some belongings, he'll see them. She sends Antonio a text, wishing him a merry Christmas, covering her sadness and regret with a long string of holiday emojis.

As she prepares to leave the house, loneliness descends. It may be waiting for her when she returns, but Jackie doesn't dwell on it now.

It's Christmas.

———

By noon, the five-year-old twins, Maria and Michael, have finally given up on arguing over whose presents are superior and wander into the den. Jackie and Nasira have erected a small tepee meant, ideally, for all the children to share.

Jackie notes their bleary-eyed expressions. She points inside at the comforter folded across the floor, and the stack of books in the center. "If you go in now and are quiet, I'll bet you can have it to yourselves for a long time."

The twins exchange a glance and crawl inside.

Maria sticks her head out. "Zeera, read to us?"

Jackie smiles at Nasira. "You're an instant hit."

"They are the cutest." Nasira crouches at the tepee opening. "Scoot over, you guys."

Jackie leaves the door ajar and proceeds to the living room, where Daniel and his father are lying side by side on the floor, puzzling over directions for a robot kit.

Jackie's mother, Cheryl, is moving around the room, stuffing wrapping paper and ribbon into a trash bag. "Do we save gift bags?"

"Seems a shame not to," Jackie says.

"Yup." Grace appears beside her. "We save them, and put them away somewhere clever, and discover them after everything is wrapped. So definitely!" She scans the room, the kitchen. "Missing two, by my count."

"Nasira's reading to them in the tepee," Jackie says.

"Postdocing is overrated. She stays right here." Grace steps around the couch. "Hector, the littles are fast asleep. Think Jacks and I can sneak out for bit?"

"Sure. We're good here."

Cheryl cinches the bag shut. "Do you girls mind if I join you?"

Jackie didn't want to talk about Miles in front of the children and, therefore, had only told Cheryl what she had told her sister over the phone the night before—the marriage was over. She can't blame her mother for wanting in on the conversation—out of concern or curiosity or both—but right now Jackie would rather talk only to Grace. After all, it was only three days ago that she saw Miles with Harlan, and her emotions are still in tatters. That said, she can't tell her mother to stay behind.

"Of course not," Jackie says. "I'll just make sure Nasira is happy where she is."

They set out along an old logging road that threads through the woods bordering the backyard. The leaf litter under their feet has thawed and frozen a few times and no longer rustles as they tread on it. Low clouds rest on the distant hills, softening the air.

Since last night, Jackie has struggled over what to say to Grace and how long a version to tell. The threads of the story are tangled, and the ends are loose. Having Cheryl along adds another layer of complexity. Her marriage, she decides, is most relevant, and most painful, so she starts there.

"Three days ago, I found out that Miles has been sleeping with Harlan."

Her mother and her sister stop in their tracks.

"Are you sure?" Cheryl asks.

"Yes. No one's disputing it." Jackie waits for her mother to comment that this is what happens when husbands travel too much, or some variant of I told you so, but she is silent, her brow knitted.

Grace pulls Jackie into a hug and rocks her back and forth, then holds her at arm's length and scrutinizes her. "Your face says there's more—more than what you told me last week."

"A lot more, unfortunately." Jackie splays her hands. "It's so complicated and distressing, I don't know where to begin."

"I'm so sorry, Jacqueline." Her mother sighs, and Jackie braces herself for the inevitable anti-male diatribe. Weirdly, part of her welcomes the predictability of it. Miles's infidelity is the letdown she was raised to expect. Cheryl shakes her head. "And with Harlan. Of all people. How terribly disappointing for you, dear, but try not to take it personally. I imagine Miles is suffering as well. Martin tells me it's helpful to take the other person's perspective." She brushes a lock of hair off her forehead with a gloved finger. "I've been practicing—not too strenuously, mind you—but I do see the benefit."

Jackie sends Grace a surreptitious look of astonishment.

Cheryl isn't finished. "And you don't have to tell us the rest if it's too painful right now, and I imagine it is." Her mother squeezes her shoulder. "Why don't we just walk? When you're ready, we're here to listen." She sets off.

Grace's eyes are huge. "Well, I can't explain that, but I want to hear everything as soon as possible. Right now works."

Jackie glances around her at the stiff gray tree trunks, the few dead leaves clinging to the otherwise-bare branches. She swallows, and an ache expands in her chest. "Remember Jeff? Jeff Toshack?"

CHAPTER 30

New Year's Day, snow falls, impossibly large flakes that take their time finding a place to land—on their edges it seems—delicate stacks of white lace piled on every surface. At a brewpub near the police station, Jackie shares a window table with Detective Cash. They had arranged to meet right after Christmas, but he came down with the flu. He's back at work today, catching up despite the holiday.

Cash makes his way through his burger as he listens to her story, asking several times for background info, infill. Her delivery has become more practiced through repetition, but as far as her emotions are concerned, the protective scarring has hardly begun.

When she finishes, he promises to follow up with whoever is handling the break-in at Nasira's.

"Your observations are interesting, but none of the other incidents are criminal. We let the university deal with hacking issues unless they request help from us."

Jackie picks at her french fries. "That makes sense."

"I agree with you about the pattern, though," Cash says. "If this Crispin really did all of the things you think he did—even most of them—it points to an extreme need for control. That's a potentially dangerous pattern."

"Potentially dangerous? I get that he seems to be trying to control my life, and maybe has gone to extremes to punish me for leaving him, but he's never been violent."

Cash leans in, lowers his voice. "How do you know, Jackie? He seems to be pretty good at hiding things."

"That's true, but—"

"You're the psychologist. You tell me what happens when someone with off-the-charts control issues doesn't get what he wants."

Jackie knows the answer, and she knows the label Cash wants to apply to Harlan. Her mind had excluded it from conscious consideration because to consider it would mean it was possible. *Sociopath.* Goose bumps pinprick her neck and the backs of her arms. It's only a thought, a theory, but that is enough to cause an invisible membrane to close over her throat and mute her.

Cash acknowledges her realization with a nod. "Be careful, Jackie. It won't hurt to be careful."

Open your eyes.

———

After lunch, Jackie is on her front porch, stomping snow from her boots. She takes two steps inside to ditch her bag and retrieve the broom from the hall closet. Beginning with the porch steps, she sweeps away the snow, sending drifts to the left, then to the right. By the time she reaches the end of the walk, the steps are white again. She pauses to brush snow from her shoulders and blow on her bare hands. Six inches are forecast, a nearly debilitating amount for DC. She's delighted about the storm because her plan is to hibernate.

Jackie is sweeping her way back to the door when a car door closes on the street behind her.

"Jackie!"

Her breath freezes in her chest. Without turning, she hurries up the walk. She reaches the porch, puts the broom aside to free her hands.

"Jackie!"

She turns. Harlan is most of the way up the walk. Cash warned her not to confront him, but she doubts she can get inside before he reaches her. If he sees her fleeing, it might annoy or anger him. What is she going to do, run and hide every time she encounters him?

"What is it, Harlan? What do you want?"

He's at the foot of the steps, snow falling between them, each flake a moment of time. "You weren't running from me, were you? I just want to talk."

Harlan comes up the steps to stand in front of her, not quite at arm's length. Snowflakes are dissolving on his black wool coat. He brushes a gloved hand over his hair, wipes it on his coat. He tips his head, smiles. "Beautiful, isn't it?"

"Why are you here?"

"I came to say goodbye. The snow's a bit of a nuisance, but my plan is to leave for Madison in the morning."

"Madison?"

He grins. "It's been in the works for a while, but I didn't want Chen getting wind of it. Sorry to leave you on the outside."

Jackie struggles to assimilate this information, as welcome as it is. "Why now? Why didn't you just stay after your sabbatical?"

"I think you know why, Jackie."

It's hard for her to accept, but yes, she does know why. He came back because he was compelled to teach her a lesson. And now that the lesson has been delivered, he can leave, start again, and she is left to pick up the pieces of everything he shattered.

The supercilious smile on his face is infuriating. "Damn you, Harlan." She is dying to unleash a long string of invectives and accusations, but she's uncertain enough about him to quash the impulse. *Be smart, Jackie. Don't throw fuel on it.* Harlan is here for more than goodbye, and he'll get to it in his time. Meanwhile, she'll employ his tactic: deflect. "What about your students?"

"Don't worry, Jackie. I won't leave them in the lurch, not the useful ones anyway. And Madison's offer was quite generous." He slides a half step closer. She inches back. "Kind of you to be concerned."

"I'm not concerned for you in the least."

He makes a clucking noise and frowns, feigning hurt. "Before I go, I want to show you something." He unzips his coat, reaches into his chest pocket, and extracts a piece of paper. He holds it by its edges with gloved fingers, displaying it for her. Two images from a photo booth strip, black-and-white, worn at the edges.

Jeff and her.

She inhales sharply.

In the top photo, she and Jeff laugh. In the bottom one, they kiss. They are so young. So happy.

They had divided the strip. Her half was lost, God knows when.

Her fingers itch to grab the photo, to reclaim it, but the significance of Harlan possessing it sends ice through her veins and paralyzes her.

It can't be true. She cannot reconcile the information. Her thoughts dart away from each other, refusing order, logic. She stares at the photo, her mouth dry, and shifts her gaze to the fingers holding it, belonging to the man she devoted herself to, the man she slept with for five years. Sweat breaks out on her forehead, along her back. Harlan is confronting her with evidence, taunting her, because he knows, and now she does, too, that there is only one explanation for it. The truth of it is inescapable. And damning.

Everything she suspected is true. He followed Jeff that night, murdered him.

She looks up at Harlan, not bothering to hide her fear, her distress. He'd see right through it anyway. Her mind hunts for a course of action, a way out. If she pushes him hard with both hands, he might fall backward off the porch, giving her enough time to get inside, lock him out.

Too risky.

Be careful, Jackie. Be smart.

Her hands are shaking with nerves and with cold, and she slips them into her pockets. Her right hand finds her phone.

He smiles down at her. "Surprising, isn't it? That he kept this photo of the two of you?"

"It's more surprising that you have it." She's stalling. In her pocket, her finger finds the on button, presses it. She touches what she hopes is the Voice Memo icon, bottom right, then bottom center to start record-ing. If she's lucky. "Where did you get the photo, Harlan?"

"Where do you think? I was right to be suspicious of his motives; I read it in his body language the night you two had drinks at the hotel. Old friends, catching up." He laughs lightly. "I don't think so."

"So you followed us to the hotel."

"Anyone can have drinks there, Jackie. It's not a crime."

"But you followed us more than once, right?"

"You really ought to change your passwords, even for innocuous sites. It's simply not safe."

"Not with you around, apparently. So, what? You took his wallet. Is that a souvenir, too?"

"I'm insulted you'd think me so careless." He waves the photo. "I only have this because I wanted you to see it. He was stalking you, Jackie."

"I doubt it." But she wonders why Jeff would have that photo on him. Maybe before he left Seattle, when he thought he would see her, he dug it up. Maybe he meant to show it to her and changed his mind. What does it matter now that he's dead? She closes her eyes to quell her panic, then forces herself to look at Harlan again. He's less dangerous, she still believes, when she can hold him like that.

He presses on. "Twenty years is a long time to keep a photo, don't you think? Maybe that's what you wanted, too, Jackie. Maybe you knew things were coming to an end with Miles." He cocks his head, a raptor considering the rodent in its talons. "Maybe Jeffrey—or is it

Jeff?—represented your next step. How perfect! What is old is new again. Women like to build a bridge to a new happiness before the old bridge collapses. Is that what you were doing, Jackie? Preparing to move on?" He steps closer, reaches as if to stroke her hair, or strangle her.

She pulls away, steadies herself against the door behind her. The broom is within reach, but if she grabs it, she's escalating. Her eyes land on the doorbell. The camera. If her phone isn't recording their conversation, the camera will be storing video, at least in ten-second bursts. It's something. The realization steels her.

Jackie keeps her tone level. "I'm getting cold, Harlan. If you don't have anything else to show me, why don't you get going?"

His eyes widen; he's annoyed at being cut short. "I'm not surprised you haven't invited me inside, but I was sure you'd have more questions."

"Like what?"

"You're the curious one, Jackie."

"Okay, then. How did Jeff lose his wallet?"

He shrugs. "He probably dropped it. Promise me you won't go down to the towpath after dark. The lighting is inadequate." He sighs, returns the photo strip to his pocket, zips his coat. He spreads his arms. "I suppose a hug goodbye is out of the question?"

Jackie glares at him. It takes all the self-control she can muster not to slug him in the face. "Leave, Harlan."

For a moment he stands stock-still, and the light in his eyes turns to flint. Jackie braces herself for a blow, an attack. She keeps her eyes trained on him, her attention the only power she has left. She cannot breathe.

"Goodbye, Jackie." He descends the steps, strides down the walk.

She wills him to continue, to not change his mind. She's locked in place, breathing in shallow gasps through her mouth, her body rigid.

He reaches the sidewalk, clicks his car open. His hand is on the door.

He turns to her. His posture, his expression, have softened, become human once again.

For one unbearably long moment, the distance between them telescopes in, and Jackie believes he is coming toward her, coming for her.

But he merely raises his hand.

She closes her eyes, hears the car door shut, the squeak of tires on snow.

He's gone.

———

Once inside, Jackie secures the door and pulls out her phone, her heart pounding. The Voice Memo app is open and the button is red.

"Got you, you bastard."

She stops the recording and leans against the door in relief. She calls Cash and relates the gist of the encounter.

He lets out a low whistle. "You sure you're okay?"

"Yes. I'm fine. Or I will be in a minute."

"I'm sending a car around to be sure."

"Okay, thanks."

"Jackie, if you can do it, send me the file now, the one from your phone and also the door cam. That way they're safe. I'll give them a quick review, then come over and take a statement."

"I'm sending it now." She finds the share button and sends it via text. "I've never accessed the camera's video before, so give me a sec." She clicks around the app, locates the link, enters the password. Her fingers are trembling, and she has to reenter it. Success. She presses send.

Seconds later, Cash says, "Got it. I'll see you in twenty."

Jackie makes coffee, spilling the grounds as she measures. She paces between the kitchen and living room, her mind scrolling through the conversation with Harlan and the indelible images of the last two weeks: Jeff walking away, Miles's texts, the police at her door, the boarding pass, the caution tape, Miles and Harlan. If only she could erase them all, delete the images permanently. But it doesn't work like that. She has to live with it, with her culpability. Harlan might be a sociopath, but she played her role, played into his hands. And not just in the last few months but from the moment she met him. What that says about her is something she cannot yet face, much less comprehend.

Cash arrives. They sit at the dining table, and he takes her statement. After, they listen to the recording and review the door-cam footage. Jackie's pulse beats in her throat as she watches Harlan's body language in the video; somehow, without the sound, he appears more threatening, as if his smooth voice were a syrup that rendered his behavior more palatable. She is more afraid for the woman in the video than she was for herself in the moment.

Jackie turns to Cash. "Is this enough to arrest him?"

He rubs his chin. "Probably not all by itself, but it's something. We'll definitely take a closer look at the security footage on campus, but either way, I think we've got enough to bring him in for a chat." He takes a sip of coffee. "When we interviewed him, he told us he was at home that night. On the recording he admits to stalking you, and he used the victim's name before you did, which he wouldn't have known unless he'd seen some ID or the victim introduced himself."

"I hadn't picked up that he said Jeff's name first."

"It's the sort of thing you get used to looking for. Even careful people, smart people, make mistakes."

"No kidding." Jackie shakes her head.

Cash studies her for a long moment. "You're not blaming yourself for any of this, are you?"

She studies her coffee mug. "I did a lot of foolish things, so yes. I was blind."

"Guys like this, they count on it." His voice drops a notch. "They count on you being human."

"In this instance," Jackie says, "I wish I'd been a little less human."

"Don't beat yourself up." Cash slips his notebook into his jacket pocket, pushes back his chair, stands. "It was a smart move to record him. Not many people could've pulled that off. And lucky for us it's admissible in DC."

Jackie's relief that she's helped implicate Harlan is mitigated by the knowledge that if she hadn't been with Jeff—hadn't been seen kissing him—he'd still be alive. Harlan might've been satisfied with the trail of destruction he'd already run through her life and left for Madison quietly.

At the door, the detective promises to keep her informed. "Lie low in the meantime. We'll ask him not to leave DC pending the investigation, which maybe isn't great news for you, but I'll keep the squad car prowling."

"Thanks."

It isn't quite three o'clock, but that doesn't stop Jackie from pouring herself a glass of red wine. Outside, the snow continues to fall, the flakes smaller now that the temperature is dropping. She is grateful for the storm; it insulates her. She moves to the living room, unsteady on her feet, and sits on the couch, placing the glass to the side. Pulling her knees to her chest, she hugs herself. A wave of nausea rolls through her. She closes her eyes, but all she sees in the darkness is Harlan, a smirk on his face, the photo of Jeff and her pinched in his fingers, as if snuffing them out.

She hugs her knees tighter as her chest constricts and a sob escapes her. Hearing the shape and size of her own pain opens a gate inside her, and she sobs, again and again, shoulders heaving, tears flowing. The full realization of Harlan's monstrous actions, his absolute ruthlessness, hits her. As soon as her crying eases and she catches her breath, the horrifying truth crashes into her again. Jackie buries her face between her arms and rocks. If only Miles were here to comfort her. His absence, the finality of it, ushers in a different pain, born not of fear but of heartbreak.

She loses track of time. Finally she lifts her head. Outside the windows, dusk is settling in. Snow falls thick and slow through the beam of a streetlight. She makes her way to the kitchen, washes her face, drinks two glasses of water, and retrieves her phone—out of habit. There is no one she wants to speak with, no news she wants to hear.

Her head is light, and she returns to the couch. Her mind spins, repeatedly turning over the same questions. How did she allow her life to unravel to this degree? Why didn't she see Harlan for who he is? And why, after having the sense to end their relationship, did she become enmeshed with him again? He preyed on her; she doesn't discount that, but neither does she excuse herself. Even after she glimpsed his dark side, she buried the experiences, and a man—a good man—is dead because of it. The path to forgiving herself, if there is one, will be long.

In her hand her phone vibrates. She reads the screen: a text from her mother.

Happy New Year, Jackie. You've had a tough time recently, so I hope you're starting 2019 taking care of yourself. I am! 🥬, 🍷 xo Mom

Jackie types: Not really, Mom. I'm blaming myself for a murder. Happy New Year!

She deletes it before she accidentally hits send and starts again: Happy New Year and good for you. Cheers! 🍷 ♥ J. After she sends the text, Jackie takes a drink from her untouched wineglass and considers her portion of the blame for Harlan's actions. Highly intelligent sociopaths like him are expert manipulators, skilled at hiding their true nature behind a facade of charm.

But Harlan did more than charm and deceive; he read her perfectly, deliberately placing himself in her blind spot. Everyone has blind spots—literal visual ones and conceptual ones. Jackie teaches about human perception, and the blind spot is one of her favorite examples of how the brain works. Inside each of your eyeballs is a layer of receptors called the retina. It captures light and sends signals to your brain, which creates a visual experience: you see. But there's a bare spot on each retina where the optic nerve attaches, leaving a hole in your vision, one for each eye. You're not aware of it because your brain guesses at the missing data and fills it in. A little white lie to keep things seamless.

Blind spots are one example of the guessing and filling in that go on routinely in the brain, all in the name of efficiency. The world is fairly predictable, so it makes sense for the brain to rely on expectations, to see what is usually there, and not bother to build the world from scratch every time you open your eyes. The object on the side of the highway appears to be a truck tire, not a dead body, because that's more likely. Most of the time, the truth doesn't matter.

Jackie sips her wine and considers the pitfalls, because shortcuts always have them. The system works well enough—except when it doesn't. Sometimes what you need to see most is sitting in that blind spot, and your brain guesses wrong. Dead wrong.

Because what you can't see, or what you refuse to see, can hurt you. Harlan tried to warn her, but she didn't heed him, and he reeled her in more often than he played her out. She would like to blame him, and she does, but it's not that simple. People share relationships, and whether they explode or dissolve or endure, the responsibility must be shared. Jackie can blame Miles for his infidelity, but not for the demise of their marriage. It had cracks from the start; he happened to be the one to fall through.

Jackie returns to the kitchen and refills her glass. The alcohol has smoothed out the emotional aftermath of her encounter with Harlan, at least for the moment, but she's still deeply worried about how the investigation will play out. She has confidence in Detective Cash, but doesn't underestimate Harlan's ability to slip out of the authorities' grasp and get away with murder. In her heart she knows her essential fear won't dissipate until Harlan is brought to justice, and by that she means punished. Whatever the ultimate burden of her culpability and her regret, it will never outweigh murder.

Harlan's Story

~

I went sailing with my father one day off Nantucket, just the two of us on a thirty-eight-foot sloop. My aunt Fossie was supposed to join us, and her preteen son, but he came down with the stomach flu the night before, so she stayed to care for him. My mother was expecting friends and had never been a keen sailor. She preferred lawn games and reading under an umbrella at the beach.

The weather was typical for mid-August: sweltering. My shirt was already sticking to my skin as I carried supplies to the dock. Over early coffee, my father had instructed me to ready the boat so he could simply step aboard and take the helm. I already knew that when we returned, it would be down to me to rinse the decks, stow the sails, do all the necessary chores. I was almost nineteen, soon to begin my sophomore year at Dartmouth, long past the age when I questioned the peccadilloes of my parents. When it suited me, I went along with them; otherwise I ignored them or stayed away.

The sound of my feet on the wooden deck, the weight of the warm air, the taste of salt on my lips: I remember all of it. The circumstances that led to this atypical father-son outing must have pinned my attention to these details before the day achieved its significance. As I removed the hatch cover and stowed the boards, I felt a sense of inevitability, the way legendary battles are foretold long before they occur. I didn't put stock in crystal ball nonsense then any more than I do today, but I won't deny the clarity and strength at my core that morning.

My father arrived around eight thirty, wearing a blue button-down rolled to the elbows, khaki shorts, and Top-Siders—the Cape summer uniform. The only item lacking was the sweater draped over his shoulders, but it was too hot for that. He added a Harvard baseball cap, which no self-respecting Boston Brahmin would ever do, but he couldn't stop himself from worshipping the symbols.

He stood holding his travel mug and made a cursory inspection from the dock. A true seaman. "Got everything organized?"

I nodded. We switched places—dealing with the lines was my job—and in a few moments we pulled away from the dock and motored out of Hither Creek. There wasn't much activity yet, just a couple of fishing boats and some kids running along a dock as we passed. My father waved at them, friendly, magnanimous person that he was, and pointed the boat out to sea, toward the bright line of the horizon.

I tossed him a life jacket and put on mine. Safety first.

He slipped his arms through but left it open. "Where should we head today, son?"

I hated being called that, being claimed and belittled at the same time. I added it to the thousands of casual insults my father had tossed at me over my lifetime, raising himself up by taking me down. The list of things my father resented about me was long. I was large, implying I was coarse; I was quiet, implying I was thoughtless or dull; and, worst, I had a detached poise, which my father wanted most and never possessed. It pissed him off that his son inherited the offhand elegance and ease of his wife and her family, something he got close enough to touch but never owned. He hated himself for wanting it so much, enough to tear off his humble Kansas skin that stank of cow shit. Being small-minded, he could not bear to see his son succeed—without try-ing!—where he failed so mightily. I had no sympathy. Why should I? My Nobel Prize–clutching father was pathetic.

I took a seat at the stern. "The weather's good, so no reason to stay in the sound."

"South, then?"

"South."

We tacked a few times, not paying much attention to exactly where we were going. It was just a sail. The summer had been unusually warm, and a haze had set up over the last couple of days. We could see maybe a half mile, which was plenty of notice for other boats and the occasional ship.

My father stood at the wheel, looking out to sea. There was just enough breeze to fill the sails, make a little chop. I had my feet on the rail, wondering if I ought to trim the jib.

"When do you need to declare your major, son?"

Here we go, I thought.

"Sometime this coming year." He knew the answer. He worked at a fucking university.

"We should talk about it some more. It's a big decision." He glanced over his shoulder at me. I had sunglasses on, so he wasn't getting much of read on me, not that it would've helped.

"It's not a big decision at all. For med school, pretty much any major works as long as you take the classes. Which I will."

My father gripped the wheel tighter and made a point of twisting most of the way around. It looked uncomfortable, but it's hard to assert your will on someone without facing them.

"Medical school. You know what I think about that."

"Yup." *But one more time. Please.*

"Doctors are mechanics." He threw a hand into the air. "Mechanics!"

"When your body needs repairs, a mechanic is handy."

He scowled. "Always with the smart-ass remark. There are plenty of doctors."

"Actually—"

"You have a real brain. A scientist's brain. Don't waste it applying what other people discover. Discover things yourself!"

I dropped my feet from the rail and sat up. "Want me to steer for a while?"

He wasn't expecting that. "This conversation isn't over. Remember who pays your tuition."

Mom.

I took the helm. My father sat where I'd been and stared at the water. I ignored him. Ten minutes or so later we tacked, after which he announced he was getting a beer. It wasn't quite eleven. He wasn't a big drinker, but he liked beer in the summer.

"Want one?"

"No thanks."

He emerged from below and set up on the bow, unbuttoning his shirt to get some sun. The hair on his chest was graying, and he had a gut, although it was smaller than two years ago when he had been diagnosed with a heart condition. I scanned around for boats and saw only one fishing boat. The haze usually lifted by that time of day, but if anything, the visibility was getting worse. I wondered if it might storm later.

I let him finish his beer.

"Dad. I have to go to the head. I'll just put it on autopilot for a sec."

He'd been lying down and lifted his head. "I can do it."

"Nah. I'll just be a sec."

Since the last tack, I'd decided on the fire extinguisher rather than a board from the hatch. Wood can be messy, and a fire extinguisher is easy to replace should that prove necessary. I went below and ducked to retrieve it from the side of the sink cabinet. I tried out different holds, but only for a few seconds. My hands were shaking a little, and it would only get worse.

I climbed up and surveyed the sea once more. No one. I didn't try to hide the extinguisher as I stepped onto the deck. I was counting on his astonishment and my size, and I had a little luck: his feet were pointing at the bow, so his head was right there. I tightened my grip on the rigging with my left hand and held the extinguisher by my side.

"Brought you another beer."

"Wh—" His eyes opened, and he registered that something was off. Perhaps he saw a red form, or that I was too close.

I swung the extinguisher into his skull.

"Oof." A cartoon sound. His skull had a dent in it. He rolled away from me, onto his side.

I swung it again, into the back of his head. The occipital lobe, seat of visual processing.

My father moaned a little.

I must've swung harder the second time, because blood started to spread across the deck. I didn't want a mess. I stood over him for a long minute, ready to hit him again. One leg bent a few degrees, but that was it.

"Who needs a mechanic now?" I shouted. That made me laugh.

The hard part was over. I crouched and leaned over the side to rinse the bottom of the extinguisher. I'd decide later whether to chuck it. Now I needed something to make him sink. I scanned around me. My eyes fell on the locker near the bow housing the sand anchor. I opened the hatch and hoisted the length of chain connected to the anchor on one end and a length of rope on the other. I judged the chain heavy enough, detached it, and returned to my father. His life jacket was mostly off, so I yanked it free and wound the chain around him as best I could, securing it with the clasps, then used the life jacket like an oven mitt to push him under the lower cable and over the side. He made a satisfying splash. I tossed the life jacket in.

No time for goodbyes.

I assessed the sails and trimmed the jib. The fire extinguisher looked clean to me, so I put it back, rinsed off the deck, and went below and made a sandwich. I wasn't hungry—I'm not without feeling—but I needed to have been doing something when my father fell overboard. Back at the helm, I switched off the autopilot and put some distance between me and dear old Dad.

The rest you can imagine. I circled back a ways, as if looking for him, and radioed the distress call. The Coast Guard showed up and pulled alongside. The officer at the wheel asked me what happened.

I acted tense and worried, but didn't overdo it. I kept my story simple. The biggest mistake liars make is showing off. Of course I didn't know that then, but my instincts were right.

"I don't know what happened to him. I went below to use the head and make a sandwich, and when I came back up, he was gone."

"Was he wearing a life vest?"

"He had it on, I think, but he never liked to zip it up."

They called in another boat and searched for a lot longer than made sense. They put a guy on the sailboat with me, and we sailed back to Madaket. I stayed quiet. People can read whatever they want into quiet.

My mother and her family were shocked, but they didn't let it get the best of them. The kind of institutionalized wealth they had gave them inherent fortitude. No crisis would overwhelm them. By sundown, everyone had given up hope my father had survived. If the Coast Guard and the police searched the boat, I didn't know about it. There was nothing to find, so I didn't give it much thought. I was simply glad I wouldn't have to put up with him anymore. That thought occurred to me repeatedly in the hours after my return, and I had to fight not to smile when it did.

I learned a lot from that day. I learned I could do something immoral and irreversible and get away with it. I learned that people see what they want to see, even people trained to look deeper, like law enforcement. I learned it was not difficult to kill someone should the need or the desire arise again (which, as you know, it did). I learned that my mother got along just fine without my father. There was, curiously enough, a sense that his departure from the world had restored the rightful order of the Appletons, and this led to the final lesson. Some people, even seemingly successful and important people like my father, are not valued much less cherished. He should have stayed in Kansas.

You might be wondering why, after killing my father because he belittled my career choice, I didn't become a doctor. Three weeks after the boating accident, as it came to be called, I returned to Dartmouth. My introductory psychology class was taught by a revolutionary man, John Gregory, who jumped over the field's arcane history (who really cares what Freud thought?) and commonsense interpersonal nonsense (optimistic people are more popular!) and lectured instead about the brain and behavior. I was hooked.

Yes, yes, how fitting that a narcissist should develop a fascination with his own brain and use what he learns to manipulate the behaviors of others. What would you prefer I study? Empathy? Attachment? Morality? Perhaps instead of judging me you ought to feel sorry for me, you who have empathy to spare. I was born this way, after all, and cannot be trained to care more about others than I do. And I do care about other people, to a degree. The reason I didn't want Jackie to move in with me, the reason I would not marry her, was, in part, selfless. What Jackie and I had was working—for both of us—but I had no confidence that I could tolerate more time together or greater intimacy or a firmer commitment. It might not have been healthy for her. If I had allowed her deeper into my lair, so to speak, she might never have left.

Look what happened to Jeffrey. I didn't plan to murder him, but the moment I saw him kiss Jackie, I knew I had to, very much like I made the decision to kill my father. I was appalled and enraged. There simply could not be a world in which dashing little Jeffrey Toshack would replace Miles, replace *me*. I followed Jeffrey to the river, keeping to the shadows, waiting for my chance. The longer I waited, the more my outrage was transformed into cunning. My concentration became laser-like, and as he walked ahead of me, my mind took in the possibilities, calculated the probabilities, and eventually revealed the correct strategy.

Seeing his trajectory, I took a shortcut. He neared the boathouse, and I was ahead of him on the towpath, pretending to be searching for my keys on the ground using a flashlight app. Nice guy that he was, he stopped to help. Our search strayed toward an alley where a broken oar became a convenient weapon. If it hadn't been there, I'd have surprised him by knocking him over, kicking him in the head, something like that. But improvisation is risky, and the oar was handy. The first blow was well placed and the second laid him out cold. I finished him off, took his wallet, and dragged him into the water. I was wearing gloves, so I left the oar in the alley. Job done.

My lawyer says Jackie's recordings are problematic but not defini-tive. It's now two weeks after the body was found, and the cops have no clear physical evidence, nothing placing me at the scene, as they say. (I told them I found the photo the following day during a walk, thought it might be Jackie and her friend, having seen them at the bar.) The lack of evidence is vexing for the DA, as is my unflappable nature. I've answered some of their questions, but their efforts to get me to impli-cate myself have been futile.

As for moral quandaries, I'll leave you with this: if you think about what happened, really think about it, all I did was show Nasira, Miles, and, most important, Jackie who they truly were. That makes me less of a monster and more of a mirror. What did I tell Jackie? Open your eyes.

Jackie's Story

~

Brownsburg, Virginia, 2009

Grace's wedding was so, well, Grace: perfect precisely because she never cared about perfection. She was the anti-bridezilla, caring about everyone, but not everything, remembering always that a wedding is a celebration, not a show. I'm certain that even if she and Hector had all the money in the world, they would not have spent a dime more.

Grace's best friend, Kendall, grew up on an old farm in Brownsburg, ten miles from where Grace and Hector now live. Kendall's parents offered their barn as the wedding venue. I was doubtful when Grace first told me about it, but it was, in fact, an oak cathedral. On that bright May afternoon, the ceremony—officiated by a minister friend of Hector's—took place in front of the open barn doors. The guests sat on folding chairs and logs, listening to bluegrass music played by whoever picked up a fiddle or a banjo. I was stunned by how many musicians were present; in my own life, I didn't know a single one.

I wasn't in the wedding party because Grace and Hector decided against that structure. My mother told me she disapproved of this break with tradition, but her disapproval of marriage as an institution was greater, and she knew her protest on either score was futile. Before the ceremony started, Cheryl perched on the edge of a folding chair, as if poised to leap to her feet should the chair snap closed beneath her. Elegant but unduly formal in her navy shift, she seemed to be reminding herself to smile.

Hector wore a simple gray suit, a white shirt, and a tie the color of fresh-cut hay. He stood, with his hands clasped in front, next to his friend the minister, and waited for Grace. All the children in attendance had been given wands with colored ribbons and waved them as they ran around the perimeter. Their laughing and shrieking became part of the music.

An elderly man sitting at the front turned his chair toward the group, took a harmonica out of his pocket, and sent the first exquisite notes of Pachelbel's Canon in D into the air. I was so transfixed I didn't notice Grace had arrived. A hush poured over the crowd like cream.

She wore an antique ivory dress with an Empire waist—right out of a Jane Austen novel—and held a bouquet picked from the meadow behind the house. No veil or tiara or headband, just her wavy auburn hair falling over her shoulders instead of in its usual ponytail. She looked exactly like herself in the very best way. Her joy was everywhere that day. Hector's was, too. Their shared joy was as wide as the blue Virginia sky.

This wasn't just my perception. Everyone sensed the magic of the day and would remember it always. I could see it in every beaming smile, in every gesture. People danced to every tune, helped with children who weren't theirs. Even those who drank to excess—and there were plenty—didn't turn mean or sloppy. The scent of spring fields swept in through the barn doors, and sunlight streamed through the chinks. On the notes of fiddles and banjos, laughter rose to the rafters of the barn and rained down on Grace and Hector's loved ones, soaking them with joy, and sending music and laughter high once again. That day, the feeling of it, would forever run through Grace and Hector's marriage like a golden thread; it was undeniable.

I shared in it, drank it up. My sister, my little sister, bathed in the grace for which she was named. I don't know how many times I hugged her or how often I caught her eye and felt my heart swell. We were replete with wine and love, helped along by the most glorious spring day I'd ever witnessed.

Sounds incredible, doesn't it? And unforgettable; my memory is vivid. At dusk, white Japanese lanterns were lit, casting a gentle light, and the first stars shone through the open barn door. I went out.

I wasn't alone in the night air. The celebration had spilled over, and people had gathered on the logs and by the carriage house next door. Children raced through the fields, arms outstretched to skim the tops of the grasses, releasing daredevil screams as the night closed in.

I'd taken only a few steps from the epicenter of the party, but it was enough to expose the other sensation I harbored but had not acknowledged. It was as powerful and convincing as the joy I shared with my sister, my brother-in-law, and everyone who gathered to celebrate with them.

I knew with certainty I would never know a day like this, or a love like theirs.

The feeling wasn't pity, nor was it envy; I didn't want to be Grace. Rather, as I stood at the edge of the night-dark field, I had a solid sense of being walled off from the love radiating behind me. I was happy for them—I've said that before, but it bears repeating—but I would not carry that happiness away into my relationships because I could not imagine, much less replicate, what they had. Their love was a faraway city, and I lacked a map and the courage to wander.

Did I want it, though?

Not then. I had Harlan. Or, rather, Harlan had me. He had discovered me. His attention toward me was a sincere expression of his delight in his discovery. Even a thoroughly deceitful and ruthless person can act with honesty, nurture a bond, and become deeply attached. Harlan's emotions are real, as real as anyone else's, but for him the correspondence is of intellectual interest only. He knows other people have emotions; he simply doesn't care about them. He may act as if he cares, but it's a performance designed to attract something he wants. Or someone.

I allowed Harlan to decide for me what relationships ought to be, what love was and wasn't. Having no map and not knowing where to search, I closed my eyes and could not see for myself. He saw for me, and I mistook my relief for satisfaction.

I mistook a great many things.

Perhaps everyone has stories they keep in a lockbox, stories they are not willing to own much less share. But if you don't acknowledge your own history—all of it, especially the underside—then aren't you creating blind spots of your own?

CHAPTER 31

On January 2, the day after Harlan confronted her, Jackie is making chili and corn bread, tired of takeout and makeshift meals. She's listening to the podcast *This American Life*, which features a story about a phone booth in Japan, in the coastal city where the tsunami hit in 2011. The phone inside isn't connected, but people come, alone or in family groups, to have one-sided conversations with their lost loved ones. It's heartbreaking and beautiful at the same time, the way intensely human things often are.

Her phone warbles beside the chopping board. It's Vince.

"Hi, Vince." It's odd for him to call during the break, and Jackie steels herself for bad news.

"Happy New Year, Jackie. I hope it's okay for me to call."

"Of course. What's going on?"

"If you haven't found someone already to audit your data, I've got a lead."

Jackie had shoved the necessity of the audit to the back of her mind. "I haven't. Who is it?"

"A friend of mine. He's between jobs. The start-up he worked for was bought, and he wasn't part of the package."

"I know you wouldn't recommend him if he wasn't qualified, but what does he do?"

Sonja Yoerg

Vince laughs. "Paco's not qualified. He's overqualified—a data manager. And don't worry, he'll do it on the cheap."

Jackie shakes her head. "I don't know what to say, Vince."

"You're welcome."

She laughs. "Thank you. You're a lifesaver—again." Her thoughts cast back to Vince's sleuthing to uncover the problems in her data. "Hey, Vince? Do you happen to be free this evening?" He's shuffling around; she's made him nervous. "I want to tell you about some things that've been going on, connected to the data breach."

"Oh, okay. Where should I meet you?"

"How do you feel about chili?"

———

Before Vince arrives, Jackie has already decided to tell him everything. It seems the best way to get his help, and he is too smart not to catch her skipping over things. She relates the whole story over dinner. At first, he's clearly uncomfortable being in her house, but as she unfolds the incidents of the past three months—the ones he hasn't been privy to—he is as quiet as a stalking cat.

She finishes telling him about yesterday, about the photograph and Detective Cash's assessment of the voice and video recordings.

He moves his bowl to the side, slowly, as if it were delicate. "So the detective is hoping the security footage will show Harlan on campus that night."

"Right. But Harlan was probably aware of the cameras."

Vince frowns. "I never liked that guy. And I'm sure the feeling is mutual."

He's quiet for a long while, staring into the middle distance. Jackie watches him, as if she might view his thought processes, observe his neural networks sorting and analyzing the data. She sips her wine and waits.

He turns to her. "You're fairly certain Harlan saw you with your friend near Wolf Hall the night he was killed?"

"I'm guessing that's what triggered it." She doesn't mention kissing Jeff again. Earlier, Vince frowned at that point in the story.

Vince nods. "If the police are on the ball, they will have subpoenaed his phone records already. But I'm guessing Harlan was smart enough not to leave his location services on when leaving his house to commit a crime—assuming that was his intention."

"I'm not sure what his intention was, maybe just to follow us, see what the relationship was about."

Vince leans forward, holds Jackie's gaze. "It's not his intention that interests me. He says he was at home, and I think his phone says something else."

Jackie's not following. "How?"

"When you walk up to Wolf Hall, what happens?" He reads her blank expression. "Ah, well, you probably have the notifications off, but when you come within range of the Wi-Fi there, it automatically connects you, assuming you have the Wi-Fi turned on. Most people do."

She sits up straighter. "So if Harlan had his phone on him, he might've logged on to the Wi-Fi without realizing it."

He grins. "And guess who's got access to those records?"

———

Four days later, Detective Cash calls to say they arrested Harlan. Using Jackie's recordings and testimony, the police obtained a search warrant for Harlan's house and phone. Vince was right; the phone placed Harlan on campus, close to where Jackie had last seen Jeff. Tests revealed that a black woolen coat of Harlan's had recently been dry-cleaned. Blood along the sleeve was detected via luminol and matched to Jeff's. Harlan either didn't know about the stains or was unaware that regular dry-cleaning wouldn't remove them. When he was first questioned, he tried to implicate Miles, knowing nothing about the MedFit data, thereby digging a deeper hole for himself. The judge refused him bail, and the DA is confident of a conviction.

Jackie cries after Cash delivers the news, relieved she no longer has to look over her shoulder when she leaves the house and gratified that Harlan will likely receive the punishment he deserves. Harlan Crispin, always in control, is no longer. Jackie doubts there's a lesson in that for him, but that has always been his problem. He isn't capable of change, of learning how to live, only of putting on a different mask.

It doesn't take long for the news to spread of the arrest of a prominent professor on murder charges. Three days after Harlan is locked up, someone leaks information about Jackie's link to the victim. To avoid the media vans outside her home, Jackie hides in her lab, working sixteen-hour days. When she's absorbed in her research, she forgets—at first for minutes, then hours at a time—what has befallen her and everyone else in Harlan's path.

A week after the news hits, Amy Chen, the department chair, calls Jackie into her office.

"I heard reporters found their way into your lecture and caused a disruption. I'd like someone else to take over that class."

Jackie suspects Chen is less worried about a disruption of learning than she is about negative attention. "Simmons is a large hall with lots of entrances. The reporters foiled campus security. All this will blow over soon."

"Maybe. But what about when the trial starts?"

Chen has a point. Jackie has been focusing on getting through each day, putting her life back together, but the media isn't going to let her forget about Harlan anytime soon. The thought exhausts her, and she fantasizes about escaping somewhere until the storm passes. It's an impossible fantasy, however; her commitments to her research and her students will keep her right where she is.

"If you insist," Jackie says. "But since none of this is my doing, I expect the lecture credits."

Chen reluctantly agrees, and Jackie brightsides the development: she now has a few more hours a week to work with Vince's friend to sort out the mess Harlan made of her data.

———

Jackie sits cross-legged in the upholstered chair in her office, her laptop balanced on her knees, reading a draft of Kyle's dissertation. It's Martin Luther King Day and the lab—in fact, the entire campus—is empty. Her plan is to read the first three chapters, then see if she can walk into town for lunch without reporters dogging her. She's adapted to being recognized by students who stare at her not so surreptitiously, but having a microphone thrust in her face still rankles her.

Someone enters the lab. A moment later, Nasira appears in the doorway.

"Hi, Jackie. Do you have a sec? If you're busy, later is fine."

"Now's good. Have a seat." Jackie's been worried about Nasira, who confided to Jackie that she hasn't been sleeping well since the truth about Harlan surfaced. Who could blame her? She and Nasira have distracted themselves with movies and takeout dinners at Jackie's house, but there is no papering over the horror of having slept with and having had feelings for a murderer.

Nasira removes her jacket and settles herself in a chair. "My parents called last night. They'd been in Jordan and in France and hadn't seen the news about Harlan until now."

"And obviously you hadn't volunteered it."

She spreads her hands. "It's so much to explain, and over the phone? I didn't know how." She sighs. "Honestly, I didn't want to get into it. They disapproved of him, and boy did they ever turn out to be right."

"Right for the wrong reasons. What did they say?" Jackie cannot imagine the magnitude of their concern, their only remaining child in the nest of a killer. That she emerged unharmed must be their only solace.

"Not very much. A combination of relief and scolding." Nasira's eyes well with tears. "They wanted to hear my voice, they said."

Jackie reaches for Nasira's hand. "Of course they did."

She wipes away the tears streaking her face. "We've just been so broken. This only makes it worse. Infinitely worse."

"Does it have to, though? Maybe this is an opportunity. They clearly love you, Nasira. Imagine how afraid they have been, and how sad, the same as you."

Nasira is pensive. "I don't know. How do I talk to them? They don't even know who I am anymore."

"How did that happen? Because of what happened to your brother?"

"Yes and no. It's a long story."

Jackie smiles. "Feel like a walk?"

Outside, the day is bright and windy, bending the tops of the pines on the slope below. Scraps of cloud hunt across the sky. They head toward town, and Nasira tells Jackie about her trip years ago to the refugee camp in Jordan, about the wounded children, about her father's disappointment. About her shame. The story is a private window Nasira opens for her gingerly.

When Nasira is finished, she stops in the path, but her gaze is ahead. "Maybe that's what made me susceptible to Harlan. Unlike my father, he thought my new career path was worthy, noble. And he did boost my confidence."

"That makes sense."

Nasira turns to her. "But I still don't know what to say to my parents."

"You've already been saying it. The fact that you're worrying about it means you want them in your life. And the fact that you haven't given up on your own goals shows your integrity means as much to you, maybe more."

Her expression is solemn. "I hope they don't make me choose."

"I don't think they will."

Nasira gives her a half smile. "Maybe I'll take a few days off to go home. Try to explain everything to them."

Jackie pulls her into a hug. "As long as you need. I'll hold down the fort."

———

While Nasira is away, Jackie falls into a routine much like the one she adopted after Harlan and before Miles, spending her free time chatting with Grace, reading and cooking at home, or on the river when the weather allows. Nasira calls after four days to say she and her parents are talking. She's been tempted to flee the pain of peeling back the scarred layers of regret and disappointment and failure in hopes of finding the generosity of forgiveness underneath. "But we hurt in much the same way," she says, and asks for more time, something the family has not enjoyed for too many years. "As long as you need," Jackie says.

Although Jackie is wary of isolating herself, she does allow for quiet moments, while rowing or at home, to own her broken heart. How else will it heal? She told Miles she doesn't want to talk to him for now and can't predict how long it will be until she does. She misses him, sometimes with a force that surprises her, but she doesn't want to muddle those feelings with his. This isn't a joint activity, at least not yet.

Miles and Antonio moved into a rental two Metro stops north of the home Miles and Jackie used to share; Miles moved out his belongings during days while Jackie was at work, but Antonio left some things behind, which is fine with Jackie. She texts with Antonio frequently, and they've shared a few meals in town or at her house. She doesn't mind news of Miles if that's what Antonio wants to share. For all the disruption, Antonio seems steadier than he's been in a long time, perhaps since she's known him. He has a girlfriend, Isobel, and brought her to Jackie's one evening. Few things have pleased her as much recently as that trust.

Jackie now blocks out time in her schedule for her friends. There's Nasira, of course, and Ursula, whose bluntness she's learned to value. And Vince, who, in helping nab Harlan, came to know more about her than her own mother. She trusts him implicitly. IT guys are like lawyers, right? Find a good one and keep him close. Joking aside, he's taught her how to play pool, of all things, and not to worry as much. Once a microcosm of two with Harlan, Jackie now cannot envisage her life within such narrow bounds.

———

In early March, a burst of warm weather explodes from the drear of winter. Jackie walks to work three days in a row, the morning sun warm on her shoulders. Tree buds swell and the air contains a sweetness. Outside Wolf Hall, a cluster of daffodils pushes through the earth, first one, the next day ten, the next day dozens, their closed buds nodding on lengthening stems.

Thursday afternoon, she returns to the lab from a graduate seminar, meets with Tate about her upcoming comprehensive exams, then opens her in-box for the first time since 8:00 a.m. There are two dozen emails, but one from Deirdre Calhoun catches her eye. The subject line reads "Grant Application." Jackie clicks it open, her smile widening as she reads.

"The board is pleased to inform you . . . fully funded . . . impressive interim results."

Jackie sends a silent thanks to Vince and to his friend Paco, who conducted the audit. It spanned four weeks and uncovered no irregularities beyond those Vince discovered, so Jackie had every reason to be optimistic about returning to the good graces of the Autism America foundation. But optimism is one thing, and a guarantee of continued funding for her life's work another. Calhoun's email is hard proof that her reputation has been restored.

Jackie reads the email again to ensure she wasn't hallucinating and hurries to the shared office. Kyle, Tate, Nasira, and Rhiannon turn toward her. "We got the grant!"

They erupt in a flurry of cheers, hugs, and fist bumps.

Nasira rushes over to embrace Jackie. "The best news."

"The absolute best." Jackie can't stop smiling. "We need to celebrate—all of us, plus Gretchen and Reese and Vince and Paco. Does tonight work for you guys?"

———

The fine weather holds through the weekend. Sunday morning Jackie rows along the Potomac, the water rippling away from her oars in silken folds. The river moves under her, broad and steady. She skims the surface, her speed a celebration of precision, touch, reach, and strength. If she can hold on to this, she might reclaim herself. Her abilities harbor an abundance of raw material for success, the real kind, the kind suffused with love and with joy. Rowing, she thinks, isn't easier when you love it, but loving it does make the effort worthwhile. The same, too, with her work, and with the trickiest of all undertakings, the ones in which you give your heart to other people.

She tires at last and heads toward the boathouse. Jackie slips alongside the dock, holds the ends of both oars in one hand, and steps out of the shell. She squats to detach the oars, lays them behind her on the dock, and takes hold of the gunwales to lift the shell out of the water.

"Hi, Jackie. Want a hand with that?" Antonio approaches her, dressed for sailing in a windbreaker and a baseball cap, cheeks red from the sun and wind.

"Hi, Antonio. I've got it, thanks." She stands up and glances past him at Miles, who is hanging back, giving her space, she supposes. She waves to him, and he lifts a hand in return. "You guys sailing?"

"Just finished. We saw you coming in." He smiles at her. "You were cruising."

She gestures to the river, the sky. "It's a gorgeous day. Makes it easier."

"I was thinking of giving it a try. Rowing." He shuffles his feet. "I was just talking about it with my dad."

Jackie looks at Miles again, who is facing upriver, his cap pushed back from his forehead. She feels a pang but isn't sure what it is. Missing him is her best guess—him, not the marriage.

"Here." She hands Antonio the oars. "Your first demo: how to pick up the shell." She hoists the shell onto her shoulder.

As they near the spot where Miles is waiting, Antonio hands her the oars. "I gotta run. I'm late for meeting Isobel."

"Oh, okay. Text me when you want to get together." She watches him go, wondering if he is really interested in rowing or just saw the chance to set up an encounter with his father. It doesn't matter; while she might not have chosen this moment to talk to Miles, neither does she feel compelled to avoid him.

He smiles at her, hands in his pockets. "Hi, Jackie. Good row?"

"The best." She sees he's waiting for her cue. "Let me get rid of this and we can talk. If you want."

"I do."

A few minutes later they are sitting on a bench facing the river. The white sails of the dinghies and small yachts glint in the sun. At the shore, several people wearing life vests huddle around an instructor demonstrating how to maneuver a kayak.

Jackie pulls a water bottle from her backpack and takes a long drink. Sitting beside Miles is both familiar and uncomfortable; she knows so little about what Miles has been going through, but perhaps that has been true for a very long time. She opts to launch the conversation with their most obvious common interest. "Antonio seems really well."

Miles nods. "We've had a lot more time together. When he can, he comes along on scouting trips, but I've also cut back on traveling." He doesn't meet her gaze, and she knows he is aware that only months ago he refused to adjust his schedule to make room for a child. Jackie lets it slide; the deeper meaning of that conversation has since become clear. Miles continues: "Antonio's been helping me work through things."

"That's a big step—for both of you."

"I think he's relieved he's not the only one with significant challenges to face. He said I could borrow his freak flag." He shrugs, smiling.

"Cute. But I don't think either of you are freaks."

"I was only joking."

"I know. But like all jokes, the center of it hits the truth." She turns toward him and holds his gaze so he cannot miss her intention. "I don't think there is anything wrong with you, Miles."

"Thanks, Jackie. I wish I'd had more confidence in that." His shoulders drop an inch. "I'd never appreciated the sort of message I was sending Antonio by being less than honest about who I am. I told myself it was better all around, but that was just another lie."

Jackie sighs. "Sometimes I don't think we can survive without lying. I mean, we all have to let certain things go, smooth the way forward, or just get through the night. It's hard to know when to stop." Miles is staring at her, his brow furrowed. "All those years with Harlan, I lied to myself about so many things, but I kept going, thinking it would resolve, that the knot would untangle itself. I thought he would change if I could just hang on and be who he wanted me to be a little longer."

"I can see that. But what about with us?"

"I'm still figuring it out. Maybe you shouldn't have married me, knowing you liked men, but maybe I shouldn't have married you, knowing that I didn't know what the hell I wanted."

Miles grins and a spark lights in his eyes. "You see? Your penetrating insight is irresistible."

Jackie laughs, and when Miles laughs with her, she cannot stop. They are doubled over, not knowing what they are laughing about, except that it feels wonderful.

Miles sits up, wipes his eyes. "I do love you, Jackie."

"I know. And me you."

———

As the sun sets that evening, Jackie wraps herself in a shawl and carries a glass of wine outside to her deck. She sits on the steps to the yard and calls Grace. After catching up on her sister's news, Jackie tells her about her conversation with Miles.

"I always liked the guy," Grace says. "I mean, that was rather a large oops he made with Harlan, but I can like him again now, right?"

"Yes. Like him as much as you want. I plan to."

They talk about plans to get together over Jackie's spring break, then say goodbye.

Jackie rewraps the shawl and sips her wine. The sun has dipped below the tree line, drawing the shadows long, chilling the air. But today's warmth, the unexpected beauty of it, still fills her and touches her memory of Grace's wedding, the magic of it.

When Jackie stood at the edge of that starlit field, she was sure she could never have what Grace and Hector had. Like the stars themselves, it was beyond her reach. She had her relationship with Harlan, what she could make of it, and her career. There was nothing more for her, certainly nothing touching the joyousness radiating from the wedding scene behind her. She would be a part of Grace and Hector's life, but she could never be *of* it. It is one thing to love, another to trust. That night, and on every night of her life, Jackie's heart was full of love, but she lacked the ability to share it completely. She didn't dare.

A mourning dove calls from the oak tree above Jackie's deck, the notes haunting and pure and wide enough to fill the world. The dove calls again, and Jackie's eyes fill with tears.

She was mistaken.

What Grace and Hector have is trust in the beauty of life. That's it. Their trust is so strong that everything they touch becomes beautiful, a wish that creates its own reality. Of course, they aren't immune to the ugly or unfortunate things that happen to everyone, but because of their steadfast faith in the beauty of life, the misfortune will also be beautiful in its pain, in its loss, in its grief, in its humanity. If you fall in love with life itself, happiness is yours for as long as you live.

The best thing about this trust? Hard as it may be to find, and to hold on to, anyone can have it.

Even Jackie.

ACKNOWLEDGMENTS

My first and largest debt of gratitude goes to my agent, Maria Carvainis, for her wisdom, patience, and steely support, and to my editor, Chris Werner, for believing in my stories and turning them into books. If that sounds easy, it's not. Thanks to everyone at Lake Union Publishing who helped create and promote this book; your work is invaluable. Thanks also to Tiffany Yates Martin, who wields a red pen like a scalpel and, when necessary, like a cudgel, and does so with humor and style.

Special thanks to Karyn Cossello and Michael Renner for advice on data management and security and to Steve Crowder on police procedure. Any errors are mine.

Heartfelt thanks to Kate Moretti, Heather Webb, and Holly Robinson for advice, hand-holding, laughs, and critical reads and to all my sisters in the Tall Poppy Writers for their friendship, insights, and support. To my daughters, Rebecca and Rachel Frank, thank you for reading, for cheering me on, and for being generally fabulous. Love to all of you.

Thanks to the readers, reviewers, bloggers, and Instagrammers whose love for books and reading makes writing worthwhile. I appreciate every gesture you make to express your support of authors and books, and when it happens to be me or one of my books, you make my day.

Love and gratitude to Richard, my husband and emotional support animal. Finding you proves I'm lucky beyond measure.

DISCUSSION QUESTIONS

1. Jealousy is a powerful emotion with potential for hurt or even destruction. Could you sympathize with Jackie's jealousy of Nasira? How did Jackie's jealousy play into Harlan's hands? If you have experienced intense jealousy, or been the target of it, how did you cope with it?

2. Jackie and Harlan become friends after their breakup, in part because they are colleagues. When Jackie starts dating Miles, the men develop a friendship. Are friendships between exes tenable? What does it take to be able to move from intimacy to friendship?

3. Even when Harlan was in charge of the narrative, he didn't tip his hand right away. When did you begin to suspect he was out to get Jackie? Did you foresee the extent of his vengefulness? Do you think Jackie should've suspected him sooner?

4. Grace is more grounded and content than her sister, Jackie. Is this a personality difference or the result of being younger and not experiencing their parents' conflict in the same way? What role do you think having a career outside the home plays in the difference between the sisters' lives?

5. Nasira is the first of the four main characters to tell her story. How did it change the way you viewed her, if at

all? How did her estrangement from her parents affect her susceptibility to Harlan?

6. What did you think of Jackie and Miles's marriage early in the book? Were you worried for them, or did you suspect something else was amiss? At the end, do you expect them to stay friends?

7. Jackie's mother, Cheryl, is entrenched in the past, but Jackie finds a way to respect and even admire her. Did this surprise you? How does Cheryl's status as a working mother factor in this, and, more generally, what do you think about changing relationships between mothers and daughters as women struggle to "have it all"?

8. Imagine if Jackie had remained content with her circumscribed relationship with Harlan, never asking for more. Do you think the relationship would have lasted? Why or why not? Harlan claimed he loved her more than anyone. What does that mean, given what you know about him?

9. Stepparenting is never easy. What did you think of Jackie's role as Antonio's stepmom? Did Miles ask too much of her? Not enough? Jackie wondered whether Antonio's knowledge of his father's sexuality might have been a barrier in the stepmom-stepson relationship; what's your take?

10. The stories reveal salient background information about the characters that reframe how you think about them. Behind the stories themselves is the idea that we all hold part of ourselves in reserve and thereby resist the ability of others to fully understand us. Is this true? Does everyone have a story they've never told?

ABOUT THE AUTHOR

Photo © 2017 Tamara Hattersley Photography

Sonja Yoerg is the *Washington Post* bestselling author of the novels *House Broken*, *The Middle of Somewhere*, *All the Best People*, and *True Places*. Sonja grew up in Stowe, Vermont, where she financed her college education by waitressing at the Trapp Family Lodge. She went on to earn a PhD in biological psychology from the University of California, Berkeley, and wrote a nonfiction book about animal intelligence, *Clever as a Fox*, before deciding it was more fun to make things up. Sonja lives with her husband in the Blue Ridge Mountains of Virginia. For more information, visit www.sonjayoerg.com.